US
DISCORDIA

THE LEGEND OF FOX CROW

BOOK TWO

JAMES DANIEL ROSS

| CINCINNATI OHIO

Edited by T.R.Chowdhury
Interior Design by T.R.Chowdhury

Published by CopperFox,
an imprint of Winter Wolf Publications LLC

ISBN: 978-1-945039-09-6 (paperback)

The Radiation Angels

The Chimerium Gambit

The Key To Damocles

The Defending the Future Anthology Series

Breach the Hull

So It Begins

By Other Means

Chronicles of Rithalion

Elvish Jewel

The Fireheart

(release June 2018)

The Troubadours Inn Anthology Series

Tales from the Hapless Cenloryan

The Whispering of Dragons

The Last Dragoon

The Echoes of Those Before

DEDICATION

Where do you go to give up? The world keeps spinning, the mortgage payments will come due. My daughters and sons will need to be fed, to graduate and go on to college. The truth of life is this: When backed into the corner the only way you can collapse and cry is if there is someone there to pick you up, care for you, and nurse you back to health. If not, will you die in that corner.

Better, then, to stand tall. To roar proof of your life into God's creation. To attack that which you fear, because if you are not giving up, then you might as well go all in.

For to leap into the air from the crumbling cliff is not madness. It is the only sane course left. And if you fall, well then, everyone was already expecting you to fall.

But if you fly, they will never forget the sight of you for the rest of their lives.

Table of Contents

Act One

Act Two

ACT THREE

PROLOGUE

MIND YOUR OWN BUSINESS

I WAS quickly coming to the conclusion that my life was never going to be the same again. And by the same, I mean normal. *Fine*, maybe that was a lie, for it had never been exactly normal, but dammit, I did everything right this time! Well, other than this first thing.

I had stolen through the little village like a ghost. I was wearing various shades of near white, off white, strips of light brown, and stained white, blending perfectly into the terrain buried in flakes of snow that fell like a funeral shroud in the high mountain valley. I attained the top of the hulking log cabin, itself half buried in ice, without making a sound. All tracks up to the building would be obliterated already by the self same wind and snow. The wind had been important, blowing the strange whiff of sweat, musk, and death toward me from the target and not from me to it. I waited for the target to roar a challenge before loosening my sword, muffling the grinding sound of the metal throat of the scabbard with a wrapped handful of cloth. I hefted the brilliant blade, ignoring the sounds of rending flesh and tendon being torn from bone as the bleating screams went from frantic, to resigned, to listless with blood loss. I crept forward, the sound of crunching ice and snow muffled by the nearly verbal mastication and sound of animal contentment.

I saw the target. I did not freeze at the massive shoulders, bundled with muscle under a coating of white fur. I refused to acknowledge the corpse, a violent red splatter in the snow. I simply cocked the sword, winged crosspiece and long, silvery blade glittering in the moonlight. I leapt from the top of the building as the moon shot through the breaking storm clouds with vicious spears, forgoing a mighty grunt or heroic battle cry that would alert my target. Still, it huffed through a flat nose over rows of fangs and turned as my sword, driven by every muscle and the weight of my whole body, spun to enter its neck at the collar bone.

The blade, flared in the elvish style, rang as it severed bones and sliced through muscle, gristle, and tissue with equal abandon. I slammed into the hairy thing and, leaving my precious weapon behind, immediately launched myself off of it to avoid blindly thrashing claws.

Launching was the important part, believe it or not, since the creature was still alive. It roared to the sky, but half the noise came out in an arterial spray of dark red blood. This didn't stop it from thrashing around with the last vestiges of its might, and of course the aforementioned perfect-for-disemboweling claws. One dying fist cracked a log belonging to the home I had jumped from, still surely strong enough to turn me into a long hot smear in the snow. This is the principal reason I was no longer anywhere near it. I rolled through the snow, shifted downwind, and drew forth the short sword worn at my belt.

This precaution was unnecessary. I had cleft the creature from shoulder to stomach, the point of the longsword protruded from the belly like a broken mast. This unleashed a waterfall of steaming blood that only intensified as the thing took a wobbling step toward me. For all of its fury, blood is the fuel that feeds the fire of any mortal body, and all it owned was melting the snow at its feet. The thing collapsed.

I waited.

And waited.

And waited, dammit, because a moment of caution has often saved me from a new ugly scar.

When the beast's mouth did not steam with breath after four of my own, I sheathed my short sword. I walked forward, still cautious, and reached for my Angel. I yanked at the blade, annoyed that it was stuck on some bone or protrusion inside the damned thing. Otherwise, I was satisfied, for I had stalked silently, struck viciously, and escaped all harm dexterously. I had done everything right.

Except for that first thing.

I yanked the Phantom Angel free and shook it once, briskly. Blood slid from the blade as if it were greased. I glanced down at the body that had been the beast's feast. It had been a boy, almost a man, and had been torn limb from limb like a roasted hen to become fist sized tidbits that fit in the creature's mouth. Mercifully, the boy was dead now, and there had never been anything I could do about it. He had already been in the hands of the creature when I had heard the first screams. Even so, I had gotten involved.

Which, of course, is always the first mistake, a habit I can't seem to break myself of these days, and which will surly get me killed. I also believe that this is the point.

There had been a time when I could have looked upon the gristly death of another human being and been unmoved. That time was gone, but I'm not sure I was glad of it. Not moved to tears, or wholesale grief, but moved nonetheless. I flicked out the point of my sword, caught the edge of the boy's heavy fur cloak, and draped it over his face.

That was when the roar of incalculable rage detonated on the other side of the village. Instantly I identified the other creature, white fur blending into the snowy curtains and showing only the big black nose, yellow teeth, and eyes.

I cursed out loud. I spun the Phantom Angel, cocked it back by one ear, and fought the urge to urinate. Before it had been mechanical, methodical, planned. This creature was fully aware of me, and would not be taken in ambush. This was far more like a fair fight than I ever liked to have. The beast was like a giant, twisted man wrapped in a carpet of matted fur, but the hands, the claws, the teeth were more powerful than those of a bear. Deathly white, it charged like a ton of rolling boulders, and the rage that came from it caused my face to heat in response. Even the elvish sword I carried seemed puny and thin in comparison to this maniacal berserker. Still, I lifted it in defiance and took a deep breath as the snow creature charged.

Dammit.

Act One

The Question

ONE

UNLUCKY BASTARD

ASSASSIN.

Everyone who knows the word thinks they know what it means. Sometimes they are more correct than not, but it's long odds. Some people think assassin means death. This is untrue. Some believe them to be ghosts made of poison and blades. Also untrue. The story sounds good, and it makes it seem less unfair that the brave and mighty could be erased from the living by just another person. This is the truth, though– they are simply men and women. Sometimes they have demons inside them, other times they have a broken and painful life that drives them to visit blood upon the lives of others. What they do have is a great deal of skill and no compunction about how those skills are used to get silver, gold, and riches of all kinds.

Assassins are, more than anything, cheaters. They look for strength and avoid it. They look for a weakness and exploit it. Of course, they do it to take innocent and not-so-innocent lives for coins of silver and gold, but that is the why, not the what. The what simply is. The why is what matters most. I have to believe that. I've had a long time to think about this.

I've had good reason.

I was an assassin. I got a chance to start over. The trouble is, contrary to the poxy bards and their warbling tales, chances are not given. They are sold on credit. And the interest? It's a killer. I suspect that I'm going to be spending each day paying for every drop of blood I shed in my former life. That doesn't mean my life is painless, quite the opposite. Take my current conundrum.

Take it, please take it.

Months before, I had shaken the kingdom of Noria by getting mixed up in a deadly plot amongst the highest of nobility. Turns out, (surprise-surprise) peasants (like me) do not ever, (ever) get the princess (no matter how charming or effective one is). Also, it turns out that the kingdom does not *like* to be shaken. In fact the kingdom downright disapproves of being shaken, nudged, or even farted upon. The nobles show the disapproval of said kingdom by using axes, nooses, and pikes of the head-bearing variety.

I had saved the life of a lovely, courageous, intelligent young woman. In so doing, I had made myself a target. For those that are wondering, this is the no-good-deed-is-kept-on-account theory of sin management. There is a corollary to that law that goes something like: Nobles have long memories and longer knives. I struck out from the Kingdom of Noria southward, over the Hammarfold Mountains, intent of becoming lost in a nation where nobody had ever heard the name Fox Crow.

This plan would have been the essence of wisdom if I had made it through just before the first hard snow, allowing me through and trapping any pursuit behind me. In fact, when I remember it, better to say if I am forced to remember it, I will remember having made it through just fine. I will not get bogged down in Mothers' Valley by a constant state of cold and storms, threatened with starvation and death by early snows, and only to be brought up short by a warning horn.

I suppose it would have been wiser to detour, or even just turn around. But then, like an idiot, I got closer. Then I heard the screams of the boy being chased. So I got even closer. And then I killed one beast, only to find out the mate was not far afield. So now I'm so extremely close to being killed, gutted, and eaten (and in that order if I am luckier than I have any reason to expect).

So, you may be asking why I got close in the first, second, and now third place? I'll be buggered if I know. It's the way my last long, painful adventure started and, memory troubles aside, one would think I had learned my lesson.

None of that mattered now. The thing had seen me and was charging like a living avalanche of ropy muscles, white fur, and yellow eyes.

Left hand, gloved against the cold, desperately tugged at the securely tied throat of a pouch attached to my belt. Right hefted the seemingly slim sliver of silver up as the hairy white beast shook the ground with every step. It held its freakishly long arms wide and low, looking to cut off a dodge to either side.

I only had time for a glance left and right, find no escape, then curse and yank the whole pouch free of the belt. I slit the throat of the bag with the sword and flung the whole bundle forward into the beast's face. Then there was nothing to be done but hurl myself backward toward the squat building behind and hope.

The bag, freed of the restraining cord, became a simple circle of cloth, unleashing a glittering cloud of black and silver powder. Tiny flames burst and crackled from inside the shiny black fog as it consumed fat snowflakes. Merciless claws were sweeping toward me, hooked to disembowel, when the cloud of dust hit the beast's muzzle. The claws instinctively slapped to the beast's face. I hunkered down and planted the long elvish hilt against the hard, frozen ground directly in the path of the charging brute. The tip barely touched the beast over the heart when I flung myself to the side like a mouse making for the safety of the barn.

Blood, red and hot erupted from the back of it even as a bone-shaking howl racked the sky as it impaled itself, blew past me, collided with the cabin, and then tumbled into the snow, thrashing. I stood and ran from the scene of misery, leery of the area in case the finely ground dust still hung in the air. I could see where it drifted to the snow, blackening it in some places, and sparkling in others as the metallic alkaloid brought fire from water. Yet, even then, Right hand drew the shortsword while Left hand was unlimbering a hidden knife from inside my vest, cracking the wax seal holding the blade into the sheath.

I stopped six paces from the beast, wincing as the face smoldered, and calculated the number of spins between it and I. Even with a sword in the chest and the dust eating at face and lungs, it still moved, showing a near supernatural constitution. The creature was spitting into its hands, seeking to clear the dust from its eyes. Every drop of water that came in contact with the dwarven alkaloid metal caused it to smoke and heat, sometimes even burst into miniature fires. Every touch rubbed the other half of the mixture, tiny shards of obsidian, further into the eyes, mouth and face, shredding the flesh.

That was when I chose to sink the knife into its back, just under the heart. The gooey, tarry poison was enough to kill a man, three times over, nearly instantly. It still took several minutes for the thing to die.

I approached cautiously, retrieved and resheathed the knife, and sighed over the necessary use of so much of my expensive black glass and alkaloid mixture– all of it in fact. The alkaloid metal conjured fire from water, and gnat sized razors flung into the eyes were useful in a self explanatory way. Yet, it was hard to make and dear to purchase. Still cheaper than my blood, and everything is cheaper than dying. So, as you can see, I am no longer an assassin. I am, however, still a cheat. And because of that, I'll keep breathing.

Good thing too, since I am becoming more and more convinced that the whole world is trying to kill me.

I, with great difficulty, wrenched free the elvish sword that had been my constant companion since my rebirth. I studied it, because that was easier than the alternative.

The blade was flared near the end, imbuing deadly weight to aid in slashes. The surface was mirror bright and featureless except when the light hit it, and the vague shadows of foreign script appeared. The hilt was a hooded figure, holding a glittering blue heart in robed hands. The body became the hilt of the sword, wings from the shoulders creating the crosspiece. This was my Phantom Angel. I wiped the blood from the blade and, out of habit rather than alarm, used the surface to scan the world behind me.

The cabin at the battle site was larger than most, set away from the village and half piled with blown snow. The doors of the rest of the village opened quietly, cautiously, but all stealth was shattered by the woman that wailed like a lost soul. I adjusted the blade and saw a man much closer to me than I expected. I spun to meet him, careful to keep the sword low and to the side. He was two dozen paces away, yet still he drew up short.

We stood still, taking in the measure of one another. His entire pose was tense rather than confrontational, yet I could pick out evidence of at least two hidden knives, so he was no fool. His long moustache trembled a little and his work-worn hands shook as he slid calluses across his bald head. Even in the severe cold, his fur hat was in his hand and the thick snow was already forming into droplets on his pate.

He held his hands up, as if to caution or placate me. He said something. Like most Norians, I knew a smattering of words from the realms on every side including *HammarSpiel*, but these I did not know. He swallowed hard, glanced at the bloody blade in my hand and tried again in a thick accent, "Move slow?"

I shook my head, looking at the two fresh corpses. "I am pretty fast." Then I pointed to the human corpse messily splayed on the snow. "Your boy?"

The man nodded, then contradicted himself. "Nephew. But must move."

Ok, it was freezing cold and I had just avenged the death of this poor kid and removed a threat to the village, but was it out of line to expect a feast? Perhaps a meal? A beer, maybe? Instead, this bald buffoon as telling me to move along before the corpses were even done steaming. The aunt, or mother, continued to wail at the body of the boy, but the remaining villagers stood at more than just a respectful distance. Behind them a priest, a huge bearded man built like a wrestler, waded easily through the crowd. His huge gut was still overshadowed by powerful arms that could split wood with ease. He was listening to the whispered comments of his flock, but his eyes were troubled. Everyone was pointing at me, but none acted welcoming in any way.

Well, it wasn't like they were family to me, were they? And I suppose if I start doing stupid things in the hope other people will find them heroic and reward me, I should expect to die hungry, unremembered, and soon.

The kid was already as good as dead. Why, dear Lords and Ladies, why did I have to get involved?

Somewhere behind me there was a rough caw of a bird. I spun, but did not see the damned thing. And that, no matter the language, was the signal to go. I never found it healthy to come to the attention of authorities, and whenever there were ravens there was trouble for me. I backed away from them all, but nobody took even a single step closer.

The Phantom Angel was almost too long to carry on one hip and still be easily mobile, so I adjusted the belt and sheath onto on my back after I slid it home. Yet, even this did not end the tension in the crowd. They were peering on, like an execution. One woman gestured me toward the crowd, but her hands were slapped out of the air by the man beside her and he lashed her with his tongue. The huge priest was looking over at me with knitted brows. I was at once glad for the language barrier. It allowed me to mutter a simple, "Lords and Ladies protect you all." And then stop trying to half shout in pidgin *HammarSpiel* and simply leave.

Or, at least, try to leave.

I turned and took a single step around the huge, lumbering log cabin where the short battle had happened. The entire group gasped audibly. The mountain man called out something, but I didn't catch it. My body was starting to come down out of the rage of battle and my legs were a bit rubbery. Rather than show weakness, I reached up and put my hand to a snow covered wall. That's when I noticed it wasn't a wall, but a scaffold. There was a sound of a hundred ravens cawing as they took panicked flight. I spun to see them but found none, in fact the only other person to seem to hear them was the priest, whose head also craned to find the invisible murder.

Then I turned back, and saw that the protruding wall wasn't a scaffold. It was big, round, and disappeared into the ground at my feet. There was a sound of cracking glass as I took two steps back, heels contacting the second dead carnivore, but still able to get a better view of what was obviously the waterwheel of a mill.

And that meant–

Then I turned and placed one foot. The world exploded into a deafening roar, ivory white, and bitter cold.

I floated, feeling at first nothing but frigid blood pouring over me. I thrashed, reaching for a world that had disappeared in diffused blue and white. Bubbles rushed in every direction, released from my clothing in a storm, giving no clear way up and out. The hairy corpse slithered from above, slapping weightlessly into my face and pushing me further down. I picked a direction as my arms numbed and legs cramped. I kicked twice pulling at the water as my lungs began to burn, desperate for life, for air. I felt frozen mud come up in clumps between swimming fingers, and blot out all sense of day or night. Gentle warmth cupped me like a kitten in the hands of a giant. I exhaled, and let the giant take me.

Then there was a harsh hand grappling me, yanking me. Bright light speared into eyes that throbbed. Someone smashed me on my back, blasting water from my lungs only to be replaced by air laced with razors. My skin felt like living bees had taken residence beneath the skin. The light hurt like barbed needles, and I screwed my eyes shut against the pain.

I heard a raven cackle gleefully.

I was dragged into the snow, which felt oddly rough and warm. I could not move, yet my limbs began shaking as if in palsy. There was muffled shouting, but I felt it was I that was muffled and not the voices. I was dragged by four men through the snow into a small church.

The door was opened before us and slammed behind. I risked opening one eye, and saw logs being loaded onto a fire with great abandon. One village woman began using a bellows on the flames, another was taking down gargantuan priest robes from where they steamed on the drying lines by the fire. Knives cut me out of my clothes. There was a shriek, and I was dropped to the floor.

Utter silence froze that heartbeat in the church.

A deep voice barked, and warm, though wet, layers of wool and leather robes were wrapped around me. I was set just before the fire on a lounging chair. Men left and returned with smoking metal pans, containing coals as it turned out, and placed them beneath me.

Strong as I am, I could not find enough power left in me to lift my head. I faded in and out of lucidity. A few times, broth was brought and dribbled between my lips. I slept. I dreamt. The dreams were always in steel and crimson. I awoke as the priest removed the metal pans from beneath me and tossed out the cinders to load new coals into them and slide them beneath the chair.

I didn't even realize I was watching, rather than dreaming, until the priest smiled and nodded.

"Good, you will live," he said in flawless Norian. The words rolled from him as easily as one mentions that the sun is up, or that the road is muddy. And yet, there was an extra hint of relish, as if it was going to be a sunny day, or at least he was looking forward to splashing in the puddles.

"I've got to go," I said. Well, I slurred. Well, I slurred while mumbling. I also rocked a bit in the chair which was as close to standing as I could manage. "I need my things."

This seemed to only amuse the priest. "You are not going anywhere. Maidens' Pass froze solid three weeks early this year. This snow surely has Crones' Cut, at the other end, just as impassible." He slid the last metal heating pot underneath me and then moved the dried bundle of my fox fur cloak from atop a pile and picked up a thin metal rod out of a collection of leather and cloth.

In an instant, I was fully awake. Those were my clothes, and he had just picked out a heartpin. Long and slender, it was made to slide beneath the ribs to kill a target by puncturing the heart.

"I was going to ask you about this..." he said absently. Then he set it down and pulled out a small ring. Unremarkable, simple, the only adornment being a wickedly curved razor hidden on the inside facing the palm. "...or this." He set the ring down, then began pulling out knife after knife out of the bundle, letting them drop to the stone with musical tones. "But, I think I shall first ask you about this."

He held up a piece of leather. Upon it, sketched in black, was the symbol burned haphazardly into my back. It spread from one shoulder to the other, a twisted mass of ropy flesh badly healed and shadowed with ground in charcoal. It was unmistakably the mark on my back, the mark of a raven or a crow.

For an instant I was back in the cistern of Carolaughan, the eyes looking in from all sides, spawning gaping maws as they pressed me into the spilled coals.

I jerked. I patted drunkenly as if it would be set by my side. "Where's my sword?"

The priest pressed me back into the seat with huge, though gentle, hands. He waited a long time before speaking, staring right through, "*Dine schwert*, your magnificent sword, sits at the bottom of the mill pool."

I felt my insides lurch. The big building with the half sunk wheel under the snow, a mill with a millwheel. The huntsman had been calling me back because I had been standing on the frozen–

"It is unusual that the mill pond was not frozen through by now." He shrugged. "But Richter, the uncle of the boy you avenged, dove in and brought you back out. You will live, and his debt to you is paid. This is good, for you seem a dangerous man to be indebted to."

"I must have it."

"Your sword will sit under the ice until spring. This is bad, since you seem in a hurry to quit this village."

I don't know exactly what sound I made, or how my drawn face posed, but the priest patted me with meaty hands. "My name is Hans Blutwolfe. I am the shepherd for this village. Like it or not, you are stuck here for the winter. Considering everything involved, I think I will hide this murder kit. You will not be needing it while you are here."

"You can't do that," I rasped, weakly.

"Well," he replied matter-of-factly, "you will be unlikely to stop me until it's been well hidden for several days." He sat down in an oaken chair opposite me. "You know, I'm pretty good with people. I can feel the wounds inside of you, and I think I can help. If you let me."

We stared at each other, the day waned, the night waxed, and still the silence grew.

Finally he sighed and nodded. "It will be a long season to carry your burdens alone."

And it was.

TWO

THE LONG PATH OF DISCORD

"YOU ARE marked by Death, Crow," Hans rumbled, then continued in his native tongue, "*Es gibt keinen Schatten so gross wie die Sterblichkeit, die über der Menschheit hängt.*"

"There is no shadow as big as mortality that hangs above humanity," I translated, smiling sadly. The winter had given me time to speak the language, if accented, "There are darker shadows, priest. Trust me."

Hans nodded acceptance of my word, then moved back into the crowd. Everyone had turned out to watch me commit suicide. It was almost flattering in a macabre kind of way.

Richter came forward, brows knitted. He handed me the end of a braided leather rope. He spoke his native *HammarSpiel*, "Don't do it, Crow. Just leave the damned thing."

The snow was melting, every day exposing a little more brown, green, and gray. Maiden's Pass was still frozen solid, but Crone's Cut was clearing, and I had the chance to get a jump on any pursuit.

I had been in Matron's Rest for the entire season. The bald, droop-mustached hunter and I had spent the entire winter hunting, foraging, moving, and conversing in his native tongue. Richter had taught me more than I had ever known, or guessed, about archery and woodcraft. I felt some kind of strange blockage in my throat, and alien wetness in my eyes. I blinked furiously. "I can't."

He shrugged. "Greed is a trap with sharp teeth."

And, though delivered like a folksy oracle in a language as poetic as hurling rocks, he was right. I looked past him, to the roof of the strange church across the village. There, three ravens sat in patient silence. A chill washed over me, and I suppressed a shudder. I kicked off my boots. The shock of melting snow stabbed into my naked feet as I shook my head. "I have to. Play me out some rope. Three tugs and I need to be hauled up. After thirty breaths, I should have found it. After sixty breaths, I should be back to the edge. After one hundred breaths–."

"I'll come in after you," Richter said. *Again* was the word he didn't say, and yet he meant it.

I smiled and faked the shocked tone of the entitled, "Of course you will."

He smiled back, but despite the intense cold of early spring, his skin was sallow and dotted with perspiration. I nodded at him solemnly and turned toward the pool of ice. It wasn't just that Richter was giving, or generous. It wasn't just that he could be satisfied with silence, a trait so rare it should come with pay. It was that he felt, *knew*, I was dangerous, but refused to let it bother him. He was absolutely certain I was on his side, that I meant him no harm. And that was starting to mean something to me.

But that had nothing to do with the fact that I was now rushing to get out of Matron's Rest. Honestly.

So, I fought with myself, bucking deeply ingrained training as I pulled off my shirt. Once it would have exposed a green, black, and gold tattoo, a symbol of the owner of my soul. Now there was nothing but twisted skin where the symbol of the raven was burned. Or maybe it just signaled a change in management. The crowd had seen it before, on my first night here, but even so, they gasped. I looped the end of the rope and tossed it over a shoulder. Silence then descended upon the village, and the eyes on my back became a source of heat that faded a bit with my first step forward.

My eyes locked on the icy path out into the mill pond, ears strained for every sound, feet searching for any give in the surface. My hands took a second to kiss the knives sheathed at my hips, prepared to be drawn and cut through the ice. I breathed deeply, looking to stock up on precious air as I moved forward, further from the heat of the crowd and toward the heart of the frozen pond.

The truth was, I could stay here. There was enough gold coins sewn into the lining of my backpack, hidden about my equipment, and melted into the bottom of a nondescript clay bottle, to buy this place many times over. I could live comfortably for the rest of my days hunting, eating, and drinking. I could build myself a home and even take myself a wife, one of the pale, plump blonde girls that the principalities of Hammarfall are famous for.

A foot touched the ice and I heard it crack. I paused, looking down at the blue white pathway. Bubbles were dancing visibly beneath the transparent road. In the sheen of wetness on top, I could see my own eyes reflected back. It was at that moment I knew I could never stay. These were the eyes of a hunted man, and not one inhabitant of Matron's Rest deserved the kind of hell that would visit here if I stayed.

I may have been spared oblivion by the God of Death, but I had betrayed the God of Murder to do it. Gods, like nobles, never forget a slight or let a debtor escape. Gods, unlike nobles, live forever, see forever.

I shifted my weight, and the ice crackled again.

The God of Death had never appeared, never manifested in winged fire or descended upon thunderbolts. He had never erupted from the earth or even coalesced out of smoke. Still, I was unmistakably marked as his servant. Wherever I was going, I was heading into pain and blood. In order to survive that, I would need the Phantom Angel.

I was a little far from where I had remembered breaking through and losing the sword, but it would have to do. I gathered myself, listening to the pond groan under my feet. I crouched until my buttocks touched my ankles. Then, starting slowly, building to a crescendo of motion, I leapt.

I entered a graceful arc, my scarred but muscled body stretched into a simple curve as my fists balled to meet the thin ice. Hardened by a lifetime of combat, my knuckles would break through. With any luck I would conserve my motion and continue to dive deep, grab the sword, and surface in an instant. Long before the cold could paralyze me. Long before I could drown.

At least that had been the idea.

My hands crunched against the ice, sending thick chips flying and scraping skin clean away. I crumpled ass over head and my back slapped flat against the ice without any amount of dexterity. The crashing sound reverberated across the village and people winced and moaned as I left even more skin to stain the surface red. My feet slammed into the ice, and one ankle screamed in protest as it tested the frozen water and was found wanting as either hammer or pick.

I skidded to a halt. Flat on my back. Staring into the sunny and smiling sky, I felt ice and snow beneath me melt and nibble like sharp toothed fish at my exposed skin. I could feel blood trickling from my knuckles, back, and one heel. Far more injured was my pride. The ravens were cawing.

"Crow?" Hans called from the bank, "Crow!"

I raised a hand, waving at him and wishing that he would just go and take the whole village with him. At the first sign I wasn't dead, the worried silence began to titter and giggle.

"The ice! It must be too thick, yet!" Richter shouted.

I felt my temper light and sizzle dangerously as I sat up upon one elbow, facing backward toward the smiling huntsman. The harsh

HammarSpiel words tasted sharp in my mouth, "Really? Do you think so?"

Carefully, cautiously, I stood. The children of the village giggled and let out a half hearted cheer. I straightened up to stand full upright and wave to them with a lopsided, entirely faked, smile.

That is the moment, of course, when the ice gave way.

What I found really rude is that it failed to give any warning. It did not slide me in gently. At one moment there was perfectly firm, back-scrapingly, knuckle-batteringly thick ice. Then it just collapsed as if it were the thickness and strength of a razor edged wafer.

Just in case you were wondering if this was a miraculous event, and whether it was a foul joke perpetrated by the God of Murder or the God of Death... my bet would be yes, and both.

Cold collided with every part of me. Despite the three months and being within bowshot of spring, the cold was an elemental presence that fought with my very soul for possession of my body. I tumbled, weightless for a moment, and I saw the leather rope, impossibly cut by the edge of the ice, flutter away. I reached for it, but my tumble put my face toward the pond bed where the Phantom Angel glittered.

I stopped my spin, and glanced up at the disappearing tail of the rope, then down toward the implacable hooded phantom that stared at me from within darkened cowl. The bright blue heart in the hilt winked at me. I started to rise, buoyed by my lungful of air, when I spun in the water and kicked downward.

The ice above was a sheet of sunny white, but the water below was black as death and twice as cold. I kicked and kicked again, hoping and praying– that's a lie, I was only hoping– I could find the sword and escape because I didn't know if I could do this again. I kicked and paddled, lungs beginning to burn as pressure pushed in on my ears like the massive hands of a wrestler. I exhaled a few bubbles and descended faster, heart throbbing in my head as water on all sides sought to rob me of breath, of warmth, of life.

Then, it was there– a slice of light amongst the dark, round rocks. I pushed harder, coming down to the stones and scooping the long handle up the way a child does a favored doll. I lifted the blade to point upward, so I could break through the blasted ice above. I caught a flash of snowy movement behind me in the blade's surface. I spun.

Floating there, perfectly preserved by the intense liquid cold of the winter pond, was the carnivore I had killed months ago, floating with wide arms and thousands of tiny cuts and burns all across its face. It hovered there upright, arms spread as if in welcome, or preparing to lunge.

Air failing, lungs screaming, I spared it barely a second thought before gathering my bare feet against the numbing rocks to propel me upwards.

Then the thing opened its eyes. And more eyes. And more eyes.

Every wound, every scar, every puckered door to its tender vitals I had made, yawned open and produced a bulbous eye. Hundreds of mosquito to beetle-sized eyes across the face and neck, one the size of a fist in the middle of the chest that looked left, looked right, then centered on me and became very, very angry. Every eye a bottle of rage, a seer of secrets, an agent of the Lord of Murder.

Precious air escaped me in a yelp, and I flung myself backwards, but the water made movement sluggish and slow. The only advantage was that the thing was even slower. It missed my head, but razor sharp claws bit into my shoulder and raked flesh from me in five runnels. Another burst of air left me in an involuntary gasp and I slung the Phantom Angel in a short arc. Both hands on the hilt, counter pulling to create the spin, the blade cleft water as easily as air, or flesh. The flared blade took the incoming arm at the elbow, and severed it cleanly.

I launched from the muddy bottom, but the beast latched onto my left calf with hooked claws and pulled me back downward. The last of my air escaped, and I had to clamp lips together to keep from inhaling cold death. The carnivore, beyond such considerations, opened its mouth and let bubbles of rot poisoned air bubbles out of it in huge, roaring burps. I brought the Angel across, feeling the jarring satisfaction of the head leaving the body of the ape-thing. But the central eye in the chest was still alive, still angry as our momentum carried us both to the bottom. It let go to rake again as I collapsed on top of it.

If an eye could smile, it did, for a claw came for my face as we lay tangled in the murk, sword trapped between us. Right hand brought up a forearm that was wickedly slashed by the claw. I was seeing stars spiral behind my eyes, and I could feel a buzzing in my head as the carnivore's hand clasped over my arm. But during all this time, Left hand was planning for its own survival. It plucked the knife from the leg sheath and plunged it up, up, into the eye in the central chest. Bubbles of horrible decomposition gasses erupted in all directions from the stomach and the thing thrashed as whatever bale demon held it as a puppet tried to keep the strings from tangling. Right snatched the Angel and my legs pushed off of the body of the creature that sat against the bottom.

Soon, too soon, the point of the Angel smashed though the layer of ice. I waved it about and thrashed through the irregular hole into the air. I vomited two waterweights and gasped air past a frozen throat. Richter, who had not missed the fact that the leather rope was cut, had secured a stool from one house. This primitive grapnel fell next to me, and I clung to it as he dragged me and The Phantom Angel back through thin ice, then onto thick ice, and then to shore.

The people gasped at the red wake I left behind, but were heartened as I managed to kneel, listing heavily and falling but for the sword that for so long had been my only companion.

Richter collected a huge white fur cloak from a villager and draped me in it, cursing, "The ice has torn you to pieces friend."

I reached down to my savaged leg and pulled out the broken tip of a claw. Blood trailed behind it, but the look on Richter's face was worth it, "Yes, the ice is vicious at this altitude."

I awoke hours later, a mass of aching joints and burning wounds. Hans entered the dark, narrow church and settled down into one of the carved wooden chairs by the fire. He let the silence be undisturbed for a long, long time.

Then he sighed, "Well, Crow, you are as lucky a man as I have ever seen. Not many people could survive the frozen pond, let alone twice."

I nodded, sipping at the mulled, hard cider, relishing the heat as it washed through me. Richter let himself in, a jug of more flammable fare under one arm. He smiled and waved as he set down the jug and went to fetch another chair from deeper in the church. I felt Hans tense and I swept his huge frame with my eyes, looking for signs of attack. Whether he noticed or not, he pursed his hairy lips and slapped his thighs.

"Dammit, Crow, you've been here months and we still know nothing about you. Don't you think, after the second time we've saved your life, we are worthy of your trust?"

I coughed, "My trust? You think it's safer for me to tell you anything?"

Hans leaned forward as Richter set down the chair, placed the jug and three clay cups on the floor. The priest pressed, "I think you carry some kind of horrible burden. I know you carry many tools whose only common link is blood."

I spat into the fire, the hissing sizzle underlining my words, "Then you know too much, and you should do as much as you can to forget."

Richter shook his head, drooping-moustache ends wobbling. "I am not likely to forget a man I have taken as a brother."

They were kind words, but they brought no comfort. "It would be for the best that you do. Should you not be able, and any ask, you should remember always that you are my friend, and I would have you tell them where and when I traveled and do it without guilt or guile. I have slim hope it will buy your lives."

Hans' face remained stony, but Richter barked once in laughter, before looking from priest to me, almost confused. "I don't understand."

Heavy silence descended upon the room. But for the crackling fire, there was no movement to disturb it. Inside my own head, I was looking for an escape route, desperately searching for a way to keep everyone in the village safe. And then I realized that it lay not in the thousands of lies that flipped past my eyes, but in the obvious truth.

"I am a bad man." I said simply, unpoetically. I looked at the fire, unwilling to meet the eyes of the other two, "Evil. I have taken lives indiscriminately. I have shown mercy sparingly. I have caused pain and misery wherever I go."

Richter, a simple man completely without guile, looked at me askance for many moments, the silence pounding the clear unspoiled confessions in like nails. The pressure of each moment built until he silently stood from his chair and left. There was a blast of cold as he left, the door thumping closed behind him.

Hans huffed and his eyes narrowed at me after he tossed a fresh log onto the fire. "And tell the rest."

"There is no more," I shot back. "Nothing that can serve you ought but pain."

"Pig shit," the priest growled. He scooped up the jug and one of the cups. He poured out a measure of clear, caustic liquor into the cup, swallowed it, and filled it again. "I believe what you say, and they have the weight of truth, but they are not your story. What about the crow on your back? Who are you? *What* are you?"

"I have betrayed the God of Murder. He and his agents will search for me until I die." I met his eyes as I reached out weak hands and took the jug. I shakily filled the cup, corked the jug and sat it down. I took the whole cup of spirits into my mouth. It burned. The priest's brows came together like clashing clouds. His knuckles turned white on the rests of the thick oaken chair, and he leaned forward ever so slightly. That's when I sprayed the mountain spirits into the fire.

Assassins are taught to fight. This should not impress you, everyone gets taught how to fight. Guards, soldiers, mercenaries, knights, most nobles, even peasants know how to throw a punch or two. What assassins are taught, and I've said this before and cannot stress it enough, is how to cheat. This means that while you are walking through a festival, enjoying the sweetmeats and baked goods, looking to buy new boots, or a bolt of cloth, or even getting drunk on the kind of powerful drink mountain people imbibe, I am watching the fire breather. I am planning to follow him to a tavern, and convince him to teach me how to spray drink into a fire to make a bright, lingering ball.

And in case you are wondering, the secret is to not spit it, but to put enough air to spray it.

The cloud of atomized water rolled into the fire and burst into a bright cloud. Hans lurched back into his chair and blinked away the ghost of light, shaking his head as he searched the big blue spot for the source of the sound of breaking crockery. But when his vision cleared, I was not there. The large man started to rise, but the broken shard of cup at his throat stopped him.

He took a breath.

He took another.

I whispered into his ear, "I am a shadow. I am a predator. I am a weapon." I flicked my wrist, tossing the shard into the fire. I stumbled from around his chair and reached for my pile of clothes, cursing my muscles as they ached. "And somewhere in my wake there are men that make me look like a half blind puppy. Do you feel safer now, priest?"

Several minutes passed, the only sound being the cloth being pulled across my skin. It felt like the soft cloth was covered in tiny needles, but I didn't stop. I didn't face Hans, giving him my back. I don't know if it was to show him I trusted him, to show him the crow scar to keep him from striking out of fear, or simply because deep down I knew that if he lunged for me, I could kill him three times before he ever touched me. I wish I did know. In my life, I must be honest. I am a shadow, and a predator, and a weapon. And as sure as there was something in the water made of eyes that would have killed and eaten me, there were other things chasing me that were far more deadly than I. I pulled the thick, peasant made shirt on last.

Then I turned around. I was ready for wounded pride. I was ready for righteous indignation. I was not ready for wide-eyed fear. That's what I had. Beneath the heavy black beard and bushy brows, his weathered skin was almost blue. He was a mountain man. He was tough, practical, and used to the dangers his life presented, but to him I was a small and fuzzy creature they had found that had turned out to have fangs and claws dripping with poison.

I faced him, saying nothing. What was there to say? Who would welcome a creature such as I into their home? I had lied by omission, telling them nothing of this. But now he knew, and he knew too much. I heard a dripping against the crackle of the fire, and looked down. I had torn open a stitch in my leg. I was bleeding again.

Hans made a sign to ward off evil. And nodded at me, not affirming, but accepting. "You are wounded. You must stay." Fatigue pawed at me and I so much wanted to sit down and just sleep, but I shook my head. He raised a hand to forestall me, "The passes are still sealed for certain. You need time to heal from your wounds. Rest now. Heal." I looked at him and I know my eyes were stricken. I did not want these people to suffer for me. Then he convinced me, simply by taking a deep breath and surprising me with what came out of his mouth, "What do I tell those that come after?"

After who I did not have to ask. I shambled painfully to the chair and sat heavily, hurting for the effort. "Tell them the absolute truth. They will know if you are lying, and there is nothing you can do to protect me that won't put the whole village in danger." I drew another breath, relishing the warmth, "I need the rest of my kit now."

And despite all my plans and work, the priest was right after all, because I spent three more weeks in his church, being put right with needle, thread, and salve. He was a man used to being kept in confidence, but he no longer sought mine. I am a man used to giving up nothing, and I am an expert at silence. The first week was easy. I slept and hurt, alternatively. The next week was not as easy, since I spent a lot of time running, lifting, and generally pushing my body to regain tone and muscle lost during the week on my back. The last week was hardest. I had stashed several miraculous restoratives in my pack, but I could not waste them, for the chances of getting any more was slim beyond imagining. I had to heal the hard way, and I was nearly ready to make my way. At least Hans had the decency to be quiet. I could feel him holding himself away from me. Richter didn't come back, or seek me out, which made him wiser than I gave him credit for.

Even if it broke me a little inside.

I awoke and felt the chill in the air fading. The snow had a slick, wet look to the top. Sharp edges of last night's footprints were rounded and softened by the tiny lessening of cold. I awoke knowing it was time to go. Hans had brought my kit when I had asked weeks ago, and I assembled it silently. Hans pretended to sleep. I did not try to wake him or say goodbye. I simply left the clay flask with the bottom filled with gold on his table. I left a note. It said BREAK ME. A puddle of gold was all but untraceable, and it was the least I could do. It was, unfortunately, the only thing.

An hour later, I was forcing my legs to continue fighting against calf deep snow, wet and sticky. I pushed on out of the valley up to the high mountain pass. My legs were already rubbery. Sweat soaked my lowest layers of clothing as I forced them past the pain of the deep freeze of the pond, past the march into the wilderness. The wind was reaching inside my battered fox-trimmed cloak, sneaking icicles like knives into my tender flesh. I missed the warmth of a home, and friends. Even unknowing ones. I reached and felt the comforting hilt of the Phantom Angel. For a moment, a small, greedy, twisted part of me was satisfied and said it was all I would ever need.

The rest of me, at least the rest of me that wasn't burnt to cinders by evil, was rendered hollow by the thought, for I was afraid of that little part being right.

Then I crested the Crone's Cut. The world spread out before me like a carpet of white dissolving into green as it reached out into the sliver of barely seen, twinkling sea beyond.

Next to me, some romantic fool had spent endless hours pulling rocks from the native soil, mortaring them flat to make thick walls of sandwiched stone. It was a silly thing, serving no purpose to the one who built it, surely. A stiff, frozen wall of air blasted into me and I had to take a moment inside the shelter.

Sitting on the small bench inside was a bundle of white. A single, wooden shingle upon it bore the symbol of a raven in flight. My hands shook as I pulled the twine knot loose and let the heavy white fur fall open. Then I could not see, the world smeared into glinting pools of color. I wiped tears away as my fingers traced the powerful curve of the bow, the straight hungry intent of the arrows, the hand-tooled beauty of the leather quiver. The heavy fur was a cloak made from the mountain creatures I had killed months ago. I put on the cloak, slung the quiver and picked up the unstrung bow.

I stood at the entrance to the shelter and raised the weapon high in farewell. I would not string it until I needed it, for keeping it eternally ready for battle would weaken the string and the wood. Richter had taught me that, and he had made these things for me. And now he was somewhere out there amongst the pines. I'd never know where, for there was no one better at blending into them save the elvish, but I knew he was there, for he had left this here as a way to say goodbye. I lifted the bow again to do the same. Then I brushed sweaty black locks out of my face and turned my feet toward the slope. I leaned into the wind, grateful for the heavier cloak to keep me warm against the furious death throes of winter.

I was tired. Tired of running. Tired of being dangerous. I was tired of giving up homes in order to play in some divine game of chess between two mad Lords. I wanted to find somewhere to be anonymous, to rest. My heart hardened and I knew that was my goal. I left Matron's Rest, and I prayed for everyone in it. I prayed harder to never see it again. I prayed most of all I had not destroyed it by partaking of their kindness.

As always, I tossed the prayer out into the air, and I felt like it just flopped around on the ground, slowly dying without breath. I continued on my way.

THREE

OUT OF THE MOUNTAINS

THE WORLD exploded out from the peak into rank after rank of layered mountains. The more my feet ate at the road, the hungrier they became, pulling me onward out of the austere heights of white cold to the delicately budding green of the valleys.

The kingdom of Noria behind me was a land of rolling hills and impenetrable forests where men lived at the mercy of nature. Before me the principalities of Hammarfall were the domain of dwarves long before it was the habitat of men. Rocky, lightly forested, and ultimately broken, it had acted as a port while they drilled uncounted tunnels into these mountains looking for wealth. They had descended upon the country with their indefatigable tools and tamed the world into precisely measured squares. Eventually the dwarves pulled back their borders and abandoned fortresses and ports across maps of which only they had seen the edges. But unlike Wisteria across the ocean, that had grown a life standing on the pedestals left by their forerunners, in Hammarfall it was a history that impregnated every facet of the people and their culture.

Perhaps it was the eyes of a killer, or an orphan, or even just a northerner and Kingsman, but these people were soft. They had never had to hack their homes from the green heart of the wild. They enjoyed gentle winters and mild summers, fertile soil and copious rain. The peasants smiled and waved as they saw a lone stranger pass by. It was… strange.

The first night I spent in one of the roadside inns I was desperate to know any kind of news there was. I had resigned myself to hours of quiet listening and wheedling through the cold night. Much to my surprise when half the town came out to enjoy the first brew of the year. And they all wanted to talk. To me.

Faced with hundreds of smiling, robust people, I felt my mental hands throw open the wardrobe of personalities stored in the back of my head. It was a deep closet with thousands of people to fit every occasion, to fit in anywhere. I grabbed the boisterous one that spent money like water. Within seconds everyone in the tavern had a free pint of the cuttingly bitter but powerful bier Hammarfall was known for.

They plied me with questions from the banal ("What kind of crops are they getting in Noria?"), to the common ("Are the Norians gathering for war again?"), to the practical ("How far along is the thaw along the pass?"). I answered vividly, almost theatrically, using beer - or rather the almost toxically bitter bier - and the answers themselves to capture the minds of the simple folk, virtually guaranteeing that my features went largely unremembered. But still, I felt the cold, hollow spaces in between the mask I wore and my own self and was sad, and a bit confused.

I was sad, for after being pulled from the freezing millpond of Matron's Rest I had never felt the need to be anyone else other than myself around the terse, simple residents. Here it separated me from them, but felt so necessary I could not resist the macabre mimicry.

I was confused because I was a Norian, of course. Strangers in Noria are reason for care and suspicion. Here, along the soft spine of a softer country, they were welcomed heartily and buried under a barrage of questions. My only thought was the same as any Norian's: who would trust the word of a stranger anyway? But they asked, and I answered. Honestly, for the record, though there was no way for them to know that.

The whole village was abuzz, expecting caravans to begin trundling through, a few each month. I learned the first city I was to come to was Forgeringer, and then Hammarfall on the coast. Either could be the place I was looking for: peaceful, comfortable, and anonymous. I would have to walk those miles to find out.

The next morning I was up before dawn, out of the inn even before the young children woke to collect water and start the kitchen fires. I looked back to the dark windows, gaping holes into the skull of the building without light or sign of life. A man named Hans had spoken at length about his new baby. A woman named Hildegart had smiled at me shyly, her bright blue eyes beautiful and full of hope. Gilfreid, barely a man, had seen my sword and immediately thought me some sword for hire. He had pestered me all night for stories of heroism and danger. The people of Hammarfall were musical, and it seemed everyone had an instrument at hand. It filled the building with bright mirth and allowed me to dodge questions easily.

Oh, they got some information about me personally; a patchwork of lies, loosely strung together with assumptions and unsaid linkages. It may even dawn on them this morning that nobody ever got a name. Might not even bother them, for I had spent freely, pennies tinkling on the table to let the bier flow until I was sure they would be fuzzy today.

For an assassin, any bit of information may be useful, and you train to remember details as well as possible until they are not needed. But now it just reminded me of a hundred happy people, living simple lives in a simple place, far away from hurt or…

And there she was, behind my lids. I closed my eyes like lowering myself into a steaming bath, memories parboiling my intimate anatomy and sending blood racing to my face– the princess I could not have.

But I did not stop walking, or even pause in my step anymore. She had her timeless duty to her people, her family and her station. I had mine. To what or who I was only beginning to understand as the miles passed beneath me while I held course toward the city of Forgeringer. I needed a larger city to hide in, to blend into the shadows. And the road did not help on this account. The miles became lonely, and for me that is saying something. The road was magnificently cobbled even this far out, and bore the signs of constant use during the good seasons. But was the first crack of spring, and there should have been merchants everywhere moving goods from where they were made cheaply toward where they could be sold dearly. The road was utterly civilized and had inns that had set up every wagon-day worth of travel apart. My coffers full, and my food supply light, I stopped at many of them along the way. Day by day they became no less friendly, but far less festive.

Then I reached Forgeringer. The city was a pleasant surprise, until it wasn't, which is usually how things go in my life. I came in through the north gate, and because of that, I had no idea there was anything wrong at all until I spoke with the guard. Yet the gate was wide, and all but unused at the moment. The moat was composed of flowing water diverted from a nearby river, which whisked away the worst of the sewage smells from the outer wall, even if it could do little to freshen the streets of the city. This was where it bypassed the city, and took the waste with it. The smell was indescribable.

The man at the gate was resplendent in dirty leather armor reinforced with rings. He wore a full, albeit slightly rusty, helmet, his nearly discarded heavy shield languishing against a wall, and his spear was currently being used to lean against. He was relaxed to the point of being bored, which was good. I knew he would want to close the gates soon so he'd be disinclined to chat. I just needed to pay the tax and be on my way.

Normally guards were just there to collect a nominal gate tax, per the foot, which went directly into the coffers of the ruling class to be used for clothes, parties, food, and all the other luxuries those who paid the taxes normally lacked. I had long ago slipped a few coins into an obvious scrip on the outside of my person, keeping the much larger, richer purse hidden from view and questing fingers as I approached the opening.

He raised a hand, "Is peace your business?"

It was a question that stopped me in my tracks. The harsh *HammarSpeil* tongue was not especially complex, and I could not have mistook his words. I shook my head as if trying to clear my ears. "Yes?"

The man straightened immediately. "Yes? What do you mean yes?"

I shook my head again, and took the risk of playing up my Norian accent when I answered. "I am a foreigner. We must have misunderstood."

The man relaxed a bit, leaning back on the spear. "I mis-understood nothing, outlander. I ask again...what is your business?"

I smiled as if a little embarrassed, not entirely an act, I continued in slightly exaggerated pidgeon *HammarSpeil*, "I am sorry. Passing through to the sea. Big boat."

The guard shook his head. "We've had nothing but people fleeing Forgeringer. Do you have a silver and a halfsilver?" I dug in my scrip, thinking the tax outrageous and handed him the coin and the halfcoin. He shook his head and handed back the half coin. "Half silver per leg to enter, but when you wind up sleeping on the streets the watch will fine you half a silver to keep out of prison. Now go in."

His tone brooked no argument, and I gave none. He said nothing about the swords hung at my hips, and that was all I needed. He waved to the dark window of the gatehouse above. Immediately, titanic chains began to squeal and screech as they pulled the huge drawbridge up over the moat. Before it shut, before any of the guards gathered for the end of their shift, and long before anyone could take any more interest in little old me, I had faded into the darkening streets of the city.

Within minutes, I was past the mass of warehouses that choked the north gates, over the wide bridge that spanned the river that cut the city into threes, and then to the residential and business areas. At normal times, these would be bustling streets from dawn till long after dusk. Now they were packed with shocked people standing in tired packs, wrapped against the cold night but unable to find more than that for shelter. They took out portable instruments and sang quietly, hoping the notes would warm them against the night.

The guard's words were true: I would likely be paying a fine, for every room, floor, and stable had been filled to bursting. Even a casual ear could pick out tales about the unrest in Hammarfall which brought on some confusion in me.

These brilliant southerners had named both their country and their capital Hammarfall. Only through a subtle use of suffixes that made one singular (the capital) and the other plural (the country) could one tell what they were talking about. Many times they used both in the same sentence, and all but lost me. Seriously, nobody could come up with a different name?

As I wandered, I was truly shocked. There were no beds, chairs, or floors available. Normally this means there was none affordable, but that was not true. They were charging a week's rent for a small room above a kitchen for a single night on the floor of the common room. Yet, still, these spaces were taken. Soon I was desperate enough to check the churches, which were all always looking for donations, had the added rent of being preached at, and yet were again all out of space. Not only the city, but every building was packed like a rat warren left unchecked.

I left the Temple of War and meandered down a couple of alleys, each one home to dozens of refugees. I did not stop. What I needed was to clear out some urban cave, making sure it was not the home of any other lion, wolf, or bear, and then eat something. My legs had done their part and got us here, now they wanted their tithe from the stomach.

I was thinking too hard, I have to admit it, and looking too hard up into the eves for unused lofts or boarded windows. I was so surrounded by the press and noise of people that I filtered out everything around me, which was a recipe for death anywhere in the world. I turned the corner into one of those places I never wanted to be.

Four toughs turned to me, forming a wall with their thick rounded shoulders. There was a shivering old man behind the buttresses of flesh, cart of foods shaking in his hands. The robbery was obvious, and I was too slow to leave or pretend to be a very blind witness.

Each of the thugs was dressed in a mockery of the upper crust. They had pointed shoes with toes that were as long as a forearm, kept from folding under by bell festooned-silver chains that tied them to the knee. They had blousy short pants over their hose, kept in place by woven leather suspenders and clapped to groins by comical codpieces featuring impossibly large stuffed leather phalli that dangled half to their knees. Also, I might add, decorated with bells. The short jackets were tied together loosely like the high nobility: lower sleeve to upper, upper to vest and both halves of vest together. Again, the laces were covered in bells. Lest you think this was done simply in the name of style and grace, the material of the jacket was thick, rough, and able to turn aside a wicked slash from a knife or dagger. Tied to sword belts with simple tug-loose knots were short, brutal hammers and sheaths holding long knives.

For once, no bells. There was also a small wooden tube, which I dismissed as hollowed out for some herbal entertainment to be contained. It took less than a second to take in the entire situation.

The best fed of them sneered at me, "Is peace your business?"

This time the words hit me like a fist. I startled, taking one step back and eyes narrowing as the phrase echoed inside of my skull, "What did you say?"

The thugs glared, for it was not the answer to the question they think they had asked. Muscles on the leader's jawline danced in frustration. "I said... is this any of your business?"

Another one said, "A foreigner! I bet he don't know about the foreigner tax."

The thugs moves forward slightly, jingling as they started to crowd one another, sensing blood and eager to partake. Their hands were inept at casually moving down to the thongs that were twisted to hold the hammers. Their shoulders almost touched now, one on my far left, all the way to four on my far right. It was far too late to turn, too late to run. They had seen me and knew that one swordsmen against four was likely dead in this alley, and his valuable gear ripe for selling. I felt old memories boil up inside; growing up in dark alleys, long before I learned to fight, I learned to brawl.

Fights had a timing to them. Swordsmanship was a deadly dance I excelled at, but this was nothing like it. Brawls were like explosions. And the one to move first often won. So I stopped my mind from racing, took a deep breath, and when I blinked, the animal inside me took over.

My iron shod boot was made for travelling hundreds of leagues, and could stand up to any road, trail or rocky climb. It smashed down onto the dainty city shoe of number two, and had him screaming. Then everything happened at once. One struck, but two was pushed into his way and the hammer meant for my delicate skull hit his instead. My Right hand drew a dagger (not mine), blade down, but used the pommel to smash the nose of number three as he got his hammer free. Rather than hang around, Right zipped further right to deflect the blow from number four. Once the blade made contact with the wooden haft, it slid down, lopping off two fingers as Left continued to push number two in everyone's way. Thug one looked up from the comrade he had injured just in time to get a knife-filled fist in his face. The extra waterweight of steel and hilt inside my gloved fingers spattered his nose with the sound of crunching celery. Three opened his watery eyes over a broken nose just in time to catch an aforementioned reinforced boot in the groin. He toppled over as if axed.

The explosion of violence was shocking, even terrifying. It was also, and I cannot lie, accompanied by a hundred bells jingling festively. It was only slightly ruined by the sniveling half screams of number four, who could now only count up to eight as he cradled his wounded hand to his chest.

I stood back, surveying my handiwork and trying to rein in the quiet murmurs in the back of my head to just knife each one and be done with it. Instead I stepped past the injured and bawling brawlers, quickly chose two hunks of cheese and two large twists of brown and salted bread and plunked down one bloody knife (still not mine) and two copper coins into the old vendors cup on his cart. I jerked my head back down the alley and he nodded his thanks as he fairly ran back toward the relative safety of the busy streets.

I stowed my cold dinner and started to swiftly saunter away from the scene of battle, feeling invigorated. It was hard enough to take on more than one man at a time, let alone leave them alive at the end of the conflict. I was justifiably proud of myself. That was, of course, when I heard a high, shrill tone behind me. It was at that moment I realized I should not have dismissed the short wooden tubes on the belts of the toughs. It turns out that those were the most dangerous items by far. Because these thugs were obviously in some kind of group and, now that there was nothing I could do about it, it appeared they had a way to call to each other. One of them got another shrill blast away, and another.

If someone does not know they are chasing you, or that it is you that they should be chasing, the worst thing you can do is run. Running men, when someone is chasing, are fleeing. And in such cases, men are much like hounds. They cannot suppress the urge to chase that which is fleeing. Knowing there was little chance that my tall bearing, my glittering sword, or white fur cloak could possibly go without notice, I maintained my calm pace to the mouth of the alley to at least appear uninvolved.

I exited the alley into a bubble devoid of people all looking down the alley at the poor food vendor who had been stopped at the mouth of the far alley by four more of the bell wearing morons. On the ground, his cart overturned, he pointed a shaking finger back up the alley, at me. Which, of course, is what I should expect to happen if I do something noble.

The four toughs turned in unison.

They came in a rush, but the first caught a throwing knife in the chest before he took his second step. He was dead before he slumped to the ground. *So much for a bloodless coup*. I spun off the heavy, restrictive white fur cloak across the second one of them, because as nice of a gesture it had been, I needed movement. The third raised his hammer and I leapt forward to catch his arm in the air. As we separated I had his hammer and he had a hole in his chest from my freshly pulled dagger going in and out-with-a-twist. His blood ran like wine from a bottle. Number Four fled into the crowd as I viciously clubbed the thug struggling under my cloak. His skull made a sound like a ripe melon under the stolen hammer, and I pulled my white cloak off of him before he could fall to the ground.

It was over, as fast as that. A very definite silence settled all about.

Ok, so this was some kind of gang, or guild, or family, or however crime is structured in this place. That was clear. Yet, somehow I doubted that the magistrate would be shaking my hand for this little act of survival. Officials were officially charged with maintaining the peace, and as long as you bleed quietly in the alley, the peace is maintained. You fight noisily and well…

So, problem number one was corpses I now had on my hands. Even the one I had hammered was dead, so to be caught was to have my neck stretched. If, that is, I was caught by the good guys. Get caught by the gang/family/syndicate and it would take a long time to die. I could run, but there were dozens of witnesses. They would definitely tell anyone in authority anything they could about me, and would probably do so to a criminal organization just out of self preservation. Number two is one was running, and since he knew the streets and people would get you of the way of a thug, I'd never catch him. I had to disappear.

I threw the cloak over my shoulder, stole a whistle and absently tucked the hammer into my belt. As another shrill blast of notes sounded down the street, I blew into the alley across the street at a sprint. I needed everyone to think I was heading for the other end, but about halfway down the alley it took a dogleg. There, masked from being seen at both ends by the twist in the path, I scrabbled up the cracking mortar along the brickwork and began to climb. Normally, I use much more finely pointed city boots to do this kind of thing, and thin climbing gloves to protect my tender digits. Climbing in road boots and traveling gloves was like seeing through muddy water. Plus the Angel was on my damn hip and it kept clunking against the wall when I tried to balance close. No time to move it to my shoulder. I had to pause and remove the gloves, knowing every second meant life or death. I shoved the leather into my jerkin, but the way was only marginally better. The cracks were just smaller than my fingertips, meaning I had to wedge the damn things in there. The stone had not gotten word it was spring and was freezing cold besides. My boots could use only the largest of footholds, and my need to be silent surpassed only my need for speed by a hair. This is why when the city guard noisily showed up in the alley beneath, I froze.

They had come in numbers, showing a wisdom I don't usually equate to men who sign up for the watch. They were moving slowly, far too slowly to catch a man running down the alley. My paranoia ran rampant for a moment until I realized that all was perhaps on purpose. I had appeared from nowhere and killed several men in less heartbeats of time. It was damn likely that the watch had no interest in meeting up with someone (me) who could commit that much concentrated mayhem, let alone try to arrest him. Instead I stay utterly still, listening to half heard whispers as they stalked along the alley. I tried not to shuffle, tried not to gasp, tried not to breathe. Then the leader, for whatever gods-awful reason, decided to leave one of his men at the dogleg.

What? Was I going to come up behind them, circle back around to ambush this group of men out of fecund morbidity? No one had looked up or else spears, rocks, and arrows would have come soon after. No, for reasons I will never know, I was left with a babysitter five manheights below, who was just waiting for me to continue so he could hear me and summon my doom. There was a brief exchange below, and the rest of the watch was cautiously off.

Look, I am in fine shape. I run (quite often for my life.) I train with rocks and logs, climb sheer surfaces, and practice with my blade whenever it is not in use in a frozen pond as a nefarious trap by the God of Murder who wishes to kill me. Yes, I am a fine specimen of manhood. But how long do you think that training will allow me to hang, motionless, upon two clumsy boot holds and two precarious finger holds? In the cold? After a long day of slogging to get here, AND two fights? If I ever find out it is actually a fair universe for everyone else I am going to pass water onto the altar of one god or another, perhaps all of them, because I truly do not deserve this at all.

So forgive me when a few moments later, I tried to reposition a leg that was starting to cramp, and slipped. The boy below, who had just removed his helmet to wipe some stress sweat from his eyes, of course heard. The young man looked up into my crotch, and then dropped his helmet and began to fumble at his belt. It turns out he also had a small whistle, this one of tin, which he blew. I told you these were a musical people. He got half a note off– clearly different from the gang whistle– when the gang hammer at my belt met his face at high speed and dropped him like a sack of excrement. Then, no other plan coming to mind, I blew the stolen wooden whistle excitedly, in gasping blasts. Then

I dropped it also onto the corpse, and shot up the wall as if my arse had been lit ablaze, noise be damned.

My fingers were bleeding, one fingernail tore half off, my right leg was threatening to seize up, but the wall continued up, up, up, forever. I froze again and glanced downward as shouts echoed past me. But they were not aimed at me. Several of the gang of toughs had come to the whistle. So, of course, had the watch.

Allow me to paint a picture I call "I Hate You All". There, his brains exposed, was a dead watchman, a gangster hammer, a horde of dandy thugs, and an equal sized mob of the city watch. I would paint you the resulting portrait "You Deserve This Because I Was Just Looking For Somewhere To Sleep, You Damned Bastards". I just didn't have enough red.

I tried to be quiet as I finished the climb, but I might not have bothered. The scuffle down on the street, followed with dozens of blasts of wood and tin brought more and more combatants, with heavier and heavier armament. The sound of jingling bells mixed with screams to become something childishly sinister, bordering on demonic. Long before they were done, I had found a window high up on the wall– well, an opening– and drew myself inside.

I fell from the lip into the top of a tower. I rolled to a stop next to a gargantuan bell and simply panted. A quick glance showed the rope system leading off to a more comfortable ringing position, and the debris by the door said nobody came up here unless they had to. It was far from perfect, but also far from jail or death.

Everything hurt, and everything throbbed. Every muscle not pushed to its failure point was twitching from the surge of survival. I am sure I passed out several times, but there was little I could do about that. I quelled the urge to look over the edge down to the alley. No matter who won down there, the chaos had served my purpose– I had escaped. Then the cost of the young watchmen crashed home again.

There had been a time when I had been able to shrug off the death of some random stranger easier than walking through a fog. Now, however, it caused a deep ache to my very core. Certainly I could tell myself that we had been on different sides on what amounts to a war for survival. Had he worked for a sane and patient law that would take into account that I had saved a man's earnings, spared four before being forced to kill a few more to save my own life… well in my experience, that kind of law does not exist. I would be just another obstacle to one sheriff, or undersheriff, or anonymous functionary claiming the Phantom Angel, my sack of coin, and anything else they fancied. I would be dead, imprisoned or fined into a workhouse long after they had claimed my property for their own. And the men who died fighting the thugs? *What else were they supposed to be doing?*

Yet, the death of the man who had spotted me haunted me into the night, making sleep harder to come by the more rested I became. I ate sullenly from the purchased bread and cheese from the man who had fingered me. Then I took off and folded the great white cloak into bedding. I drew the thick fox fur cloak over top of me on the floor. Finally, finally, the last blows were struck and the last jingling scream heard.

Yet it was a tin whistle cut short that invaded my dreams.

FOUR

THE PRICE OF ESCAPE

I SAT up, the cold stone floor of the bell tower was well padded by the no-longer-quite-white fur cloak. The lighter, fox lined cloak had acted well as blanket. I had only wished I had kept enough presence of mind to undress, for now the uncomfortable wet in my clothes was like standing in a rainstorm. The pre-morning wind came by and licked at my bones, chilling them everywhere the damp cloth touched. After a few minutes more I moved, and felt the cramped cages of heroic effort followed by cold repose clamp upon my limbs. I let the cloaks lay there, but picked up the Phantom Angel and stretched out my sullen muscles.

Taking time to survey my surroundings, I noticed the thick ropes and heavy timber showed little signs of decay, which meant the church must still be active. I gave a glance down into the alley from which I had fled. I should not have bothered; in the dregs of the night, the cleft was as black as a tax man's heart. I crossed to the other side of my perch. I derided my luck, for I had picked the one point on the whole building where I would have to climb three times as far to get to an opening or roof. The church was built on the foundations of much older buildings, probably catacombs of some kind, and then the tower was made to pierce the sky far above the church itself and every building around. At least it gave me a view, but it was not beautiful or comforting.

Forgeringer was laid out like a giant tick, full to bursting with people. I shuddered. It was indeed under siege. Out on the road, campfires spread like an invading army of the penniless, the homeless, and the desperate. Beyond the road, to the southwest, the terrain became even less forgiving as the mountains that made the northern border and western spine of Hammarfall (the country) crowded to the shore. It was a cloudy sky, blotting out all the heavenly bodies and their merciful light, yet I thought I could detect a glow against the far off clouds. The pattern shifted against the sky making skulls and leering faces and at least once a lidless eye inside of a complex golden knotwork of blades. This was dawn, such as it was.

I shook my head, because whatever powers there were in this city had completely lost control, showing they had no right to that control to begin with. In any case, there was no way I was putting my head in that meat grinder. I just needed to find someplace quiet, serene and far away from the push and pull of the damned world.

Then there came words that nearly pushed me over the short wall and to my doom far below. "Is your business peace?"

The Phantom Angel rang from his sheath, only instinct and a lifetime of practice keeping the blade from nicking stone or bell in the tight quarters of the belfry. It made a moaning arc in the air and came to a sudden stop, point barely a handspan from the nose of the speaker.

It was an old man. Well no, that is a lie. Despite the fact that he perched on a forgotten rain barrel, his ankles bopping together and feet dangling like a child far short off the floor, this man was truly ancient. His hair was simply a forgotten wisp that settled around his skull as a halo. His teeth had long since gone, giving his mouth the caved in appearance indicative of great age. Even his dark eyes had withdrawn to hold council with his deepest thoughts beneath protruding and balding brows. Yet, he was older still, with wrinkles upon wrinkles and loose folds of skin where his arms and legs had deflated due to the ravages of time. His skull, feet, and hands looked too large for his body. He chuckled at the deadly tip of the blade, apparently too overjoyed at every moment of life to be perturbed at anything. He had naught but a long white shift between he and the cold, but he paid it no mind.

My first instinct was to run him through. Madmen and prophets are dangerous, and in my life I had suffered both to my peril. Yet the point wavered, and I lowered the Angel, figuring any man who had no fear of a blade may have a reason for his courage beyond mere insanity. My eyes darted between my guest and the door in the wall, still unconvinced he was real.

Finally the words he had used hit me again, and I looked foolishly around the tiny platform suspended dozens of manheights in the air. When whatever explanation I was expecting to materialize did not become evident, the obvious question popped out, "What did you say?"

The imp of a man giggled, relishing every second then leaned forward, as if sharing a secret, "Do you have business here?"

I stared at the wrinkled, bronzed little man. I was certain, certain to the core of my soul, that this was not what he had asked. Yet the guard and the thug from the evening before had acted as if I was the one who had misheard. Besides, what reason would three far flung men have for asking the same puzzling question? I sheathed the Angel; it had been a long night of sleeping on the stone and I was unrefreshed. At this point, I just needed hot food and means to escape the city before the watch, or the unnamed criminal gang, found me and repaid me for using them to ambush one another.

"Well?" The old man interrupted my thoughts with a voice honed with the authority of age. I blinked at him blankly before he repeated, "Do you have business here?"

I was in a belfry for no good reason and, even worse, the solid wall containing the door faced the front of the church where all such identifying religious symbols were located. However, it is important to note that I have a rule for situations such as this: NEVER ADMIT GUILT. Well, that's not entirely true. The Rule is: NEVER ADMIT GUILT UNTIL SUCH TIME AS YOU CAN KILL ENOUGH PEOPLE TO ESCAPE. Which, I know, is a little bloody. But that leads me to another rule of mine: BETTER YOU THAN ME. That is why I nodded imperiously, strode to my bundled cloaks, and gathered them into my arms and lied like a street orphan. "Of course I do."

The old man looked left and right. "Then why-ever were you housed up here?"

I sighed as I twirled the fox-trimmed cloak over my shoulders, giving myself a moment as words assembled themselves behind my mouth. Then, as I picked up the white fur cloak, they emerged easily. "I have spent half a year on the road and the silence of indoors disturbs me. I feel closed in unless I can hear the wind."

The old man's eyebrows, what was left of them, shot up. "It is awfully cold to sleep outside in order to entertain the wind."

I affixed the thick, black iron clasp to the fur cloak, pulling it tightly about me. "What is a good price for a peaceful night's rest?"

And, as if I had stumbled upon something crushingly profound, the old man set one deep pit, where an eye hid, upon me. "Oh, too true. The price of a long, peaceful rest is, indeed… dear." But then he slid to the floor, as spry as an adolescent. "Well then, if you have business here, we best see you fed before your meeting with the new abbot. We may have been lax in finding you a drafty enough room to keep you, but at least we can find you something to dine upon."

"My thanks." Certainly I had not forgotten about escape, but then again, escape is easiest to accomplish on a full stomach.

The old man opened the door, the hinges protesting in a grumbling bass, and started down the stairs beyond. I followed, thankful to yank the musical portal shut and block out the bastard wind that had stolen my warmth all night. No wind was a great improvement, but it came at the cost of a rickety set of stairs that soon disappeared into darkness. The old man seemed not to mind, taking each squeaking step in turn like a child one tenth his age. At least his insane bravery was explained– now that we were indoors, the man smelled like he was pickled in the strongest and harshest of spirits. Though he spoke well and did not stumble, it was not unusual to see a man of his age almost inured to strong drink due to a lifetime of exposure.

I had to move carefully, but soon the ghostly light of the ill-fitted door below cast enough illumination to see the outline of the wooden planks. It was clear, however, why the rain barrel was in the belfry, for anyone who climbed these stairs and then pulled at the giant rope would the need a repast or two.

Churches were normally cold affairs, but upon exiting the bell tower, precious heat slapped my numb face and tingled in my fingers. The halls may have been dark and gloomy, but expensive braziers were lit against the cold.

He motioned me to a side passage and after only a few moments, we were in a small back room to the kitchen. A fire burned and several black cauldrons containing unknown, but delicious smelling concoctions, burbled. He bade me sit and disappeared for only a moment. Then he returned with a plate piled with hard biscuits, fresh sausage, and– in dwarvish style– a salt crusted potato. I dug in without further encouragement.

The whole place seemed all but deserted. A novice or two went scurrying past the door to the corridor but they never even paused to glance inside. They could hardly have seen me, for even with the warning of their flopping sandals, I barely caught sight of them as they went by. All the better for me, for the hot, roasted sausages were heavenly. The hard biscuits crumbled into cheesy lumps, with a slightly beery and pleasant aftertaste. The boiled potato had been slit expertly, and a lump of butter inserted into the center. Then the outside crust of salt crumbled with each bite, flavoring the inside wonderfully.

The old man nattered on, but I barely gave him notice, as my instincts were tuned to listening for a hue and cry at my presence. But then it happened again...

"Is peace your business?"

My eyes snapped up and fixed the old man with a steady glare that was in no way friendly. "What?"

The old man did not notice, which made me doubt the power of my glares nowadays. "I asked, what is your business?"

"Why do you ask?"

His voice was low, given burrs and rasp by a lifetime of use, "Oh, I think you will find a man's business is everything in this life. So, tell me what do you do?"

I thought about the heavy pouch of coin inside my jerkin, the life of comfort and peace it meant, and I shook my head. "I don't do anything anymore."

His expression fell, casting eyes into further shadow and making his face take on the aspect of a sunken skull. "Oh, that is a horrible thing. In Hammarfall a man is defined, esteemed, by those things he does in life."

Visions of blood and suffering flashed before my eyes. Scenes I had built with poison, blade, and garrote. The words tumbled out before I could catch them, "I am no man to be esteemed."

The old man nodded sagely. "You are correct, but then you must ask yourself what can you do to purge yourself of your unworthiness."

My eyes narrowed. "How do you speak to me in such a way?"

The old man chuckled, "I have fed you, wanderer. I have spread my breadcrumbs before a crow and I imagine I can speak to you in any way I like." I sat up straight as shouts started, far off but inside the building. I looked to the exits, then to the old man. He shrugged. "You have the look of a man who is ready to take his farewell."

Complex emotions boiled up inside of me like a witches brew left on the fire far too long. I had urges that spanned from thanking the old man and darting off on my own, to cowering behind him lest I were caught roaming the halls alone, to stabbing him and everyone I saw in the face until I made daylight. Instead I made a fist on the table next to the wreckage of my breakfast and tried to stare the man down. "Your words are twisted and unclear, but you seem to know me, old man. Speak plainly."

The man stood briskly and spoke as he walked out of the room in his white shift, "Oh, I know you better than you know yourself, I think."

I bounced to my feet and dashed into the corridor, but in the instant he had been out of sight he had seemed to sprint to the end of the corridor. With no better offers for guidance forthcoming, I raced after, my equipment bouncing on my shoulders. Of course travelling this way made the angry voices grow louder and louder.

I caught him, doddering along the next corner as if this were his top speed. I felt my brow furrow and my heart begin to pump madly, waiting to fuel my fists for a fight. I hissed in a whisper, "Who are you, old man?"

"Nobody important. Who are you?"

My answer was instantaneous, "Nobody important."

The old man stopped and whirled upon me, poking my chest with one boney finger. "Good. Because I would hate for you to think you had paid your debts." And then he opened the door next to us. I followed instantly and we disappeared inside as some monks came around the far corner. He shut the door behind us and put a finger to his lips. We might not have bothered, for the shouting crowd was obviously on the other side of the wall, and nearly drowned out anything we might have had to say. The room beyond was all but unlit, with just trickles of dawn coming in from a window only a hand wide and far above.

"What debts?" I growled quietly.

The old man took up a white sheet from a table and wrapped it around himself. The smell of crushed flowers, alcohol, and incense slapped me about the face. His cheery demeanor faded into nothing. "You know, of course you know– the debt to the gods, to those you have murdered."

I staggered back from his accusing glare, hands raised as I scanned every patch of darkness for an ambush. The old man harrumphed and popped himself onto the table. With deft hands he began working the sheet around his ankles. "Do not think the gods have forgotten you. Do not think your debt is paid. Every second you cry out, asking why you deserve such treatment, know you are far luckier than most in your position."

And there it was...the loss of home, wealth, the woman I loved– all of it boiled into a single molten dagger I hurled at the old man. "Luck? You call my life lucky? You think I am over-gifted with mercy from the heavens?"

He deflected it without even looking up from his work around his thighs. "Yes. But for the mercy you so easily disregard, you would surely be dead, your soul devoured to feed some minor sycophant to the God of Murder." He continued to fuss about his hips, and I finally took notice of his fingers. Old though they were, they danced like magic, an almost invisible needle flying like the wind. Like a plague victim, he was sealing himself up in a funeral shroud.

My voice raised, and gained a hysterical edge, "What are you doing?"

"I am delivering a message, as my Master wills it." He huffed, lay down, and continued sewing from the inside of the funerary cloth. "You have been asked, and you have not answered, Crow. Is peace your business?"

My sins were laid bare, my life behind me measured in knife edges and piercing weapons. I felt the question take the wind from me. "No," I answered.

"Then what makes you think that claiming a quiet life is the task left to you by those you have wronged?"

Then, he was there, my old friend, Defiance. He flared to life in my chest and spread warmth across my body as my face twisted into a sneer. "Who is to say what debt I owe?"

The old man was working at his neck, the rest of the cloth pulled tightly about him and sewn into place. He smiled at me, but it was the smile of an old man watching a young man about to learn a painful lesson. "The one that holds the tally books, Crow. And you know that. What I am here to say is, and what you must remember is– you are not bound for a peaceful end. You have not earned one, and you do not deserve one. Glorious. Legendary. Maybe even heroic. But not peaceful."

Immediately I looked down to the bulge that contained the hundreds of golden coins beneath my leather. I slapped a hand into it, feeling the clear metal, the weight and mass. I looked up to call the old man a liar, that I had the means, and thus the right. But somehow, impossibly, he was now cocooned from head to foot in the shroud. I reached out to shake him, but the freezing flesh beneath the thin cover sucked the feeling from my fingers. He moved, not as a man, but as a single solid piece of mortifying meat.

Take it from someone who has seen a city worth of dead bodies in his day... the old man in the shroud was past dead by a matter of long hours. My legs shook, and deposited my knees onto a small wide padded stool made for the purpose, allowing me to kneel before the body as incense censors smoldered into life and candles shyly fluttered into brightness on all sides. Carved everywhere were skulls, angels, and ravens past counting.

I was in a mortuary.

Then the door flung open, framing me in torchlight. It was from there that things began to happen rather quickly.

"You, there, what are you doing here?"

There simply was no escape. Only one way in, one way out, and an argument brewing on the other side of the wall– everything appeared grim. On the other hand, when discovered, ADMIT TO NOTHING. If possible, LOOK LIKE YOU BELONG. When trapped, a useful cover is to act important and indignant. I summoned up a haughty tone and shielded my eyes from the light– and by extension my face from the monk's eyes– and sneered for all I was worth.

"How dare you interrupt me in my prayers for my kinsman?"

And that, of course, made the poor man's mind skid to a complete stop. "The Abbot never mentioned kin."

An abbot, then. An important position usually attained only by the moneyed and titled. One hand genuflected the symbol of the raven even as the other gathered several secret coins from pockets sewn inside my sword belt. I stood and towered over the small robed figure, growling deep in my chest, "The Abbot kept you in his confidence, then?"

"Well, y-y-y-y-ye– Well, no."

I reached down to the monk's thin, limp arm and picked it up, laying three heavy gold coins into the palm as if they meant nothing. Inside I wanted to scream, imagining all the comforts and necessities I was giving away without a fight. The monk stared at the coins as if they were rare and colorful bird eggs. "See to it his funeral is... special."

I started to push past the monk and he gave way. "Of course, of course, sir. Let me show you the way out."

He scuttled ahead of me as I smiled at his tonsured head. A much better, and oft unused, rule: IF POSSIBLE GET THEM TO SHOW YOU THE WAY OUT.

So he opened the door and strode into the next chamber. Angry noise exploded all around us, reminding me far too late this was where the commotion was coming from. Sensing the exit so close, however, I quickened my pace, hoping to find it before the furious voices found me. And of course, that's where everything fell to pieces.

Oh, we had only entered the main worship hall for the monastery. Thick, black fabric fluttered up the walls and then into the center of the room, forming dark archways through which the penitent had to pass. At the altar there were wreaths made of raven feathers, and a statue of a cold, distant man welcoming those passed into the afterlife. It could have been me, but I felt like he was looking at me and smiling. At the altar, at the head of two crowds bearing white sheeted bodies, was the new abbot, maybe just the prior, and he was shouting to be heard. "You must go! We are not a church! We are not authorized to do burials for the public. Only priests have that power, and they are busy with the refugees!"

"Our men deserve proper burials!" screamed a tough with an enormous fake phallus, vest, and hammer.

"Your men were thieves and dung munching perverts!" a city watchmen matched him. "Our men deserve rest in hallowed soil."

But these two were not alone. Oh no, of course not. There were crowds of each. This is what the loud argument had been about. Each wanted burial for their lost fighters, and had mistakenly brought them to a monastery of the God of Death instead of the church, the church– like all churches– being overrun with refugees. I had to go, slowly, calmly, I had to turn around and just slip out unnoticed.

Then someone bellowed, "Oi!"

As if lit on fire, I drew the eyes of everyone in the room. And, just like that, I was a dead man. I smiled charmingly, mostly to see if it would buy me a second or two to speak. It did not.

Someone squealed from within the ranks of the thugs, "The winged sword! That's him!"

"That's him?" A sword rang off the steel throat of its sheath as the watchman yelled, "Get him!"

Everyone glanced at the speaker, then back to me. Only now I was armed with a smile and the Phantom Angel.

The closest of the watchmen, watchwoman to be fair, pressed the men around her back. With a discrete pull, she effortlessly relieved one of them of their sword while drawing her own. The long tongues of bright metal began to weave, began to dance. Faster and faster they twirled around her, becoming a moving shield of razors as they whipped through the air with high pitched laughter. She was young, and fast. While she was not as good as she thought, she might be lucky, and sometimes that was enough. The watchmen behind her grinned nastily as the blades came to a rest pointing at my heart– one tip for each chamber.

"Fancy sword," she sneered. "Do you know how to use it?"

I have to admit, I was impressed, and any other time her display would have required some kind of drinking contest that would end in hours of sweaty nakedness. At the moment, however, I just nodded and twirled the supernaturally sharp blade in a simple circle. There was the sound of rippling cloth above, catching everyone's attention. The swordswoman looked back to where I had disappeared out though the door, having severed the ropes holding the huge arches of black banners in place. As the crowd surged forward, these drapes descended like shrouds to cut off all control and all cohesion to the hall. Curses exploded on all sides, ricocheting down the hall before the thunder of tromping boots swallowed them whole. While this was happening, I was making my own way out.

Phantom Angel back in place, I shifted the belt with two tugs to move it from my hip (good for fighting) to my back (good for running). And run I did. Ran like a rabbit, for the wolves were indeed after me. I found a door near the rear of the monastery and shouldered through it at a sprint, rolling across the ground as I lost my step. The world spun and I heard the wood lining of the sheath on my back crackle and snap. I came to my feet and my legs pushed harder to send me along the rear wall. I had found outside, luckily, but I had also found daylight, offering me no easy escape. I spotted a scaffold ahead as dozens of mixed pursuers vomited forth out of the door behind me.

I leapt and caught the lowest wooden crossbar, swinging my boots onto a platform of raw boards, then slithered up, jumping, climbing, and all combinations of those two to set foot on the top of the wall. I saw the shacks below, built against the wall to save on expense, saw the wide open gates that lead to safety and freedom of the wild outside the city.

I took two, glorious steps on top of the wall when unimaginable pain exploded on my side. I toppled outward, slamming a manlength down onto the sloped roof of a shop. I tried to stand, gripping the crossbow bolt that protruded three hands up from my belt, and felt my legs go out from beneath me. Left reacted without being told, gripping the bolt as close to the chest as I could and twisting, snapping the shaft so it could be pushed in no further. Yet, it was this safeguard that sent a paralyzing blast down one side, and I fell. I curled around the wound into a ball as I rolled.

I came off the roof like a child on a sled. My body bounced off an awning, thudded into the soft mud of the street like a sack of potatoes, and slid on my back to the very center. Oh, you could say I was lucky. The mud was at least half a foot deep after last night's rain, and I landed on the side without the bolt sticking out of it. I discovered less than a second later that this 'mud' street was largely made of cobblestones with the massed buildup of excrement from passing horses providing the brown padding. I felt again at my wound and my hand cupped a huge tumor. I struggled to my feet and gingerly pulled away my hand. There was a lot of blood, and a stray coin.

The curse I made up on the spot would have drawn applause had it not been delivered with such seriousness. I ripped at the shirt, slid the pierced moneybag off of the bolt face, and grabbed the exposed shaft. It had barely gone in a thumb width, spending all its piercing power on the tightly packed bundle of gold coins. I yanked, and remembered that a thumb width was enough to hit, and break, a rib. The world spun in swirling colors, and mental fingers might as well have clawed at a muddy pig as I tried to get myself under control. The bolt fell from a numb fist, but it was the sound of bloodthirsty shouting that brought me back.

Refugees were pouring into the city, huskers surrounding them on all sides trying to strip them of wealth the very instant they entered the gates. Beggars pressed to the outer edges and into the alleys by these more affluent seekers of coin. Behind me, there was a shout, and all the time I had to suffer was gone. Instinct for survival alone blocked out the grinding halves of rib as I launched myself into the crowd. Which mindless reaction caused me to rip open the bag, I'll never know. What I do know is hundreds of pinky-nail sized golden coins poured into my palm and I ducked and sprinted into the middle of the crowd as I launched them into the air.

The coins flew into a cloud, lighter coins arcing higher, heavier thicker coins falling first from lower heights. It gave everyone just a heartbeat to stop and feel for what had clunked into their hands, chests, and heads before the true rain of wealth descended upon them. I disappeared into the jostling mix between the first moment and the second. My pursuers arrived as the riot really got started.

For those that don't know, I grew up as an urchin on the streets of a city like this one. I had long ago perfected the art of slithering through holes in the crowd, crouched low so I was easily missed. I was also expert in giving one last push to clear a space to be visible to pursuers, then let the crowd swallow me whole. This is, of course the point where it is best to change direction.

It's a gamble of nerves, for you pick a space and stick to it. The whole art of stealth is not about wearing black in the middle of the night. In fact, that is pretty much the antithesis of stealth. In order to pass, or be passed, unnoticed, you must blend in. This is why the watchmen and thug storm that ate into the crowd howled with frustration, pushing men and women to the side roughly, pressing forward into the massed group at the mouth of the city, and coming to the inescapable conclusion that they had lost me through the gate.

Not to be outrun, they formed groups and departed Forgeringer with areas of responsibility; to beat the bushes and collect me as man or corpse.

Back in the city, in the second eastern side alley, one beggar asked another. "Pardon me, sir? I don't suppose…" From underneath a stinking, smelly, fully street-excrement covered fur blanket, a coin appeared. The beggar took it gleefully. Seconds later he cleared his throat, "The price of schnapps has gone up, with all these strangers in the city…" Another coin appeared, and was snatched. The beggar on the other side of the fur covered lump took notice. The first beggar again cleared his throat, "And to only have one night of warmth almost seems a torture–" A knife, blackened but as sharp as vengeance itself lashed out from underneath the fur. The first beggar barely made a noise as he died and the two coins coldly recollected.

Under the brown-matted cloak that hid me from the world, I cast a glare at the panhandler on my other side. He stayed silent. I watched the groups leave. I watched most of them tiredly return. I watched dusk fall and the gate lock. Only then, stiff and sore, side blazing in pain, did I stand. Deeper in the alley I drew out some water from a flask, spiked it with grain alcohol, and anointed the shallow wound with clenched teeth. I then cleaned my hands and applied a medicinal salve, finishing with a wrapping around the whole torso as tight as I could stand it to keep the cut ends of bone from rubbing together.

I had three of the miraculous potions of health in my pack, but what had once been a lifetime supply, now I had no manner of replacing. If it came to it, I would take one to survive, but it would have to be survival itself and not simply searing, crippling pain. I repacked my kit for the last task of the night.

Going up the wall was easy. Oh, yes, they had guards. Bored, half-asleep men who stood as single sentries and not more effective pairs. Having a man guard a staircase, however, that already led into the city he was protecting was not an effective use of manpower. So, I was silently up the stairs and on the wall in an instant. In a few seconds I had a rope looped over a merlion sticking into the air on the edge of the wall, and tied around my right thigh. From there it was a manner of edging painfully, slowly, over the wall and letting the rope through my gloved hands. It traveled up, around the stone, and down to lower my thigh, and thus all of me, down to the drawbridge. A simple glance said that the gates may have been closed nightly, but the bridge hadn't been raised in so long it may not have been possible.

And, for once, my luck had changed. While the north entrance to Forgeringer was barren, this side was like the site of a mighty campaign. People had come from Hammarfall, the city, in a continuous stream. Here they pooled into a malaise of suffering. Little food, less clean water, the smell of the city was only overcome by the wretched stench of the camp. Yet the collective conversation of the few awake, along with the sounds of thousands sleeping, allowed me plenty of cover. The instant my feet hit soil, I pulled the rope down, coiled it tightly and put it in my pack since sauntering away from a locked gate with loose rope was bound to raise suspicion. I could not do it especially quickly, or silently, but as I said, guards rarely look straight down and there was no need.

I collected myself, my feet carrying me into the camp. I checked my weapons reflexively, satisfied they were there, and the pouch of gold and silver, assuring myself that it was indeed gone and I had not just had a nightmare. I sighed. I had scattered coins sewn into the edge of my cloak, the collar of my shirts, and into pockets in my belt. Yet, it would not sustain me a year, let alone a lifetime. There was no comfortable home in my future, no warm chair by the fire to sip spiced wine. I suddenly wanted to stab someone, anyone, but the tensing of my core muscles shifted the arrow wound and sent waves of pain through me.

"Is peace your business, sir?"

My head whipped around. It was just a small girl, thin and still short of puberty. She had not asked that damnable question, her begging hands made that clear. I reached into my pack and produced one of the dark, salted loaves I had bought yesterday, then topped it off with a small gold coin. She nearly fainted at the sight of it.

Maybe it would be enough to see her and her family through this, maybe not. All I knew was I had less than I needed, and having even less than that did not hurt as badly, somehow. She started to get excited, but I shushed her and sent her on her way.

I put one foot in front of the other on the way to the city of Hammarfall, sure of only one thing...

Peace was not my business.

Then the skies cracked open and rain began to fall from broken clouds.

FIVE

A MAN OF VIOLENCE

AS YOU may have noticed, dear reader, I am mostly lucky in the unluckiest of ways. This often leaves me confused as to whether to complain bitterly, or be humbly thankful. Until directed otherwise, I'm sticking with bitterly thankful.

The rain was early spring rain: hard, harsh, and cold as a knife in the kidney. I pulled up the hood to the suddenly, much heavier, fur cloak, and pulled the Angel down off my shoulder and tucked it beneath it, crosspiece under my arm. It was not hidden, exactly, what with half the winged crosspiece bulging out the front, but while I had never known the Angel to rust, I was not tempting fate further. I was coming up to the beginning of what Hammarfall people called a forest. I crossed the threshold and was immediately embraced by rows of trees that marched out in every direction like lines of soldiers.

The pines here had grown high and wide, casting boughs that caught light rain, and concentrated heavy rain, allowing you to be hit with fewer but far fatter drops. It was darker here, and quieter, with wet needles underfoot absorbing the sound of every step. I had managed to develop a stiff walk that left my injury as only a wailing misery rather than a debilitating scream. It was somewhat hampered by having to carry the Angel low, yet as lightning flashed overhead, I was suddenly glad I had hidden my polished steel away from all light.

Ahead, inside one of the saddest, most makeshift tarp-and-stick arrangements I had ever seen, there was a fire. Well that is not entirely true. It was the shelter built by city folk, and only did its job when aided by the pine shelter provided by the God of Wild Places. There was a fire, and coughing, and complaining, and bawdy jokes, and almost certainly drinking on rickety stools brought for the purpose. What purpose you ask? Finding and murdering little old me. Paranoid, you say? Well you didn't see one of the men turn, casting his comically large fake phallus in shadow against the fire. It was like a mythical wyrm set to devour the forest whole, I swear. Though to call this wild was more than a stretch.

I hunkered down, no doubt in my mind they were looking for me. And it may have been that there were others just waiting down this road. The city watch may even pursue me all the way to Hammarfall (the city) or to the borders of Hammarfall (the country). Either was unacceptable, but increasingly unlikely as the rain pounded down turning the roads to... No, the roads of the lowlands were paved. Even so, it would cause them to give up sooner than they would like, and none too soon for me. Though that did not help right now.

I pictured the maps of Hammarfall I had studied before leaving Noria. To my east a short distance there should be a river, the same that went around Forgeringer on one side. From there would be a series of paths where oxen tugged barges up and down the river. It would be far less pleasant than the shaded, sheltered, cobbled road, but far less likely to be guarded. I departed the road like a shadow, leaving the laughing, drinking, much-more-dry-than-I group behind. I was at the river before long, but I had to fight through the short brush that had grown up in the unrestricted sunlight beyond the reach of the pines. Not that there was sunlight right now.

I emerged onto the path covered in brambles, injury at my side gnawing away at my strength. I was already breathing heavy, but as my feet began to point downstream, I was grateful for the thick layer of gravel over the mud, for the wide path needed to keep the oxen sure footed, and for the lack of trees to limp over whenever the wind took mood to push them over.

It was pleasant going. Fine, that is a lie. It was excruciating going, and I made several hours of time. I never stopped to congratulate myself on losing my pursuers in the finally abating rain. It was a good thing, for when the "HALT!" crashed into my ears, I almost expected it.

Dawn was rising and she had been out all night. Though at least ten years my junior, she was not gorgeous as one would determine a woman, but her strength was written in her eyes and jawline. Her build was decidedly masculine, and her stance confidant and comfortable. Her watch uniform was probably the one she had used last night, and the more I looked at the chest piece, the more it looked homemade. The leather especially appeared substandard and thin. It was her, the swordswoman from the monastery. *Dammit.*

I sighed, and with great force of will kept my hand from my side where I was sure my wound was just waiting to tear open. I had three healing draughts in my pack, but no way to get to them, drink them, and then wait for them to work before she cut me down. Not unless I could stall. A lot. I dredged up a friendly, easy voice and spoke in *HammarSpiel*. "Good morrow, fair maid."

"Draw your sword, highwayman," she shot back.

A laugh died halfway to my throat. "Highwayman? What say you?"

She took off her cloak solemnly, as if this moment held great significance. She had two similar swords on her hips, and she fingered the pommels. "You are a brigand and a murderer, and I shall bring all of you or part of you back to Forgeringer to answer for your crimes."

I could not keep my shoulders from slumping, nor the air from huffing out of my lungs. "Be reasonable, I just saved an old man from being robbed. That's all."

"And the watchman in the alley?"

Pieced that together did you, or are you fishing? "I don't know what you are talking about. All I know is a gang of toughs attacked me. I ran and escaped," I lied, mostly.

"You lie!" she shouted, drawing her swords.

Dammit. "I am not lying!" I lied, again, brain racing for an escape.

"Enough!" she roared. "Draw your blades and match to me, villain!"

I raised my hands, stepping back. "Any blades?"

She pursed her lips and took a lunge forward, but did not strike. I jumped back, opened my wound, and fell to one knee groaning. "Quit foxing. And tell me your name, knave, so it may be entered into the books of the justly executed."

My shoulders slumped, as if defeated. I brought forth the Phantom Angel. She eyed it lustily, then backed off half a shuffle as I tossed it to the side of the path. Then I removed my much shorter sword and, again, tossed it to the side.

At that, my opponent began to blush, to huff. She shouted, "You cannot surrender!"

Then I produced another, plain knife. Without crosspiece, blade as wide as the palm, needle sharp point, it was made for throwing. They looked pitifully small next to her swords. My other hand reached for the iron clasp that held the fur cloak in place. My voice held no mockery, no light, only serious death, "I have chosen my blades."

She recognized them, but almost dismissed them as a sideshow trick. For while every farmjack thinks what makes a knife bite is force of the throw, it is the spinning of the blade more than anything. You must calculate the revolutions and have the tip enter as it hits. Throwing knives in combat is something that takes years of practice. I have had that practice.

Her face became a rictus of rage, as if I were mocking her. She lunged forward, covering half the distance between us, but no more. Instantly, the one knife slid apart into three blades in my hand. Two folded down into the palm while one was perched in the fingers. I whipped it down with a half turn, piercing her thigh midway from crotch to knee. She paused and shrieked as the still somewhat excrement-covered cloak fluttered off my shoulders and over her head. She pawed at it for a moment with hands full of hilts when she finally dropped one sword and clawed it from her face. That was when the second knife entered the shoulder of her weapon arm and she toppled over.

She reached for the knife, wrenching at it and making the wound worse. I planted the last knife in the dirt a finger from her eyes, blocking her sight of the wound. She looked up at me, gathered titanic desperation and fed it into a roaring fire that was her will. She desperately gripped the knife from her shoulder and slowly, slowly struggled to her feet. She smiled as she reversed the knife, ready to plunge it into my body. She stabbed the air, a challenge and an anticipation. From underneath the fox-trimmed cloak, I brought a hand. It held a throwing knife. With the movement of a thumb, it fanned into three. All flight went out of her and she slumped to the ground.

Tracking her to her camp was easy. Getting her back into the woods was easy. Binding her was easy. Tying her to the tree was easy. Deciding what to do was not.

A fine horse shuddered and nickered at the smell of blood, but was otherwise quiet. The rain ended, but under the canopy of the grand pines it would drip all day at least. I checked and rebound my own wound. Only afterward did I move to her, hoping her blood loss would head off any further attempts to kill me.

I started with a small knife sharp enough to cut starlight, and began to peel off her cuirass of leather. I had been right, for much of it looked less than well made, and had no chance to stop the knife. I pulled it free and her breasts were beneath, bound by a long length of cloth wrapped around her many times.

I took her pot to the river, filled it with water, and returned to the coals of her fire. She had collected wood and kept it beneath a blanket to fend off the worst of the rain the forest canopy did not keep away. Soon I had a roaring fire, the tallest tongues of which did not come close to the lowest branches of the forest. Onto it went the pot, and when it started to steam, I began to unwind the cloth from her breasts. She cursed and kicked at me, bit and tried to smack her skull into my face. I backed away marginally and put one firm hand on the oozing knife cut on her thigh. She wailed and almost passed out. Then I continued my work until her breasts were free. Even at that moment I did not know what I was really doing.

I turned away from her and she spit, "Go ahead and try to rape me. Anything you put in my mouth I will bite off. I will chew out your neck. I will–"

She went on at some length as I again took the small sharp knife and cut away the leather over her wounded thigh. I could smell her musk, and I would not be human if it did not move me. But she was bound and bloody, and as bad of a man I ever was, I was not that kind of man, and helpless was not my kind of woman. Her build was taut and broad, with impressive musculature. She had studied swordplay seriously for quite some time.

Using hot water, I cleaned the wounds to everyone's amazement. Well, at least mine. She hissed, but otherwise remained quiet. When that was done, I put salve on them, then went back to the boiled cloth. Taking one of the arrows Richter had made for me, I created a stiff clothesline in the tree and let the long lengths loop almost to the ground, giving them enough air to hopefully come close to dry. Out of my pack I gained a small, curved needle made of silver and some fine silk thread. First, very slowly, I sewed the small gash the bolt head had made in my skin and pulled it shut.

She watched with horrid fascination and mounting tension as she came to realize I meant to do the same to her. She hissed as I sewed her wounds shut, an elvish trick learned long ago. *Because a dead assassin brings no money to the guild.* At some point she stopped threatening me. I could feel something from her, a desperation, a longing for purpose. It was so utterly familiar, and it touched me. I picked up her blanket from the small woodpile and shook it free of splinters and small forest life. Then I covered her nudity and went back to the fire.

Inside her pack was a few choice morsels of food. She had planned to be out after me for five days, maybe more. I helped myself to what I found. Mind straying back to the small silver vials of healing draughts inside my pack, longingly remembering a life without pain. Measuring the idea of survival now to survival later.

"What are you doing?" she finally asked.

"Repaying you," I said simply.

"By stealing my food?" I paused, eyed her warily, then offered her an open cloth sack of hard biscuits. Her face twisted in ill humor. "Repaying me for what?"

"Your horse," I said matter-of-factly.

"You can't have her!" she exploded. Her rage was immediately swallowed by the forest, the rain, and the gloom. As bare whispers echoed back, I imagined riding the horse, rocking back and forth with grinding rib bones. I went to my pack. "I sold everything to get her! You cannot have her. Do not ignore me, scoundrel!"

She lunged, but succeeded only in dislodging the blanket that hid her modesty. I took out one of the silver vials, broke the seal that stood for the woman I loved, and tossed the entire contents into the back of my mouth and down my throat. Immediately, great fatigue washed over me, and I felt quite distant from my body. I staggered over to the watchwoman, covered her with the blanket, added another blanket from her bedroll, and then used the rest of her bedroll in addition to mine and my cloaks. The very last thing I did was strip down to skin and slide between them, no less than half a dozen weapons within grasp.

"I will see you dead," she proclaimed through clenched teeth.

I may have said, "That would be rude after I saved your life." But I may not have. The draught had me fully in its fist, and it pulled me down into the waters of dreamless sleep. In my dreams I remembered a very old, plump cleric.

You are a hero, Fox Crow and you always will be.

Even in my dreams, I balked, but she believed in me so much. I awoke instantly, completely, as was my habit, only far too late. The healing elixir had kept me asleep too long, and the only safety I had was appearing asleep longer still. I came awake at the slithering sound of a sword slipping free of a cheap leather sheath. Their voices were lowered to whispers, but their footsteps sounded loud to me.

The first hissed, "Well, hello Raina. What have you been up to all night?"

The tied up woman responded, "Quiet, Armin. Just get over here and untie me!"

Dammit, there were two.

"What's wrong with him?"

"He took a healing draught; he's completely out. Now get me free," Raina answered testily.

Gods dammit, there was a third one, who was bolder than the rest because he didn't whisper, but just pitched his voice low. "Well, it looks like you had a good time."

There was the sound of movement, and then Raina cursed softly, "Give me back my blanket, Stein! Or untie me!"

And, just my luck, there were four. The last was no nonsense, brutal, quiet, grim, and efficient. "Shall I kill him?"

There was a sound of Armin going through my pack. "Wow, there's a lot of high quality stuff in here. You don't think he's a noble, do you?"

But Stein was not listening, he was too busy appreciating Raina's nudity. "So tell me, girl, if you studied in your youth with some kind of fighting master, why is it you are tied up to a tree all naked-like?"

If possible, she may have hated this man more than she hated me. "Stein, I swear–"

The brutal one was tired of waiting for an answer. "I'm just going to kill him."

One was keeping his distance, voice quavering, "Yes."

You could almost hear Stein put out a hand to stop the grim one. "No! The Codpiece Louts will pay more if he's alive."

"Not the Justice?"

"They won't pay except in thanks."

And the scavenger, Armin, said reverently, "There's the sword."

And that was it. I was already moving as my eyes flashed open. Two men were at hand, Armin kneeling over me and the grim one standing on the other side. I rolled forward toward Armin, seized his neck and sunk a wide, thick-bladed knife from under a blanket into his ribs from where I lay. I rolled back, pulling him on top. Grim was already hacking downward with two hands. His slash cut deeply into Armin, who I held like a shield over top of me. I plunged my knife into the top of his boot, then as he crumpled forward, into his chest. Startled by the screams, and smelling blood, the horse pulled against its tether but was held firm. Grim went one way, Armin's body went the other, and I came to my feet, naked but with the Phantom Angel in hand.

Stein lunged forward and his sword and our blades rang like bells as I circled around to be clear of the fire and bedroll. Then I edged a bit away and provoked an attack by glancing around. The last unnamed watchman I was fumbling with a crossbow, managing to spill a dozen bolts from his quiver and finally get one into the slot. He was pale and dull, blond and scared to death.

Stein was handsome, with a cruel cast to his eye. He did not waste what he thought was a perfect opening; he drew his sword expertly and lunged. Too short, his sword did not come within three hands of my chest. I riposted with the longer Angel, catching him under the chin in the hollow of the throat. The crossbowman shrieked and dropped his crossbow, lighting off for parts unknown. Amazingly, the normally finicky contraption did not go off. I spun the elvish blade once and severed Stein's head as I ran past. I got to the crossbow, scooped it up as I dropped my sword, and aimed at the retreating back.

And aimed.

And aimed.

"Lutz!" Raina called out.

I pulled the release lever on the weapon. There was a short scream, and then the sound of agonizing pain. Raina could not see around the tree to which she was bound. She just saw me drop the bow, regain my sword, and walk off into the woods. Seconds later, Lutz was silenced.

I dragged the body back to the camp and let him fall. I cursed, because there was blood everywhere. You could no more sleep in a bloody bed than travel in bloody clothes. If contagion did not kill you, suspicion would. I took a spare moment to cover Raina's breasts from the needles of the cold morning air. She just sat there, stunned.

First I took out a razor, cut and pulled out the stitches in my side that now straddled yet another scar. I got dressed, started packing, taking what could be salvaged to the water and washed, though it would likely mildew during the day and need to be aired out tonight. Tomorrow night would end with a cold, stiff morning but it could not be helped. Luckily both cloaks had escaped even a spattering, and I moved them to be sure. Once dressed, I laid out the attackers like four lonely pieces of cordwood. They had all been young men, hungry and eager, and they all were wearing uniform and armor of the city watch. I tossed the bodies but came up with little more than a good set of light gloves, the crossbow and ammunition, and a few spare coins. I started the final phase of packing.

Raina finally broke the silence, "You didn't have to kill him."

I looked up at her, taking in the golden locks of hair, the light green eyes, the firm set to her jaw. There was something noble in her even as tears leaked from her eyes. I looked back to the four bodies and then again to her. "Which one?"

"The last one," by which she meant crossbowman, "Lutz."

I began saddling the horse, which took some calming before it was even possible. "I should just let him run and get reinforcements, should I?"

"You are a murderer!"

"I didn't murder you, Raina." The reply was sardonic, but inside I was wondering why that was, and why he seemed so familiar.

"You are a thief!"

I sighed. "I am less of a thief than most. Look at the watch for example. I would have been taken in, summarily fined out of most of my belongings, and then cast out to starve in a sea of refugees for saving an old man's life and coin."

"You broke the peace," she replied weakly.

"The old man I saved didn't look too peaceful. By all rights they were not turning me over to the Justice, but to those thugs, anyway."

"You killed a watchman!" she accused with some force.

My words were hot, but gently put. Not for her benefit, but so I could finally slip the damn saddle on to a horse utterly convinced that the next corpse would be horse flavored. "Only after he came after me for saving an old man's life. In fact, young lady, the only thing that really separates the watch from any other gang is the blessings of the nobility." She soaked that in, horrified at even the thought, until at least I got the belly band snug. Then I noticed the beast was holding his breath. I waited. Waited. Then he exhaled and I tightened the band up further. "Besides, what do you care? They don't seem to care for you."

"That's untrue!"

I looked at her the way a parent looks at a lying child. "Really? Because they seemed a lot more interested in killing me in my sleep, laying claim to my possessions, and staring at your exposed body than helping you escape torture, rape, or slavery."

She shook her head weakly, feeling the barbs of truth latch into her. To her credit, she stopped weeping for Lutz, pulled herself together and spoke to me as an equal, "They were jealous. I studied with Master Martin Gotzplatz, the best swordsman the land has ever seen."

I couldn't help it, I snorted in distain. "If you think you are some kind of master swordswoman, it may be time to think about getting married and having children."

"How DARE–"

And then I was there, in her face, noses touching. My voice dropped to a dangerous whisper, "I dare what I like because in all this world, your

Master Gotzplatz lives because he has never had cause to face the likes of me. You are headstrong, half trained, and totally ignorant of how the world works. Worst, you have thrown in your lot with a group of people who would rather see you naked than ensure your safety." I watched the words smash into her, break her apart, and then– as it became clear to me– I added, "You mortgaged your life for that horse. You never had any intent of going back, did you?"

And there it was.

It is a hard thing to find oneself in a place of one's own choosing, then to look around and find you are not at all welcome.

But in admission, there is freedom.

She looked at me, searching my face, "You are better than Gotzplatz. Take me with you. Teach me."

And there it was, the traditional student teacher bond, forged in fire, sung of by bards, a transmuting process that breaks the hold of mortality and lets sacred knowledge travel the eons. There was only one response.

"Hell no." I was packed, the horse was ready. It was time to go and leave this psychotic little vixen behind. I leaned over and cut Raina free.

She rubbed her wrists and gathered the blanket around her more effectively. "What? Why?"

"Look, I am not teaching the woman who tried to kill me to kill a little bit better so next time she succeeds." And I nudged the horse into a trot, headed to the river.

"But this isn't about you!" she cried.

"Then why should I care?" I tossed back.

And then I was out of sight, out of the forest, but not out of the woods by any means.

Six

The Bond

IT IS often not appreciated that a man-bearing horse travels, in a day, as much as a healthy adult. The advantage is not speed so much as bursts of speed and, of course, not having to actually carry every damn thing you decided to bring along. It is this reason, and no other flaw or quirk on my part, why this was the second morning in a row I woke up with a blade in my hand.

The gravel path had provided the perfect amount of sound as feet pressed against it, and even before I was awake, my foot was lashing out into the back of a knee. My blade came up as the sword tumbled, knocking the dull edge away even as my arms hooked the attacker and pulled the shape across me, facing away.

A sudden wave of soft scents and powerful urges fought the desire to begin carving flesh with wild abandon. Then my captive said, "I could have killed you. We are even."

I growled into her ear, "No, you could not, Raina," and I roughly tossed her off of me.

She had two - no three! - of the swords and all four of the daggers from the dead watchmen strapped to her. So when she kicked into a roll, she came up with a fresh sword held lightly in her right hand. It was long before dawn and I had no patience for this, but my command of, "Put it down," was not in the least heeded.

"Make me," is what she replied. I bent down, eyes on her like a mongoose watches a viper, and lifted the Phantom Angel from the ground, letting the brass throated sheath grind against the blade all the way out. I dropped the sheath. She tensed up as I loosened my muscles. She focused as I diffused my attention to absorb everything before me. She stopped breathing while I took in deep breaths and hooked my foot under the first, discarded sword on my bedroll. I felt my hands tighten on the Angel.

"Gladly," I said.

Then I kicked my foot. The dropped sword arced into the air toward her. Seeing opportunity, Raina dipped one sword to the side while she watched the hilt of the second come toward her, holding out an hand to take command of the blade when it fell. I leapt forward, batting the first sword out of the air. The other attempted to come up, and it, too, was batted to the side. I continued my rush and reversed the Angel, striking out viciously with the pommel that cracked Raina in the sternum. She fell backwards, weapon tumbling, ribs cracking, head thumping against the only barely forgiving gravel. It happened in less than a breath, and once it was over, I turned away from her and went back to my bed.

As I started to pack, she tried to rise. I had knocked all breath from her. She was red and purple in the face, one hand clamped to her chest, and the other grasping at her last sword. She drug it free as she managed to perch on shaky legs, gasping sounds accented by tears of pain and panic deluging her face. She lifted the point to my heart.

Then she toppled over.

After a moment or two, she began to breathe normally. I checked to make sure she had not ripped the threads holding her ruined skin together on her shoulder or leg. But by the time she awoke, I, my camp, and her horse were long gone.

I could only imagine her crawling to her feet, perhaps gathering all three swords, and then walking, painfully, home. I had felt the sternum pop under the impact of our combined weights, and I knew it had to be utter agony for her. Still, it was her own ignorance. Thankfully, pain was a wonderful teacher.

I comforted myself with that thought throughout the lonely day of riding and as I prepared my bed. I blinked as I looked into the modest fire I had burning, for a fist full of stray thoughts hit me from nowhere. I bundled cloth, saddlebags, satchel and pack into a humanlike form beneath the dirty white cloak. I lay my swords down to act as obvious bait, then took up the crossbow and bolts. Within minutes, I was safe, warm, and hidden from view. I dozed.

The stray thought was still there, every time I awoke enough to actually know I was awake. I would focus on my camp, see that the fire was nothing but coals, and doze off again. In the interim a thousand cawing questions would lift from my brain and begin circling my head. *What would I have done at her age, to escape crushing loneliness and lack of respect from all sides? What had I done?* My eyes opened, and I saw her as plain as day, a shadow at the edge of the river. She lifted herself from the frigid waters fingernail by fingernail, the icy blue of her skin lighter than the dirty rags that bound her breasts and closely covered her loins. In the center of her chest was the bright purple splotch I had given her. A thought slapped me and I blinked hard, *You were her once. That is why you could not kill her. Too proud of your skill with a blade, too ignorant to know it was nothing to be proud of. You were this exact same person long ago.*

She slipped a dagger from her loincloth, and held it low to not catch the light. I nodded approval as she slowed further, placing hands only where mud showed through the gravel, where stones would not roll or rub and give her away. I watched her, admiring the spirit it would take to come all this way, to suffer this much, to persevere.

But are you really a teacher?

Maybe I could be. Maybe I could.

She pulled herself out of the water, barely dripping from hair pulled tight into a knot to hold as little water as possible. She had a sword across her back, but it was held only with a thong. The sliver of steel would hold no dripping mess to betray her.

But another thought came sauntering into my head– what gift is it, the gift of murder?

She was slow, taking time to dry slightly as to not rain on her target, to be quiet, to notice every tiny thing in the moonlight. She was learning so fast on her own, though the water downstream from the city would do her wounds no favors. She came even with my head under the blankets and shifted her weight to her legs.

To those who have nothing? This girl already had the gift of murder. Soon someone else will find her.

But can she learn?

She reached out toward the cover over my face, knife poised in her other hand, ready to speak, and paused. She shook her head, sensing the same wrongness of something just beyond thought that I had.

She has the instincts; everything else can be taught.

She backed off only a fraction, then her head snapped up. Shapes detached from the forest and entered the gravel path. I cursed silently, so intent on her that I had shut out all else.

Quietly, carefully, she raised her hands, careful to retain the dagger in a loose grip so it didn't hit the ground and wake me. I saw the spear point flash in the night, jabbing at her to back away.

She obeyed, face unreadable.

Then a man came from behind, blade snaking around her throat as the free hand sought soft places tightly bound in cloth. "Hello Raina," he hissed in her ear. "Keeping him warm for us?"

She looked at my bedroll and saw no movement. Her eyes went wide. I waited.

"He's mine, Lars," she said, voice pitched low, but still far too loud. "I tracked him."

The man behind her chuckled darkly, his hands still roving. "You did more than track him, looks like." He took hold of her naked sword and cut the thong that held it place.

She was looking everywhere, in the trees, in the shadows, still painfully aware that she held a weapon. "He knows we are here."

Lars snorted. "Bullshit." His empty hand snaked back around her midsection and pulled her into him, but his sword hand motioned to the spear carrier. "Wake him, Ivan."

The other man giggled like a moron, then lifted one heavy boot. The rest leaned forward in anticipation, and I made out all four men–watchmen all, stripped of almost all uniform and armor in their search of me. Then the boot came down on where my head was supposed to be. There was the sound of crackling wood.

Raina shook her head again. "Mistake."

In my defense, Ivan was a big man, larger than me and twice the girth in the middle. That was why, when the massive whip snare went off, it didn't lift him from his feet, but only snapped his leg to the side, turning his ankle, knee, and hip into flopping uselessness. He shattered the night with a scream.

The other three were instantly alert, three swords acting like eyes searching every patch of gloom with vicious jabs. The one called Lars yanked Raina close, fingers grappling her breast binding. He hissed something I couldn't hear.

"I don't know." She replied, voice an icy monotone.

His voice raised, "Don't give me that, slut! Where is he?"

"I don't know." She appeared utterly unmoved, but her fingers were bringing the dagger more fully into her fist.

Struck by the knowledge that he had a vulnerable back, Lars spun, hand on Raina's neck, blade at her throat. His breath was coming fast. "Where? WHERE?"

She was fast, one hand snaking up and catching his sword hand while her own knife lashed down and back, sinking it up to the hilt in his crotch. Lars gagged more than screamed as blood poured to the ground. She took her weapon from his numb fingers, abandoning her knife as she gracefully turned, took hold of his sheathed sword and kicked him away, freeing a second blade. Lars went pale and fell to death, crotch raining blood. Her voice was loud, strong, and defiant, "I do not know."

The last two may not have been bright, but they could identify power. I didn't think she was going to attack, but they saw her defiance as a threat, and fell upon her.

She parried both blades in a flurry of steel, naked feet keeping painful traction on the raw rocks of the path. She moved well, her actions decisive, her intuition predatory. Then, there it was– an attacker one gave her an opening and she took it. Her right sword slid half to the hilt, killing him most assuredly, but not instantly. Then the second one struck. She deflected the heavy strike with her left hand sword. Then, the first one, screaming in pain, tried to grab her. She planted the free sword in the hollow of his throat, but the second one was slashing down at her again. She did all she could do... she fell to the ground and the strike rung off the first sword blade impaled in the first one, who promptly took vengeance from beyond by toppling across her.

The second one put a foot across his dead compatriot, pinning her to the ground as he raised his sword above his head. He roared in exultation, blade bright in the night. She did not shut her eyes, she did not look away. She didn't even flinch as a red rose of blood, a twisted iron bolt head at the center, blossomed halfway from his sternum to neck. He fell, gurgling, and died on the growing pile.

It took longer than I would like to climb down from the tree where I had hidden amongst the lower branches near the edge of the wood. I retrieved the Angel first, then lifted first one watchman, then the other off of Raina. She lay there, dagger held loosely but definitely in her right hand. She watched me warily for what seemed to be forever.

"Why didn't you kill me?" she asked.

"Because I don't have to."

Her face twisted. "Because I'm not a threat?"

"I have killed many women, and I am alive only because I do not underestimate them, but I think you want to learn from me more than you want to kill me." I offered her my right hand. "You do want to learn?"

She very purposefully let the dagger roll from her fingers to the rocky ground and then took my hand. I lifted her gently to her feet and said, "As long as you can keep from killing me, you will learn."

I looked across the devastation of the camp. Lars had bled out in moments. A bolt during her fight with the freshest two corpses had silenced Ivan forever. The last two were cooling in death, and only the slightest flicker of remorse troubled her face. Still, she forced herself to look around. I didn't like the pallor of her skin, or the angry red spreading from her leg and shoulder wound. But her words were strong. "What do we do first?"

I turned to her. "Strip and dispose of the bodies. Find things of value, get ready to move on to put more distance between us and pursuit."

She frowned. "So, you are just a bandit, after all."

I rolled Ivan's body off of the fur cloak, which I doubted would ever be white again. It had served its purpose, hiding the rolled blankets and clothes to look like me sleeping. "If you will remember, I spent almost all my hard fortune escaping thc city."

"Yes, why ever did you do that?"

"Coins can only purchase a life, not restore it." I shrugged. "Seemed like a wise trade when the opportunity presented."

"You are a very odd thief."

"And you are a very odd student, wanting to study swordplay from a thief, and at this point you have killed nearly as many watchmen as I have. Go get your gear and hurry back. We have to move on."

She went, and I got to work. Unable to remove the marks of the watch from the swords, they went into the river. Same with the tabards. Like most young men of limited means, they kept their wealth on them with the idea that if they died defending it from thieves, they would no longer need it. I took a similar trail of thought and pocketed the measly sums. Yet they had four bottles of drinkable wine, food for days, fresh bedrolls, and other gear needed to outfit Raina completely. She came running back down the path, excitement betrayed by her messily bundled life in her arms.

"You're here," she said, somewhat surprised.

Again, I eyed her critically. She cast me a foul look as she dumped her load to the path and began dressing. Yet her nakedness– though appealing– was not my focus. It was the slight rivulets of blood from the even more agitated thigh wound I had both inflicted and sewn up.

I sighed, feet objecting to what my head was already planning and my mouth already saying. "Get dressed, and then mount the horse."

She pulled a shirt on over her head and looked at me sourly. "Of course, he's my horse."

"Not for about a day or so." I fixed her with a withering glare as I dragged the last corpse off into the forest, hopefully to be devoured by scavengers. I returned and slipped the Angel from off my back and under the flap of the saddle. I took a little bit of time to wrap it in a blanket, but all that did was make it look like a sword wrapped in a blanket. Finally, I took Richter's bow and the quiver of arrows to bulk out the shape. My short sword I kept close, as well as a cloud of murder implements that had precipitated all over my body in hidden places.

Raina was clothed by then, her pack reclasped, but she was leaning against the tree behind her, eyes closed and an indiscreet red stain spreading on her leggings. I sighed.

Not so long ago, I had seen people as little more than bags of muscle and bone with cores that were either bags of gold or bundles of sharp knives. Since my… *what could it be called? A conversion? A rebirth*? Ever since I had abandoned murder and had begun drawing crows, those walls were gone. I saw the young woman in front of me, the burning need she had inside. She didn't want blood, not really. She wanted control. Control of her life and her destiny.

If I didn't give it to her, someone would. And they would bring with them emerald and gold ink for a tattoo. I reached for her, and gently helped her up onto the back of the brown gelding.

"I'm not going to sleep with you," she said tiredly, slumping forward as I bundled her pack behind her.

"No, you are not," I replied, wrapping her in the huge, no longer white fur cloak. Despite the slight damp left from washing out the blood and the stink of all the ground-in dirt and sweat, she hugged it around her. I took it as another bad sign.

I was worried that the watch of Forgeringer would have sent a runner ahead to contact the city of Hammarfall and maybe even raised the national soldiers of Hammarfall to scour the countryside for the dark, long haired man with the Phantom Angel sword. In response I hid the sword, tied back my hair, and tried to look like a middle income man of some anonymous tradition. The girl, possibly even presented as a new wife, would provide even more concealment.

I needn't have bothered with any of it. Long before we made the walls of the city, the signs of rot were unmistakable. They say armies march on their stomachs, and while true it is myopic. All of society lives on its stomach. In a world of ten men, all men farm, until one man can feed two. Then nine can farm and one can be a smith. The smith makes a plow, freeing up another man to raise oxen, to pull the plow and provide milk. Eventually you have five men plowing, and five doing other things. The collection of these other things is called a city. But while everyone looks down on the dung-footed farmer, living in drafty houses and doing mindless labor, what everyone forgets is the instant he cannot do his job, everyone dies. Everyone.

That is why, on the way into Hammarfall, when we saw empty farm after empty farm, fallow and untouched since the previous year, we would see nothing but trouble. Against my better judgment I scouted one out. The door had not even been fastened, and everything of any value had been cleared out. Check after check remained the same. It boded disaster, but maybe not yet. I settled us into an outflung abandoned hut and lay Raina down on a sleeping roll. I started a fire, then opened her wounds. The smell hit me like a hammer, and I had a silver vial dug out of my pack before I even knew what was happening.

There I stopped. Other than perhaps the Phantom Angel, this vial and its sister hidden away were perhaps the most valuable things I owned. Raina's face was pale, but covered in sweat. Her breathing was already shallow. She barely moved when I uncovered her and pulled down her breeches. The sewn wound was not just red and angry, but looked like a violet and crimson spider lay along the line of the cut, broken limbs spreading up and down her leg in purple lines turning black.

I cracked the wax seal on the silver vial, and a tingle passed down my spine. My thumb held the stopper in place as I stood and spun, Phantom Angel hissing from the sheath and clearing the room all the way to the door with a deadly whistle.

There was nothing there.

Then, from above, a harsh caw startled me to the bone. I stood there, tincture in one hand, staring at the black feathered bird that looked at me mockingly. There I was, with two options in my hand, one cool and soothing, the other hot and sharp. I felt the weight of both of them and the eyes upon me. The question was obvious. I had been asked it enough times already.

"Go to hell," I spat. "This is not about who I was, but who I am and who she is."

And it was. She had come with me as a student, and now she was my responsibility. I uncorked the vial and put it to her lips, dripping a few drops of the remainder and wiping the cork on her shoulder and leg.

She slept.

I don't know when the damn bird left, but it wasn't there by morning. That was fine with me. I didn't need anyone, man or God, telling me what kind of man I am.

SEVEN

THE WOUNDS OF HAMMARFALL

IT WAS then, dear reader, that I remembered why I had spent many of my thirty years in this world hating every single person in it.

It started with Raina waking up and being surprised by that fact. She checked her wounds and found them closed behind the sewn threads. Now she may have been young, but she was not stupid. The pain had vanished, the wounds had knitted around pale scars, and she couldn't even remember the infection or fever.

"NO-no-no-no!" She said, a murmur raising to a shout, "I will NOT owe you this much!"

That was just how the morning began. I heated some bread in the coals of the fire with some sausages and we ate breakfast, but she still glared at me like I was about to ask for something. Since she was well enough to complain, once we packed up, I determined she was going to walk. This led to the second argument of the day, her first lesson in fisticuffs, and a black eye. But, in retrospect, I had to pick her up off the ground and put her across the saddle for a quarter of a mile. Once she woke up, she slid herself from the horse, walked around the damn thing and got in my way so we couldn't go forward.

"Show me," was all she said.

I was going to refuse, but I decided I wanted to hit her again. I remember my lessons pretty well, and passing them on wasn't the problem. It was slowing Raina down so she could absorb the material. She was insistent, hungry for the knowledge. I had once taught a gaggle of beardless youths and they had not pressed like this. Finally she performed the fist combo perfectly and smacked the outer ocular ridge of my eye with her knuckles. She hadn't pulled her punch the way I had taught, even a little. I saw stars.

"So, that was lesson one, Master?" Then she was flying through the air, slapping against the ground and startling the horse that immediately galloped off the road and into a muddy, unplowed field. She gasped and wheezed to catch her breath, and I could tell when she finally had managed it because she demanded, "What the hell was that?"

"Lesson two," I growled. "Go get the damn horse."

And she walked into the muddy field to get the horse, but rode him back. I let her perch on the foul beast until afternoon. We paused and ate cold biscuits and cheese, and I rode until nearly night. Then I noticed that her legs were wobbly and she rubbed her thighs as if they were on fire. Raina was not only a fresh horse owner, she had never owned one before, nor ridden one for more than an hour at a time. She did not argue so much to be allowed to ride the next day.

The smells of the sea wafted to us on the breezes traveling leagues from the shore. It let us know we were close. We pushed ourselves to get to Hammarfall before nightfall, but it was not to be. I resigned myself to a cold night outside of the walls, but it wasn't as bad as all that.

It was far worse.

I dismounted as soon as the walls of the fortress city came into sight, the sky above stained bloody by the setting sun, and motioned Raina into the saddle. She visibly thought about asking why, but decided the correct thing to do was to claim the seat, THEN question my decision. As soon as she was settled I started to jog, racing the setting sun and letting the horse trot next to me. Expert horsewoman that she was, even just at a trot she held on for dear life and bounced everywhere.

But our rush brought us no closer to the constantly rising peaks of Hammarfall. The day expired. We began to hear the distant crash of surf. The sky grew dark, and yet though we forever came closer, we were not there. We passed a outlaying inn, the scene of some horror. The whole structure stank of fresh fire and smoked in the chill night. I tried to look everywhere at once, but could detect no hint of men or ambush. Just as I was beginning to doubt my choices of destination, a black shadow separated from the wreckage of the inn and flew off in the direction of Hammarfall.

"We should stay here and skirt Hammarfall during the day."

I sighed heavily. "Hammarfall is where we are going."

"Whatever fortunes you were promised in that city, they are likely lost, Master."

I sighed again. "Sometimes, Raina, it is more than just promises that drive us."

"Such as?"

"Threats." And though I said it lightly, the massive shadow of the city was across us, and lent that one word the power of prophecy. Raina did not ask further, and I did not explain.

I did not want to stop in the evil shadow with its totally silent farmhouses, burnt carriage inns, and, other than one harried wine merchant that did not stop to hail us but scurried onward, the complete lack of traffic or camps. I kept a knife handy but hidden. The night unfolded, but we pressed on until the horse hung his head low in fatigue. Then, at the base of the black hunk of rock speckled with faint fires, there appeared a light just for us. I began to smell the sea even with the wind at our backs, and the city shot up further as we descended out of the high ground down to the city gates. I pressed on, even for another hour until we attained the entry.

As I have stated, the point of gates is for them to be shut at night, for reason of taxes if not for defense. Yet, here four men sprawled around the entrance, as sodden as any that have ever been seen. We approached the massive arcing gates, horse hooves tiredly clacking on the street stones, then over the long bridge that lead to the city proper.

Of the four, only one came even partially awake. He snapped (well, sloshed) to attention, his entire uniform consisting of a battered guardsman helm. The rest of him appeared to be part farmer and part thug. He snatched a spear and barreled our way with it, but not in any way seriously. He was squinting past the ghosts of alcohol and wobbling on his feet.

"Halt!" he ordered, and despite any 'sh' sound in the word, he still managed to slur it. Halt we did, and I cast an eye about. Four guards, three drunk. Outside only because the booze made them so warm. The guard shack was cold and dark. He looked to be more or less alone. I weighted this fact against the price of his life before I tried to remember that wasn't who I was anymore. When he pointed his spear at me, remembering that became more difficult. "Halt! in the name of The Volker."

We had already halted, and had no way to halt further, so we just stood and waited. He set the spear down as a staff and leaned on it, nearly falling asleep. I cleared my throat and his eyes snapped open. "What is your title?"

I blinked at him, then glanced at Raina, who was just as nonplussed. I shook my head. "I have no title. I am a common man."

The drunk's face spread into a gap-toothed grin and stood aside, gesturing to the city behind him like a carnival showman. "Common men and women are welcome here. Find a revolutionary place to bed down, and report to The Volker after dawn. Just stay… away.. from… loyalist… scum…"

The edge of the gate had proven too comfortable for the guard, and he was again drifting off. I was reminded of the harried wine merchant that had escaped this city hours ago, and the men in front of me spread out like tenpins by the fist of the grape. I don't know what they were here guarding for, but if they had been only a tenth as drunk, I doubt I would be entering this easily. If watchmen were generally corrupt and looking to shave silver off of the population, revolutionaries were worse. I owed that merchant, who had doubtlessly passed by passing out samples, a debt.

The streets were lit by dwarven lights, pinpricks of ghostly white flame fed by a gas reservoir somewhere far below. The pillars that held the light were built to withstand an angry ogre, and so in the dark were more intimidating than comforting. They did cast enough light that we saw that paint had been liberally spread across the town. In certain places there were red blobs I thought looked like fists if you squinted and turned your head just so. Then there were yellow crowns. Finally black X's on places that looked dark and lifeless.

Raina shook her head. "It's worse than I had heard."

Her voice had wisely been pitched low and soft against prying ears. I matched it. "Do you know what is happening in Hammarfall?"

She looked at me askance. "You do not?"

"I was the first through the pass, then got chased by corrupt officials and a street gang into the wilds, then chased by watchman thugs and some crazy swordswoman."

"The watchmen are not thugs," she snapped adamantly. I noticed defending corrupt didn't enter her mind.

"What do you call the men we just passed?"

"Those are not watchmen, those are revolutionaries."

"I find that the only difference between the two will be who wins and ten years of time." We continued in the darkness. "Now, speak."

It was not a story of fairy tales, to be sure. Everyone had too much shit on them for it to read that way. Each of the great cities in the country of Hammarfall were ruled over by a prince or princess. Each was somewhere in the line of the noble families to rule. The king ruled the whole of the country and saw to its taxation, management, and defense.

As one dies, another noble pops into the top slot to carry on a-noble-ing in the finest tradition. Some are tolerated, some loved, and some not so loved. His majesty, King Hans Grieger Von Hammarfall was of the latter.

The shocking thing was that he knew of it, and cared about it. In fact, he cared about it so much that each year paranoia ate at his brain a little bit more. At first he needed a food taster, then an army of them. He strictly limited the people who could see him to the point where he assigned a commoner judge to sit over high court cases involving nobility. The nobility finally started taking care of things themselves, poison and blade rather than subject themselves to the judgment of (ick!) commoners. But the king refused to appoint nobles, lest they become the face of justice in his kingdom. If the commoners got too popular, they could be sent to the headsman much easier than nobles. Things got worse from there.

"Here," I motioned, interrupting Raina in her narration. We slipped up to an unmarked gate and I plied my hand to it. It took several tries before an innkeep, built like an aging barbarian blacksmith opened the gate and cowered away from it as if expecting a beating. I must have looked at him as if he were mad, for it would easily take five attackers to even begin to make a man such as this breathe hard.

I fished a pouch with enough silver to jingle and shook it. He looked Raina and I up and down then motioned us inside quickly. Like most of the buildings, this one was a half timber affair with an abbreviated stable built on the side. We stripped the horse (had Raina ever named the thing?) of everything then carried it inside. Raina made a face at me when I sent her out to feed and rub him down, but being the teacher had advantages.

Inside, the place was gloriously homey. The walls were covered in furs, the low coals in the fireplace were surrounded in thick iron that had absorbed the heat of the fire and still radiated it into the room. The thick pieces of wood, from rafters to tables and chairs, were a deep chestnut, filed and waxed until no splinters could be found.

I sat down heavily in a chair. "Keep, I need something to warm me and wash away the darkness of those streets."

Though fairly certain he was not to be beaten, he still seemed almost timid, despite clearly being able to carry a cow in to be milked at the bucket rather than the reverse. He bobbed his head, almost in relief. "Food?"

I tried to be conciliatory, considering I had gotten the man out of bed. I was in desperate need of a friend right now. "If it is not too much trouble."

He brightened and spread his hands as if performing a trick. "Certainly! Stay and rest, master. I will have you at ease momentarily."

I lay back and rubbed my eyes, the strong wood feeling soft and inviting compared to the wilds and the road. Raina came in and fell into the chair next to me. I felt, more than heard, her open her mouth when the innkeep was back, setting down thick clay mugs and a copper pot filled with steaming goodness. He ladled out the reddish golden mixture into the cups and set out platters of the strangest fare. Apples dried to a rubbery consistency, mated with a strangely sharp cheese. Cold, but cooked, bacon speared onto pungent black bread cooked with onions throughout that had caramelized to the edge of sweetness. A strange fruit that was incessantly hot filled with a soft cheese that spread the warmth from a mouth numbing explosion into a raging fire that filled the torso and drove away the gloom. I took one of these last, then washed away the fire with a mouth full of the spiced apple drink. The warmth of the drink accented the exotic spices that mulled the whole, not quite covering the belly warming tingle of extremely strong wine or weak liquor. The drink was dangerous stuff, but the simple, yet wonderful tastes of the food demanded nothing less to stand up to their power on the palate.

The big man set fists on hips, massive muscles straining at his tunic as he himself was fit to burst. It was then I realized Raina and I both had been stuffing our faces without pause.

"Sir," I said, with no sarcasm, "you look as if you were built to wrestle bears, but you seem to have found your true calling as a cook."

He laughed and took the liberty of sitting next to us. "Ah! You are a northerner. I can tell by your speech. My mother was a northern girl, brought back by my father who was a horse merchant." He took a mug, which it turned out was hanging from the far side of the pot with a few others, filled it, and drank to our health. "I was raised amongst the horses, and became a powerful boy with work and trail food. Yet, my heart called for a stable place. Though a mighty man, my father, Lords of Light watch over him, died in an avalanche years ago. I sold off his stock, along with all his brood mares and purchased this place. Horseman's Home has done well by me all these years. I am Konrad Pferdmann."

His hand could have crushed mine easily, and for him to describe his father as mighty conjured up the kind of robust musculature that would laugh at natural disasters, but I let that lie. In fact, I added a lie of my own, "I am called Crow. I am a swordsman from the north. I have heard of many opportunities for work inside of Hammarfall, but so far it seems a country of refugees and strange gatemen."

Konrad looked left and right, as if fearing some hidden listener, then went and dropped a log on the coals. Within moments, the fire was going again, and he sat down close to gossip.

He confirmed Raina's story in the broad strokes, though he was far kinder to the king than she was. That being said, it still wound up with the king half mad with fear of assassination. Finally he ordered all doors, gates, and portals, everywhere in the kingdom, be locked. Guards were set everywhere, meant to interrogate anyone going anywhere. Ships were held in ports until their goods rotted. Food spoiled. Cloth mildewed. Ironworks rusted.

So, in came Oleg Volker, a charismatic firebrand. He was a wonderful leader and wanted all the best for his people. They loved him. He had organized riots in the city of Hammarfall and called for greater freedom, lower taxes, and so on. The king, who had been waiting for just such a thing to happen, withdrew every single one of his forces to his palace to fend off the inevitable assassination attempt or storm of peasants to break down his doors. Neither has happened, mainly because people are much stupider, and far more evil, than that.

Immediately upon taking power of the streets, Volker began raiding the homes of the wealthy commoners. With no guards to protect them, all they could do was protest or be executed. Many escaped in the early days, and so now Volker had the gates locked down to stop anyone leaving that might be squeezed of coin.

Konrad spread his hands helplessly. "They tax businesses almost at whim, and have raided - they say taxed - all the farms within reach, bringing food and bodies into the city to bolster his numbers."

I swallowed an apple and cheese wedge. "Surely, there are armies on the march to put an end to this?"

Konrad took another mug of hard cider, his payment for the news of the day. "With what food? Volker will be alive until harvest, that much is certain. What is less certain is who will bring in that harvest, or who will be alive to eat it."

"Alive?"

Konrad again checked for listeners even in the deserted bar, then leaned in. "Volker is a man who loves his freedom. Freedom for all is his rallying cry, but freedom for himself is what he loves best. Those that disagree, are apt to disappear."

I took that at face value and nodded. "Nevertheless, I need work to continue. I shall need lodging for my student, the horse, and myself. At least two meals a day, linens and washing, for a week."

He quoted a price as my hands secretly fiddled with the edge of the fox fur cloak. The little pocket sewn into the lining came open and dumped its cargo into my palm. He set a high number, and I clunked the gold coin onto the table. Konrad was a man wise enough to accept lots of money now in lieu of slightly more money later. He nodded graciously and took the coin.

Within minutes Raina and I had been scooped up and deposited in our rooms. Well, truth be told, we walked, but the massive brawn of Konrad allowed him to scoop up our saddle and horse load of packs, carrying them as if they weighed no more than a set of dry towels.

The top floor had but one room, but it was richly appointed. Raina would be but one floor below and I was too tired to think of that as a bad thing.

Once alone, I stripped. I leaned the Phantom Angel in the corner next to the bed, set the saddle in front of the door to alert me to intruders, tied down the latch to the shutters with metal wire, and fell into bed. I really should have checked on Raina, but my paranoia did not extend that far after a forced march of a day, half the night, and then at least six cups of hard cider. I was asleep the moment after I noticed how soft and supple the sheets were against my skin, and I congratulated myself on the choice of inns.

EIGHT

THE REVOLUTIONARY AND THE FOX

SOMEONE kicked in the door. I responded to the rude interruption by trying to kill them. It seemed only fair as I had been very short on sleep.

I found out several somethings very useful just then, as the first thug kicked open the door, got far too little movement out of it thanks to the saddle in front of the door.

The first something I learned is men from Hammarfall run toward the priggish. Seriously, nudity outside the confines of their bedrooms really seems to disturb them. A roaring naked swordsman is right out.

I snatched the Phantom Angel from its sheath and swung it in a horizontal arc. As the lead thug backed into the next in line, I learned the second something– the dwarves taught the smiths of Hammarfall absolutely nothing. Oh, the thug's sword didn't shatter like a wineglass, but it did snap at the hilt and leave him holding a handle and crosspiece. Or maybe all the thugs carried cheaply cast swords. That would be typical, and likely, because I looped the Angel over my head to build momentum and snap off the sword of the second in line as cleanly and mercilessly as the first.

One nude foot lashed out and hit the lead man in the sternum. Already off balance, he tumbled back into the hall, taking one, two, three and number four with him. I lunged forward and made them scrabble like rats with the lantern unshuttered. Number Five, however, appeared a higher class of thug. He appeared as the others scrambled out of the way. He had Raina's gold hair twisted in his hand, the other holding a dagger to her throat. Her eye was purpling and swelling, but she was more furious than frightened. My respect for her ticked up another notch as she continuously scanned everyone who came within reach of her sloppily bound hands, those paws working covertly to loosen them toward freedom.

I stepped back, and Number Five came into the room. He pressed the dagger, which had to be pretty dull, against Raina's skin. There was no blood, but she flinched.

"Get dressed. Volker wants to see you." The command brooked no delay.

Oh, he does, does he? It took half a heartbeat to decide to take Number Five's arm at the elbow, a spinning strike directed downward like a guillotine to pull the blade from her neck and sever his control of it immediately. There was another half heartbeat where I was certain I could do it. My entire body hardened in preparation to take the arm, and naked that I was, it was enough of a signal that Number Five ducked back behind Raina, pulling his dagger and arm with him.

"Get dressed!" he repeated, pulling at Raina's hair.

Banking the flames inside me to a low, long-lasting grudge, I reached somewhat sullenly into the corner and took up the Angel's sheath. The blade snapped home and I lay it on the bed. I picked up my breeches, paused and cast a nasty glance at Number Five, "You want to watch?"

The man sneered and reached forward to pull the door closed with his already full knife hand. He never saw Raina's elbow as it turned his nose into a bloody explosion. She snatched the knife from his nerveless fingers and shouldered him into the side of the doorway, knife perched in the hollow of his throat. The men outside dared not lunge at her, but I am not sure she would have noticed in time. She was whispering a long string of instructions, or curses, or maybe dire promises to her prisoner, who immediately urinated in his pants. I smiled and decided, despite how often she had tried to kill me, I liked Raina.

"Enough." I said, like I was in control. Raina's face snapped toward me. "Let the poor buffoon go. Go get dressed. We will meet the anarchist."

She let him go, but kneed him in the crotch first. She even replaced the dagger in his sheath without him noticing before turning and leaving for her own room one floor down. The men were disillusioned and disheartened in the hallway as I shut the door. If this was the quality of revolutionary they were breeding nowadays, Hammarfall was in serious trouble.

I dressed, careful to bring the Phantom Angel to draw all kinds of attention, as well as a dozen other ways to kill, secreted away to be easily missed. I appeared in the hall, pulling the door and locking it behind as my only moment of pause, and turned immediately without waiting for the gaggle of morons to even think about leading me as a prisoner.

Raina was already waiting in the hall, owing to the fewer weapons she had to secret about herself. Actually, I wasn't sure if she had any and I wasn't about to ask in front of the thugs. I discretely passed her my short sword and its sword belt from under my cloak. Number Five, the great urinator, saw and started to say something, but I fixed him with a flinty stare that gave Raina time to put the damn thing on, and shut the thug up. I was reasonably certain that nobody here had ever heard of Fox (Simon to be technical) Crow, but an audience with the head thug in a clustered array of them was likely to be messy if at any time I acted like a common man. I was not a common man. I was a predator, and I tried my best to let that show in every movement and every look.

Downstairs they had Konrad and the pretty little thing I assumed was his wife at spear point. I sneered, a facial expression made so that it could deafen everyone within the room.

My words were commanding, sharp, impatient, "Let go of the poor man and lead on to Volker." The tone had been precise. I was not a prisoner, I had an *appointment* to speak to the revolutionary. When they did not move I snapped, "Your master will not wait all day and neither will I. Move!"

And as I have always said– walk into a den of thieves and start yelling, and your throat gets slit. Walk into a barracks and shout orders, half of them will be done before anyone thinks to question who you are. They left the muscle-bound innkeeper and his wife as we took to the streets.

The sun was bright, but distant and cold. It stabbed at the eyes without warming the heart. I thought about being fussy and calling for my saddle to ride to the meeting, as befitting my made-up station above these men, but then I remembered what they did to nobles and kept myself quiet. Orders were one thing, airs were another.

Raina walked just behind and to the side. She was holding together well, only a sheen of sweat in the cool morning light betraying her fear. I could not fault her, for as we turned down a side street, we left behind the human construction of half timber houses, and entered the old dwarven stone buildings.

dwarves are pragmatic about things carved out of native rock. The rock was there before, will stay after, and so they don't really own it.

They simply lease its use as they try to dig as much ore, minerals, and crystals out of it as possible. They don't view it as theft, more like midwifery. In the end, however, they will abandon their mines, forts, and tunnels without a second thought the instant the treasures wear thin. Thus they have left mine-town ruins all over the face of creation.

Men have, since every man was nothing more than a barbarian, abandoned their tents and seized these structures. Normally built hundreds, if not thousands, of years before to fend off creatures long since killed off by the dwarves, the men had no trouble using these fortresses to fend off one another.

Hammarfall was built on the edge of the Long Night Sea. It was shaped like a horseshoe, with the long tines facing the water, and the hollow belly filled with the bay. From the northern spike to the southern, the ground rose in a gentle angle to the magnificently appointed palace far above on the southern horn. Somewhere along that route there was a gate, and behind that gate were the nobles cowering from this crisis. At the base of the carved cliffs, men had spread out from cliff's edge to outer wall with buildings of his own design. This, however was not where we were heading.

We were lead deeper into the city along the northern arc, to the higher class neighborhoods that boasted dwarven architecture in their foundations, if not the walls themselves. That is what they meant: safety, stability, permanency. City buildings, homes of wealthy families, and royal buildings were housed in the dwarven carved structures. It was one of these that Volker had taken as his mayoral seat.

Had this been a meeting hall? A bier hall? A home? Whatever it had been, now it was a cross between a church, a tavern, and a throne room. Most bizarrely, the walls were painted on every flat space. I have seen, and stolen, a cathedral's worth of art. It was always meant to inspire, to flatter, to speak quietly in the presence of power, or to simply revel in the beauty of a captured moment. This was something far different.

Everything was in caricature, exaggerated seductively. It was a kind of art that would never be put to canvas because of its simplicity and lack of skill at capturing life. Yet, this lack of adherence to life allowed the painter to capture emotional truth as he saw it. He wielded it like a hammer. Inept and cruel guards were everywhere, royalists marked with the crown. They were holding leashes upon the peasants, riding yokes upon them, stealing from them pots of coin. Over them all was the purple shadow of a man who, even a foreigner like myself could tell, was supposed to be the king.

Some had words, but they were few and far between. Easy mantras that anyone could learn, but sparse since so few of the audience could read. "Sir is the word used as a chain a man puts on himself. A crown is not a halo, it is a ring of horns." And so on. Easy to remember, easy to chant, short on thought.

We continued down the great hall toward the end, and the constant pressure of the simple, powerful messages thundered on all sides, demanding an emotional response. I mentally pushed them aside and concentrated on the room itself.

Drunks sprawled everywhere, and sullen women were chained by the fire, fine dresses in stained tatters as they provided a constant stream of food for the people coming in and leaving. The servants all had the air of nobles fallen on the hardest of times. As I watched they were abused, groped, and even spat upon once. The abusers/patrons they worked to feed all looked like guards of varying degrees. And by varying degrees I meant all lacked the full complement of equipment and most lacked much more than a helmet and a weapon. Watching them slouch around the tables, drinking from barrels of beer, they lacked far more than equipment.

One glance at Raina and I could see the muscles of her jaw dancing. I fixed her with a hard stare and the expression of enduring unpleasant smells may have faded a little. On the other hand it was possibly my imagination.

Apparently they used cloaks to designate the lieutenants, for it was one such guard that came to us, typical lieutenant-level scowl in place, and demanded our weapons. I glanced back at Raina, wishing I knew her better so that I could give a clear nonverbal signal that I was about to start trouble, but I did the best I could while being subtle. She nodded in return imperceptibly, and I turned my head back to the man.

Directly behind me there was the sound of flesh meeting flesh, a male yelp, a sword singing its release from a metal throated sheath, a peel of steel on steel, a deep thud and the sound of a man in agony, a clatter of a fallen sword covering his groans. Understand that this happened faster than it took for me to glance back, partially because I had focused on the cloak owner. He was shocked, not smug, so I was hardly surprised when I glanced back to find the two guards behind us rather less than battle worthy. One was missing his sword and was hunched over his cracked pair of eggs. The other had been leveled to the floor with a surprise throat punch where he still lay, eyes rolling. Raina smiled grimly, flipped my short sword she wore end over end, caught it, and sheathed it.

I mentally filed the look I had just given her from *Follow my lead* to *Do something violent, would you*?

I gave my attention back to the lieutenant. "No."

The word was not shouted, but it echoed off of every wall, since all other motion, sound, and breath had stopped. This was it, this was the dagger's edge. If our fate tilted one way, we would have to fight our way clear of a dozen barely trained men, but then out of a city full of them. If it fell the other way–

"Heins! Stop wasting their time and bring them to me."

I was barely able to keep the shock from my face. History would indicate "fight my way out" to be the option fate chooses, but not today. Instead we were guided to the head of the table, which was now occupied by a tall, thin man wearing glorious purple robes. The suit of rich violet that washed out his face and made him seem slightly feverish cost more than a set of plate armor.

Let me take a second to go on about color. For me color is a matter of survival. For most, it is a matter of frivolity. For the upper ranks, it is a sign of station.

Natural colors were cheapest and easy to obtain, and thus signaled a peasant. Making natural fiber white was more expensive, and difficult to maintain, and thus relegated for formalwear for peasants and the most common of clothing for the upper classes. Then came colors. Most dyes are used in the same bath many times. Meaning deep crimson is a first bath cloth, and is expensive, the dull pink cloth is the last bath in the dye, and is cheaper. Some peasants could afford one or two special pieces, but otherwise would ornament clothing with colored thread. But all dyes were not created equal. At the upper end of expensive was the deep, full bodied blue of the royals. But at the top, aside from the dyeless threads made of silver or gold, was the rich purple of kings and emperors. Oh, in the past, laws were written to say that nobody without so-and-so blood line was allowed to wear the holy color of puce, or whatever color was considered holy at the time. Now it was recognized that such laws were, by and large, unnecessary.

It was useful upon occasion in a society where someone could take offense to just about anything a peasant said and have his head off with the snap of his fingers. It pays to know who to bow to, and the color scale of society helped that happen. This is why I could identify the speaker immediately. I took him in from across the room, and the closer we got, the scarier he became. Oh, he was not big; his build was typically thin with a growing belly and chins from access to suddenly plentiful and richer food. It wasn't that he was imperial, for he was surrounded by lackeys and lickspittles of every kind, little different from the half equipped 'watchmen' from around town. They wore expensive mail, carried better quality steel, but they had spent little to no time actually in combat, at war, or facing someone who wanted to kill them. It wasn't because he was powerful, or rich, for he wasn't. He didn't even keep his seat as we were presented to him, and though it may have been from an overabundance of brotherhood with the common man– whatever that meant– he offered his arm. It was that he was wearing velvet clothes sewn from the king's purple, the most expensive dye on the most expensive fabric, over black stockings, shirt, and so on. I shook his hand warmly, for he was clearly a power of a kind and it would be best not to antagonize, but I privately wondered if this man realized he had turned himself into a mirror of the caricature of the king drawn upon the walls.

He was calm, cool, and looking to impress. His warm voice was framed by a cunning smile, "Good to meet you, swordsman. I am sorry if the men were overzealous in bringing you to me."

I returned his smile, with exactly the same amount of sincerity unless I missed my guess. "Mr. Volker, I have heard of you. You are accomplishing awe inspiring things here."

He nodded gracefully and gestured to the chair on his left. "All the way from Noria?" he assumed with an air of surprise. "Well, we can only hope to keep it going until next winter."

The men all around stiffened as I sat. Each of the seated men had taken off their weapon and placed it on the table in front of them. Without being told, I did the same, the silvery elven steel of the Phantom Angel reflecting light in rainbows and the blue heart in the hilt glittering dangerously. Raina started to settle next to me, but a subtle head shake and hand gesture told her to stand. I could only hope she knew enough to keep my back from sprouting a knife unexpectedly, but I doubted it. I needed to start her on training the very second there was time. I sensed her glowering at the back of my head, but I ignored her. Steins, full of warm, bitter beer, arrived almost immediately.

"So, you have me at a disadvantage. You know who I am, but I do not know you… your title…?"

Which was as clumsy a trap as I have ever seen laid at my feet. Even if I were a noble, unless I were already drunk, stupid, and perhaps a touch inbred, I would not tell these thugs. I waved at the purple monster before me. "I am just a commoner, coming from the north in search of a master. I am Fox Crow."

Volker's head cocked to the side. "Isn't that an unusual name?"

I nodded, not willing to get into the long story. I simply replied, "It is the one I was given."

Volker's face became slightly wry and a little worried, "A devotee of the God of Death then?"

"Unwilling servant, I suppose. As are we all," I replied, sipping on the beer, wondering what possible thing the people of Hammarfall could have done to be inflicted with this drink. I swallowed and could feel the unaccustomed heavy bite. I had to be careful with this wicked brew.

Volker smiled. "Good, isn't it?" and took a few healthy gulps. The rest of the men around the table did likewise, almost in time. I kept the amusement and disgust from my face. These armored men were more a dance number than a war council. "But let us down to business, Crow. Come summer, we will be facing several challenges to what we are trying to do here. I need as many warriors on my side as I can gather. I would like to hire you on."

And there it was. I shook my head. "I am not a soldier. You'd find me worse than useless to your task."

"I disagree. I think all skills are worthy of learning at this point."

"I agree they are worthy of learning, but not of teaching. I see quite a few captains and generals here." I motioned around the table, they frowned even more fiercely. "I am sure they can drill the men into order."

Volker smiled and leaned forward, hands clasped tightly. "True, true, but there are so many uses for a man of your talents."

Aside from the fact that this man had no idea what my talents were, I'm sure I knew what kind of uses he had in mind. I was careful to keep my face blank. "I'm flattered," the next word had to be choked out, "sir, but I think I will make my own way."

There were wordless explosions of disbelief around the table. The loudest came from across from me. The man was high enough in the service of Volker to be wearing a full set of chain and plates, helmet, and shield. He had laid a longsword like the rest and judging by the delicate filigree on the hilt, it was not cheap in the least, nor had ever been used. Still, he was the kind of man who wore plate and chain to a meal of any sort. The only purpose was to remind everyone of his station, too newly won to be comfortable.

Volker pressed, "I can offer you food, board, and safety."

I nodded, sadly. "I think I can do better."

"We have many enemies. I can offer you a cut of the treasures pillage from their homes."

I sat a little straighter, feeling the throbbing need for gold in the pit of my stomach. Gold had always meant freedom, power, comfort. If I understood him correctly, even only cupping my hands beneath the stream of wealth he could squeeze from the town would allow me to personally drink gallons of the stuff. Volker's eyes sparkled as he sensed the need inside me, but I shook my head somewhat painfully. "No."

The purple champion of (some of) the people stifled a glare. A serving girl came by and dropped a set of freshly baked loaves onto the table rather sullenly. Volker turned the full heat of his glower upon her. She shuddered and put the bread into a neat pile. Volker reached out for her, pulling her limply into his lap. His hands wandered across her breasts. "There are other spoils to be claimed."

I am not naïve. I know the ways of the world. But being brought so close to the facts of this matter lit a fire inside me that burned my greed alive and replaced it with a cold, hard flame. I may not have been able to stop this revolution, but I didn't have to partake in it. I stood as if burned by the chair, my word coming out in an echoing challenge. "No!"

Volker turned red as his man across the table started to stand as well. The idiot started to reach for his sheathed weapon on the table. I snatched up the Phantom Angel and brought the pommel viciously down on a band of iron that held his wooden sheath together. With practiced ease, I slung the belt over my off shoulder, grabbing the clasp with my free hand, securing it, then giving it a quick double pull to bring the Angel up to my shoulder outside my cloak, arms free. It wouldn't stay there long without being further secured. I hoped it wouldn't have to, or else we would have to drink blood in order not to drown in this room.

The standing lickspittle roared, "How dare you speak to the Great Man like that? I challenge you, villain!"

I sneered so hard it was a physical slap to the face. "Draw when you are ready then, lackey."

Volker kicked back from the table but kept the girl in front of himself as a shield, red face draining to pale in a heartbeat.

Volker's man snatched up the sword in the slightly dented sheath and gripped the hilt. He grunted. He lurched. He cursed and tried again, and again. He yanked and spat and heaved, but could not free the sword of the pinched iron ring I had deformed.

I drew forth the Phantom Angel, the mirror-bright blade growling on the metal throat of the sheath for what seemed like forever. I brought it forth as languidly as the falling night, the winged monk crosspiece dull and heavy as the final judgment even as the glittering point pointed unwaveringly at the armored henchman's chest. His sword, still imprisoned in the sheath, fell to the floor.

I slowly, professionally took the sheath and belt from my shoulder and twirled The Phantom Angel in a tight arc and sent it home before securing the thing to my waist.

Volker's face was stoic as he pushed the serving noble to the floor. He began to clap slowly, sardonically. His words were matter of fact, bitter, but at least honest. "A man with a sword like that one had best be a master of its use or lose it to the first bandit on the road. Come with me, Crow. Together we can do great things."

I stood tall before him, ignoring everyone else in the room, then I offered my hand to the girl on the floor. She quivered for a moment, then allowed me to help her to her feet. I pulled her closely and she had not bathed in days. I whispered, "We would do truly terrible things."

"All the truly great things are terrible to behold."

I shook my head and sighed. "I have taught your men a lesson and I shall take this girl as payment."

The room again galvanized. Even the girl stiffened in my arms. I passed her to Raina, who took her like a watchman takes a prisoner.

Volker sputtered, "What lesson, pray tell?"

I affixed him with a level, dangerous glance. "Learning to take no for an answer can be healthier than forcing the alternative."

Now there was nothing but red hot hate inside his eyes for me. His mouth twisted into the exaggerated frown of a spoiled child. Again he began to clap his hands in a slow cadence. Without further word, or turning my back on the procession of thugs at the table, we backed away. We turned once in the center of the room, hurried to the entryway of the hall, and passed the slightly stunned guards who watched us go without even lifting a finger.

Outside the air was crisp and cold. The plump, pixie faced slave girl shuddered and I slipped off my cloak to wrap her, taking the opportunity to tighten the Angel's belts. I immediately regretted my generosity, since it was frosty even in the daylight, but I suddenly didn't want to be seen as the kind of man who would take it back.

"So," I addressed Raina, "What did you learn?"

She answered without hesitation. "You never back down. You serve no man." She glanced at the noble girl, "And you are a better person than I gave you credit for."

I shrugged, honesty bubbling up again at the worst time. "You should have learned that I am an idiot. I only serve rich men, and I nearly got us all killed." I too, focused on the girl. "You have noble blood?"

"Yes. Far from the throne, but blessed, nevertheless." She looked resigned to fate, golden ringlets limp and despondent as well she should. Rape and then marriage was not unheard of and was the easiest way to get into a lesser noble family. Being in any noble family was like having any kind of horse, if you did then you were a rich man– fields were plowed, goods got carried, and you need not walk. Peasants had only their own two feet.

"They caught you on the street?" Raina asked.

The girl shook her head. "Our house was modest, in the lower city. They burst in and took us all, killed who resisted, enslaved everyone else and stripped it bare."

I nodded. Unless I missed my guess it was a common story as of late, and how Volker was funding his revolution aside from confiscatory taxes. "Is there anyone who will take you in?"

She stared at me for long heartbeats, then glanced at Raina. Tears began to stream down her face uncontrollably. "My Uncle! He will take me in! But there is no way to get to–"

"Let me worry about that." I said. "Point the way and we will have you to him before noon."

And so we began winding through the streets, stopping only to claim our horse and put on fresh, more presentable clothes from the Inn. I let the girl, Winifred, ride as we walked beside her like guardsmen.

The city became more gap toothed. Many blocks had crowns painted over doors, which were then X'ed out. The world was silent as to what happened to the occupants, but I'm guessing Winifred had guesses.

Finally, we came to a sloped section of road that seemed to double back toward the main city gate on a whole raised level. We then traversed the city again, coming across the wide belly that overlooked the forest of ship masts and the crashing sea beyond. The hypnotic swish of far away waves only highlighted the clop-clop of the horse and the terrified city that hid behind closed doors and cowered in silence. Finally, legs throbbing from the uphill path, we came to an impressive gate that crossed the rock from edge to edge, abutted by houses nearly nice enough to gain entrance. The massive gate was shut and barred, traces of ice along the bottom and cracks saying it had been that way since long before winter ended.

"Hail the gate!" I called.

Two men with crossbows leaned over the edge, taking aim. I felt my belly go cold as the hungry tips gazed at me. They gazed at Raina too, but it was hard at that moment to be too upset about it. I found my voice and even managed to force some manliness into the call, "I have Winifred Ironschlager here, snatched from the claws of Oleg Volker. She seeks reunification with her uncle, the Grand Conductor Swan Lampedocht."

There was a flurry of activity above. The crossbows shifted from us to down the road, as if a horde of unwashed, half-armored thugs were about to pour out into the road and hammer into the gates in a stinking wave. In fact, that was probably exactly what they were waiting for.

A call came from above, "Dismount and come through carefully, on foot."

I helped Winifred down and we walked through one at a time, leading the horse. Winifred came through into a circle of armed men, then I.

A voice murmured, "Look at that sword!"

The Phantom Angel winked at them in its sheath, the noon sun burnishing the antique finish of the crosspiece. Then the horse came after. Next was Raina. I handed her the reins and she took them without comment. I pulled myself up to my full height and shook my hair out of my eyes. Every second, the guardsmen relaxed further. The plump girl had the clothes of a noble at the correct level of disrepair. The sword was too rich for a common man, and a horse besides. My 'manservant' painted me further as some kind of minor noble, and thus an ally. The captain took no chances on offending a noble. I, and I want to be absolutely clear about this, did nothing to dissuade them of this. He saluted me and I saluted back smartly, as if reflex. She smiled knowingly, "I'll send a man along to escort you, sir."

And so she did, but it was men, not a man– enough to keep us in line. It took only minutes of walking through the tidy, well tended streets. The first thing that struck me was how human the buildings were. Then I saw past the façade and decided I was an idiot and Volker would have a far harder time taking these homes than those built of wood below.

The dwarven architecture had not been abandoned. Rather, it had been absorbed. Human additions had been bolted to the outside, molded into the background seamlessly, to give that same half-timber feel of Hammarfall (the country) architecture. It was all a lie, for underneath, the solid, man-thick walls carved of living rock remained.

Despite thc nightmare of fighting house to house through a hostile city built like this, and thus the supposed safety, there were no children playing out in the streets. Upon occasion, people looked through beautiful panes of clear, dwarven mercurial glass, but they quickly shut the curtains. Stranger yet, the top of every flat building had a man-made cistern, a spindly tower holding a massive barrel designed to catch and strain rainwater into the wooden container. I turned to mention it, but as we marched down broad lanes to yet another massive manor, Winifred broke loose of the group and dashed across the foreyard to the door. There she pounded as if demons ran after her. Her fists hammered in time to a panicked heart, and when the door opened, she fell sobbing into the arms of a gray haired scholar who could not be any more shocked if she was actually being pursued by demons.

This is how we met Swan Lampedocht.

NINE

THE LEGENDARY CONDUCTOR

WE WERE greeted as honored guests and guards dismissed themselves back to the gate. We still had to give up our most obvious weapons at the door, but we did it without comment. I didn't sense an ambush, or even armed servants. It was the house of a minor lord, and not a jail by any stretch.

For those counting, this counts the seventh time in my life I have actually been rewarded for doing something noble in my life with something pleasant, and the tenth time ever I had not been lied to while speaking to a pretty girl in distress, and the very first time these two events coincided.

Lampedocht nattered over the girl as you might expect, tears rushing down his face. Within minutes it seemed he had cooks, servants, and tailors fluttering about. We were given leave to bathe, which I gave Raina permission to enjoy, fed, which I gave Raina permission to enjoy, and dressed in fine garments, which I thought I would deny her pleasure, but instead thrilled her when she found out she could get man-clothes tailored to her instead of living in ill-fitting secondhand rags from a store.

She mock thrust all around the small room we had been given, tumbling about and relishing the fluid fit of the clothes. The seamstresses were scandalized. Ladies should wear this or that, et cetera, whatnot, and all that. We ignored them.

The house was a testament to music and it silently inhabited every part of it. There were marble busts of famous composers. Framed glass were tattered scraps of ancient runes I vaguely knew had something to do with music, but nothing specific as to their meaning. Every spare scrap of space was the same. Then there were display cases with rebecs, harps, drums, lutes, flutes, and hundreds of others I could not identify. Soon we entered a hall of more practically and accessibly displayed.

"Come here," I called to Raina, who was still enjoying the new, clean man-clothes far too much.

"Yes, Master?"

I nodded to the case. "What do these instruments tell you?"

She stared at them, but within seconds shook her head. "I don't know."

I went to the next. "And these?"

She barely gave them a glance, and shrugged. "What?"

I took her to another rack, then pointed out wear marks on them.

"Oh!" Then she lowered her voice, "you are saying the Lord is a dilettante, unable to keep with any one thing for long."

I affixed her with a hard glare. "Fortune forefend you think so if you enter the house of a master of murder and look at his collection of tools. These cases along this hall are not antiques; they are all modern made and played nearly to death. This is not the collection of a man unable to keep with any one thing, but a man so talented at what he does that he needs dozens of ways to do it in order to stay interested. He's a master of his craft in a way you may never be a master of yours."

She scowled at me, but remained silent as we went downstairs to again meet with our host. We were given subtle presents of new purses, expensive things made of thick leather, strung with metal cord. They were presented full of silver coin, enough for a month of hard living if it came to that. Not quite equal to my retirement pouch, but fresh monies, all the same. Then we were brought to his table to sit and talk.

When questioned, Lampedocht could focus his amazing intellect upon a problem like a dwarven lens, searing a problem to ashes in moments. The trouble was, he never stopped long enough, leaving only a smoldering idea behind without much in the way of heat or warmth. His hair was constantly springing away from his head in cowlicks the color of rain clouds, and his beard could be considered well trimmed days ago, and since then only half trimmed as he had been distracted in the middle of the job. Swan Lampedocht was a man who would be brilliant if he only drank enough hard liquor to bring his thoughts to heel for more than a half second, and no more. Balanced on that knife edge, I am sure he was a stellar mind. Balance was not his forte.

I tried to reconcile the man before me with the man who had nearly played through the instruments upstairs and couldn't. Raina gave me a snide glance, but I was sure I was right.

You may have noticed that I have neglected to describe the reunion of Winifred and her uncle. To that I say there were tears, and there was laughter. She made a selfless and somewhat fearful recounting of the abuses inflicted by the bandits. I am sure she thought she was to be disowned, disinherited, or shuttled off to a nunnery somewhere. These fears were real and as common as they were horrible, stacked upon the abuses that triggered them. I shall not add to her burdens by recounting them here in public. I will say that Swan accepted his niece with love and devotion of a man who knows that a person can easily stain themselves, but never be ruined by wounds inflicted by others. Ugly is a state of the soul. At least he was good enough of a man to know that.

Still, there was little of a reunion, and the reason soon became clear. Society is a lot like a tree. There are those at the very top, the throne, that got all the sun and water they wanted. Beneath, those that were closest to the throne were eclipsed by it, yet protected by it. Fewer leaves, but less chance of being pruned. The further down the tree one goes, the tree spreads to catch more sunlight. The further from the trunk, however, the larger the chance that a branch would be lopped off.

That's what had happened. Volker had taken axes to the lowest branches, those furthest from the king, and let them rain to the ground. So, few came by to give Winifred their condolences because her ties to the higher families were so fragile, and those closely related in status or blood largely lay severed on the ground below.

Swan, for his part, doddered unconvincingly from one subject to another, his aged mind stuttering as he tried to make sense of the worst kind of stories told turned out to be true. Winifred ate very little before being excused. She flashed Raina and I a strained but heartfelt smile. She sat in the next room at a complex dwarven machine instrument. It was a box of pedals and white keys that made tinny, harp-ish, twangy sounds, but somehow were soothing. She played it as if taught from infancy, quite possible in noble families, and provided song after song for our lunch.

Swan lit a pipe with rich brown tobacco, graciously offering me one, which I puffed as he lit it from a taper transferred from the fireplace to first my own, then his face. Servants appeared from nowhere and cleared dishes like wraiths. Lampedocht sucked in silence, listening to the mournful, nearly mechanical tunes from the harpsichord beneath Winifred's fingers. In that relaxing day we spent the day until the night seemed to press in, and I felt the dark begin to stir.

His voice, soft and educated, was sorrowful. I wish to say I understood, but if it were my niece in the other room, bruises barely hidden by a large frilly dress, I would be removing Volker and most of his men bloodily off to the halls of the damned right this instant. Granted, I am a man of such talents. If I were not, I assume I would be demanding someone else do it.

Nevertheless, Swan was taken by a mounting sadness as he gazed out of glass panes onto well tended streets patrolled by the finest guards, "I do not understand it. Never have. The king may have been restrictive, but not as much as he might be. And his constant fear may have been a burden upon the people, but it was less burden than those preoccupied by lust, or greed, or even this evil of civil war. We are men of Hammarfall. We are countrymen, all of us. We should be as brothers."

I coughed on the smoke as the words slapped me. I set the pipe down on a plate made for the purpose on the table. Winifred's fingers stuttered on the keys. I glanced to her, and saw the pain flit across her face in an instant. It was then I decided that I did not like Swan Lampedocht.

Yet he continued, "There has to be something to bring us together, to unite the people again."

He sighed.

I am no priest, no wizard, only a man. Yet since being marked by the God of Death, I felt things. Mostly things hard to describe, things I wish I hadn't. I heard whispers, and tossed my head to clear my ears. Swan turned at the movement, his brow creased. I glanced over my shoulder to Raina, whose blue eyes glittered impishly as smoke curled out of her mouth and up across her face like a veil. She drew in deeply again and then set the pipe Lampedocht had given me back on the plate.

"Good tobacco," she said, smoke blasting from her nostrils like dragon's breath.

Lampedocht smiled as if he had just watched some amusing animal trick. He gestured with his pipe stem, "It is getting late and I have kept you. Still, Master Crow, if I may be so bold, may I ask for you to call upon us here again for dinner tomorrow?"

I stood like a shot, because ignoring a noble dismissal was dangerous no matter how distracted and harmless the noble looked. "Of course Lord Lampedocht. Only, it might be troublesome to get in past the guards at the gate without one of your relatives in tow."

"Oh!" The composer jerked as if coming out of some kind of dream. He rummaged in a box on the mantle of the fireplace for a moment. "Of course. I shall send word to the guards to expect you. They will know you by this."

He handed me a ring. The jewel was large ,topaz unless I missed my guess, and the whole gold setting was inscribed with more music runes. I nodded gravely to the man and we took our leave.

Out on the street, we buckled our weapons on. "Did you give up all your weapons when they asked?"

Raina obviously thought about lying, but shrugged. "No, Master. I have a knife in my boot. Shifted it from one to the other when the seamstress was done."

I nodded approval.

"How many did you have?" she asked.

"Five," I replied.

She started to bark a pejorative at me, but a caw shattered her reply. Above us, upon the eves of the magnificent home, cloaked in darkness, a raven sat. It cawed again, then took flight.

I don't know what she saw in me, put whatever she saw made her turn pale. "Was that a sign?"

I nodded.

"Good or bad?"

I sighed and shrugged. "Damned if I know. Let's get back to the inn. I need to start you on swordplay, knife throwing, and secreting blades."

And we did that, and more. But first, we stopped by a blacksmith, who shrugged helplessly at empty shelves. Apparently he had been visited by Volker. He brightened when we bought half wasters, otherwise known as wooden practice swords, in different sizes. He was taking home money for the first time in weeks, probably. The wasters were hard wood without edges, slats glued together around a thin lead rod that gave it the heft of a real weapon. They could break a bone, but it was not likely in armor.

We got back to the inn, training weapons and bundles of old clothes, and in minutes had changed from our new finery and met in the back yard of Konrad's inn. She was an endless sponge, drinking in everything I put in front of her. She analyzed every time I hit her. Without ego, without rancor, she would apply it immediately to her deck of tricks. She was tireless. She was relentless. She was instinctually ruthless. If only she didn't have her endless fixation on fighting fair, whatever that means, she would be ideal material for molding into a whirling wind of death.

The sound of the wasters clattering sounded to children like any number of games they played together, and started to peek at us from around corners and through knotholes in the courtyard fence.

She struck high, and I lunged. In a second we were chest to chest, hilts locked and the smell of our sweat mingling together. "How many do you think report to Volker?" she breathed.

I smiled, proud she had spotted it. "Let's give them something to report."

Faster, and faster we went. We had drawn quite a crowd of children by the time it was too dark to see. They perched on every available piece of fence and stared with wide eyes. We finished in a whirlwind of strikes, blocked in perfect time to make a staccato drum beat. She tripped me and I slammed into my back. I stared at the blunted tip of the waster sword for only a second. Then she pulled me to my feet.

Once again, we were very close, our smells mating in the primal air. I pulled her near, then whispered in her flushed ear. "Tonight, we are sleeping in the same room."

I let her go, and she flopped to her bottom, sputtering. The clouds in the sky, heavy all day, finally let go with a gentle, though freezing, drizzle. I turned in it, grateful that I would not have to spend coin for another bath tonight.

Raina staggered to her feet. "What did you say?"

I stripped like a Norian, the children giggling on every side. As clothes came off, I exposed four hidden blades she had doubted I possessed. I tossed them on the pile in her arms one by one. That one forearm was slightly lighter in color than the other was overlooked by all as I tossed my clothes to my apprentice.

"What did you say?"

"I said clean up the yard of our equipment, bring it in and oil it to keep the wood and leather from souring. And spend some time in the rain; I don't want to smell you tonight."

Raina rushed me, dumping the clothes, waster raised as she lunged. "What did you say?"

Nobody saw what happened next, but from beneath the flesh colored strip of cloth on my forearm came a thin, black dagger. I rolled Raina up in my arms, flinging her into the wall, then planting the thin blade a mere hand-width from her left eye.

"I said I hid five blades from the tailors, and I meant it. Next time, so will you." I let her go and sauntered into the inn. "Now collect and clean our property, then spend some time in the rain to get rid of your smell. We share a room tonight."

And I was gone. It took only a few minutes to get dry by the fire in my room, then get dressed, including three new blades and a heartpin. I had everything arranged so that by the time Raina dragged herself, wet and cold, from the impromptu training ground, her room was locked and empty. But as she kicked at the door, another oaken portal opened slowly and silently at the end of the hall.

The room was softly lit by candles, the smell of roses and sandalwood wafting out from the cracked door. She opened the door like a parolee being shoved back into a cell, but there she found two beds inside the expansive room. She staggered in with the armloads as I sat, freshly dressed and sharpening another blade. I wrinkled my nose.

"You didn't spend time showering in the rain, did you?" She still blinked at the room, at the small brass censor putting out incense smoke, her gear and my gear in a heap on the floor, two beds set far apart. I sighed as if weary. "Take coins from your pouch and buy a bath. These clothes are horrible, please pay the Konrad's wife to wash them properly, also out of your own funds, then go bathe and meet me back here."

She left, and came back an hour later as if her grand execution had only been stayed until this exact minute. On the table by the fire there was a hunk of dark black bread, and a ramekin of golden butter with herbs sprinkled through it. She ignored it all as she stood, tall and proud. She shut the door behind her and walked to the center of the room. There she let her towel fall and stood like a statue to a warrior goddess.

I set aside my make-work, then stood slowly, intently. Her irises narrowed to pinpricks and her hot breath came fast as her face flushed and her hands clenched. I circled her, nearly but not at all touching as I took one, long, interested look in every curve and feature of her hardened body. I took her by the hand and lead her to the bed. Still she stood, rigid and proud, and so I pushed her down. She lay back immediately, so I pulled her up to sit. Her brows furrowed as I knelt before her. I placed one hand on her thigh, then spoke slowly, as if to a moron, "You have not been injured."

She blinked once. Then she blinked twice. She made a noise but it said nothing but confusion and disbelief.

"Well, not all true." I produced a small pair of flat pliers and a blade the size of a finger, one so sharp it could shave a shadow. "Your leg and shoulder have knitted thanks to the potion. Now that we have the opportunity, we need to remove the silk before it rots."

She slumped, then tensed, then shook her head. She opened her mouth again and then yelped. The knife had cut the strands easily, but once pulled forth, the strings had to part the skin that had grown up about them.

I yanked quickly, but she still winced as each thread jumped free of her flesh. There were many tacts to take, but for once, just once, I looked into her confused and hurt eyes and decided to be gentle. "Your training is coming along very well. In fact, I think we can dispense with swords. You said you studied under a swordsman?" She nodded, hard pride, or maybe hard purchased pride. "You learned well. You must have started very young."

She swallowed, nodded. Again there was that steel beneath the tightening of her jaw. I pulled out the last thread out of her thigh and pressed a cloth to the weeping holes. "I can imagine that the tuition a swordsman would require of a young woman would be rather high."

Her breathing came faster, her skin radiating heat like a campfire. I began to work on her shoulder, cutting and pulling free silken threads, "You know, there are things one has to do to survive. As long as those things keep you fed, keep you breathing, I don't think anyone can fault your methods. Especially not someone who has never been out, alone, and fending for themselves."

Raina cleared her throat. "My family already had too many daughters."

"No they didn't." I replied immediately. "Look, you wear a sword long enough and you are going to wind up killing someone who probably didn't really deserve it. If you are lucky, you can get past that. If you are not, then you are going to be drinking a lot just to get to sleep." I pulled the last thread loose. "But what matters is it is much easier to survive if you understand what actually is and what is not your fault. It is not your fault your family had a lot of girl children. It's not your fault Martin Gotzplatz used you as more than just a student. Feeling guilt over these things does nothing but leave you hurt, and weak. Someone can completely ruin all your concentration by making a pass at you." I dabbed at the weeping pinprick wounds and then stood and turned. There was a sharp little jab at my kidney.

I glanced back, where Raina had a small, razor-sharp knife poised to bleed me nice and slow. She whispered in my ear, "Completely ruin my concentration?"

I turned around to stare down at the sharpened spike. "Where ever did you hide that?"

"I am not telling." She smiled wolfishly.

"You are learning," I replied, "And I just might be in love."

Her eyes narrowed and she lifted the knife to eye level briefly in threat. "Give me the key to my room."

I chuckled. "Oh, no! You are sleeping in here, apprentice. I am not waking up to one of Volker's dogs holding you hostage again."

"I freed myself!" she exploded.

"After I agreed to his terms!" I snapped back in a whisper. "Now lower your voice and next time break his nose sooner!"

I blocked off the door, and mindful of our adventures that morning, I slept in hose and a shirt. Sparing me only a glance, Raina followed likewise. As the final candles were extinguished, I filled and emptied a cup from a pitcher of water, over and over down my throat. We set our weapons near to hand, and burrowed into the covers. The fire was low and the night had turned chill, which was good. At least for me.

I awoke hours later to the pressure of a full bladder, but it was the sharpness of the cold that woke me. I emptied it into the garderobe down the hall and then crept back into the room. I stirred the coals of the fire with a poker, then I shook Raina awake. She came to groggy but with a knife in her hand. I secured the hand and put a finger to my lips.

She glanced about the dark room and then hissed far too loudly, "What is wrong?"

I sighed silently, then answered with only enough breath to reach her ears and no further, "You are too loud. Sometimes you are not going to want to fight, sometimes you will be unable to fight. Either way, you are going to have to get away without being seen or heard. Seen, we will cover later. Heard, we can do tonight."

She shook her head to clear the last of the sand from behind her eyes. "What? How?"

"You are going to go downstairs. You will take four eggs, half a loaf of bread, a portion of bacon, some potatoes, two mugs of small beer, a bottle of watered wine, a pan, two plates, and utensils. Bring them here with four logs for the fire."

She listened as if to a madman, then rolled her neck to clear out the stiffness and fixed me with a harsh look, though her voice was softer. "You want me to go downstairs and steal you breakfast?"

I huffed. "Not steal. Here are two silver coins. If you get away clean, leave one coin. If you are caught leave two with whoever catches you."

"Two coins is a lot to pay for breakfast."

"Not to worry, I'm only paying one; the other is from your purse."

She affixed me with another nasty glare. "And If I decide it's worth a silver coin to finish my night's sleep?"

I smiled, calculating quickly. "I thought you'd say that." I hadn't but I had an answer. "So I guess you'll be doing the whole thing naked."

She laughed, still convinced, deep in her heart of hearts, that this was just a joke. "And the logs? We have plenty of wood."

"Not after we cook breakfast. Now strip and go." She paused for a full minute, staring at me incredulously until she finally pulled the shirt over her head, exposing her breasts, but stopped short of standing as I upped the ante just a bit further by handing her sword belt, dagger and short sword. "You must learn to keep these from banging into things as well."

She strapped on her weapons, muttering fiercely. The look she gave me was positively murderous. I put two logs on the fire as I flopped down on the bed and they caught in the hot coals. From my perch near the peak of the house, I could hear the occasional thunk of wood, or bonk of metal, but I was listening for it. At a certain point she realized my order had been long for a reason– it made her bring everything up in several trips.

It was within a few candlemarks of dawn when she finally walked in to the room, arms full of wood. As if the crash of the quartered logs into the metal bucket was a release, she let them fall with a discordant clatter. She still glared at me as the crackling fire finally heated the thick iron pan I had requested. I sheared off the traditional square slices of bacon and added them to the pan, setting it on the small iron rack inside the fireplace. Normally used to heat kettles and bed warmers, it was doing a fine job of setting the bacon to popping. I used the same knife to quickly dice some potatoes and onions, which waited their time under a drizzle of salt.

"Hungry?" I asked. She made a noncommittal noise. I waited, and waited.

"So, what was that all about?" she demanded. I didn't turn, or look at her in any way. I could hear her shuck her weapons and pull on her nightshirt. The edge of to her voice would be unmistakable in any case. I sighed. When I didn't answer, she asked, louder, "What was that about?"

I removed the crispy meat chunks from the popping, sizzling soup of raw grease and then sprinkled in the salted potato. It spat into the fire, causing random flames like faeries around the pan. Then it settled down and got to cooking. I turned to her. "You feel yourself unfairly used?"

She curled up on her bed, arms folded defensively. "To get your breakfast for you naked? Oh, of course not."

I sniffed a bit. "It amazes me that when people complain the loudest that they are not being treated fairly, it is very often when they are given far more than they deserve."

She sneered, which brought forth a laugh from me.

"So you got food for your master, naked."

I huffed out a half laugh. "I should be so lucky. During my tests I had clothes, but no money. We weren't staying at the inn, so I had no idea of the layout. If I had been caught, it would have made for either a hasty retreat, beatings, several nights in prison, or worse."

She cackled humorlessly and unbelievingly at me. "You were taught to be a thief?"

I blinked at her, face placid. "An assassin."

She stared at me for a moment then she started to shake her head. I turned my face from her and added the onion to the sizzling mixture, which I stirred as she found words. "No. No, assassins have a mark on them somewhere. Unmistakable. I've seen you naked! You are not marked!"

I pulled up the back of my tunic, showing her the ugly, twisted flesh that made up the raven spread across my back from shoulder to shoulder, up my neck and down my spine.

"What happened?"

"Sometimes, not often, but sometimes you get a chance to do something different."

"And you took the chance?"

I laughed at the memories, bitter but not as angry as even a few months ago. "Or had it forced upon me."

I could hear her turn pale. She glanced about as if to escape. "Why train me to be an assassin? I never asked for that!"

"Keep your voice down!" I hissed. "And I am not training you to be an assassin." I cracked the eggs, dumped them in along with the reserved bacon. I began stirring it furiously, to break up the yolks and mix the whole mess together as it finished cooking. "Assassin is just a word. A soldier paid to kill a specific enemy might well be the same. A reeve told to quiet a dissenting voice in the crowd. A judge paid to make an inconvenient body swing from the gallows. They are all informal assassins, as well. But you want to use a sword, and so that makes it noble? You already know how to use a sword, Apprentice. Now I need to teach you everything else. Believe me when I say that there is very little swordsmanship involved in being a real swordsman."

"I don't understand."

I sighed, but I didn't take my eyes off of the fire. "When we are done, you will be more than a soldier, more than a swordsman."

There was a deep pause, full of echoing darkness and crackling fire. "What will I be?"

"What you always wanted. You will be able to change things." I doled out a plate heaped with food. I passed it to her, and while she shook her head I pressed it to her again. "You will eat. The day starts early in a candlemark. We may not get another chance with Volker's men about, we have a great deal of preparations to make, and only until dinner to have them done."

She took the plate and ate some of the steaming mixture. "Preparations for what?"

"Lampedocht is about to hire us for a job." I began eating my own serving, relishing the buttery saltiness of it all.

Raina started. "How do you know?"

"He fed us, clothed us, gave us money. But still he asked us to return. Most nobles you will meet want little to do with us after the coin has changed hands. That means that the interview is not over."

I ate, banked the fire, moved the iron grate in front of it to block the light and catch sparks. Raina set her plate aside as I got into bed, glancing to make sure the saddle was in place before the door and my sword standing by the bed within easy reach.

Ten

The Infant Assassin

"NO!" I snapped at the continued redirection. The blacksmith's hackles rose in response, but I plowed on, "If you have nothing better than this, we'll look elsewhere."

The short, bald man with a braided beard fitted with hundreds of small beads huffed. Around him were swords cooling in boxes of clay. *Cast* swords. It was like eating spoiled meat, better than starvation, but not by much. And he kept trying to pawn these barbarian blades on us.

It is of course my luck that the most important stop of the day was with the one merchant who had no time. Every other store, shop, or kiosk we stopped in had proprietors with a few extra lengths of belt and were falling over one another to snatch at our coin. Here, he wanted to unload his dross and so only offered this steel, barely worthy of the name, with huge visible impurities and mostly made of iron. His forge was the only one in town set up to do the work I needed, but all he had was the kind of blade carried by–

"The Volker has me working as fast as I can in order to get enough blades for his men. I can't take a break from this."

The Volker, eh? Not just a name, but a title, now. I set down a stack of coins on the anvil. "So there is no way to take time out for a bright-sand steel blade?"

The smith glared at me askance. "How do you–?"

"Can you take the time for one?" I asked, setting another stack on the anvil. This was an illusion, already far too much for the work I was asking done. But it was important to get him thinking the stacks were big before negotiations begun.

"It takes a great deal of time," he hedged, looking past me out onto the street like a man engaged in a criminal venture.

I nodded, "I know, and I will know if I am lied to, so speak truly. Can you make one and will you?"

Behind me Raina did not bother to hide her confusion. To her credit, she kept watch on the street all the same. There were few out this cold morning. Fewer once people opened their doors and saw layers of ice on puddles in the street.

I set a third stack of silver on the anvil.

The smith swallowed hard, as if on a huge silver hook, and nodded, "Go now, come back tonight and you'll–"

I leaned forward into a punch he never saw coming. It rattled him and knocked him back. As he tumbled, I swept the top halves of each stack back into my hand. The smith stood and I spit into one of his glowing molds, the spittle cracking like the fingersnap of a demon. "Fool! I told you what I want. Even at best times it would take until tomorrow night, working straight through to forge what I am asking. Any but a masterful smith would need measurements, or at least ask who the blade was for. You are trying to sell us a normal blade at bright steel prices. You have wasted my time." I reached for the bottom halves of the stacks.

"Wait!" the smith bellowed.

Raina whistled, a warning that came almost too late. A quartet of Volker's thugs - correction, Volker's high-class thugs– pushed into the smithy. They were wearing chain armor, swords, shields, and long, red cloaks to mark them as supremely important people in a sea of common men. Two of the ruffians took up flanking positions upon me. I could smell their stench through everything they were wearing. It became worse when they smiled and deep brown clouds could be imagined huffing between their teeth. Dogs had better breath.

The shortest one shouldered himself to the center of the room once it became clear nobody was dying and hitched at his belt as he glared at me. "So what do we have here?"

I am convinced that somewhere, in the most foul, barbaric tribes of the far mountains, places where they eat rotten foods, relieve themselves in their tents, and wear rancid animal furs, there is one man who acts as a watchman for the chief. And when he turns up anywhere he says, *So what do we have here*?

I took a half step back, leaning nonchalantly on a post and by complete coincidence clearing enough space to draw a blade and stick the first thug beneath the chin. From there things would get dicey, and dirty, but probably survivable. In the short term, at least.

Shorty smacked his lips and cocked his head. "The Volker has deemed that dueling is an oppressive institution to the people. It is punishable by death." He licked his lips again, looking at all the valuable stuff he could see and imagining everything he could not. "Any free man can kill a duelist and claim his property as his own."

The smith held up his hands in front of him to forestall such a sentence, "Oh, sir–"

The leader snapped, "Sir is the word used as a chain a man puts on himself." He droned as if by rote, "We are all fellows here, equal of class and station."

The smith recoiled as if struck, paling to grey beneath his ruddy skin. "My apologies, Fellow. But as you can see, there is no dueling here. I do not duel. I cannot duel."

"Not you!" The leader sneered, then turned to face me. "Him."

I took a long time moving my head downward, giving my own belt an exaggerated examination. "This would be the first duel in history to happen in a room full of weapons, where not one was in hand." I looked left and right. "Or an opponent."

"I have reports of you fighting at all hours of the day and night. Even in the nude with some harlot!"

The silence left behind was deafening.

I tried to catch my temper, I really tried, but the words that came out of my mouth were acid, "The 'harlot' you describe is my apprentice. She's standing behind you and has spent more time with her sword in her hand than you have pulling beetles from the soiled forest of your anus. We were not dueling. We were practicing. And unless I miss my guess, if you call her a harlot again she will shave your arse into bristles and use it to scrape her boots clean every night."

Mentally, I shifted gears. I was done talking, everyone was done talking. I made plans to kill these men, and I let the declaration seethe through my eyes.

The leader gathered up his rising gorge at being so addressed. He thought about arresting me, he considered executing me. But as these ideas flashed across his face, he also realized he was within my reach. Most likely he would die first. Then he met my eyes, and he knew I meant to make that happen, and the bottom dropped out of his bucket of courage. He raised a finger, but he kept it close to himself, lest he lose it in a flash of steel. "You just better watch yourself."

And, again, when said shit-covered tribal barbarian retreated from the hunter that would rather brain him with a club than take his fecund orders, he said, *You just better watch yourself.* It's as if there were a script, or a guild, or both.

But leave he did, taking his less intelligent, but more violent, companions with him. Raina watched him with eyes sharpened to fine points.

The smith watched them go, head shaking and mumbling curses. He had a head full of steam, but an empty belly was a powerful agent of forgiveness. He wiped blood from his mouth and spat on the ground, eyes darting to the coins.

I produced a freshly purchased bottle of honey wine. I uncorked it and drank to prove it was safe, then passed it to him. He drank, watching me the whole time, then nodded grudgingly to accept the wordless apology as I passed him the cork to show he could keep the rest. "The Volker pays pennies for his damned cast iron blades. I cannot survive even with the endless culling of my stock he makes. The cost of materials is barely below the price he demands to pay. But to forge the sword you want, it would take all of until tomorrow night. I would risk making The Volker angry." I shrugged and turned away. "Wait! Wait. Wait. Wait. I will forge the sword you ask for. I have an old dwarven recipe. We will take measurements. I and my sons will work until it is done."

I put a stack of coin on the anvil. One quarter of my last bid. "The other half on acceptance of the blade."

The smith mentally tallied the coin in food and warmth, his face screwed up at the loss of my last bid, and nodded painfully. I turned and motioned Raina into the smithy.

To his credit, the smith then took the measurements correctly. A hilt heavy sword 'blank' was provided her. Iron weights were slipped on the end until she was comfortable with the balance, then adjusted, adjusted again, and again to find the exact weight and balance. He watched her move the long blank about, took notes on how she had to pull to get it free of an imaginary scabbard. He noted how close it came to the ground when she moved it through its paces, and finally took a flensing knife, carved at a flattened section of one pole in the smithy, and made notes in charcoal there. Only then, after he called for his sons in the roughest of terms, he came forward and swept the coins into his hand off of the anvil.

"Tomorrow. Midnight."

I nodded at him, then we departed.

We traveled the street for a few moments in silence, the few other travelers scurrying by wordlessly in the cold-bleached world. Finally Raina broken the silence. "Well, it looks like you have earned me a reputation."

I took a high-handed reply that was dripping with sarcasm. "Be respectful, apprentice, you address your superior."

Despite herself, she laughed. "Master Crow?"

I huffed. "That sounds ridiculous."

She looked at me askance, as if sure I was japing. "Master Fox?"

Which I was. "No, that's even worse, go back to the other one."

"Master Crow, what is bright-sand steel?"

"The exact proportions change from smith to smith, but it's a certain kind of sand, charcoal dust, a dusting of other metals, and iron. It's put in a clay crucible and then dropped into a lamp furnace or a forge with horse drawn bellows like the ones at that last smith."

"How strong is it?"

I smiled. "Not just strong, but supple. I will teach you."

We continued well into the day, but we spent little more coin. In reality, I was teaching Raina the skills I had hoarded for years in order to be an effective assassin. We walked down an alley to a blind spot between two closely set buildings.

"How do you get to the roof?" I asked. And when she shrugged, I moved to the wall, showing her where to find finger holds. I showed her how to climb one wall, flat, to climb two walls, spread between them, and two walls with back against one and legs against the other. Her only lacking was confidence.

I began teaching her Norian, for having a foreign language in common could not hurt, but she proved useless at it. I showed her how to be quiet, or at least how to blend in so that the noise one made was swallowed by the world around. I made efforts to talk to her about blending into the background at night.

Assassins do not wear black. At least not for sneaking. The art of blending in requires that a man not look like a man. To make that happen, assassins gather many swatches of cloth and tie them around their limbs, giving birth to the street name for an assassin: A Ragman. We spent some coppers on rags to begin her own ragman suit. Finally, we approached a group of beggars, and pulled our cloaks low and tight, rolled in what could loosely be called dirt in the alley and blended in between them.

It was horrid, smelly work, and after we headed back to Konrad's inn. My eyes picked up the movement of predators in the crowd. It took only moments to tell her what to look for, and less for her to notice the men who were trailing us. Raina tugged at my sleeve.

"I see them," was my reply. "Right here, down the alley, then sprint."

We ducked into the alley and took off at a run. We spun around the corner, and could hear our pursuers coming. Yet, when the thugs of The Volker turned the corner, they found nothing but empty alley. Poor boys, the area was used so often they could not even pick up our footprints out of the mob. They banged on a few back doors while the fastest one ran to the end of the alley and looked both ways for us.

High above, Raina suppressed a girlish giggle, the excitement of the moment bursting upon her like a mug of strong bier. It was good to see her enjoying herself. I had too many memories of clambering up walls and barely escaping packs of dogs, or men with knives, or guards with nooses, all chasing me to the roofs in order to escape. Often as not, I was bleeding, and it was a matter of life or death. I shook off the bad thoughts.

We leapt from roof to roof, and finally came to ground a few streets over. We made it back to the inn where we bathed, snacked, had our cloaks laundered, and then dressed in our brand new clothes for our second trip to the haven of the nobles.

Eleven

The Mother of Symphonies

WE CAME to the gate to the upper city. I hailed the gate, the ring held high. The hail was answered, guards came out and hustled us inside. They examined the heraldic device almost to exhaustion until they passed the gold back to me. This time they did not escort us to Lampedocht's home. We felt the eyes, nonetheless.

Clothes and faces freshly washed, we walked up to the door and rang the bell that hung from a delicate collection of metal spirals. "Did you notice?"

Raina looked at me, face devoid of humor or prevarication, "The three men outside by the gate? They seemed interested in us."

"Make no mistake, Volker now will believe us enemies."

"Are we?" she asked honestly.

"That all depends upon him."

Then the door opened, and the nameless servants escorted us inside.

We were relieved of our largest blades, but in the same way we were relieved of our fashionable cloaks provided just a few days before, politely, efficiently. I let the Phantom Angel go only with a jaundiced eye that noted exactly where it had been placed and in which closet.

Winifred was left to carry the conversation largely on her own and I would have to be blind to not notice how informal and warm she was to me. Do not mistake, even with Raina occupying the space of my apprentice, Winifred waited upon me as if the low noble were nothing more than a common servant. Her eyes and hands would linger on my person as she moved about the table as an animated hostess. I smiled graciously at her and hoped to dodge the implicit complications. What Lampedocht thought of this, I would never know. To say Swan was distracted would be like saying I am a little suspicious.

I was convinced he was in the precise same clothes he had yesterday. They had not been removed and laundered, or laid out and reworn, but instead had ridden his slim frame all night. The wrinkles marking the movement of his spindly arms, legs, and birdlike neck were just too freshly impressed for anything else. His hair was again blasting from his skull in unruly curls. He had not scraped away the whiskers from yesterday, and the full growth on his chin and under his nose was sprawled in every direction. It was not just this, but his hands had the dried, nearly powdery texture I associated with men who handled old, dry books for hours on end. The fingertips on his right hand were splattered with purple, confirming that thought at least.

Clearly more effort had been made for tonight than last night. In fact it was a great deal more favorable faire than even last time we had dined. The potato based soup with the tiny cubes of fried bacon and strips of just barely done onion, the mushrooms, the two ducks, one with a spicy glaze that seared the tongue, and the other with a sweet glaze that was both sugary and tart.

"The spices are luxuriously used," I said.

Lampedocht barely registered, murmuring, "All things from foreign lands come here– silks... spices... fireworks..." And just like that he was lost once more.

I, again, attempted to lure our host into conversation. "Late night composing, Milord?"

That, at least, snapped the small man out of his distraction. "What? Oh, no!" And though he was pleased at the mistake, he acted as if he had to be somewhat scandalized by the implication, "Oh, no my good fellow. I am no more a composer than a gardener is a breeder of beautiful, rare flowers. I am the conductor of the Royal Concert Hall, but, alas, I am an infant in the blending of notes and instruments."

I nodded, taking a delicate sip of the fruity, mild wine to wash down the strongly spiced venison stuffed mushrooms. It was excellent, it all was, and it was just another hint that we were being set up for something here.

"Nonsense!" Winifred exploded, "My uncle is far too humble, and too timid. He has whole concerts written that have never–"

The conductor pounded his hand on the table, making silverware rattle. His long eyebrows crinkled as he frowned deeply through his unkempt bush. "Silence, girl. I have seen the masters of the ages, and heard their work brought to life by the fingers of far more talented men than I. There is no comparison. I am not a composer. I can lead an orchestra, but I cannot feed them the art they need to thrive!"

Winifred looked rather stricken at the words, her eyes sorrowful and helpless. "You cannot compare yourself to the masters of any given age.

If you will not start the road that early, you will never gain those heights."

He did not look angry, really, but resigned and cranky to have his hope's hibernation poked so thoroughly. "More's the pity, then, for I have waited until I am an old, old man and I will never have a chance to catch up." It was then he affixed me with those dull gray orbs and they started to sparkle. "But perhaps you can help me yet, Master Crow. You see, I am not just a conductor, but something of a collector of historical facts and tales about the musicians and their work."

And there it was. Not that I minded the dancing, whispered nothings, and romance portion of the courtship– eating this well could become addicting– but it was nice to finally know why I was there. It was no mystery that he wanted to offer us work, but now I wanted to stop flirting and get down to the job at hand. I told him quite plainly by saying, "Yes, sir?"

"If you would, come with me." We stood and exited the dining room together. Raina made to follow, but I made a 'keep still' motion. Lampedocht may have finally understood she was my apprentice, but she could not shake the idea of her following me around everywhere. Within a few minutes, we came to a spiral stairway and took it upwards. It ended at an ornate, curved door that Swan opened with a gold plated key. The door lead to a beautiful room, paneled in plain wood, but equipped with musical instruments of every age and description. The walls were festooned with winged musical angels, agents of the old God called The Muse. Her worship had declined in the north, but not here. He spread his arms, encompassing his kingdom. "A harmonically resonant room. My conservatory."

I glanced across the room to the stools of different sizes that had been laid out. Even a barbarian could recognize the wrought iron stands before them and guess these were the seats for an octet. Yet I remained silent. On the journey here, Lampedocht had nattered on about the history of music and I had pretended to listen politely, but now he drew me close and I could sense the reason he had brought me here had come to his lips.

"There is one figure in the musical history of Hammarfall–" (the nation I was sure) "–that is more mysterious than any other. It is a woman shrouded in the fog of war, in the evils of her time. She has been called the Witch of the Hidden Caverns, the Enchantress of Strings, the Burning Composer, the Mother of Symphonies. She was…" And then he just stopped, caught up in his own world encompassed by music only he could hear. I awaited, and waited. Finally I cleared my throat. Swan caught himself in the middle of his fugue and shook his head. "Of course, of course. This is not the way. Not the way at all, really."

He snapped his fingers, and instantly became the noble blooded lord that I expected them all to be. Eight immaculately coiffed and dressed musicians, each bearing their tools of the trade, entered silently. They sat on the stools in the center of the room, arranging themselves for play. Lampedocht became nearly a whole other person, snapping his fingers faster and faster. The octet acted as if it were the cracking of a whip meant to part flesh. The speed only barely hindered their precision as they found seats, arranged sheets of music, and readied instruments. They pressed fingers, lips, and bows to instruments and, like hunting dogs, trembled slightly. He offered me a seat in a dusty red plush couch and I took it. Then he walked before the octet and seemed to grow in power and size.

Lampedocht, unable to stop himself, raised his hands. "The Seduction by the Fairy Queen, by Annalirya Von Zeitheim."

And then there was music. It hit me like a velvet wave. It was sad, it was yearning. The world rippled away into a pool of images from inside my head. And there she was. Auburn haired, blue eyed. Barely stepping into womanhood but wiser than a dozen charlatans and a dozen warmongers combined. We were so close to forbidden love that I crossed a kingdom to be away from her.

It was love unrequited. It was love undeserved. It was the sweetest of sour wine poured onto the tongue at the first flakes of winter. I felt it. I understood it. It bypassed all my defenses and filled a gaping wound in me. I blinked back tears.

The music ended. I felt heat pounding at my temples, a sheen of sweat covered my face, which I discovered when I raised a shaking hand to rub across it.

"Superb!" Lampedocht beamed. "Exceptional. Now, Master Crow you can see what I mean? The performance is precise and worthy of commendation, but it is the composition that is almost–"

"Magical," Raina breathed.

I glanced back to her and she was the same: flushed, sweating, shaking. Winifred had brought her demurely to the room and now showed her the seat next to mine.

Lampedocht's face twisted minimally at being addressed by a servant, but this was overwhelmed by the choice of word. "Yes, that is the common thought. When done well, her work takes everyone on a spiritual journey. She is a cipher for all souls, an artist for the ages, a beautiful muse that speaks to all men, and all races so I hear. The elves who have heard her revere her as a master of her field. The dwarves, in their jealousy, have banned her performances from within their realms."

However, in my experience, magic was not something light and airy that came along to help mankind like a fairy godmother. It was dark, and required sacrifice, and often was a siege engine where a hammer would do. Winifred, less effected as her uncle due to previous exposure I am sure, poured out glasses of brandy from a set in the corner and I quaffed mine immediately. The burn helped me focus.

I took a deep breath as Lampedocht began the next song. I turned to stop him, but then was enveloped in a cloud of sound that swallowed me whole. Suddenly I wanted to fight. I needed to fight. Not violence for violence's sake, not a senseless battle, but to fight for something rational, noble, and pure. I felt it pick me up and light me on fire. It was the sound of pure murder, of power, the hidden desire of a dark soul damned. The music ended and I felt the spell snap around me. I downed another splash of brandy. Somewhere inside my head there was an alien whisper, barely heard. I shoved it aside, "And you think that there is one of these songs that can bring an end to the civil war?"

Lampedocht smiled as if upon a prized student. "Not exactly." Which gave me pause to breathe in relief. Because the idea that there was a song that could end a war was– "There is an entire symphony."

Again he directed his crew, and I felt as if concussed, the sounds and sights of an alien age, of an far away realm showing across me like a boiling rain.

It sounded like a lost soul, a damaged beauty that wandered alone in the darkest of places. On the notes were carried the footsteps of a person who had tasted the blackest fruits of the human soul and would never be able to stand in the light again. It sounded like someone like me. It created such an unimaginable longing inside of me that it hurt.

Finally, Lampedocht turned away from the musicians and came over to me, spry beyond his many years. He took up a stool and sat very close to me, leaning so closely I could feel his breath. "Master Crow, out there is the last completed work of Annalirya Von Zeitheim, The Magnum Opus Discordia. Will you bring it to me?"

I nodded dumbly, for whatever it was, whoever had made it, however it sounded, I wanted to feel like that again. I needed that music.

"Another?" Swan asked, smiling as he raised his composers stick.
I nodded. More.
Of course, that should have been my first clue.

Act Two

The Quest

ONE

PREPARATION FOR DISASTER

THE SONGS followed me all the way back to Konrad's, filling my mind to the exclusion of all else. Several times Raina nudged and made not quite subtle gestures to Volker's men as we passed street after street. I would come out of the fugue, take note and nod, and then sink back down into the passages of crescendo and diminuendo that the song had imprinted upon my soul.

Even then, had I been paying attention, I would have known the shape of things to come. Sadly, I was as blind as a boy finding first love. I failed to even take into account the tripling of the number of lookouts for us. It would have warned me so that when I opened the door to Konrad's Inn, I would not have been shocked to see every available space but two taken up by armed and armored members of Volker's guard. The two spaces were at the center of a sea of stinking, gaped toothed grins and cast swords. Across from the empty chairs were Volker and the lickspittle I had humiliated the other day.

Music still cascaded through my brain and I kept my face placid and stony. It became harder as one man stood directly in my face and smiled nastily. I didn't recognize him until he said, "I'll take that pretty sword," and reached for the Angel. It was the same lackey from Volker's hall who had wanted to disarm me before. Apparently the last lesson hadn't taken.

I made a slight, casual movement. It didn't even draw a reaction from the crowd of men on all sides of us, but the functionary screamed and withdrew the hand, the inner swell of the base of the thumb effortlessly sliced to the bone. "Careful there, mate. Swords are sharp," I said into the silence when he gasped for air. "Might just take a whole hand."

The man screamed again as some of his buddies dragged him out of the taproom and plugged his noise hole and bleeding wound with dirty bar towels. The mood was quite a bit less festive now.

I caught Konrad's eye, he was all but held at knife point behind the bar. The huge man's face was a sheen of sweat, his shirt soaked with it. "I need heavy bier for everyone. Honey wine for my table. Bring out the large steins and keep them full until I am poor." He started to go fulfill my order, but one of Volker's men moved to stop him. Everyone looked to the revolutionary, but it was not the look of men awaiting orders. Everyone had heard the words 'heavy bier'. The stuff was almost black, fine bodied, bitter, and not watered in the least. Some of the more well off of them may have once had it on a special occasion. To the rest there were only legends. These were the eyes of begging dogs hoping to accept the nice stranger's bone.

And this was the problem with being a popular leader. Nothing wrong with it, as long as you were respected for something: wit, honesty, loyalty, whatever. I was not one to cultivate such luxurious sins in myself until lately, but I understood them. I had a hunch that Volker was the kind of weasel that bought his men. He looked to a situation, proclaimed it unfair to the common men, pillaged it until dead, and passed out the spoils to keep his mean loyal. But here they were, being offered what really amounted to a pretty thin bribe, and they wanted very much to keep it. Lucky for me that the more I 'bribed' them in this fashion, the less use they would be to the grand revolutionary.

I reached the table, but one of the slightly more indigent thugs put a hand to my chest to stop me. Volker nodded and men almost cheered. He had agreed to let them be bribed, of course the man with his hand on my chest thought he was being nodded at and allowed me to sit, fully armed. The thug behind the bar let Konrad get back to work, and he began grabbing ornate drinking tankards the size of a well-developed forearm and filling them with black bodied, golden foamed liquid out of a tapped keg. I sat gracefully across from Volker, and at some point unnoticed, slipped the bloody knife I had used to cut the guard onto the table. Thick, red drops fell from it onto the surface, and Volker kept looking at it as if it were alive.

Within seconds, Konrad's petite, beautiful wife set two bottles of honey wine before us, along with six globular glasses and then wisely retreated. She was casting me nasty glares, as if all of this was my fault. I didn't know what she was thinking, even if the place did now smell like a cross between the inside of used armor and a pig sty, I hadn't invited Volker here. I popped the loosened cork from the end of the bottle and poured out four glasses, gesturing for Raina to join us. She sat down eagerly, and took a long, loving sip at the expensive treat. I drank from mine, Volker barely let the mead touch his lips, and his companion didn't drink at all.

There were several moments where we just sat, taking the measure of one another. Finally, he asked, "And so, Crow, can we ever expect there will be a day where you do not hurt or humiliate one of my guardsmen?"

I took a deep breath. Two kegs were already empty, and the wife, I was starting to feel foolish for not knowing her name, was filling the steins with beer, while Konrad's obscenely muscled form took the two empty kegs out and, more shockingly, brought two full kegs in. Tossed one over each shoulder, they had to nearly weigh as much as a man apiece. A large man, in fact. That he could be intimidated by even this room full of scruffs offended me on some level. Don't get me wrong, fighting all these men in a fair fight would end in any man's death. I just never intend to fight fair.

Realizing I had not answered Volker, I nodded my head. "Just as soon as they stop trying to take my sword."

He smiled. "You think your sword would do you a bit a good in a room full of my men?"

I stared straight through the artist. "Don't you?"

A word on bravado... sometimes it makes you look like a complete fool. At other times, if you can inspire just a tiny seed of doubt in an enemy, it will allow you to avoid a fight altogether.

I took a drink from the globe of heavy dwarven glass.

His voice took on a sharper edge as he forced his nonchalance passed the breaking point, "What you don't seem to understand is that, one way or another, you are going to wind up working for me. Maybe not this year, but next year, in the next city. Unless you flee Hammarfall completely, you will belong to me, and the sooner one or the other happens, the better it will be for you."

Men were starting to argue over the steins of beer. Those in the back thinking it had been too long since those in the front had begun enjoying themselves.

I smiled as the noise covered the words from traveling much past our table. "You are already lost."

He breathed through his teeth to keep control of his words. "You are wrong."

"I am not."

"My army of the common men will crush all opposition."

I laughed at him softly. "Have you ever seen a mounted knight ride his destrier through ranks of conscripts? They will mow you into the soil like the cut stalks of reaped wheat."

Volker's eyes narrowed as his cheeks flushed. "Is that it? Are you a spy? Working for the nobility?"

"Volker, we live in a world that requires coin. Nobles have coin. We work for them and they give us coin. But not everything they need done revolves around you."

His face reddened and he balled his fists. "Damn your insolence, I will have you."

I blinked, nonplussed. "If it is inevitable, then you can afford to be patient."

He stared at me without comment for many minutes, the crowd around us becoming more inebriated, more rowdy. The heavy bier was powerful and it was doing its work. He must have thought we were playing some kind of high class mental game. The problems being: Volker was not high class, Volker was not capable of playing mental games, and Volker was an idiot.

"What if I have one of these men cut you down?"

I pointedly leaned the Phantom Angel in its sheath against the table and smiled tolerantly. "Find one that is sober, first." The man across the table from Raina smiled wolfishly. I motioned at him. "And for the sake of his manhood, don't make me embarrass this one again."

The man started to rise and Volker's hand slapped him down into his seat by the shoulder. Volker's face twisted, eyes wide with rage. "I'm afraid we are not going to be friends, Crow."

I took a long drink of the mead, sat it down, dabbed at a droplet on my lips with my sleeve. "Pity."

Volker stood. "A lesson is in order. Oh yes, a lesson indeed. Not here, not now, but soon."

I nodded to him, still seated. Volker motioned to the heavily armored lickspittle next to him and started to walk out.

"Alright you louts, put down the cups! Time to move out! Your Volker is walking, and you have sworn to him your service. YOU! MOVE!"

Men scrabbled, spilling bier and dropping steins. Some men were bitterly complaining they had not been served, others desperately tried to finish off the dregs of the high proof beer, others had just received the container the size of their forearm and began to chug greedily. Still, fifty men take a few minutes to empty a business through only one door, and they had time to quaff a huge portion of the bier before racing out shakily onto the street.

In the middle of it I stood, full of honey wine and Volker's last proclamation of future pain. I crossed the two paces to the armored lackey in the shadow of men the table provided as they bustled out. I took him by the arm and he tensed to attack. I pulled him till our bodies touched, capturing his eyes with mine.

"He can't be serious," I said through clenched teeth.

The ersatz knight shook off my harm, pushing himself into the stream of clunking men. He straightened, tugged his ill fitting armored chest plate back into place, and jutted his jaw at me. "He is as serious and unknowable as the sea. And as powerful. He will wash you away."

I dialed for a facial expression that said, *I am seriously considering this*. "Tell him we will meet when this job is done and discuss terms."

The lackey stared at me. Then he barked a laugh. Then it became a torrent of mirth that spewed from him as he followed his men out. My face reddened, I could feel it, but I let the fool have his precious moment. He had paid dearly for it, after all. I turned, grabbed the bauble from the table and drained it. Then refilled it. I could feel the world starting to distort, but it was no matter.

If the exalted armored commander of minions outside was smart, he would march the men until they vomited the bier back up as a way of punishing them for drinking from the "purse of an enemy". Their commander was a dolt, however, and I saw no reason to correct him. Plus, I saw no reason to pay for the bier myself. Little bier had a bit of alcohol, and was consumed all the time by everyone. Heavy bier, like I had ordered, was as strong as a troll's fist, and very expensive.

I again drained the full glass. Raina's eyes heavy on me.

"What?" I snapped.

"You were not as quiet as you think you were–"

"Really?" My voice filled the finally empty room. "And how quiet do you think I needed to be?"

She swallowed. "Master, are you thinking of making a deal with The Volker?"

I rolled my eyes and drained the heavy glass. By the time I was done with my second mead, the strong honey wine buzzing in my head, I got to meet Konrad's embarrassed glance and his wife's tiny glare. I filled my glass and Raina's, then walked to the bar and dropped silver onto the polished wood. From this angle the room looked even worse. There were clearly broken steins littering the room. Bier had been sloshed everywhere. Seats and tables now sat listing in a nonexistent wind where joints had been torn asunder by rough treatment.

I produced a strange purse I flaunted in the air. "To whoever said I would deal with Volker, and call him Volker, for he has no title, and deserves none, I say...a pox on your privates."

Raina relaxed and drank her measure of wine, but Konrad's wife hissed, "They will be back as long as you are here."

"Well, Missus, you appear quite sour for a woman who had a bar full of patrons tonight." I tugged the strings loose on the pouch in my hand and upended it upon the bar. The haul was impressive, indeed, widening the innkeeper's eyes and shutting his wife's mouth at the same instant. Before I could stop myself, I snatched back five golden coins from the mix, but there was still enough to buy a horse let alone pay for the heavy bier, repair some furniture, and replace some eatery.

I tipped a nonexistent hat to the peevish, wife. "Not to be contradictory, but I believe that you are stuck with them, with or without me." I continued in a stage whisper. "They seem to have taken over the city, my good woman." I drained the mead in one long pull, which was a waste in compared to savoring it, but a deal next to leaving it to rot. "I only wonder if this started as high-nobility against everyone else, and how long it took to move to all nobility. Soon it will be luxury merchants, if not already. How long then to all merchants?" I let the thought hang there as I filled the glass to the rim, emptying the bottle to the last drop. I sipped enough to carry the full dwarven bauble upstairs, spinning at the last moment and lunging back to snatch up the Phantom Angel like a prized infant. Then I began to wobble back upstairs. "In any case, you shall be rid of us in a few days."

I dismissed her glare and Konrad's sheepish eyes and perpetually shrugged shoulders, and made my way upstairs.

It was true... Volker was a dog of a man. I despised the naked and random use of power most nobles possessed, and not only did he share the vice, he was horrible at it. That was where we deviated. The art of his meeting hall said it all– he was so offended at his loss of personal liberty that he would rule with an iron fist to take it back, robbing the rest of the world of liberty to do it. He was like a man who had lost his purse, only to steal from another random man to even the scales. As long as his personal scales were even, the whole world was.

More, he was a man who complained about an army of guards that did not treat him with respect, and so he collected his own guards and paid them in rape and pillage. Were I a civic minded man, I would definitely end him. With so many thugs, however, it was likely to be suicide.

I cracked the window, and I could hear the distant hammer strikes, vaguely musical in their destruction and creation, carried on a cold breeze. I glanced to Raina who paused in changing her clothes.

"Is that mine?" she asked, jerking her chin outside.

I nodded. Indeed, it was her sword being born. Thousands of strikes performed over two dozen hours and it could be heard blocks away. It was a punishing undertaking, once started it could not be stopped, and one we were paying a pittance in comparison thanks to Volker starving the city. I shut the window, face dark. I drained the golden liquid from the globe. After the rich meal and fine vintages earlier, my head was already swimming, but this town was getting more dangerous by the second. The faster we got away from it toward the Opus Discordia the better.

I stood and wobbled to the fireplace where I gently set down the dwarvish glass, and then tossed the now empty pouch into the fire. Raina wrinkled her nose at the acrid smell of burning leather.

"Why did you do that?"

I staggered back to the bed, collapsing in a hug around my sword. "Never get caught with a pouch that doesn't belong to you, full or empty."

There was a slight pause and then her words came out, sharp with scandal, "You stole The Volker's purse to pay for the bier?"

"Don't be stupid." I pulled covers over my head, frowning. "It belonged to his armored lackey. Besides, the bier went to his men! I wasn't going to pay for it."

"A cutpurse. My master is a cutpurse!" She said in wonderment to no one in particular.

I sat bolt upright, flinging covers in an explosion. "It is a better skill to have than standing in one location for hours and pretending not to sleep. Now, go to bed watch-woman. We have to be away day after tomorrow and there is still much to procure."

Then I flounced back under the covers.

***

The next morning my head thudded like an out-of-time giant's footstep. I saw with some distant pride that Raina had positioned the saddle in front of the door. It was from there that all that was good and light, everything that contained even a shard of optimism, was destroyed.

At my insistence we woke early. We packed everything we owned into tightly bound bundles, there was no telling when we would have to be off in an instant. We set them aside, and then I sat Raina down and quizzed her on the contents of the bundles. She failed. Miserably.

So she unpacked the bundles, repacked them, and then passed the quiz of what was in them, but not what was missing.

I sighed, but wasn't really disappointed. She was learning to retain information she had once thought useless and beneath notice. She was doing it quickly at least, and soon she would see how it came in useful if emergency overtook us.

Next was breakfast. Konrad was a man who grew up on the road. As such, it was his opinion that breakfast was to be a feast, a reward for making it through the night alive. Awake at dawn on the road, lunch was a far off thing and the stomach needed its fuel to burn for the rest of the body to stay warm.

There were eggs, sausages, kettle bread and light bier mixed with apple juice and honey to make a refreshingly sweet beverage. There were also far more exotic dishes like potatoes, mild peppers, onions, and spinach smothered in garlic, spiced and fried in some way to keep the spinach mostly fresh while the rest was tooth soft and warm as a loving bosom. There were three different pan baked cakes, two of which were sweet with herbs and honey, the last which was savory with butter and bits of ham baked into the thin outer layer.

All of it was awful.

Awful, you say. *Crow you must be mad to describe such a repast as anything less than heavenly*!

You have forgotten my previous night of excess.

My mouth soured at every savory concoction, my stomach lurched at every sweet confection. Konrad deposited a stack of cakes before us and sprinkled them with sugar that had been crushed to powder on a rolling mill, his face radiant with expectant glory. I ran to the privy and threw up.

I returned to Konrad's suffocating worry and his wife's pointed smirking. They produced a firm rice flavored with chicken broth and slightly salted. It went down and stayed down, absorbing the sourness in my belly. Still, I watched Raina devour her food with a gusto that made me sneer at her delight.

We left soon thereafter, the bright sun stabbing me in the eyes like a thousand recriminating souls. I muttered darkly and shivered in the morning air as we set about our business. New boots for her, since the ones she wore were ill-made for true cross country walking. A dozen small blades to be hidden about her person. High grade alcohol for cleaning wounds (an elvish trick), and heavy oil to cover weapons and keep them from corroding even if dipped in water (a dwarvish trick), and a sheet of old sailcloth cut into sturdy strips, then folded in half around raw cotton to form long bandages (a trick I made up myself, thank you very much.) We rolled the bandages and stuffed them into our packs. I'd need a few more silver needles and silk thread for closing wounds. We bought small canvas tents, rope, a steel grapnel that simply weighed half a ton instead of the whole lot. I even let the smith talk me into a neat contraption. It was a knife hooked like an eagle talon, but even more so, creating a little more than a half moon. It was connected to a sleeve by thick chain links. The sleeve went over the belt, and the knife in a sheath. It was used in climbing or even securing oneself in a tree for a night of rest. I gave him perhaps a bit too much coin for it.

Raina looked on with a sour face.

"What?"

She shrugged. "Looks useless to me."

I grumbled as I packed away the purchase. Only then did we stop to eat. It was not up to Konrad's fare, but my stomach had settled. The sausages and pasta were hot, and there was plenty of it.

"Are we going to be able to get the Lost Symphony and get it back to Lampedocht?" Raina asked, fingers trailing toward a hidden knife to make sure it was secure.

"Stop!" I hissed, staring at her heavily. Several times while we ate I barked sharply at her as she fingered half a dozen hidden blades we had secreted upon her person, for what use was hiding them if she was going to point them out to all who had eyes? "As long as Lampedocht doesn't decide to make this more complex than it is, we will be fine. If he can get a royal order, so much the better. Find the family, produce the royal order, exhume the body and make off with the pages in hand."

Oh, if only.

Next was a tailor, where we paid extra to have several sets of clothes made. Less expensive than the finery provided by Lampedocht, these were hardy clothes with folded, triple stitched seams. They would be too heavy by far come summer, but if we lived until summer, chances were we would have the coin to buy lighter clothing then.

Finally, wearing our thick travelling gear, we set out further into the city. One hand spent silver like water pouring from a pitcher, the other grasped at it to hold on to as much as possible. Food, rope, supplies of all kind flowed into my hands and into the packs, pouches and sling bags. I was unable to refill my pouch of burning glass, used on the white-furred creature, because apparently alchemists have the good sense to test how the winds were blowing and the means to escape post haste. What surprised me was the preponderance of fireworks. The people of this city were crazy for them, and used them at all kinds of celebrations. We passed them by, since I saw no need to make more noise in order to get done what I needed. We were so loaded down, we had to return to Konrad's and deposit our packages before moving on.

A modest donation to the most impressive church gained us entry, and another secured a brother to pour over the contents of a dozen dusty books and even dustier maps. Annalirya Von Zeitheim may have been long dead, but she was a noble, and nobles found it harder than the common man to hide. Her palace, the place of her death and burial were the same. Easily discerned with only a few hours taken. I took copious notes from half a dozen maps and tipped generously as we left.

"Master, did I mistake the monk, or did he say the family line was dead?"

"You are correct.," I said, smiling for once, "and that means no need for a royal writ, just a pair of shovels. Nobody will even know, so there is little chance of thieves chasing us to relieve us of our prize. By the time people know what we went to get, we will be back with it. For once, Apprentice, our lives are getting easier."

Which goes to show, again, I should keep my damn mouth shut.

Finally it was the dinner hour and we passed the gate to the land of the nobles, a routine occurrence to the guards now. I cast eyes about, and caught at least five men lounging entirely too casually, smoking pipes, speaking in low tones, paying far too much attention to who was entering and exiting the Lord's Quarter (which was just us as far I could tell). I was paying so much attention that I completely missed all the signs of the party happening just beyond the wall. Typical, because that's where everything started to unravel.

Though the passing through the gate had become routine, past the gate was anything but. The once deserted streets were flooded with people, numerous buskers and vendors filling the cobbles. A cacophony of music washed in from all sides like a constant rain driven by competing winds. For all the world, it looked like a festival of some kind was going on. I gave these newcomers a close look, for they really should not be there.

Raina leaned in. "Master, has Volker ended his war of the lower city against the upper?"

Then certain facts started to pool in the back of my mind. "Remember the tailors who fitted us at Lampedocht's? I doubt they live here, even if he does have his own private cook and serving staff, which I somehow doubt."

"What does it mean?"

"What DOES it mean?" I replied.

We walked quietly for a few minutes. I caught sight of a painted clown who was genuinely bad at his job. Clowning sounds simple until you try it, then most people simply come off as clumsy prats. Though looked down on, it takes a surprising amount of skill and timing to be funny. This one, however, was worse than could even be counted by drink, incompetence, or youth. Plus he was staring at me with that look that carried the smell and taste of venom.

"It means the nobles have secret ways into the upper city."

I nodded. "And that means?"

She nodded. "So does Volker, unless he is a fool."

"So does Volker," I repeated, casting a wary eye in all directions, though the clown was the only performer who took obvious note of us. "Unless he is happy with the situation as it is and is saving the upper city for later conquest."

I quickened my pace. The lazy streets, walled by the mansions and encapsulated yards that surrounded them, wound without hurry or passion from one corner to another until they deposited us at the home of Lampedocht. At least I think it was his.

The tall, stately edifice of plain white and half-cared for green yard had magically changed overnight. What had been a slightly forgotten dowager of a residence was now a colorfully regaled belle of the ball. The lawn itself went all the way to the street as the white and black wrought-iron gates had been flung open. The ragged lawn had been tended. The bushes and trees trimmed with shears and then strung with garlands of flowers. If there was a festival, this was the epicenter, and the sound of music here was like the exhalation of a titan. We walked past the numerous carriages lining the avenue, through the crowds of immaculately dressed children clapping at dancers, puppeteers, and jugglers. Fireworks were in much evidence, spinning spitting wheels of sparks, crackling poppers, and cloud aimed rockets. Apparently they were cheap enough at this port to even be given to children to play with. We brushed past the vendors. I would like to say it was because I had better things to do, but in reality, I could hear... *Her*.

We dove into the crowd around the front yard, noting in the smallest part of my brain that there were no guards of any kind. Then we entered the passage to the side of the house, transformed into a tunnel of speckled and fresh fragrances by the roses entwined into the arched trellis. The sound of *Her* reverberated in my soul, pulled me forward like the promise of first love, with the edge of addiction that such love brings. I almost stumbled as I hurried forward and broke into the back yard and halted, conflict surging through me. I was in awe of the long, undulating lawn. I was struck dumb by the massive amount of marble used to create an intimate amphitheater, which must have cost more than most communities spent upon their churches. The edges were not crisp, meaning it had not been built just for this, rather had been freshly scrubbed to gleaming. But more than any of that I was stabbed, I was crushed, I was felled by the sounds of *Her* reverberating around me.

Lampedocht, filling the shell-backed stage to capacity along with thirty performers, jerked his hands in perfect time, coaching greater and greater emotion out of the players, out of the audience, creating a thing of beauty with sound so bold that images hovered just on the edge of vision. The last note wailed, soared, soured, and fell to earth dying. I felt tears squeeze from my eyes and begin to run down my face. Then I felt something I had all but forgotten.

A red hot bolt of pain slammed into the center of my back and dumped me to the ground. By the time I was on my knees, it was gone.

Raina sprang to my side, helping me up as my legs shuddered with remembered agony. I hadn't felt that particular punishment in over a year, and I looked left and right to find its source. No crows, no cackling ghostly figure, no shining light from the heavens highlighting my misery. Nothing but the crowd who took no notice of my momentary hell and rocketed to its feet as I stood, camouflaging my weakness.

Raina leaned in. "What was that?"

"An old wound," I growled under the thunderous applause, "one I thought healed."

But it wasn't healed, and it wasn't a wound. It was a debt, and it pulled my heart out through my spine whenever the Sovereign of Death yanked my leash.

"Wait, what?" I asked in a sudden panic. Up on stage, Lampedocht was introducing a rotund, yet fastidiously manicured man on stage to the crowd. And though I could see the blade descending toward my neck, I saw far too late to stop his words of execution.

"Alexander Jaeger Von Schwartzklippen!" The crowd cheered the plump man as he waved to them smiling. From his immaculately coiffed head, the huge glittering gold earring he affected, to his self satisfied smile as he waved to the crowd as a monarch. It took only that instant, but my teeth began to itch, champing to get a piece of him. "Noted historian and adventurer will lead this expedition!"

The bastard called for quiet and got it. "I and my team shall find the tomb of Annalirya Von Zeitheim, obtain the priceless Opus Discordia, and return to see it performed for all of Hammarfall."

And as the enormity of his words crashed in about us..."So much for quiet or simple." Raina groused.

I would have agreed, but the words poised at the edge of my mouth were pure poison, and I didn't have enough friends in this town to speak that way about a man the nobles were cheering mindlessly.

Two

The Law of Man

ALEXANDER Jaeger Von Schwarzklippen fancied himself some kind of sailor, or soldier… maybe a general, or admiral, or scholar. Well, he fancied himself something and it was always something better than anyone else in the room. He was also one of those people who did not have one name, he was too large for it. Even such a name as Alexander required Jaeger together to encompass his enormous ego.

That's why it was especially awkward when I said, "You can't expect me to follow this ruinous fop into the mountains, Lampedocht!"

Which, to be fair, was me being diplomatic. My true feelings about the man would peel flesh to the bone.

"Master CROW!" Lampedocht shrieked, albeit quietly before turning to the useless tit. "Please, Lord Schwartzklippen, you must forgive him. He provided my family a great service–"

The (very, exceedingly minor) Lord Schwartzklippen glanced at me, and in that momentary flick of his eyes there was a promise of infinite pain. "One does not kick the dog for barking. It is a dog, after all."

The sitting room grew cold, and I knew I was running into another one of those situations where coming from the wrong womb slit the throat of my credibility. There was no reason for it. I knew what I was doing. I could see all the armies of problems assembling before us. Herr Von obviously did not, and it was going to get him killed. Plus, I was sure he was the kind of bastard who kicked dogs on principal, let alone for barking.

"Frankly, Lampedocht, I appreciate you finding these mercenaries, but I seriously doubt we will need them. My thirty men will be more than enough." He rested his hand on the ornate hilt of his sword. The only wear on the sword was at that place, where he rested his hand upon it.

I barked a laugh. "Without Raina and I, you won't even make it out the front gate."

His mouth twitched. "We shall see."

"No, you won't, you'll be hanging from a rafter long before then, the birds eating your eyes as –"

"Gentlemen!" Lampedocht exclaimed. "Lord Schwartzklippen, I understand your feelings, and Master Crow can obviously be… abrasive. At the same time, he is an expert swordsman and hero. He single handedly stared down The Volker's men to rescue my niece from the anarchist's own lair." Then he turned to me, hands heavy with small pouches. "Understand, Crow, how important this is for the culture, the history, and the peace of Hammarfall," city and country I was guessing, "and I could not bear the burden of that grave cost alone."

"What grave cost, Lampedocht?" I sighed, exasperated.

"This expedition must be successful. It has to be. For that we need the best. I believe in you, but the nobles of Hammarfall demanded Lord Schwartzklippen's leadership in order to protect their investment. But that investment allows me to pay for the best. We must pay for the best." And he handed me both pouches. They were heavy, leaden, almost chilly through the soft leather. I hefted them, not believing. Then I finagled them around to jerk open one string. Inside the coins were heavy and glittering, newly minted and shaped lovingly by blinded slaves at the mint. The color was as honey, but sweeter by far. I became aware I was not breathing, but Lampedocht was talking. "If you can work with Lord Schwartzklippen…?"

"Under me, actually," he put in.

"No." I jerked the strings shut, then deposited the bags inside my shirt against my skin. "But I can work alongside him."

Schwartzklippen made a drawn out throat noise halfway between a groan and a whine, "That isn't going to work for me."

I faced him down where he sat, tiny glass of highly concentrated wine in his fist. "I don't care. Lampedocht wants this symphony, and I will bring it back to him. You will not stop me."

He spoke from inside his wineglass, eyes narrowed. "Ooooh, I think I could stop you."

I crushed the urge to put a dart into his left eye. "You won't even get out of this city alive. I am willing to bet you have a crew of third to sixth sons of nobles of all sorts?" He nodded. Having a crew of noble blooded children would fill many needs of a man who needed to go anywhere, do things of questionable legality and morality, and give him access to numerous back doors and cellars that would be open and waiting for him to use as bolt holes if the need arose. In short, they were a way for him to be a bastard and get away with it. I took a deep breath to begin my assault. "You must have them strike all insignia from their equipment. We will be–"

But he simply was not there when my words landed. "I tell you what, Master Crow," He rose and bowed to me in a fashion that was exact but not at all respectful, "I shall do better than bring you along, I shall put you in charge of the men. Second in command, as it were. You are going to take care of all the detail work. Who could have a problem with that?" And, having trapped me neatly in front of Lampedocht, slithered from the room.

Raina stood as stunned as I, but the conductor was ecstatic. "There you go, my good boy! Second in command! Who could have a problem with that?"

Second in command? That, ladies and gentleman, was even worse than not going at all. In one smooth motion, he had foisted all the grunt work of making this succeed while keeping himself in charge, guaranteeing it would fail. Worse than anything, I had to go, because I needed to hear the symphony. And if I'm honest, also because there was no way I was giving any of the gold back. This did not mean I was going to make this easy, or pleasant. Herr Von could call himself in charge all he wanted, but the person in charge of making hi journey easy or pleasant was little old me. I already had plans.

I met the men a short time later. I had hoped for a group of scabrous bastards with missing teeth and dislocated morals, men willing to do anything for a bit of coin. Those at least were practical men I could deal with. I had once even had a chance to lead starry-eyed man-children into battle. Though untutored in intimate war and unbearded, I was able to connect with them and lead them to ultimate victory in the name of their princess. Either would have been fine. When I was shown to the attic of Lampedocht's mansion, where the men had been bunked on pallets of thick straw and given bedding, I saw that not even the comfort of having simple, corruptible minds was meant to be.

The two dozen some odd man-boys that lounged in the attic, playing cards, sipping at high proof bottles, one in the corner molesting a serving girl, were neither world weary, nor jaded, nor innocent, nor malleable. They were, in a word, worthless. Some called them rascals, others hooligans, or rakes. Whatever they were called they were lazy, overfed, uninterested, and far too self-satisfied. These were the products of lust, bastards in the literal sense, of wealthy nobles, or the useless teats of the high born who had enough heirs already. They had no responsibility other than to enjoy themselves, spend less than they were given, and perhaps garner a little glory and respect for themselves by latching on to 'Klippen as if that made them less than pirates.

One of the boys, easily in his early twenties, turned from his cards to follow the eyes of others. He took in me in an instant, then lingered on Raina as if pricing a nag. Then his lips twisted sardonically and he passed back a brandy glass to me. "See this filled and my bed turned down and there's a silver in it for you, my good man."

Laughter filled the room.

There are lessons in leadership. The first is, if you are seen as an almighty, fickle rockslide of a man, nobody goes poking at your pebbles. I had no desire to be in charge of these little pimples, and every heartbeat I spent guiding them away from the path of utter stupidity took time away from my life. I did, however, like my pebbles unpoked. I needed to make an impression, and it had to be memorable in a way they had never seen.

So I took the glass, patiently held it in the crook of my arm as he turned back to his game and I pulled on a glove. I turned away from the room toward the exit and shifted slightly. Raina watched me with wide eyes and I tried to silently comfort her, but I was busy concentrating on not spilling anything at the moment, glass at crotch level. Almost lost in the hubbub of the room, the sound of the glass being filled occupied a higher and higher octave. Then I shifted again and turned with a full glass of deep yellow fluid.

"Sir?" I said. "Your beverage?" Then, protected by the thick leather, I brought the fine glass down over his head with a musical crash and shocked splash.

The whole room stopped, except for the one man who smelled strongly of urine. He popped to his feet and had his sword half out of his sheath before I kicked it back home and leaned in, every ounce of power in my legs and arms focused into my forearm. *Ahem.* My *armored* forearm. Beneath the simple leather covering lay plates of metal made to protect me while falling, or being slashed or when I felt the need to elbow some lousy cretin in the face. Oh, and I felt the need...badly.

My whole body focused behind my blow, which homed in upon his pathetic snarl. Teeth and pieces of teeth went flying, and the blonde, blue eyed angel fell to the floor as if splashed there from a bucket of shit. The room was shocked to utter silence, so I took the opportunity to ply a steel reinforced boot into the groin of the fallen man...once. Fine, it was twice.

"My name is Master Crow, and you will do what I say or there will be trouble and pain." I barked into the silence, words eating up the space and leaving dread behind, "My second is Raina. You will treat her words as if they are my own. I don't care who squeezed you out or who seeded you. I am in charge. If you don't see me, she is in charge. If you don't like that, stay here." I coughed to give them a second to soak that in. "Klippen says we leave at noon; I say we will meet him outside the town at noon. We will leave at dawn. We will wear no royal insignia whatsoever. We will wear simple clothes. We will be humble and pass as peasants." There was some grumbling. I produced a knife from nowhere and flung it into a clay pitcher of wine, knocking it off the table and into the lap of the loudest boy. "We will pass as peasants because they will kill any noble they find or suspect. I will cut any throat with my smallest, dullest knife in the middle of the square if that's what it takes so the bulk of us can escape this city and Volker. Even if the throat is one of yours." Again, silence. I nodded. "I will be back a candlemark before dawn. Pack tonight. Do not make me wake any of you."

I gave a disgusted glance down at the man at my feet. "Now scoop up this bag of offal and get him to the healer to see if any teeth can be saved. No need to bother Lampedocht or Klippe. Your own coin can pay for it and he can owe you. Move."

Pebbles thusly safeguarded, I turned and left. There was not a whole lot of shuffling, so I guess Blondie was going to lose his teeth. Pity.

"Master?" Raina ventured timidly, "I know you are upset about having to answer to Schwartzklippen, but how is antagonizing those men going to make any of this any easier?"

I grinned nastily at her. Then we were at the bottom of the stairs and Lampedocht was presenting me with a small glass, eyes worried. "Please, drink with me, Master Crow. I.. uh.. I hope.."

I drained the fiery topaz liquid in a gulp, smiled fiercely, and clapped the old man on the shoulder with only a tad too much force. "Never better, Lord Conductor. I have met the men and introduced myself. Just please let 'Klippe' know we will be ready to leave at dawn, as he ordered, and will rally just out of town."

Lampedocht recovered from my overly manly greeting and nodded as he beamed. "Well, that is good. I shall certainly tell him. Shall I summon the servants to turn down your bed and prepare a pallet for your apprentice?"

Still smiling back at him, my words pranced out of my mouth as if giddy with expectation. "No time, good sir. But thank you. We must be back to our lodgings and there pack up our gear and retrieve our horse."

"Oh, good, well farewell, Crow. I hope to see you whole and hale upon your return."

"And I, you, sir."

A minute later, we were out onto the street. The lamps had been lit, burning precious oil into the night in case something hidden need be seen by the nobility. All it showed now were dozens of hired men and women picking up after the massed fundraising party and concert. We took the opportunity to scour the upper city and found the long path cut into the native rock that lead down the inner arc of the cliff to the southern docks. These also had guards and gates like the upper city, but the guards were given the uncomfortable position of being responsible for security and being ordered to largely ignore it. We traveled through the docks and crossed back to the lower town as I pondered what this meant for Volker and his battle against the crown. Was it a case of the rich ignoring the security that would keep daggers out of their eyes? Even at this late hour, upon seeing us, a man stood shakily from his seat in the shadows and ran, rather obviously ran, toward the heart of the lower city.

"Trouble?" Raina asked.

"I can't imagine it will be anything else, Apprentice." I looked at the moon, judging the hour. "We have to hurry."

Indeed, we were almost late. The final hammer strikes had taken place hours ago, and the mystical quenching to harden the edge to a killing surface while leaving the center pliable-yet-strong had been done. It was a simple thing, with scrollwork on the crosspiece and a ring pommel, with bleached leather beneath twisted wire for the handle. The blade had been hollowed out with a fuller that ran a full three quarters of the blade, adding to both flexibility and reducing weight. He had struck blow after blow to mold it into shape, then polished the blade to a high sheen. As the last polish went on, the smith's apprentices had dunked the crossguard and pommel into a chemical bath, turning them the darkest of midnight blue. Then these, too, had been polished to a mirror shine.

The smith passed the weapon to Raina with solemn, if exhausted, pride. His boys were already asleep at the foot of the forge, which still glowed. I knew quite a bit of the process, and it would have been hour after hour of non-stop hammering to make this blade, but no finer steel could a human carve out of a lump of iron. Raina's face said it all, for she held it as if she had never touched a sword.

I discretely passed the smith the promised silver, and a gold coin nearly doubling the miserly price I had negotiated. It hurt to do, but he truly had earned it. He smiled back grimly and passed over a simple wooden sheath. I passed that to Raina, and then ushered her out as if she were a child with a fancy new toy. I motioned for her to keep up and she finally sheathed the thing and slung the whole over her back.

"It is magnificent, Master. Thank you."

I shrugged. "You paid for most of it."

She took no note. "Why did the smith not speak, do you think?"

"From the very second he accepted our coin, he was working on that blade. It may have been two days and a night to us, but for him it was a long eternity. That shard of brightness you carry represents an unending ritual of heating, hammering, heating, and hammering. The sand-steel is unyielding, and has to be beaten into shape, but skillfully, lest you crack the forming blade. He didn't just sell us iron, or steel. He sold us the last two days of his life and one of the most finicky things he can make. There is a lot of himself in that steel."

"So he is sentimental?"

"I find most artists are. They get used to selling off their work, but they never quite learn to like it."

"Artist? Why did you not give such praise to the smith?"

I was honestly taken aback. "What? Give him praise before and give him excuse to charge us more? I praised him with extra coin. And after. That is enough."

I looked to Raina to see if she understood, but she was captured with events ahead. And so was I, but not the same events.

Ahead an ass of some great size was being lead toward a building. What it did not want was to go forward, nor back, nor turn in any meaningful way. Obviously a shipment had come in late, and the shopkeep was trying to get it in before morning. A tired man heaved on the creature that brayed and bit at him, drawing something of a crowd even this late. He finally managed to muscle the thing to the eaves of the shop and tie it off on a support. The ass immediately started yanking at the tether as if it meant to being the entire shop down. Given time, it might just do it, but then the shopkeep crossed behind the beast. The ass lashed out with its rear legs, hooves nearly caving in the shopkeeper's skull. He cursed loudly as it brayed at him, and responded by continuing to empty barrels, boxes, and even heavy bags of flour out of his cart and behind the beast to keep anyone who wandered by safe. He was taking up half the road, and was the focus of everyone's attention. Well, everyone but a small group just beyond him and myself.

I slipped a hand to the back of my apprentice and she stiffened. Two cold, heavy, fist-sized bags of coins slipped into the large pouch under her cloak. Then I gave her whispered instructions. She took off my shortsword and hooked on her own brand new blade, then accepted the Phantom Angel which she slung over her shoulder.

My final instructions burned the air as I whispered, "If I do not come by morning, flee the town and never look back."

And, following my words to the letter, she was gone down the alley. The men down the street who had no interest in the production of *Misery of Two Asses* started as if thinking of following her, but then I was coming toward them.

I smiled.

It was not a nice smile. It was diligently crafted to give the watcher the idea that I was hungry. For throats. I got within a half dozen paces when one of them held up a hand and I stopped to be polite. Besides, Raina needed the moments to escape.

These were, all but one, Volker's men. They all had that stench of freshly minted authority, the certainty that comes from never having to relieve someone from a guard post and finding them with throat slit. They were well grown men, but still babes. All but one.

That one held my attention. He was old, almost as old as half of the men here added together. His grey hair blended into brown skin polished by the wind into crinkled smoothness. His eyes were just slits as he watched me askance. His whole frame was lean but for his chest and arms. Even underneath the rough spun winter wear that was slowly disintegrating due to age, his arms and chest were vibrant and impressive despite his advancing years. He spit black juice from a mouth wrapped around some kind of root in his cheek. In his hand was a bow lovingly crafted by skillful hands. Strung, it was barely shorter than he and used finger wide arrows he had arrayed in a quiver. He looked like a wolf, tall, rangy, without an ounce wasted on sloth. Richter, of the Matron's Rest, liked to say that you never tangled with old wolves, for they had survived everything so far and were ready for anything else that came for them. Looking the man up and down, I saw no reason it didn't apply to him. Though he hovered at the back of the group and far out of reach, I also didn't see any way I would be allowed to avoid tangling with him.

This was obviously all scripted. "You. Outlander. You slept with my friend's daughter. He demands satisfaction."

I did not look at him, only the bowman. I was kept from easy striking distance by the wall of thugs, but when I spoke, I spoke to him. "I did not sleep with your daughter."

One of the other toughs poked me in the chest. "Ooh, now he calls us liars. What if we all demand satisfaction?"

I took a deep breath. I walked through a dozen ways to kill them all. I died, each time. It was that extra manlength I could not cover. It was the wolf and the damned bow. I sighed again, "Produce her, and allow us to marry."

Another still snorted. "So now you admit it? Well, he doesn't want his daughter to marry a dirty outlander."

Still I watched the hunter. It had been a harsh, early, winter and it was ending late. A few coins may be the difference between life and death for a family in need. All around the sparse midnight crowd, amused by the shopkeeper and the ass, now watched my accusation with morbid curiosity.

"Don't do this," I begged him.

He shrugged and didn't quite meet my eye. "A man must protect his own."

And that, was that. There were more threats, more hollow reasons for them to hate me. All that mattered was they shoved a bow into my hands along with four, thick arrows. I looked at the bladed heads, at the hand crafted fletchings, and my hands ran along the plain bow. I found no sabotage or fault. Not that they would need it. "How far?"

I ignored distractions to every side. The old wolf shrugged, adjusted his threadbare cap and picked up his bow, adjusting the quiver over his shoulder. "Far as you want. Makes no difference."

He had grown up with that damn white slabs of wood. He had carved all of them himself since he could walk. Like Richter, his family had survived because of his skill, and he was right– if he could see me, he could hit me. I loosened my left vambracer and began backing away. Step, step, step.

The thugs fanned out away from the bowman, out of the line of fire. Old Wolf sighed and tested his grip on his bow. Ideally, I would take him at his word and be right in his face. The problem is the toughs he had with him would be too close and cut me down once I killed the archer. What I needed was to be invisible for a second. I fed three spare arrows into the bracer, made sure they were easy to pull out without shredding my arm, and continued to take short steps back.

I passed the wagon, the stack of supplies. I drew level with the ass near the pile of goods.

Old Wolf readied his bow. He spit again. He noticed the pile and judged its use for cover. He shook his head, unconcerned. Then he shrugged at me, a silent apology. The wolf kills for food, not for sport. I was just what happened to be on the menu. Nothing personal.

I nodded back to him and smiled. I shrugged widely, one hand holding the bow, the other the arrow. The arrow that jabbed into the rump of the jackass tied to the store rail. The ass brayed, the whole crowd of people jumped, and the ass bucked with all of its might. The sharp hooves went high, and flung a bag of flour off of the very top of the pile, rupturing it into a dense white cloud.

Too late, Old Wolf saw it coming and loosed three arrows into the cloud. The crowd gasped, and then everyone waited. Second after second crawled by, the silence only broken by the constant and all erasing braying of the donkey breaking against the walls.

Then it stopped, the cloud cleared, and I was nowhere to be seen. It was simple really. And for that reason I had no time to hesitate for mercy, only for victory.

An arrow struck Old Wolf in the right breast and he collapsed around the wound, groaning. The toughs looked at him, when another arrow struck a thug in the head. I wish I could say I was aiming at his head, but while I had trained enough to be a decent bowman, this strange equipment precluded fussy aiming. The two remaining thugs saw me where I had ducked down an alley and scrambled to the top of the store, firing from just over the peak. I had gained surprise of just a second or two, enough to fell two men. Then I loosed another arrow and struck a thug low in one lung. He collapsed as the last ran off. I nocked an arrow, drew it back, and aimed. Aimed. I lowered the bow, and let the string pull forward jerkily. He had passed out of sight. Besides, I had trouble enough here.

In seconds I had clambered down to the street. People gasped or screamed as my sword hissed from the sheath and the short, razor sharp blade plunged into thug after thug. One tried to crawl away before the blade severed his spine just below the skull. I spit upon him. This was their doing, as was what came next.

I walked to the crumpled form of Old Wolf. I took a second to check his back beneath his clothes and see nothing but clear skin there. That made all of this even worse. I kept an eye on his hands, but knelt well within reach. I heard his lung filling up with blood, saw where the arrow had ruined his chest muscle. The first would forever cripple his pull with a bow. The second would kill him far sooner.

BETTER YOU THAN ME aside, I hoped being honest made one sound honest. "I am sorry it has to be this way."

"Fair is fair," he replied simply, words gurgling. "Good trick."

"You have a name?"

"Gunderson."

"And a village?"

He tried to move and failed against the tidal wave of pain locking him to the ground. He was panting, unable to catch his breath. "My family has nothing to do with this."

With a simple caress I lifted his money pouch from him and held it up. "Who gets this, then?"

He questioned me with his eyes, and I nodded. *Nothing personal.* "Drohnenwald."

I nodded again. The strike that followed was fast and it was instantly fatal.

The wolf may be masterful hunter, but there is a reason it does not eat the fox.

I lined up the bodies and stripped them of what coin and valuables I could. From Gunderson's body I had a pouch of coin I segregated, a stag-handled dagger and skinning knife set, his bow, and a whole archer's kit for arrows, strings and other sundries. I set them to the side as well.

I hefted the dagger and knife set in my hands, alien words echoing in my head, *Is peace your business*?

"Well, what do we have here, Sirrah?"

This guy. I wish it had been anyone but *this* guy. *Then again...* I kicked the last body into position. "Dueling."

"You killed them?" I nodded, at which his smile drew supernaturally wide. "Arrest him!" Suddenly, the borrowed bow was drawn, the arrow nicking the end of the official's nose. His next word was a shout. "Wait!"

"These men attempted to have a duel, and were summarily executed," I lowered the bow, let the string go slack, and pronounced the last word as a curse, "fellow."

The stunted official rubbed at his nose, brought his fingers away bloody and jumped in agitation. "Executed? By whom?"

"By me. The last time you saw me, you made it clear that anyone could execute a dueler, and claim all their possessions as reward. I have done so."

I brushed past the guards. The leader exclaimed wordlessly and the last in line grasped my arm. The haft of the bow came down on his fingers. I swept out one leg and brought him to his knees. Everyone held their breath because a dagger they hadn't seen me draw was under the poor fool's chin. I waited, staring at them expectantly, and receiving only silence in return. "I leave this city tomorrow. Better we not meet again, fellows."

Then the man fell to the pavers, feeling at his throat for cuts as I turned and disappeared down the closest alley.

It was getting worse. There was no way that this was the work of Volker, but his lard-headed lieutenant would be just the man to try something like this. My worry was how soon he would try again. Worse, how long before he gave up on local champions and guardsmen and resorted to a professional assassin. I had to conclude my business in Hammarfall, the city, and get out of Hammarfall, the country, before stupidity alone burned me alive.

I entered Konrad's Inn, his wife once awakened by Raina's entrance, snapped awake again as I came in. She shot needles at me as she bolted the door, pulling night shirt and robe close as she held the candle high so I could see my way to the staircase. Before leaving I made arrangements for some fresh and expertly prepared preserved food to be served at an obscenely early hour of the morning. She nodded sullenly, but did not reply.

I made my way up to the room. I entered and shoved the now piles of equipment, saddlebags, and saddle in front of the door. Raina came off of her bed as if burned. She stared at me for a moment, finding no extra holes or broken bones in my person she cocked her head. "How did you win?"

I shrugged and dumped the spoils onto the floor. "I changed the game. Now get some sleep."

I undressed, tossed a few logs on the fire and put up the screen to capture the light and sparks but allow the heat to warm the room.

Raina's voice came out of the gloom as I burrowed under the blankets. "Tomorrow we leave, then?"

I finished pouring water down my throat and set down the mug. "Very early. Hopefully before they can react to tonight and make more plans for me."

"So then we will be safe?"

I wanted to lie to her, if nothing else to stave off any further conversation, but it wasn't right. She was my apprentice, and she had to learn.

"Oh, no," I said, closing my eyes and forcibly yanking sleep near, "tomorrow it gets even more dangerous."

THREE

EXIT THROUGH BEASTS INTO THE WILD

MORNING came too soon, and too cold by far. I awoke to nothing but ashes in the fireplace and tossed on two logs to bring light to the place. The pressure from the water I had downed last night kept me from returning to slumber. I used the indoor outhouse, another Dwarvish innovation learned by the men of Hammarfall, and then commenced to kicking Raina awake. Well, to be honest, there were no kicks, because at a light touch she came awake with a knife in her hand. I was so proud.

I nodded approvingly and gestured her up. She followed my lead and then we started packing. The sun was nowhere near up, and even false dawn was hours away. The stars shone coldly and the huge circle of the moon glared madly at us from over the horizon. I would like to have said I slurred around drunkenly from lack of sleep, honestly I would, because it was more pleasant and dignified than feet curling from the cold wooden floor, and breath icing in the air. We had soon dressed, and then began divvying up the many goods we had purchased: rope, food, bandages, and so on. Half was split between she and I, so as not to overload us and provide some use if we were separated. The other half went on the horse, because it was big and strong and could not effectively complain about the burden. We poked at the burning logs and liberally spread sand in the fireplace to douse the flames. Only then we slung the bags, backpacks, weapons, and saddle.

Our packs took up one table, while the other was a kingly repast prepared by Konrad. Roasted and spiced nuts, with cloth sealed bags of candied nuts to take with us, cold sausages and sliced apples dipped in tart citrus juice, berries, and black bread slathered in butter went on forever. We gorged, but we had to do it quickly.

Stepping outside was like being punched by a collapsing house. The cold numbed the lungs and bit at the fingers, causing them to shake as we tried to saddle the horse. And of course the damn thing (had she named this nag yet?) sucked in a double lungful of air as I tried to tighten the belly strap, forcing me to wait until he exhaled, then my numb fingers slipped on the strap and I had to wait until he breathed again to get it good and snug. My reward for heading off the risk of falling off at an inopportune time and breaking my neck was a nip on the thigh from the damn thing's teeth that burned and throbbed like murder itself. I was tempted to knife the beast and be done with it but for two things First, it was a horse being a horse, and punishing a horse for being a horse is the act of a brutally stupid man. Second, I didn't want to carry all the equipment. Even now, I don't know which reason weighed in more.

Raina, meanwhile immune to the cruelty of animals, moved around the white gelding, cooing to him, covering his flanks and forelock with spare blankets to hold out the cold. A quick slit with a knife and threading of a leather thong pulled the blankets out of the way of the hooves, and closed the gap in front to keep the creature warm.

We had done all this without words, and I wondered what would happen if we were forced to fight as a pair, which we had not trained for due to lack of proper sparring partners, and had never done in real life. I made a mental note to get more mileage out of the lord Rakes in that respect, they were dumb enough to leap at the chance, and we left Konrad's Inn.

We led the horse instead of riding. It appeared whatever spy Volker had employed on Konrad's Inn and the entry to the noble quarter had either nipped off for a bottle of warmth and forgotten to come back, or perhaps just found a warm spot and fallen asleep. I hoped it would last.

The all-too-alert guards at the gate to the noble quarter let us through, and we made it to Lampedocht's estate without trouble. From there, the icy cold could not touch me, for though Lampedocht had servants mostly awake to let us in as instructed, the Lordlings of the Attic were still sleeping the sleep of the rich. And senseless. And eminently stab-able.

My rage instantly dispelling the clutches of winter, I marched downstairs to collect two large buckets of water from the rain barrel. I had to punch through the ice. Now, you would imagine that the first man got it bad, and the soaking got easier from then on. I say to you, nay! I am a fair and just tyrant, but a tyrant after all. I started pouring a stream that coated the faces of sleeping lordlings, whores, and so on, all down one row, then flung dregs at others on the far side that were awakened by the high-pitched, girly screams generated by my gentle ministrations. The last one to stand got the whole other bucket from face to floor, and I remind the dear reader that the bucket was really filled with ice too lazy to properly harden. One man did rush me, but he had no weapons and a quick kick to his bare testicles, hard enough to lift him off of the floor, ended his ill-considered coup.

"Wakey, wakey, my little darlings. Aren't you supposed to be packed?" I growled, wondering how many more of these stunts would be necessary until they understood I was in charge. Then I took in the dancing, cursing, shivering band of armed children and I decided this was a hobby I could grow accustomed to, should they prove even dimmer than expected. "Your roughest, simplest clothes if you please."

Then there was a light of reason that entered their eyes as they watched their friend writhe in pain. That reason was... Because Crow Said So. It was all the reason they would ever need for anything, and it was just now taking hold. Some dressed wet. That was fine. Others toweled off with bedclothes or clothes they did not intend to wear this moment. Also fine. Freezing now or freezing and mildewed later, I cared not. But the prostitutes they had hired scampered from the room as the men hurried themselves in packing.

That was when I noticed Blondie. His eyes were dark, and foreboding despite being perfectly sky blue. I noticed his mouth was not bleeding, meaning that his pals had taken him to a healer. I also noticed his perfect smile dissolved into shattered ivory towers on one side of his face, meaning they had done it on the cheap. I mentally shrugged. If a man spends months or years with a group of mates and they would not front the cash to keep him from having a mouth of shattered teeth, then it spoke volumes more about him than I could. I held out a hand toward him.

"No family crests. No insignia. No signet rings. Nothing that says, 'I am a noble'."

"Shut up, I will do as I like. And when my father hears about your treatment of me, you will be whipped to death," he grumbled. "Besides, we are leaving by the docks. We will not be bothered."

I held his gaze, and decided a smile, barely concealed, followed by a slight snort, would be the best message to all. I pointed at him. "Good. YOU wear insignia. And you ride first. Anyone else?" Silence reigned. "None? Good. Finish packing."

That took less time than would be imagined. Then we were outside. The horses were pulled, and saddled and I instructed all the boys to walk their mounts. I sent Raina around to cut off insignia that may have been missed, pointing out jewelry to be removed, and to have the boys wipe charcoal and fat stained cloths on their weapons and clothes, tack and harness. More slowly than I would like, the shiny lordlings of nothing became a drab group of sell-swords. They were ready.

We walked the horses for a simple reason– nobles hate to see commoners ride. The first thing any commoner does when he sees a noble is dismount, then remove his hat. Commoners are used to simply walking their horses in town, lest they have to dismount ever other minute to show proper respect to their betters. It, of course, drew all attention to Blondie, which may very well lead to his death. And to tell the truth, that bothered me less than you might imagine.

Blondie, however, got in the saddle immediately, resplendent in silks, signet ring, badge of office hanging from thick, buttery links of gold, and gloves adorned with his family's device. I nodded. "Good. Out in front. Three manlengths." He started to protest when I took the old, battered crossbow from the pack on the horse and loaded it. The weapon in my hands was not a show piece, it was meant to cast a heavy bolt straight through a lightly armored man without much trouble. The expensive bows, in fact everything expensive, had been hidden effectively away as it had been done on each of the men. The only pieces of obvious wealth were the Phantom Angel on my hip, and Blondie. Both were meant to serve the same purpose. Getting over two dozen men moving was more trouble than I wanted, and took far longer than I had guessed, but at least they were halfway quiet.

Breath still coming in clouds, anger fading and letting the cold move in, I signaled for us to start out. We wound toward the gate and out of the Lord's Quarter. Our luck had held, for there were no prying eyes waiting for us in the bitter cold. We walked the horses down and toward the gate at the docks, the rush of the far off waves and the percussion of the hooves, the wheeze of animal breaths becoming a lulling sound so early in the morning.

I let Raina take the horse, and uncocked the crossbow. Carrying it loaded would send the wrong message. I slung it on its strap and tucked the bolt into the tied straps of my purse. We exited the docks gate easily, but a boy, bundled against the cold, took off the moment I appeared. I cursed bitterly, but there was nothing for it. I had Raina mount up and gallop ahead as the Rakes assembled. She returned mere heartbeats later, the sound of her mount's hooves never out of earshot.

"They are assembling pikemen at the docks, crossbowmen on the roofs."

No need to ask who they were. This was Volker. I thought for only a second. They were ready for us at this gate. Maybe… "Mount up."

"You said–" one whining voice began.

"Or stay here." I shrugged. I pulled myself behind Raina and I motioned everyone into a gallop. I was counting on terrain to help us more than hurt us. Hammarfall, the city, was shaped like a horseshoe.

The southern half had a raised arc of stone upon which the nobles lived. We were racing from the southern tip, along the belly, to the center. From there we dismounted, allowing our horses to quit looking so much like horses that had been galloped halfway across a city, and walked them up a steep grade, across the raised ground, and down a grade.

If we were in luck, we would arrive at the gates ahead of any word that we had left the noble quarter, if indeed they thought to tell these men at all.

We arrived to the main gates of the city, flung open to all men by edict of the Volker, and I breathed a little easier. There was nothing here but the sounds of our passage. The burning torches acted more as malevolent eyes in the gloom, more than hopeful stars. Yet, it looked like all my preparations may have come to nothing when a slurry, sloppy sergeant exited the gatehouse and barked for his squad. And, by the God of Death's perfect pink penis, it was a whole squad. Thirty men in various states of drunkenness poured from the building, blocking our way. Well, to be fair they were blocking everyone's way.

The leader, who apparently had also been to the same training school as every other two-bit tin helmet in Hammarfall (country) raised his hand and cried, "HALT!"

Blondie, the idiot, actually had his horse take a dozen more steps toward the drunken commander, close enough that there was no hiding the nature of his clothes, no hiding his medallion of office, no room to maneuver for what came next.

"State your business."

"I am leaving the city, even that much should be obvious to you." Blondie of the broken teeth could have added more smug condescension to his voice, but he would need a few more years practice.

The sergeant smiled. "So, you are a noble's son, eh?"

"I am, what of it?" I was holding my breath. *The idiot had to know, didn't he*? He could not be that insulated from the goings on in the city.

"And you come down here? Eh?" That was a sentence that sounded like the drawing of a blade.

"I have. And I shall pass unmolested."

"Do you know what you have done to this country?"

"Keep your tongue before I cut it out, Sirrah! You do not know to whom you speak–" But Blondie's control was wavering as he watched the spearmen coming closer. It was then that I knew that he knew. He just didn't believe even thirty filthy peasants were any kind of threat to the power inherent in his noble blood.

"I know to WHAT I speak! Bring him down!"

Blondie drew his sword, but the guards were on him in an instant. I raised my hands to forestall any further stupidity from the rest of the Rakes, but it was hardly necessary. One of the guardsmen lunged upwards with the spear, but Blondie leaned back. Rather than being an inspired maneuver, however, it simply allowed the same spearman to slap him in the chest with the haft of the weapon and send him tumbling to the pavers. His sword went skittering under the boot of the leader who gestured to his men. I looked back to the almost thirty man-children in my command and saw them recoil as the guards forewent their spears and beat Blondie with truncheons and boots. I will give them this– what they did was not elegant, but it was thorough.

When finally they had finished, the leader came up and relieved Blondie of his heavy coin purse, silver appointed sword belt, gold medallion, assorted rings, earring, boots, and fine cloak. Then they tossed a ready rope high over the gate to the city, bringing down on one side a noose. They fit Blondie with the loop. They tightened it. The other end was tied to his own horse's pommel. A dark stain spread upon the man-child's pants and dribbled onto the street.

"Please, hold!" I called out. Surprising the hell out of everyone, including myself. It was nearly comical, for the rest of the actors in this little tragedy had clearly forgotten the large group of quiet men were there at all, waiting for passage out of town. I held my hands open as I walked forward, clearly empty as I approached the commander and the almost dead noble's son. "Lukas, you may have tried your best, but you lost this one. You owe half a mark to every man and if you skip out on the debt I'm going to make you wish they hung you."

The leader bristled to be ignored in any manner, "Here, now. What is all this?"

I sighed, raised my hands and shook my head, "I am, in part, to blame for this sham. This is Lukas. He's a gambler, a headstrong pretty boy, but as common as you or I."

The sergeant's face darkened into a storm cloud, "You had better explain, and fast."

I patted the air in his direction, "Look, Lukas here is about to ride out today, and last night he finds this nobleman's son at the bar playing cards. Well, Lukas here is like a demon making deals with the chits, and soon has everything this little bastard owns: horse, clothes, sword, coin, everything." The guardsmen chuckled as my story continued, but the sergeant's eyes only narrowed. "So, here Lukas is, feeling flush and gets himself drunk. Bet every man in the crew that he can get out the front gate of Hammarfall in his new finery." I reached out and ungently slapped Blondie across the head like a child. "I'd say he lost."

The sergeant got real close to me, reeking of cheap schnapps cut with rotgut. "You mean to tell me he was trying to make it through the gates as a noble? And you let him?"

I shrugged. "You ever try to talk a kid out of something while he's drunk?"

"So he's not a noble?"

I shook my head. "As common as dirt."

The face next to mine had a mouth that formed not so much a frown as a closed door so intense it was a curve. "Prove it."

I nodded, conscious that every eye of every guard was on me, and in the next few seconds I was going to die trying to save a dung eating moron I hated, or save a dung eating moron I hated. Neither option thrilled me, but I couldn't just let them hang this kid. So, showing open hands, I reached forward to the woosy, swaying face of Blondie. I pulled up his lips and everyone gasped.

"No nobleman would let his kid go through life like this, eh?" For all the world, it looked like he had once been kicked in the face by a horse, or fell out of a tree, or something. The shattered teeth looked like they had healed over time, but had never lost the jagged appearance of a wound long past. Then I leaned forward to my opposing number. "Look, you already took all the most valuable stuff he won from the noble. The kid's going to be paying off his mates for years. He's gotten a whipping fit for a king," An expression that got a laugh. "Can you let him live as an idiot having learned his lesson rather than die as one?"

"The horse?" the sergeant asked.

"He will need it to work the next few months, and his sword, but surely what you have already taken would buy a few horses, and will be easier to divvy up."

The sergeant hefted the take in his paw and then realized how cold it was away from fire and drink. "Let him go."

The guardsmen did, and Blondie collapsed. I motioned some boys over to toss him across his saddle. He was in no condition to ride. Then a hand closed on my arm and turned me around. I fought the urge to knife the sergeant in the eye when I faced him.

"What is your business?"

"We're going out to protect some merchant caravans coming in with," I thought quickly, "spirits."

"Why are you leaving so early?"

"We have far to go."

"I recognize that sword," the sergeant said darkly.

"Then you know I am no noble, and work for none, let alone command a flotilla of them." I gestured to the lads.

"Volker's Right Hand doesn't like you."

I shrugged. "Can't be liked by everyone."

"They say you bought a hundred men some bier the other night."

I shrugged again. "Doesn't stop me from trying to make some friends."

And though he looked like he was chewing half a worm in a bite of apple, he motioned us all along. "Get moving."

And with Blondie tossed over the saddle like a sack of fertilizer, move out we did.

We cleared the gate at a slow walk, got half a bowshot from the wall, and then mounted up. Even then, I kept the group at a sedate pace. We rode to the crossroads, then dismounted. Those who had soaked hair were shivering, but I forbade a fire. Those that had wet clothes mildewing in packs would shiver later, so I considered the decision fair. Raina was wrapped in the thick white fur cloak from the mountain monsters, and I had the old fox trimmed cloak, but most of the man-children had little more than capes or thin cloth cloaks.

There were signs pointing to each road's destination, and a tall, covered awning with three sides walled in. I directed everyone into the covered area, posted two men with the wettest hair around back of the pavilion to keep watch, and let everyone else unpack their gear and repack it. Lord SchnauserKuddle may have been a fool, but either he had the foresight to send the boys out for food, or to have it purchased and delivered to them. They had tight, efficient packs of nuts, hard tack, smoked meats, peas, beans, and dried fruits, as well as skins for water and skins of wine to clean it. What would save them from starvation were the dwarfcakes they bore.

We had nothing like them in Noria, but now I would be unlikely to live without them. Born of thick, heavy bread, they contained nuts, dried fruits, and large swathes of honey. A few had been soaked in dark spirits, adding to the flavor and shelf life. While I had fifteen waterweight of bullfists, a mix of crushed dried meat, animal fat and marrow, berries and nuts, but even after only a few days this hunter's staple alone it would pall. Plus, after the first half dozen meals of nothing else, the reason for the name became clear whenever one had to return one to nature, so to speak.

The Rakes sullenly tended their weapons, each fingering their light swords and daggers, not a shield amongst them that I could see. One or two had bows, but they were the light hunting bows, and not the heavy bows of the deceased Wolf or even like Richter left me. I pulled the shields off of the horse and passed one to Raina, keeping the other for myself. That was when Blondie started stirring.

His comrades had, at least, taken him from his horse, laid down blankets, and set his battered form on top of them. He was stirring with a piteous moan. One of the men offered him some watered wine and he spurned it with an oath.

I kicked the oaf and hunkered down to get a good glower going, "So, do you remember what happened?" He nodded morosely "You would be better off for having listened to me?"

He nodded again. Now he may have been agreeing with me, but the spoiled, angry look on his face made it much more likely that he was listening to the voices in his head tell him where to put his knives in my body.

I let it go, because, in either case, it would be a few days before he could make good on a plan or even move around enough to help out. "Stay still for now. Your boss should be along in a few hours, and then we will ride as long as he will let us."

I looked forward to his arrival, but only because it would keep us moving. The sun came up and blunted the curved knives of the nightly chill, but we were still at the crossroads, waiting instead of riding away from the city and almost certain danger. Then I had the Rakes break out the most perishable of foods and eat an early lunch. After, I switched out those who were on watch and those who were given time to rest. Every moment we continued to wait did not lead to my relaxation, but instead dripped blood into a towering inferno of revenge behind my eyes.

Not to say the day was a complete waste. From the looks I received I could see that Blondie Brokenteeth was still intent on murdering me. At least half of the men were trying to peel Raina out of her thick leather armor with what passed for charm, and the rest with their eyes. I was betting at least one would think so little of her as to use force and thus braced myself against the time she killed one of these self important idiots.

Oh, I caught a hundred flaws, and noted who could not be trusted on guard duty with whom, and who knew to sleep while they had time and who did not. I learned they still had far too much pride in skills that did not warrant it. I learned they really did not fear death in a tangible way, but only out of a childish belief in their own higher fate. I learned they were too well fed compared to normal soldiers, and needed energy constantly directed to stay out of trouble. Most important, I learned who had any amount of self control.

As the sun was beginning to set, and the whispered complaints at their early rise gave birth to low grumbles, and now to muttered conversations Then the slave chain went by.

It is often said that form follows function. This is no place more evident than in the slave chain. Made to keep people secure and jailed while still travelling from place to place, it was always the same. A rope, or in this case chain, was run from the first slave's collar, linked to every collar of every slave behind him, and secured to the last slave's collar. The collars were normally for necks, but could be done around the waist as well. Kept the hands free, feet free, and made sure unless you could get more than ten men brave, cunning, and coordinated enough to make a break for it at once, what you would have is a tumbled mass of attempted escapees you could whip to your heart's content. It is so common a way to control men that I have never seen it done any other way.

I saw the slave chain coming far off, from the opposite direction as the city, and felt a cold chill settle upon me for I had the good sense to know what was coming. Immediately I pulled in the watchmen with harsh whistles. Then I ordered an early dinner started. While the men might have complained otherwise, they were used to far more substantial fare, eating early was a treat and they pulled food from packs with gusto, I called to Raina.

"Yes, Master?"

"Get the bottle of schnapps, cut it with wine from our stores, and pass it out."

She hesitated, but stopped herself from forcing me to repeat my order, instead asking, "How much?"

"Three fingers now, three more in ten minutes." Her face screwed up in a look of distaste until I added as a desperate afterthought, "Do not serve it yourself. Get one of these knobs to do it." If you think knobs referred to a mechanical piece of a door, you have not been paying attention to my opinion of the Rakes.

She nodded and sped off to do my will. I looked back to the road, wishing I had been able to spare the coin to buy a spyglass. No, that was a lie, I had plenty of coin. But paying as much as ten swords, or three horses, for the set of glass and brass that made up a portable spyglass was simply beyond me. I understood it was a fickle thing to build, and there was perhaps only one man in the whole country that could make them correctly and without much distortion in the lenses, but I still had trouble letting that much gold out of my purse at once for something so easily broken. Right now, however, I would have killed for one. Well, at least maimed. Well, unless it was the missing Lord SchnauserKuddle.

Regardless, I did not have a spyglass, and no amount of imagined murders would give me one.

The second round of drinks was passed and quaffed with extra zeal long before the food was consumed, as was planned. Now I can hear some of you out there wondering loudly why I would serve over a dozen barely controllable lordlings alcohol. Three main reasons. The first being, these men were hard drinkers. Part of their sour disposition was about being woken from a night of heavy drinking with the normal pounding headache that brings. Without even a touch of alcohol to deaden the pains, it would have followed them even to this point in the day. Just a touch of the poison was enough to cure the condition for a while, and I needed that wash of relief. Second, I needed these thoughtless and largely worthless Rakes to be just a touch too relaxed. Slow, off balance, I could stop them before they did something stupid. They would do something stupid because, reason three, I knew what we were about to see.

The guards were pure Volker. They seemed slightly more confident, but I was guessing that it was because they were horsemen before the revolution and thus comfortable in the saddle. Also, they carried swords and whips. Swords and whips make most people confident, especially when everyone else was chained up. I have already described the chains. What I was not sure of was what the huge canvas bags on their backs were filled with. At this point I was guessing food fresh from the fields. The slaves certainly showed the signs of having harvested it.

As I have said, everyone looks down on farmers. There are lots of them, they have mud and shit between their toes, they are generally pretty poor, and did work most people assumed was completely unskilled. The last at least, was a complete lie. The rest were only lies to a certain extent. What it came down to was that city folk were just different than country folk and the two rarely interacted. Differences plus distance usually meant the country people looked upon the city folk with just as much distain. Now, however, the Volker had given them both a common enemy: the nobles. And so, I had guessed who was going to be chained together, trudging down the road, but it might as well have been a certainty.

Dressed in rags, feet wrapped against weeping sores and blisters since the boots had been stolen and sold weeks ago, only the stylish ghosts of facial hair being reclaimed by beards and the eyes haunted by past glory could truly tell of having fallen so far.

Conversation ended as if by an axeman's chop. I turned as if a guardian of the gate, waiting for someone to yell, to rush forward, to attempt some kind of mind numbingly heroic rescue.

But they didn't.

The Rakes saw the line of men, and by their births I knew there had to be relatives, friends, and in-laws chained together just close enough to recognize. I watched as every set of eyes swept the line, and every one of them caught sight of a familiar face. But, then they did the right thing. They put their faces into their cups or food, and ignored weak and plaintive calls for help. I had expected to have to use harsh language, and stand in the way of a few, maybe even tackle one. I needed not do one such thing.

And, strangely enough, though it saved me blood and sweat, I found myself loathing the lordlings. I saw the slaves and was disgusted. While I had no illusions of trying to cut them free, and thus earning mouths I could not feed and a death sentence from the Volker, I was older and wiser by far, and none of my family were chained with them. The Rakes became rowdier after the passing of the slaves. Joking more roughly with themselves. They did not look at me much, and Raina not at all. I set watches again, and we continued to wait.

It was near dark when Lord Alexander Jaeger Von SchnauserKuddle finally arrived, trailing a pale man riding a pony laboring under the weight of packed books, stacked wood, hogsheads of some kind of drink, and what looked like a pig. The boys welcomed their hero with cheers, and some backward thrust sneers to tell me that I was going to get it now.

Alexander dismounted, bringing with him a small keg and the slightly deflated and wholly naked corpse of a gutted piglet. The lordlings cheered like morons, so loud you could hear them for miles. He had brought faggots of wood, and a fire was built. It was at that very moment that I knew that Alexander had planned to be late all along, leaving us hanging out here just in case Volker got smart enough to send out a cloud of citizen soldiers and wipe us out.

At the same time I hated him, admired him, in the same way I admired a furred predator, because he had done the same thing to me that I had to the Volker. The second I had broken the boys down a bit and made them rely upon me, he came along with a bit of comfort and bribed them away from me. The primary difference was I had not been anywhere near as successful.

I wanted to cut his throat and watch him die. Well, I wanted to stab him in the guts and let him die slowly. Fine, I wanted to open up his guts, insert thirteen rabid mice into him, sew him up, and just make an evening of it.

He threw his arm around me, smelling of lilac scented bath water and brandywine. He smiled. "Good to see you out here, Crow. I hope my boys were no trouble."

The 'boys', such as they were, had taken to setting up a spit to roast the pig, a process that was going to take hours at the least. "Alexander, we need to get moving. If a babe wanted to catch us and stop us, or overtake and ambush us–"

The lord reacted as if lightly slapped, "My dear Crow! The pig is just started, the barrel of schnapps is full, and we have the services of the most informed scholar in all of Hammarfall to guide our steps. Do shut up and keep watch while the boys relax."

And he turned away with a flourish, completely unaware of the razor sharp knife that had been held to his side, ready to puncture at the least provocation. Well, he had given me the least, and I had not punctured him. I felt slightly ashamed at the softness of my character. Raina caught sight of the knife and her eyes went wide. I gestured her over and whispered quick instructions. Five breaths later, I materialized out of the darkness in front of the robed scholar. He started visibly, dropping his bedroll with a muffled shriek.

I reached an unyielding hand for him, a smoky vision of judgment. "Come with me," I ordered, voice low and hidden beneath the ruckus of the starting party, "and tell me everything you know about Annalirya Von Zeitheim."

FOUR

THE ROAD

AXEL (I could not make that up) Hundeausführer -(nor that) was a decent enough man. With a name like that, combined with a body type that could only be described as spare, he was destined to be a scholar of some kind. He was probably beaten into it more than anything. He was the kind of man who plucked stray brow hairs until he was going bald from the eyes up. The only problem with growing up beaten and ascending to a position of knowledge is an unhealthy fixation on the rules.

I have a general opinion on rules– if I didn't make them, I consider them capricious and unnecessary. Hundeausführer felt otherwise.

"I- I- I- can't tell you anything. Orders of Van Schwartzklippen," was all I could get out of him during the night, at least without applying much sharper forms of intimidation. Normally I'd jump at the chance to carve out a little of some minor functionary standing in my way, but I was trying to leave that man behind.

So Raina watched half the night and I watched the other half, and everyone else ate, drank, sang songs, and passed out. Well, Hundeausführer ate and drank a little, but only in between chapters of one of his many books. It was during that long, meatless, schnapps-less night that I toyed with the idea of leaving Alexander Jaeger the Von to his own, doomed quest and make my merry way with Raina and two, heavy bags of gold.

But that course of action meant I would never hear the Opus Discordia, nor Lampedocht and his musicians perform any of The Burning Composer's work ever again. Others may perform it, but I was sure none would ever match the passion, the expertise, I had heard from Lampedocht's people. Right then, in the cold, lonely night, I could not bear being separated from that work forever. It had moved me as little else ever had. I would feel that deeply again.

Thus it was just before dawn that I took my overfull bladder on a short walk to the hasty fire pit and let go over the last wisping, ashy ends of the wood, preventing any phoenix from rising in any short amount of time. I packed up my bedroll, loaded up the horse, and then, just as light topped far off mountains to the west and spread across the land to the far off sea, I began kicking the lordlings awake. I need not be rough, but I was a little rough anyway, and so each one came awake in a start with a groan. There had been enough in the hogshead for half a dozen glasses of schnapps per person, and now they were each feeling the thunder of their bad decisions.

I gave orders in a calm, low tone, but I might as well have raged like a giant for the pain I caused them. Still, they knew what I could do, and after glancing at the sleeping Von Schwartzklippen, got themselves moving.

Say what you want, but getting a camp moving with partially drunk and severely hung-over people doing the work is not particularly quiet. I managed to wake Raina softly and get her started on her own gear. Then one of them Rakes had his foot stepped upon by a horse unhappy with his rough treatment. The lordling screamed very much like a gutted pig, spooking all of the horses to bolt despite the makeshift rope corral I had raised. Chasing them down involved a great deal of cursing and screaming by all hands. This, finally had woken Hundeausführer, who wandered around the camp in a daze, unsure of what was going on or how to proceed. That was when Master Von awoke. His dainty beard had been twisted by sleep into a storm of brown hair, not to mention the damage revelry had done to his coif. He stalked toward me across the camp, half dressed and wearing only one boot. He clenched his fists as he got near, but pulled up short as I produced a razor sharp knife from nowhere, smiled at him, and began drawing the blade across my dry face.

"Yes, your lordship?" I asked, cheerfully.

"WHAT is the meaning of all this racket, Crow?"

"Well, your Lordship, you put me second in command. So here I am, commanding second. Readying the men to move the second you are ready to travel. Detail work, as you might say." And my smile widened by way of punctuation.

He was shaking, his face a red mask of pure rage, fueled I am sure by a late night where he had partaken of more than his fair share of liquor. "I will not be ready to leave for SEVERAL hours!" he managed to choke out, then stalk back across the camp to his bedroll.

I waited for him to settle down amongst the still, and slightly sheepish, forms of the Rakes. Then I shrugged and shouted, "You heard Von 'Klippe, put it all back, unroll your beds, and sack out, boys!"

The aforementioned Sausagelicken sat straight up and glared heavily at me. I bore his gaze easily, continuing to shave dry and wiping off the bristles onto my sleeve from the edge of the knife. He curled back into his bedding in what was supposed to be a menacing way. Instead of sweet sleep, he got to listen to the louts chase the horses back into the corral, hammer the waist high poles back into the ground, unsaddle the ones saddled, drop their gear to the dirt, in many cases go relieve themselves at the edge of camp, and then settle down. At that point they were not even a little asleep, and engaged in conversation, traded insults, or games of chance. It was not particularly quiet. Finally Alexander slung his blankets from him and shouted, "All up and prepare to move out!"

To which groans were his answer. He kicked a few of the louts to their feet, and cursed his way off to the edge of camp where he relieved himself. That was how, with a maximum of effort, confusion, and cursing, we broke camp.

"Master Crow!" Sausagelicken roared almost an hour later. I left where I was directing the boys in how to chase down the horses and moved at a reasonable, but far from hurried pace. He broke off his rage in his teeth and used the shards to form a vengeful smile. "You. Go scout ahead."

I gave him a smile and a sarcastic salute. "But of course."

Those of you who have done it, or who have perhaps heard me talk about it, know that working scout for a larger group is extremely hard work. I myself, I stripped myself of pack and goods until I had a day of preserved food, some watered wine, and about half the means of death and destruction I normally liked on my person.

"You are scouting ahead?" Raina asked, seriously. I nodded. "Alone?" I nodded. "Then why are you smiling?"

In response I turned to Hundeausführer, still clumsily assembling his pack. "Master Scholar, Herr Von Schwarzklippen, in his wisdom, has asked I lead the way." Hundeausführer blinked at me, nonplussed. "I will need your finest map."

Taking it from him was like ripping a baby from the bosom of its mother, but I managed it without a twinge of guilt. I found the first seven turns, much further than we had any chance of getting today, before folding up the lambskin and slipping it into my pack. I would study it later, at which time I would find out the good news, and bad.

But for now I was on foot, scouting for horsemen, which meant I needed to get on the road quickly and keep a brisk pace. At least I kept up my part.

I scouted ahead for half a day, entering the cool reaches of the pine forest early and keeping my eyes and ears open while moving. I only stopped at the most likely lunch location a little before midday. There was a stream to water the horses and men, a nice spot risen above the road and screened by trees to allow privacy from prying eyes. If I had designed it, there would be forty-foot tall walls manned by unimpeachable troops wielding crossbows, but I take what I can get. I unfolded the map and stared at it, taking in the details and seeing we were in for even a longer trek than I had first imagined.

I climbed a tree and nestled myself into the branches far enough up to be screened but low enough to see two dozen men on the road. There I traced the lines of Hammarfall, the country, and realized exactly what we were in for.

Hammarfall connected the country of Noria in the north with the far off sands of Andriattica, a land of deserts, sorcerers, and spices to the south. The sun set in the west onto the relatively short and wild flatlands of the Untamed Baronies. From there, eastward, the land vaulted into obscenely rugged mountain ranges called the Spine of the Hammar, then fell into rolling, forested hills and into the flatlands that lead to the sea. From the edge of the mountains to the Long Night Sea was the country of Hammarfall. From there one can cross the sea to Wisteria and parts even more foreign. While not as utterly wild nor as expansive as Noria, Hammarfall had a lot of terrain, and we were walking into the worst of it. The map showed roads in the mountains that were likely unused for centuries, and the markings on the hide gave me the impression that the Untamed Baronies were not part of Hammarfall, nor friendly to outsiders. Or maybe I misread the large number of skulls.

It was then I realized that I had been reading the map for a very long time, and I still heard not a peep from the troops. As I have already pointed out, it is a common misconception that horses make travel much faster. Nothing prevents most of them from traveling slower, however. When they did not arrive in half a candlemark, I dismounted the tree and hurriedly ran back down the road…

…to find everyone safe and sound, packed out in the middle of the road, eating, drinking, and lounging.

Von Schwarzklippen came out of the woods at my approach, holding a half empty bottle high and roaring with good cheer. "Master Crow! Do not look so sour! Not all of us have your iron constitution!"

I, too, pitched my voice to carry. "Master Sausagelicken, surely you know that if you are too far away to hear me die in ambush, I am too far away to do you any kind of good to prepare for said ambush?"

He colored at my jibe, but tried to ignore it as he pretended to think on that. "You have a point." He thought one more instant. "Do be a good chap and leave blood stains when you die."

"And you as well, since any group looking for this rabble is likely to let a single man pass and wait for the crowd of men before striking."

He thought about that, swishing it around in his mouth as if looking for a rotten taste. "Fine, take one of the boys."

"So your answer is to make me a more inviting target?" The boys heard that an perked up. "Fine, but you have to follow closely. If we are attacked it is the only sound you have that can warn you of what's coming."

But Alexander had already turned away. I was going to choose a lordling when one came up to me, picked by Schwartzklippen for some unholy reason of his own. Just looking the boy over, there seemed little wrong with the lad. I motioned to where Raina rode her (*MY*!) horse. "Turn over your horse and tie down all but the bare essentials to your saddle. Bring nothing that jingles, sloshes, or squeaks. A day's food and water will do."

Then, without any kind of malice or mischief, the boy shook his head and leaned closer, "WHAT?"

And I found the problem that Alexander Jaeger had mined my way with. It wasn't that the lordling was stupid; he was not. We finally left the group at a jog, but once we were able to slow down I was able to teach him silent hand signals very loudly. He caught on quickly. The only problem was there simply was no way to teach someone hard of hearing that he was making too much noise with his feet unless his feet be fitted with trumpets. His name was Hanner, and he was a new addition to Von Schwarzklippen's entourage. The latter, along with his penchant for yelling, were the reasons why he was given over to me.

Thankfully, the day passed uneventfully, and when we picked a spot for the night, Schwarzklippen only decided to go an extra quarter of a mile in the growing dark and then refuse to set sentries. I had a short argument with him, and was given Hanner again.

"Hanner has been on point all day, and is exhausted. We need–"

Alexander dismissed me with a generous wave. "Do you seriously think that someone could sneak into camp, undetected, kill any number of us without raising an alarm, and then escape? Preposterous!"

His last word was spit into my face. I turned to see all the lordlings in his command smirking at me, enjoying seeing me taken down yet another peg. My brain boiled behind my eyes, and I felt familiar stirrings of the Beast in my heart. I collected Hanner and set off. I pulled Raina, Hanner, and Hundeausführer into a small circle of brush, hacking one massive bush off at the base, drawing in the group into the hollow center, and rolling the thick foliage back into place. It was a perfect, if cramped, hiding spot for four. We laid out bedrolls and each went about their pre-bed business when I noticed Hundeausführer take out one fist sized bottle amongst three or four in his pack, unwrap the thick velvet cover, and unstop the cork. He dipped in a quill and allowed the nib to hover above his paper as he slowly turned his face to me and my psychotically bright smile.

"How many of those do you have?" I asked. At least one extra, as it turned out. And a brush.

I didn't trust Hundeausführer to stay awake if his life depended upon it, and it would since I would likely beat him to death for sleeping on watch. So Raina, Hanner, and I split the night. The night broke into dawn, and long before the others had woken, Raina and I were ready to do scout duty for the day. Hanner already had orders to stay close to Hundeausführer and make sure he survived.

My apprentice and I were already starting down the road when one of the lordlings awoke.

He rubbed his eyes, yawned, poked at a friend to get him moving. Poked again. Then he noticed the dark puddle beneath his partner's head. He reached around his friends neck and pulled back stained finger. His screams did the rest. Men of supposed noble blood awoke and saw dark blotches across the throats of friends and screamed, waking these men who saw their friends screaming with dark gashes across their throats. It was only moments before Alexander was on his feet, half the camp armed and yelping like scorched dogs.

"Crow!" he roared.

"Here, Alexander!" I called back from just down the road. "Getting an early start on scouting! See you at mid day!"

"You bastard, you did this!" His outraged words quieted the camp and focused them all on little old me.

I looked positively shocked and offended. "How dare you, sir! One might as easily say someone could have crept into camp last night and slit every one of your throats! Preposterous!" I roared, then added, "You have some dirt or something, right here, old chap." And I motioned to his throat.

He slapped himself there and his hand came away dark with watered down iron gall ink. I waved to him and scampered off, my work done.

Raina sighed loudly. I ignored her and we walked on in silence beneath the massive pine trees that made up the dark forests of Hammarfall. Then, again, the deep intake and loud exhale. We walked along and she scooped up a straight stick that made a fair walking staff, as thick around as the hole made by thumb and forefinger. It only occupied her for a few steps, then she drew her breath in again when I was forced to ask, "Something on your mind, Apprentice?"

But she answered much more like an equal. "Why must you antagonize him, Master?"

I answered in a manner I imagined some learned scholar would. "Because, my dear, when two large canines meet, they must know who it is that controls the pack."

"Can you not just spend time with your nose in his butt?"

"And you don't think that's what he wants?"

She huffed again, "But then one dog is going to die."

"Yes, but I cheat. So I will win."

She blinked at me. "I don't follow."

I nodded. "Fine, why did Von Sausagelicken show up late the first day?"

"To make the men hate you for moving them out early?"

I nodded again. "And why send me off too far ahead to help and stop without telling me, and refuse to set a night guard?"

"I can see he was trying to strip you of authority, but why–"

"And by painting their throats?"

"You showed them you could kill them all if you wanted to."

"No." Then I reconsidered. "Well, yes, and it helps me if they would remember that fact. But more than that, it showed they were vulnerable. It made them fear, and hopefully it will save this argument from happening every night and his lordship from expecting me to stand guard half of every night so his men can get beauty rest. The Rakes will remember this morning and set guard for me no matter what Alexander Jaeger Von Schwarzklippen says."

She thought about that for a bit, then, "I can't believe this is training for being a swordsman."

I sighed, a real, heartfelt, I Am Too Old For This, sigh. "Being a swordsman is not just about being a swordsman."

Raina laughed. "But of course! That's the egg of reason itself."

"Listen!" I snapped, perhaps a bit too harshly. "Being a sword for hire is that you are expected to solve problems. The trouble with that is eventually you run into one person who is too good for you, or two people almost as good as you, or three men who are not idiots, or a crowd of morons–"

"I understand, Master."

"Do you?" I asked incredulously. "Because the crossroads of the matter is this– matching force on force is wasteful. Better, far, to be cunning, resourceful, and smart. You still have these romantic notions of fighting fair when nobody else in the world will."

"I understand that when you speak about the Volker and his dregs, but there are still some honorable people in the world."

My shoulders sank as if under enormous strain and I shook my head. "Raina, firstly if your opponent were so honorable why would you battle them? Second, EVERYONE will drop the notion of fighting in any way fair if they think it would save them a splinter in the finger, let alone a spear in the eye."

"With all due respect, perhaps it is your training. You are a skulker, a sneakthief, a cutpurse, a pickpocket, and an…" she whispered, which was just adorable, "assassin."

I shrugged, "I always thought my methods were formed from being mortal, from having this annoying habit of bleeding while cut. Or shot with a crossbow. Now, we have ignored the world around us for too long. Let me teach you how to scout."

"Ignoring the world around us? You speak as if the whole world is trying to kill us."

"That is an excellent way to put it." I smiled at her ruefully.

She huffed. "You can't go through life acting as if–."

She set down the end of her walking staff ahead. The ground cover of dead pine needles erupted, there was a wooden crack and metal crash that rattled the bones. We both froze.

As if the jaws of some horrific beast, a huge metal spring loaded trap had shattered the end of her walking stick. Raina let out her breath in one, long stream and started to move.

"STOP!" I hissed. I put out one hand and she handed me the shortened stick. I scanned the ground carefully, then stabbed down beside her with a modicum of force. Again there was an iron thunderclap and the stick once again dissolved by the length of a forearm. "Let us…" I swallowed hard, "let us be patient and still for a moment."

And we stood there, on the road, thinking. Hard. As the whole world apparently now wanted us dead.

FIVE

TRAPS AND TRIGGERS

WE WERE exhausted and sweaty despite the cool air. Alexander and his cronies rode up, somehow amused at the whole deal. I flipped sweaty hair out of my face and watched them grimly. I was going to ask him what he thought was so funny when he said, "Whoa, ho, ho! Look at this, boys, the advantages of having an 'apprentice' are becoming all too clear."

I reached out and pulled at Raina, stopping her from running forward and killing Alexander. To hell with her, that was my job and it was not time yet. I motioned for her to get the traps and load them on the horse.

"Schwartzklippen, you disappoint me. I thought your little pig dick was already familiar with every one of your 'apprentices'. Why else all so young and supple?" I shot back, which deflated the enjoyment of his sycophants. As their leader's face screwed up into a retort, I picked up a shattered remnant of one of the sticks we had been working with (there were dozens about now) and shouted again, "So I wanted to ask how your plan for wasting time leaving, getting up late, and taking many breaks was working for you?"

"You lout!" he spat back. "My methods are my own and have carried us through dozens of adventures–"

I dropped the stick on a section of pine covered earth. It erupted with iron jaws, tossing debris high as the teeth shut murderously. It left a slightly ovoid dark patch on the road where it had been dug in, then lightly buried. Such a pattern was repeated for a hundred manlengths down the road in an almost random pattern. There had been over twenty of them. "My apologies for the interruption, your lordship. What is it you were saying?"

They were four manlengths away, but they still drew up short, just managing to avoid mating their horses' noses with their horses' chests.

Alexander was sweating into his neat beard and double chins already. "Is it safe?"

I shrugged. "Near as we can tell, yes. Still, it would be best to ride single file."

"You!" He pointed to me as if seeing me for the first time. "You will walk ahead of me as I proceed!"

Immediately, my temper seared to life. I walked up to one side of his horse, sheer malevolence leaking from me like an odor. Once there I kept my voice low, but the hatred that fueled the words burned them into the mind of every ear that caught them. "Understand this, simpleton, I have humored you until now, but this is no random occurrence. These iron traps are not rusted. They have not been in the moist soil more than a day. It is not a random trap laid by bandits and then abandoned. This was a deliberate attempt to hobble our group using sophisticated and expensive means. They also did not hover here to make good on their trap, so they must be ahead, waiting in ambush. Now unless you can convince me that your clownery ends at this very second, I have lost patience with you and will no longer put any effort into safeguarding your life."

I ended my tirade past the sailor/scholar/adventurer so that he had to turn in his saddle to see me. The shock of these words lasted for only two breaths. Then AJ Von Schwarzklippen's face screwed up into seething rage. "How DARE you?"

"Wrong answer," I replied, and slapped his horse on the rump.

I am not, all in all, a man who is cruel to animals. I also will not shy away from it if it means killing the rider. This was far more effective than either. The small barbed ring in my hand pricked the horse's rump, and thus spurred, it leapt forward into the field of iron potholes. Alexander screamed like a child, shrill wails reverberating past every tree as each hoof beat brought him further into the no man's land. Once through, the horse slowed to a trot, walk, and then a stop. Von Schwarzklippen dismounted like a cut sack and then recoiled from the ground as if it would bite. Then again, it might.

The lordlings did not laugh, did not cheer, only stared blankly at their castrated leader and then at me. "And that goes for the rest of you. I am not carrying you any further. Orders are given once, and ignored at your own peril."

It was at this time that Raina had collected Hanner, the disarmed iron traps, Hundeausführer, and the horses and were leading them single file across the contested area. I turned and, totally trusting my ability to sport these damned things which had been honed over the last hour, walked my own path across a different stretch. The men hesitated only a second before splitting into two groups. Some followed Raina, some myself. Halfway across I picked up two more forearm sized pieces of shattered log. One went into a hidden set of teeth, setting it off. The second I hung on to until we were almost on the other side.

There Von Schwarzklippen stood, his face rose red and heading toward purple. The weight of his anger ballooned him, and made his hair stand up from his skull, fighting whatever greases or glues held it into place. I wondered briefly whether this hollow crown was resisting his attack because he knew he would lose, or because he honestly thought I would win. He struck me as a man who only attacked when he grossly outnumbered his opponent, which normally I respected a great deal, but not when one puts on the airs of a duelist. I directed the lordlings to pass to one side of me so as not to come between Von Scarletlippen and myself. I dropped the log to my feet, reached into my pouch, and produced a sweetly sour green apple. The other hand wiggled in the air and summoned my shaving knife as if by magic. I sliced off a piece and popped it into my mouth, savoring the cool, juicy bite.

Men were still pouring around us when Von Schwarzklippen regained the power of speech. "I will leave your corpse along our path, foul creature."

"That shows a great disservice to a man who has saved you from harm and death. Step forward, then. I have heard you are a great swordsman. Let us see what your basket hilted slasher can do," I taunted. "Come along, then. I have only my knife drawn and you'd be hard pressed to find a better time to take me."

But there he stood, shaking and red. Impotent and unworthy.

I shook my head and the knife disappeared. "How about armed only with an apple?"

His words were distorted by clenched teeth, but he did not move as he hissed, "Your mother fornicates with animals."

I flipped a foot, tossing the log to my hand. I pointed at the fop, "My mother died when I was a boy, in a house fire. Father, as well. Burned to the ground by men who served a crown, probably men like you. Too busy burning and looting to fight on the front lines–"

Alexander roared at that last prick to his ego and reached for his sword. Before his steel could clear his sheathe, the log bopped him on the head. Much to my sadness, he staggered back into his horse and fell to his rump. "You are even too stupid to sense the simplest of ambushes. Do us a favor– drop your food, coin, and drink. Then make your way back to Hammarfall. You do us no good here."

I dropped the log into the space there had been between us, and a final set of iron teeth smashed closed. He gaped at the sprung trap, then met my eyes.

"And be assured. The next time I even sense I am being threatened by you, I will end you and send your head back as proof of your demise. Whatever vainglorious story we can muster may add to your legend, but not to your life."

And then, done, I reproduced the knife and started back in on the apple, cutting slices from the base up to consume the whole thing. I got four lordlings off their horses and sent them ahead to scout for more traps and the inevitable ambush. Von Scarletlippen hovered at the back of the group, sulking. I don't know why he was so down. I was finally in charge and that made me feel like humming a tune.

The day passed without incident. The forest began to thin and it opened up into an area where we could easily make a defensible rest. When we made camp, I did not have to set a watch, but I did have to alter it. The lordlings were used to the most powerful family names doing the least amount of work. I changed it so every man pulled his weight. I started with having them build a castra.

Castras were a Norian tradition from classical times. Soldiers would dig a trench, build a berm, sharpen sticks and mount them in the fresh soil, and generally make a makeshift fort at the end of every single day after a long march. So it was that any mount of fighting men had some kind of defense if raided during the night. The world was plenty full of foul fae and worse creatures that would pick them off, so I knew this to be a good idea. The amount of bellyaching that ensued was astronomical, but I cared little. Soon the soft-handed little lordlings were building their very first castra. It would not be the last.

This was done and rations were eaten. I noticed Blondie of the Broken Teeth and Von Swellednoggin glaring at me in what they thought was a covert manner and quietly talking. I would have to keep an eye on that.

The wind was picking up, and it did not bode well for a restful night. I set up a perimeter of guards and lit a timing candle. We covered the candle with a helmet, padding removed, taken from one of the boys and then tents were broken out. Two men to a tent, to make it harder to slit throats. Raina would stay with me. She could defend herself from rape, but I didn't need dead rapists. Outside, the watch was in full swing.

Every half candlemark, one lordling would go to bed, wake the next to take his shift. He would go relieve the first, who would have to circle camp and then relieve the next, who circled camp, and so on until the last man went to bed, waking the next in turn. The roving men kept the standing men from sleeping, and the standing men kept the holes between the roving men closed. It was a kind of arrangement I hated facing myself, and that was the best point of reference I could draw. As the first watch started, however, it began to rain.

Raina and I stripped to smallclothes and lay on our blankets. It was with the rhythmic pattern of large raindrops upon the cloth tent that finally lulled me to sleep.

I awoke with a mouth warm and wet against mine, a body pressed so close I could smell the feminine need for my touch. My eyes snapped open and it was, indeed Raina. I recoiled in shock and her eyes snapped open.

Then she punched me. Hard.

I could barely see past the twirling stars that blocked out most of the world as she fled the tent. I groaned and rolled into one corner, in quite a bit of pain, but still pleasantly surprised that while it sounded like heavy rain outside, it was dry along the inside of the tent. I take what victories I can get.

She was back as the pain settled into a low throb. She was soaked, even from just a few minutes out of the shelter, but she handed me a steaming wet cloth and sat in the corner of the small canvas house, refusing to look at me.

As long as she was dripping on her own stuff, I decided to take a few minutes to collect myself. I wiped at my face with the hot cloth. Even in the shadowy morning, I could see the dark stain on the linen. I could taste the copper in the back of my throat, so it was not a surprise. I squeezed at my nose, but felt no need to pass out, nor the crackling of soft bone.

"Is it broken?" she asked at last. I shook my head and wiped at a fresh drainage from my nose. "I'm sorry, I didn't mean to."

"Hell of an aim for an accident," I retorted quietly.

"I was having a dream. I didn't know it was you. It didn't mean anything."

I nodded, blowing out a clot from my sinuses into the cloth. "I get told that a lot."

Her shadowy face clouded over even more. "Don't make this difficult."

"Difficult? For you? Look, Apprentice, I can accept you don't love me. I can accept you don't lust after me. In fact, it makes my life a hell of a lot easier. On the other hand, for the sake of my sanity and equilibrium of my nostrils, next time you wake up, just finish the job or roll the hell over, would you?"

We stared at each other. One heartbeat. Two. Then she started to snort. "You are a troll."

"Witch," I retorted.

"Witch?"

"Bitch, then."

She threw something soft at me that smelled like it had spent the day in a boot. "I never promised you anything, Master Crow."

"No, I was there when I took you as apprentice, and I remember you promising to be the greatest pain in my ass of all time."

"So?" she sniffed.

I snorted out blood again. "Your aim is terrible."

"The targets are too much alike!" she protested around a smile.

And as we joked I began to understand that this, this is what she had always wanted. It wasn't to become the walking embodiment of sword wielding death. Nor was she wanting to become an assassin, or a hero. She had always wanted to be accepted as one of a group, to be really, truly treated as an equal, even if that meant being an apprentice. She was learning because she believed that the learning would garner her respect. I don't know if she had noticed, but most of the time all I could engender was fear. I had to convince her to give up this life, the way of the sword, before it killed her. Still, I was determined that in the morning we would continue her training, but the weather made a mockery of me.

The rain fell from the sky as if coming off a waterfall. All exposed dirt had become marshland, heavy and clinging to the foot. Even the grass managed to float the water on top of it, turning small depressions into fast moving streams. We dismantled camp. Someone had built up a lean-to over the low fire, allowing us to have kettles of hot tea. It was important for the majority of lordlings who did not dig a deep trench around their tent, as I had (well, as I had Raina do) to funnel rainwater away from the ground inside the shelter. Those men were wet, cold, and miserable. I earned no great love explaining how to avoid it next time, but when has the world been a fair place?

We ate cold rations again, gathered our gear, the tents, the sharpened poles we had cut from the forest and placed around the camp. It was grumbled at now, but would save us an hour setting up the next castra, and there would be another. We packed the poles onto the horses of the scouts foraging ahead. The roads were less paved this far from a city, and the horses struggled as they sank into the mire. It would not stop us, but we had to be careful, lest a horse topple and break a leg or its rider. It would eat into our travel time, and made me nervous. Men looked lovingly into the forest, for whatever dangers were there, they would have some sort of canopy and a thick carpet of pine needles to protect them from the mud. Had I been alone, that's where I would be, but we were far from civilization and I did not trust dead reckoning to get us where we needed to go.

We continued up into the hills to the next fork in the road. The forest continued to become heavier, but retreated from the road, allowing the full fury of nascent spring to fall upon us. The scouts were waiting at the fork in the road, little more than grey phantoms in the hurling rain.

I dared not bring my horse to a trot to hurry ahead, so we met the men as a cloud on the road. "What say you?"

This was one of the older, wiser lordlings. I had still not bothered to learn their names, only attitudes. He was still a fool, but a fool who could see when he needed to follow orders, and that pleased me enough to make him head of the scouts. He reported, "Ahead the forest reswallows the road. There's a white rope tied at neck height ahead."

"A white rope?" Alexander exclaimed.

I ignored him. "What did you do?"

The scout shook his head. "Nothing, Master Crow. You said to wait for you."

"As I did. Well done. Any signs of men in the woods?" He shook his head. "Lead on, then."

I called for bows, and the two men who had them produced them. Raina rode up to me but I shook my head. Not only was I not going to lend a bow to the lordlings, I was not going to use my own. I needed to concentrate on any ambush from the perspective of getting out, not fighting from within.

We traveled at a piteous slog for another half candlemark until we reentered the bosom of the woods itself. The trunks of trees marched closer as if an army encroaching upon us. The tracing of pine boughs above condensed into a lattice that further closed into a complete roof. Though it blocked out almost all the light, all it could do to the deluge from the heavens was concentrate it into areas of dry followed by icy streams out of the blackness. It had the unsettling quality of a cave, without the safety of having solid walls people could not fire arrows through.

The horses were wheezing, the sound of their steps slowing though the ground was dryer here. All of this could not provide enough distraction to keep me from noticing the wrist thick, bleached, white rope that was strung at neck height across the road. I trotted my tired mount up to it, and examined it closely. It was bowed not at all, and while it was positioned to either break the neck of a man on a galloping horse, or forcibly dismount a man and kill him with the fall, It was far too thick, and white, to hide. I ducked under the rope and followed the path of it where it disappeared into the forest on one side and terminated in one of the largest pines I had ever seen on the other. On instinct I reached out, and the rope was pulled so taut it might as well have been a metal pole.

"We don't have time for–" Alexander drew his sword.

"STOP!" I screamed. Actually stopping him against all odds. More calmly I motioned to everyone. "Dismount, walk your horses under. Do not touch, cut, or molest that rope." I motioned to Hanner. "Come with me."

My reins were tossed to one scout while Hanner and I disappeared into the dense growth at the edge of the road. It took only a moment before we cut our way through the screening underbrush back to the rest of the men.

I went to my horse without hesitation, but one of the other lordlings approached Hanner. Hanner, hard of hearing as he was, answered a quiet question with his usual parade ground voice, "There are three, thick trees cut almost through and leaning toward the road. If you cut the rope, they come crashing down. Would have killed some of us for sure, and lamed most of the horses."

Again, the lordlings looked to me as if I were something special as I mounted up. I wish I could delude myself, but I knew it would not last with this lot. We left the white rope behind, but soon had to make camp anyway. We had only gone half a day, but the horses were exhausted.

Again we set out watches, a berm, a trench, spikes, and tents. The rain had relented to a light patter but I noticed everyone still carved a trench around them tonight. At the edge of my mind, I could hear notes being played to a symphony that was not there. It was just a trick of the mind, a call to something more civilized from a man stuck in the wild. Yet, the notes spoke of danger, waryness, and made me uncomfortable. Once inside the tent, I gave orders. Raina and I went to work with a short shovel. We dug down three handspans, collected the dirt and reinforced the trench around the tent, and then spread out our equipment. I put up my shield at the head of the tent, and hers at the foot, laying packs, saddles and so forth so they were just shy of touching the cloth. It left a very nice sink in the center for us to lay in, and be beneath the level of the ground. There was a chance it would flood in the night and soak us, but as long as the pool was not blood, it would be worth it. It was to her credit that Raina waited until we were done before asking, "What exactly are we doing?"

The notes shivered. I shrugged. "I have a bad feeling."

"I understand. I don't like the wet or the dark, either."

It wasn't the closeness of the forest, nor the chill of the rain. I shook my head. "How long could those Dwarvish bear traps held us up for?"

She thought about it. "Minutes to forever."

"Right, but unless we had significant losses, a few hours. Only if we had been cantering the horses like idlepate morons–"

"Like our Sir Lordship Von?"

I nodded. "Like him, then we would have lost many men. Probably turned back."

"But we saw it. What is your worry now, Master?"

I hesitated, but just for a second, "Those dwarvish contraptions probably cost a few gold coins each. That is a lot of money, especially when added up. Now the tree trap, a trap within a trap. Ride into it and get knocked over backwards–"

"Cut it and half the forest falls in on you," she finished.

I met her eyes. "Whoever is out there is well funded, highly educated, and resourceful." I started to make for the flap at the foot of the tent. "Come on."

Her shoulders slumped. "What now?"

"Now we teach them not to leave their toys laying around."

She, Hanner, and I completed the job quietly, with some instructions on concealment and stealth, and returned to the camp with the explicit instructions that no one goes past the line of spikes for any reason. Then Raina and I stripped off our sodden wet clothes, hung them from the central pole of the tent to dry as they might. I smiled not because she stripped in front of me, but because she did it without even noticing.

I lay out my sword for easy reach, took Richter's white bow from its protective tube, oiled the wood, waxed the cord, oiled the sword. My apprentice did as well, prepping her captured crossbow, setting out ammunition, oiling weapon before resting.

Finally, the music faded away. I pulled on breeches and was asleep before I lay back upon my pack. Raina chose some hose and a longshirt before following suit. I should know, for it was only a handful of candlemarks later that we were awakened by the mechanical sound of iron slapping iron and a long, pitiful scream. I awoke at the first hint of a sound, and then winced as a hole appeared in both sides of the tent at once.

Without a word, I threw myself on my apprentice, keeping us both down in the three handspan deep hole that took up the whole floor of the tent. Men screamed and more holes appeared above, but my ruse had worked. The raised level of dirt on all sides combined with the lowered floor had bolts screaming above us. They were not far above us, but any miss was a good miss for the fox or hare.

There was a pause and the two of us bolted for the exit of the tent. Bows in hand, ammunition slung hastily on, we were fighting nearly naked in the night. Four guards lay dead, five were wounded, and two more lordlings had sat up or exited their tents to become crossbow fodder. Eyes as adjusted to the night as any, I fired at moving shadows in the forest, eliciting screams and cries. A man had found a good firing spot I had noted last night. From within a dark cloak he was aiming at me. Raina took a shot at him and, while it went wide, he dove to the side out of an abundance of caution. He hit the ground and it erupted in metal fury, closing about his chest and letting him die a slow, suffocating death.

More men on all sides were coming out of their tents, but to little avail. I shot once more, but Raina continued to pull back the heavy string on the guardsman's crossbow and fire at what she saw as suspicious. I tossed my bow and quiver into the tent, retrieved a dark brown cloak, shield, and the Angel, then motioned to Hanner and Raina.

We returned with the expensive iron traps we had collected from the first roadside waylay. Four were bloody. We also returned with four-and-a-bit bloody copses. It took Raina and Hanner several trips, and meanwhile I had the boys stoke up the fire, oil up the traps, and take out a huge fabric tarp from stores and raise it on the provided poles. I even had them venture out and crack open some fallen logs and axe out the dry innards so we could have burning fuel. Then my minions set the four and change corpses down, and I squatted to remove all bolts and arrows and then look at them closely.

The first was a deer, at the wrong place and the wrong time. It had caught one of Raina's spare bolts. Its presence was significant. We had been quiet, tired, and a half dozen paces off. No shock that a gentle animal of the forest would come by. Now, our attackers had been much closer to it, had even passed it in the night, and still had not disturbed the doe. I had a lordling gut, dress, and start to roast the beast over the fire.

Alex, still dressed in his night shirt with hair all a tussle, stood by one corner of the cover. "What are you doing, necromancer? Think they still have some secrets to tell?" I started to undress the first corpse which elicited, "Oh, so this is a quest for personal satisfaction. Too bad there are no walls to this tent. Still, should we leave to give you some privacy, Master Crow?"

I did not pause, did not raise my voice. I picked up a used and bloody bolt and gripped it in my fist. "Von Schwarzklippen, what exactly are you?"

The lordling straightened immediately and put his hands on his hips, face reddening. "What do you mean?"

"Well, I'm guessing that if you had a sir, or a price, or a baron, or anything like that you would use it until people's ears fell off. And since you don't..."

Alexander reached down and wrenched me to my feet. "How dare you, you common, fatherless– *squeak*!"

He did not actually say squeak, he just did it. I could understand, he wrenched me to my feet, and then there was a jab in his genitals. The sharp pain was easily explained. I was holding the point of the bolt I had taken from the stomach of a dead man and now pressed against him with just shy of the pressure needed to break skin.

I do a very nice calm voice. It is even, it is soothing. It is terrifying when I am doing something violent like pricking someone's privates with the razor head of a bloody crossbow bolt. I tried that voice now. "I am sorry Alexander Jaeger, was there something you needed?"

"Eeeeeeeeeee–" was all he managed, eyes rolling and wide.

"Well, it seems you have a hold of the front of my shirt." I pressed a smidge harder. "I can't go anywhere unless you let me go."

He let go, continuing the irritating whine, "Eeeeeeeee–"

"Now I'm going back to work. Is there anything else you need Alexander Jaeger? Any further comments you want to make?" I asked, twisting the bolt slightly.

"Eeee-heeeeeeee-heeee–" No, he wasn't laughing, but instead starting to cry.

"Then, go back to bed, and leave the real work to the rest of us." And I removed the sharpened piece of filthy metal.

Alexander bolted for his tent as if his nut sack were bleeding, which it probably was. I made a mental note to kill him, despite how many men we had lost.

Now there were less than twenty fully battle ready men. Worse, the corpses were telling me nothing useful. They were in great shape, with good teeth and no obvious ailments. Good hair, only slightly greasy, which means it had been washed within a week. The clothes were high quality and sturdy, as were the boots. They had no money on them, the swords were better steel than most, as were the daggers, but none bore the mark of a blacksmith. The crossbows were war bows, and had been fired indiscriminately at all the tents and anything coming out of them. With the rain there were few ways to tell how many there had been, but the number had been sizable.

Most interestingly was the last corpse and the partial. The last corpse seemed to be the first man to find a jaw trap. It closed over his leg and nearly severed it. He was not instantly killed, though he would be touch and go without a healer. But, instead of call to his comrades to carry him, he had slit his own throat.

I've been around and I can tell you that slitting-one's-own-throat dedication to a leader or cause is very, very rare. Of more import was the partial corpse– the arm. Someone had scrambled up a muddy slope to a firing position on hands and knees. The hand had set off the trap and taken the arm. It was the arm of an older man. More telling, according to the deep indentations at the base of the fingers, this one usually had a fist full of rings on at any given time and had done so for at least a decade. He had not brought them to the raid, which hurt a little. *If you are going to force me to kill you, at least provide some practical monetary reward.*

Practically, however, it put throat slitter in even more glaring light. The arm man was not abandoned, which meant he was of more importance, or our attackers would care for one of their own. Not brigands. Not barbarians. These were civilized men.

Which goes to show how exhausted I was. Sleeping light, waiting for a dagger thrust from one imbecile or another, was beginning to take its toll. I am certain that is the reason I missed the obvious.

We distributed the crossbows amongst the lordlings that said they could use them, but I doubted their word. They went to Alexander in order to ask what to do with the dead. In retrospect, it was a good idea, since I would have buried them where we stood like commoners, and that was sure to offend someone.

They were sending the wounded back with the dead. I left such noble details to the nobles. We were left with eighteen men, including Hanner and Broken Tooth, to continue toward the Opus Discordia. It did us little good. Hundeausführer, tiny muscled, very much a weasel but honest and quiet for all that, had taken a bolt to the face and was quite dead.

SIX

THE GHOSTS OF THE PAST

THERE WERE two announcements that turned my guts and made me want to do Alexander Jaeger Von Schwarzklippen serious and lasting bodily harm. The first was his proclamation that Hundeausführer should be buried here, rather than taken back. The second was that he would personally see the wounded back to Hammarfall.

The first drew the protest of three: myself, Raina, and Hanner. The second upset the whole lot of them. Von Sneakingoff tried to calm the crowd, to put his sacrifice in the brightest light, but even his most sycophantic saw right through that. So Von Sneakingoff was here to stay, which I can't say I was thrilled with. To his credit however, as the rain continued to build back into a deluge that came down in buckets, he managed to not only avoid digging any part of Hundeausführer's grave, but succeeded in getting himself done up in the frilliest shirt and pants he could manage, with soft boots with the massive turned down cuff. I don’t know where he thought he was going, but I bet it involved sails, anchors, and probably a cabin boy. He then prayed lengthily, piously, and loudly. Mostly loudly. He also limped slightly, and pulled at his crotch a lot, so I smiled to know that some of his actions had consequences.

We lowered Hundeausführer's body into the pool that would be his grave, watching the water swallow him before he ever hit bottom. Then we slung the mud back into the hole, covering him for eternity as we collected our goods and made off. Von Schwarzklippen rode at the front, as if to leave behind the responsibility of the dead men he was sending off in care of the wounded.

Raina came to stand beside me and watch them go. "Where are they going?"

"Sneakingoff did not say, but I think he's sending them back to his 'secret path' into Hammarfall docks."

"But we were nearly hung by that route. What if they get caught?"

"Dead," I replied matter-of-factly.

"They took Hundeausführer's pony with them." Soft words, easily delivered that threatened to start me in on a monstrous tirade. She forestalled the inevitable battle by passing to me a small oiled leather satchel of books. "These were the most often read. I hope they will help."

"You can read?"

"No, but you can."

And she was right. It was an odd skill to have, but necessary in the way I used to work. See, an assassin does not read. No need. But a nobleman reads, part and parcel of growing up. So if you are an assassin that wishes to pass for a noble, you need to be able to read and write classical tongues, as well as modern script. It cost me a handful of silver and a summer to learn at the feet of a drunk and broken syphilitic monk. It had earned me thousands of coins more than I spent, but would do me less than no good in the rain. A mournful tune began in my head, and it ran for days.

The fire would not stay lit, and the deer refused to cook. The lordlings cut up the meat, hoping to cook it tonight. We packed up the camp, again including the iron jaws and wood spikes despite the complaining. For four more days we ate cold rations and wound up tossing the deer meat. The loss of the fresh deer was a major blow to morale, but the smell coming from the meat left no doubt that it was inedible except in the most desperate circumstances. Still the music invaded me, and seemed to sap my strength along with the wet and the cold. On the morning of the fifth day, we were coming out of the pine woods. Unfortunately, my skin felt hot, my head buzzed, and the world looked distorted. The only clarity was the ghost symphony that played for me alone. I was definitely sick. Everyone avoided me lest it spread, and that was fine for me.

Again, a cold breakfast and on the road, up into the mountains. The forest became sparse again, and retreated from the road. The rain was still slammed into us out of the heavens, but we made much better time as the roads became rocky.

Though the mud had been washed away, leaving only smooth rocks and pebbles behind, the way had become steep. There was no place to stop and rest, so we had a cold lunch in the saddle, and continued on our way. Soon, we could see the scouts slowing down ahead as the sky robbed them of warmth and strength. The horses were no different, and their pace slowed. I dismounted, and several others followed suit. Alexander Jaeger stubbornly remained in the saddle, his mount becoming more and more tired as we climbed onto the base of the mountain.

I turned back, looking for the endless deep green carpet of trees extending to infinity, perhaps with just a coy sparkle of sea in the far off line where land met sky. Not so, for the torrential rain blotted out everything but the world just around us.

Then, a cry from ahead. A ragged cheer went up from the men. What conversations there were just got swallowed by the rain, but there appeared ahead two, huge, square glowing eyes. Despite myself I smiled, for those two lighted window panes meant warmth, comfort, and for the first time in days, being dry. Men were already starting to pile into the building, and an incoherent, bestial roar, my own, was required to being them back to the cloud of horses tied up in the rain. Once again, they moped like spoiled children as we brought the horses into the large stable to the side of the inn. There were only a pair of broken down nags inside, obviously owned by the stable itself as work animals, so there was plenty of space to board every single mount we brought with room to spare.

This was just like all kinds of inns found out in the wild places of the world. They lived on the purses of caravans and travelers, spaced so far that by the time customers arrived, they barely noticed the massive prices and bland fare. After a week on the road, anything but water was sweet, and any warm food was heavenly. The only difference was that this one was full. There were already ten men inside, talking low and drinking by themselves. Alexander was first inside. I tried not to care, I swore I didn't care. Then I just swore and stomped back outside, stabled Alexander's poor horse that had been wandering in the rain. I removed the saddle, then searched through the bags quickly until I came up with a small purse of gems hidden in the heel of a boot. Taking these as payment, I replaced the heel and the boots, slinging the entire sodden saddle mass over the stable wall like the others. Only then could I enter the warm inn.

The lordlings had made themselves at home. It was only barely past noon, but it was obvious we were going nowhere the rest of the day. Already the party was starting, and coins were changing hands at an alarming pace. Immediately, I noticed the ten men spread around, ignoring the boys. That was nothing suspicious. I would have ignored them to death if I thought it would work. The music buzzed at me, biting at the inside of my skull and begging me to pay attention. Instead I was distracted by days of cold and wet. Then Alexander made a scene with the innkeep. "How *dare* you? Move one of these ruffians and open the room for me!" There just had to be classes in being a selfish prick that get handed out to nobles.

To his credit, the innkeep stood firm. "There are no rooms! You must take the stables! One silver per man, two silver per horse!"

Alex spouted off in classical, a line from a classic play I could not place, "*The Innkeep is a dog and should be put down.*"

But the innkeeper responded with another line, "*This prince vexes me and needs a proper spanking.*" Which drew laughter from the other travelers in the room.

Alex Jaeger began on another tirade, but I slapped him on the shoulder and forced him to sit. My other hand slapped a messy pile of coins onto the bar. "Men and horses. Meat and bier and horse feed?"

The man hesitated a second, then nodded. I lifted my hand to free the silver and left, Alexander's murderous gaze upon me. My head swam with fever, so I stopped only by Hanner. "Make sure the horses are fed." He smiled at me and lifted his mug, but I snatched at his sleeve, my face serious in the way only a drunk, the fevered, or a madman can be. "Do not drink more than this! Keep your wits!" I hissed.

Hanner was, after all, one of the Rakes, and he was shocked, then started to frown in a pout like any of them would. Laughter at the table beat at me, pounded at the gates of my mind so I staggered outside into the icy rain. It felt wonderful upon my overheated body, washing away the sticky sweat and sickly heat. Only then, I began to shiver violently. I positively dove into the barn, but even half mad, my instincts did not desert me, and I pulled my equipment up the tortuous ladder into the loft. I picked the farthest corner, barely managed to unroll my bedclothes and fall asleep.

My dreams were paranoid, too close and at odd angles to reality. *Crows watched me like the towers of churches, bearing the same judgmental eyes. I was flanked by watchmen holding my chains. Not watchmen– they were knights. They walked me through streets that became a castle corridor. I was marched outside to the gallows. The crowd cheered my demise while ravens lined the top of every wall, watching. The executioner grabbed my face and shoved it through the noose.*

But as I passed into the noose, I was no longer on the gallows. I was in the inn. Everything was frozen in a moment of time.

Ten men. Ten men. Ten men going nowhere. Asking no questions about the news of the capital. No insignia of the Volker or the king. None sneering at or joining in with the gambling, drinking, or singing of the Rakes. I have found that there are two reactions to a party like ours, get angry it is going on or join in. The number of people who will just ignore it is infinitesimal, and ten of them at once is beyond belief. I walked amongst the frozen party, moving louts aside as I stared into the chiseled faces of the ten men. They each had swords, and long daggers. Nothing suspicious about that. Only sword and long knife personally makes me naked. Yet...

I turned around and faced the stables, our horses frozen in their stalls. The roof erupted upwards in a swirl of crunching hay. Ravens circled everywhere. In their eyes was further damnation. One bird, the size of a horse, landed so close I could feel the heat of her beating heart. My face was wrenched skyward, and the bird opened its beak above me, as if to clip off my head with one snap. Instead, hot warm mush slid into my open mouth.

I startled awake, Raina's strong arms holding me in place as I thrashed and my stomach roiled. Her worried face became pained as she pushed me down, and it was only then I recognized the taste of the vegetable porridge in my mouth. I started to swallow, fought against a spasm in my stomach, and swallowed the fairly tasteless garbage. I stopped struggling. She met my eyes and relief came flooding in.

She whispered, "I was wondering if you would wake up sane or not. You fever broke hours ago, but you have been thrashing in your sleep like a tormented soul."

I pitched my voice low as well, "What candlemark is it?"

She shrugged, "Probably three candlemarks past dusk. The last of Alexander's lords staggered in and have fallen asleep."

Then it all came back– ten men… the stables… "Alexander?"

"He complained until they gave him a room inside."

I shook my head. "Of course they did." *You are on your own, fool.* "And Hanner?"

Raina's brow furrowed. "He's holding a grudge. After so long on the road being told to only have one stein was emasculating, and he's pretty angry. If I didn't have a sick master to coddle myself I would have–"

I started to struggle to my feet. "Get him. Get all the crossbows and bolts. Do it quickly and quietly. Go!"

And, thankfully, she did. I had time to bolt down the vegetable gruel to settle my empty, aching stomach. Then I pulled out three bits of equipment I had hope to never have use for. I pushed the door to the loft open just a fraction of a fingerwidth. The rain had stopped, but thunderclouds roiled overhead. One could not see them for the thick fog that erupted from the ground like a demon's curse, but you could hear the distant rumbles coming closer.

Hanner was yawning and looking at me with no great love when I produced a piece of charcoal and cleared a section of straw from the floor.

Can you read?

Hanner nodded.

Do not speak! This is what you must do…

I whispered the plan to Raina as I wrote it down and both nodded understanding. She shook her head. "What will you do?"

Out of my pack I pulled out a small gray satchel. From it I withdrew a host of ripped, torn, irregular cloths in various shades of gray.

***

Outside, the problems were obvious.

Three to five days of hard rain had soaked into the wood of the stable, swelling the boards. This meant the easy answer, block the doors and burn the drunk men inside, was out. The wood was too wet to burn reliably and would at least allow us time to assemble and charge out. What they could do, however, was open the doors, toss four or five flaming pots inside, and *then* block the doors. The wooden frame was wet, the straw inside was not. They knew where men would be sleeping because they knew which end of the stable housed horses and where the bales of hay were stacked. The fire would kill some, panicked horses would kill a few more, and the smoke would finish the rest. Any that made it out would be cut down by crossbow fire.

It was a neat, easy plan. This was critical, because ten men have to move as a unit to pull this kind of thing off, and everyone must be crystal clear on the plan for two reasons. Firstly, they would be unable to speak for fear of alerting one of their prey. If the drunks could get awake and mobile, they could attack. Outnumbered two to one, even against drunks, meant more men had to die. Second, more than a dozen paces away they would not see each other in the opaque fog. More than half a dozen paces, it would be impossible to tell who was who. They had to stay close, and not lose each other, lest they start firing on one another in the gloom.

No, everyone had a position and they knew it. One man on the north side of the stables to block the door with the bar and then watch the loft door with a bow. Nine men to throw open the door, toss in the jars of burning sludge, and then to fire in shifts into the opened doors of the stables until it was forced closed and braced against a charge. It was a nice, neat plan.

Then I came along.

They spread out from the building, footsteps nearly inaudible in the fog. From the roof I could see one, barely an outline of a man, break off and circle around back. I could hear him setting the bar across the back exit to the stables. He drew his sword and waited.

Not now. Not now.

At the other end, nine men were making ready more complex means of death. Almost invisible in the night, they had thought to use their windlasses inside the inn to cock the heavy crossbows. Now they padded out, loading heavy thick bolts onto the strings. They lined them up on the ground, bolt facing down, stock resting on a small Y-shaped iron fitting driven into the ground. In this way three men had twelve crossbows to fire, one after another, before they had to touch a windlass to begin reloading. Two had sword and shield, and prepared silently for whoever might make exit. Two others opened clay pots of heavy oil topped with alcohol and jammed thick rags down the tight necks. Two men wordlessly padded to the doors and took the heavy latches in their hands.

Not now.

Though now it was easy to tell what was happening in retrospect, at the time, in the fog, it was devilishly difficult to tell what they were doing. My heart pounded in my chest like a caged animal, and my hands were sweaty on my weapon. My recently fevered muscles felt oddly heavy, yet empty. I wanted to sleep or kill. The leader, only distinguishable from his hand movements, signaled the last man who came forth with a shuttered lantern. Of course a lantern, for a stray wind might blow out a candle, and they must not have had a torch at hand. I stifled a snort. The lampman went to the middle of the two firepot-men. They came forward with the rags of their firepots, which sprang to beautiful life the second they touched the lamp wick. One firepot wielder swept his bottles together, lighting them all. The other hefted one and lit a second, but let the others be. In either case, they were the only shapes now easy to pick out in the gloom.

The leader motioned. The shieldmen moved ahead of the crossbowmen, just behind and inside the firepot throwers. The shieldmen knelt to be out of the way of the bolts, and the leader signaled for a charge.

Which, was their first mistake.

The doors swung wide, groaning like all the victims of murder, and the firepot throwers reached far back, though a simple toss would have done.

That was their second mistake.

The soft leather grip of Richter's white recurve bow molded to my fingerprints. I knocked an arrow and drew back the string to my lips. I could hear his voice, repeated often during the long winter, *Not where the arrow is, but where it will be. Not where the target is, but where it will be. Where those two collide, is where you aim.*

But my target was stationary, and at close I could spit upon him from the peak of the stable roof. That was fine by me; I'll take easy any way I can get it.

Then the first set of bolts leapt through the dark doorway. Not in, but out.

Inside, sixteen drunk, sleeping men were laid out in the stable paddocks. In the center, behind stacked bales of hay, were Raina and Hanner. They fired the two light crossbows we had first, and as told, picked the most obvious targets, the fire throwers. With globes of burning brightness in their fists, they were easy to see. One crumpled and dropped his pot to his feet. It ruptured and turned him into a pillar of flame, sending the second pot to join its comrade. The other thrower fell over in a wave, the bottle of oil rolling along the ground to the foot of the rightmost shieldman, who ignored it.

The bowmen were shocked for half a second, which is what I wanted, because I desperately needed to kill their leader. Two shafts, one and then the another, pierced his back as he sat hunched below the firing level of the bows. If not down, he was out, and I switched to one of the bowmen.

The crossbowmen fired, but were doing so blindly, and practice told them to aim at chest height. Of course everyone was laying down sleeping or crouched behind cover, so the bolts should go high. *Should.*

With no way to tell, I fired on. I hit the left bowman, who collapsed and set off his crossbow into the thigh of his closest shieldman. One doorman ran forward into a pool of flame to snatch at an unbroken firepot. Raina or Hanner cut him down as soon as the pot moved.

This was not a hunt, it was a culling. At these distances it was not so much shooting as it was a knife fight with projectiles. Another doorman ran for a fallen bowman and I shot the firepot burning at the foot of the shieldman as they passed close. They both were set alight. I shot the shieldman twice before one of the two below could use the windlass to crank the string back, load a bolt, and put the dancing pillar of fire out of his misery.

I turned and padded for the far end. There, the sentinel waited patiently, ignoring the screams of the dying. There were supposed to be screams. He ignored the bowfire, there was supposed to be bowfire. He ignored the dying because, until the arrow transfixed him just below the neck, he had no idea who was being sent to hell.

Without pause, I slid down the roof and hit the rain softened ground with a roll. Then I was up on my feet, discarding bow and arrows as I made the front door to the inn. I entered cautiously, and the place was lit, the equipment needed to prepare for the ambush spread out amidst the wreckage of the party a few hours before.

I heard a soft voice from the second floor, and I looked leerily at the stairs. There was no time to probe cautiously; I had not had time to scout and determine which steps were loud, and which were solid. But, as I had been taught, stealth was not about being silent all the time, it was about blending in to what the ear expected to hear. Though I had soft boots on, I brought my muddy feet down in a calm, easy rhythm on the steps, a slight bit too hard to mimic hard soled boots.

I got to the top, where only one door was open and a candle burned within. A calm, cultured voice spoke. "And it looks like your quest is at an end, Alexander Jaeger Von Schwarzklippen. The mysteries of the Magnum Opus Discordia will remain untapped for all time." Therein was the useless Alexander Jaeger, not even tied to a chair. Tears and snot were encrusted on his face around a gag, and at least one of his fingers had been snipped off. Not that I don't think having a finger lopped off is anything painless, but I flatter myself to think I would have to be tied down before they could attempt it. There were crude torture devices everywhere, none used but maybe the club and snips. The educated voice belonged to one armed man who hovered over the recoiling Schwarzklippen with a small knife. I stepped into the room. " Are there any survivors to...?"

The rest of the question went unasked. Swathed in tied rags from charcoal to off white, spattered in mud from my fall, I must have looked like a wraith from beyond the grave. I pulled the mask down to expose my smiling face, at contrast with the blackened shortsword in my hand, "Just you." And my eyes trailed down to the bloody stump of an arm wrapped in a fresh bandage. I remembered the ringless fingers back at the camp. "I would shake your hand, but I seemed to have left it back in the bear trap."

The one armed man was pale from blood loss days before, but now became positively blue with fear. At a suggestive motion of my sword tip, he dropped the knife. I looked about the room and chuckled, "How convenient. I appear to be in the correct place for me to ask you some questions."

The older man drew himself up and held his head high as he steeled himself for what he thought was to come. Hell, what I thought was to come. What I didn't think was to come was the man saying, "A member of The Redemptive Order will never–"

I assumed what he was going to say was give up our secrets. Or perhaps, break under torture. Or even, be able to keep our mouths shut if you give us spun sugar treats. Sadly, we will never know, for now that he was perfectly safe, Alexander Von Schwarzklippen sprung into action. He grabbed the club from next to his chair and swung it with all his considerable weight behind it, focusing the blow from the last fifth of the club onto the crown of our prisoner's head.

I realize my life is gruesome even at the best of times, but nothing very dramatic happened. There was a blood spot on the club, and on the crown of the corpse, but there was no doubt what fell to the floor was nothing but a body. If you were unschooled, the reflexive shivering of a body without a brain attached would be clue enough. Alexander Von Schwarzklippen hit him twice more until the face was nothing but caseless sausage meat. I stared at the plump moron in shock and loss.

"What?" he screamed at me, a question and an accusation. "Look! Look what they did to me!"

And he held up his mangled hand.

But I was already thinking ahead, and sent my feet screaming back down the stairs, outside to–

"All dead, sir!" Hanner shouted with a tired salute. The lordlings had awakened drunk and scared, soon to become drunk and angry at the attempt on their lives, and had bravely stabbed any wounded prisoners to death just as they had been taught by their hero: Alexander Jaeger Von Schwarzklippen.

The oil burned for a good long time, but ultimately came to naught. The bodies told me nothing, other than twelve men aged twenty to forty had ambushed us in the woods, and had waited here for us to slaughter us like pigs. More curiously, in the root cellar, we found the body of the innkeeper. He had been tied up, and his gag placed on too tightly. He had vomited, and chocked to death on his own fluids but it did not look intentional. They, who would kill us in our sleep, had tried to spare this man.

I ordered him buried, but they just burned him along with our attackers. It would not be the first failed order, for now that they had access to all their money, extra coin from the ambushers, and now free alcohol, they were all but unstoppable. It was barely dawn and they were breaking windows to let out the heat as they burned every log the inn had managed to save over the winter. They scraped mold from meats in the cellar and barely roasted them before devouring them en masse. It was like watching a pack of dogs with a found corpse. Actually, I think it had even less dignity.

Raina found me outside, trying not to fume too badly at the useless and wanton destruction. She sat next to me and sighed. "What now?"

I shrugged. "At this rate they will burn through the stores in ten hours. Then they sleep. Maybe tomorrow they will be ready to ride again. Make sure Hanner only indulges and doesn't drink himself stupid. We may need him if the rest of our enemies circle back around."

There was a trace of panic in her voice. "Rest of our enemies?"

I snorted, a single aborted laugh, and motioned to the stables. "Where do you think their horses went? It was the one thing that made me certain they were not tradesmen of some kind– no horses or pack animals to carry goods. No, this was a scout group meant to delay us, or stalk us, and kill us if possible. Another, bigger party is somewhere out there." Raina cursed bitterly. "Exactly." I replied. "Worse, all our attackers were killed. We know what they want to do to us, but not why."

We sat in sullen silence for a long time, then Raina shook her head as if attacked by a fly and said simply, "Maybe it is in Hundeausführer's journal?"

I turned to her, proud of her memory and a little ashamed of my own. There had been no time on the road to get dry enough to read. Now, however, it looked like I had almost a day to look over the books Raina had lifted from the scholar's collection.

The inn was an impossible ruckus of noise. In one corner, the lordlings had raised Alexander upon a chair set onto a table. He stoically glared at me, his stained traveling clothes changed for his reserved finery of velvet and silk. His injured hand was displayed like the tooth mark of a dragon. It appeared that he surveyed the room like a sovereign, the Rakes serving his every whim without question. I slid through the crowd to the kitchen. I found some food and candles. Then I slid black out the door and to the abandoned stables.

The bodies of the poor innkeeper and our twelve attackers had burned for hours. Now they just smoked on the only unsheltered dry spot for leagues in any direction. It would not last long. Angry thunderheads were already coming over the mountains like an invading horde. Spears of lighting lit them up briefly before being swallowed by the rioting tumult.

I went into the barn, fed and watered Raina's nameless nag and crawled into the loft. I cleared an area of hay, painstakingly and carefully lit the candles, and spread out the contents of Hundeausführer's satchel. The older books, read over and over by the conditions of the pages, were strange. Each was an examination of the life of the most moving and prolific musical artist of all time: Annalirya Von Zeitheim, Enchantress of Strings, The Burning Composer, Mother to the Magnum Opus Discordia. I started to read one, but the tone was all wrong. The man was accusatory, almost abusive. The book opened with a scandalous rumor about Annalirya pretending to surrender to an invading force, then poisoning the five hundred men at a massed feast. Then she stripped them of their skin, using the skin for drums, and tendons for strings. All of her instruments were inlayed with their bones. All the while she made them scream in musical tones. I tossed it aside wondering why Hundeausführer would bother with such garbage.

Next was a loving treatment of the great lady. It described her manor, where we were heading, and a few tales of woe and struggles overcome, but then dissolved into a treatise on her music alone. I set this aside as well.

Next was a dire warning to the examples set by the Burning Composer. But the whole thing was mathematical examination of her work, showing mystic numbers woven into her timing and tone. *Whatever that could mean.* I tossed it aside as well.

Losing patience with dense tomes of lies and professorial sophomoric pedantry, I picked up the much newer, far more paged through, handwritten journal of Axel P Hundeausführer.

It was all here, dissected and digested into a form I could understand. There were notes on the fantastic myths told by jealous critics to shun the lady. The precise location of the lady's castle was noted. Notes on her most famous work and various words that had been bolted to the tune like a bird burdened with fins made of iron.

It was at this time that Raina came in. To one side, in a stable bereft of any other feature, she found a brazier used to heat the chamber in the dead of winter. She hung our gear as I turned page after page. The clothes, cloaks, armor, bedrolls all dripped in front of the fire. Immediately the sky opened up again and let loose with all the fury it had spared us the last day. I kept reading, almost wincing at the awed tone of Hundeausführer's words, his fawning phrases, his obvious love beyond worship for this long dead woman. But as I read, I could not fault him, nor contradict one adoring word.

I could hear her music again in my mind, a lullaby made up of dragons and fae, circling the air above me in a spiral without end. It was a tune that warmed me, and wrapped me in a blanket of notes louder than my beating heart. A crow caw, loud and obnoxious, shattered the web of sleep, and I sat straight up.

The storm still raged outside. Down below the horses dozed and the hung clothes steamed before the fire and provided shadow in which the two of us slept. Raina had curled up opposite me, bales of hay moved to block sight of us from the floor and two loaded crossbows waiting use. Leaving a crossbow strung and drawn was a sure way to weaken the string or stretch it to uselessness. *Still, the damn things were free, so why spare the expense?* At least she had blown out the candles.

I tossed more fuel on the brazier downstairs and crept back to a place where I could use the light to examine another book. I engulfed myself in the legends and lore of Annalirya Von Zeitheim. Her *Peace to the Sleeping Knights* piece was used to lure traitors to the throne who had invaded her castle to sleeping doom, for then loyalists flooded the room and slaughtered the traitors as they slept. She had defended her own castle walls by playing the violin solo, *The Rage of the Dragons*, and inspired her handful of men to fight like demons and hold off an attacking force of one thousand. Attackers had reported there being hundreds defending the walls, dark soldiers with glowing red eyes. So many stories, legends, myths… the music leapt up to pull me down again. It was a comforting place, and the drum of the rain became the percussion of the symphonies.

Come morning, I was well fed, well rested, and ready to go. This was why, you can understand, I was on the verge of burning the inn down. Dawn had broken hours ago and nobody was moving toward travel at all. They had failed to put out a watch. Add to this, Hanner had stayed up with all his friends, so now he was just as green faced and just as worthless. Thankfully, my apprentice saved me from murderous arson.

Raina had rounded up a block of cheese, a dozen eggs, a rasher of bacon, and a whole bucket of button mushrooms. With some salt and pepper, we made breakfast fit for a king. The mushrooms especially, fried up in the bacon fat, filled me with a wholesome fullness. Was it my fault the smell of the food sent most of the Rakes running for a ditch to empty their guts of bile? I am going to say no.

As the boys were rousted, we got the bad news. One of the wounded men not sent back had drank himself to death, so another man with a flesh wound to the arm was sent back with the body. Again, I was too busy to ask questions and too thin on patience to approach Alexander Jaeger in his new kingly demeanor. Instead I went around the common room and kicked Rakes awake until they were moaning and groaning, then picked one who I hated the most this morning and sent him up to wake his liege lord and emperor.

Still, all things considered, we were on the road before noon, and I was willing to take that as a win. Even better, the road remained rocky and the rain had ended the night before we left after one, final snit. Fog hung everywhere in the chill air, but it was a low, meandering, shy thing, not the oppressive blanket from the other day. The forest, too, retreated from the road as if in respect for our shrinking group.

Hanner rode close to me, but I gave him a disapproving look and he did his impression of a scolded puppy. Raina was going to say something, but I stopped her with another look. I felt I had earned my silence, and was loathe to give it up. In fact, the only thing to spoil the silence was the barking of the insufferable Alexander Jaeger. He continued to play the part of king, snapping fingers and orders for his Rakes to bring him whatever his whim demanded. I passed near him once, and the look he gave me was positively volcanic. It was so fierce, it made me forget the slightly rancid smell I noticed following closely about his majesty. I cantered ahead, and looked back on instinct. The only two sets of eyes that were not blurry were both fixed on me. One set belonged to Snotleaken the Brave and the other to Blondie of the Broken Teeth. But by this point, murderous looks from the two of them were simply as common as muddy boots on this trail. I should have not dismissed them. Would have saved me some trouble. But there we were, the advance group advancing admirably, the main group moving without noise, and more importantly without complaints. In the distance we heard a high pitched wave of water falling, but it did not sound dangerous, and we ignored it until we were upon it.

We crested the rise and found the path turned from moving upwards to cut across a wide embankment. There was a vast lake, winding from this place off into the clefts between rising ground up into mountains far distant. On three sides the water abutted directly to the rising slopes, but the road we were on made up the fourth bank of the lake. The water had obviously been fed by the rains, washing mud and grit out of the rocks and leaving the murky depths unknowable by human eyes. More disturbingly, the water had crested our roadway, and it spilled over the edge down a steep incline and into the cut leading back down into the valley.

The group halted, but there was no sign of our advanced group. They had either crossed without trouble or died there and someone had hidden, or eaten, their corpses. Without word, or preamble, I decided to risk it. The first two steps were the hardest, but what I had guessed proved correct– the water was only two fingers deep, though moving fast. The current threw up rooster tails where it hit the horse's hooves, but didn't cover them for all its rage.

The, now quite loud, roar of water made conversation difficult, and so I simply signaled for everyone to continue. Out of an abundance of caution or some fearfully indistinct foresight, I watched the lake as the men crossed. We were, of course, halfway across when something happened.

At first it was a rumble, a deep seated vibration that could be felt even through the horses. My sword, in fact many swords, were half out of their sheaths, but the next sound froze us with more curiosity than horror. There was no way to describe it except as a great slurping sound. Like a toothless giant with a pond of soup, the sound was near deafening, a rumble felt in the chest and a great depression, not two manlengths from the road, opened up in the water.

The depression roiled, burbled, and then began to swirl with malicious intent. Huge chunks of errant ice, floating debris, logs, and jetsam disappeared into it without hope of escape. Like the most devastating of storms, the unseen monster of the lake drank everything that entered its maw. Never did the thirst slake, never did it stop nor pause. It simply continued to drink endlessly, but made no manner of movement other than to slowly swirl in the water. The pull was so strong things floating on the surface as far away as the eye could see were heading noticeably toward it. A huge sheet of ice slipped toward it, but as it came over the whirlpool, the whole thing cracked and floundered like a mighty whale. It snapped into pieces and sank from view.

I pushed the Phantom Angel into the sheath, fitting it snugly inside, but did not take my eyes off the brown storm of water.

"What is it?" someone asked.

I stood in the stirrups and leaned over as far as I could. "I cannot see teeth or tongue. There must be..."

Someone suddenly grabbed my far foot and yanked upward, shoving a shoulder into my hip. Combined with my leaning posture, I came out of the saddle in a headlong rush. The sound of someone's scream was cut off by the water, and I never made it back to the surface.

The current, as mighty as the hand of any giant, pulled me under.

SEVEN

THE KNIFE IN THE BACK

MURDER. Murder was on my mind as the current tossed me like a doll. Sticks beat me bloody, and I exhaled what air I had in my lungs in a silent scream. Needles scratched me and my head slammed into a vertical log. It was only then I realized I was being pulled between standing trees beneath the water. I curled up to protect my soft belly, but the water cared not. Almost frozen itself, it robbed me of all feeling but crushing pressure, all warmth except that of the dead, and all sound but the slurping rush of my demise.

I felt hard, cylindrical walls on either side, above and below, scrape raw flesh from beneath tender fabric. I slammed into a sharp angle downward and scraped painfully to a stop, and the water, until now my effluvium, became a raging torrent on every side as it pressed past me toward freedom. Ice chunks acted as fists, beating my body as fast and harder than any rain. My heart was pounding in my ears, my lungs aching to draw in the sweet release of icy liquid and have the blinding, crushing pain over for now and forever.

Something still living, only tamed, growled within. An animal instinct made me thrash, to buck in the tiny, constricted bend in the tunnel. I felt, more than heard, a wooden snap, and I tumbled free of the burning cold down a dozen yards encased in moving water to the bottom. I was dumped into a pool where I slammed into the bottom, then rolled to the side and again was squirted again along the water's path.

The force of the water deposited me with the rest of the garbage, a stack of debris and dirt washed there over the centuries. My body hit it with the full force of a god's expectoration, and I crashed through the already failing plug to the lake above. I rolled downhill for half a league, pain searing every nerve shut until all I could feel was a distant buzz. Momentum pushed me into a pool created by a downed tree, and I washed ashore, vomiting brown water.

I gasped in sweet, rare air, and passed out.

Fine. I tried to pass out. I *wanted* to pass out. After being crushed by the fists of a lake and dumped down what felt like leagues of uncaring rapids, I damn well *deserved* to pass out. Instead, as the world swirled away and I wanted nothing more than to let it all go, I felt a weight land on my chest. It moved. I ignored it, so it plucked at my nose like a pair of scissors.

I opened my eye to find a raven perched upon me. Again, for what it was worth. It stared at me, promising to eat an eye if I decided that this was a good time to take a day off.

"Putrescent bastard," I swore, at the God if not his warder. I swatted at the thing, but it came off as a lazy wave it evaded easily. I sat up, a swimmingly bad idea according to my head. I placed hands against the ground, marveling at how much skin had been scraped from them in all directions, and pulled myself out of the water. I stood shakily, and my cloak, the cloak bestowed upon me so long ago by the boys with whom I faced death, fell from my shoulders in tatters and floated away. It looked so much like the savaged body of a fox, pulled into infinity by the current. I turned back upstream.

Where I was, I could see a thousand paces up the raging flow to the raised road that banked the lake. I could see the exit to the tunnel I had been pulled through; it still ejected water and debris at a fantastic rate. What had felt like a road to forever from the whirlpool to the drain had been less than a bowshot.

Focusing on the problem at hand, I saw no way up the steep walls of this wash back to the road, at least in my condition. Still in a daze, I stumbled off. I broke from the wash and went up into the woods, avoiding the deathly steep route to the road. The grade here was more gentle, but it still moved higher and higher into the woods as I tried to turn back toward my company. I had to stop often as I shivered violently, the constant buzz in my extremities a torture I could live without. My mind wandered from moment to moment, vision blurry and breath coming in knife hard gasps.

I was not a fool. Of course, I understood what had happened. The path we were on was an earthen bridge over a cleft with a spillway drilled to allow for drainage. This man-wide pipe had been filled in with dirt, plugged sometime last year or after a week worth of the hardest rain anyone could imagine. Then that rain, collected and focused by the slopes of five mountains, had formed the lake. From luck or fortune, the plug had started to let go as we crossed, making the whirlpool. Then, quite simply, someone had used it to try to murder me. *Then again, maybe they succeeded.* I shivered violently again.

I came across a well worn path, and my feet were drawn to it. I followed it for only minutes when a small shack came into view. I tried to call out, but my voice was weak. I tried to knock and fell through the door instead, pushing it open. Inside, a skeleton in rags occupied the only chair, a spindly, homemade thing as ragged as it was. The fireplace was of stone, and the bed covered in blown dust, twigs, leaves, and cobwebs. I shuddered violently again. All my warmth was collecting in my chest. It felt much better, because my hands were not buzzing. Sadly they were doing not much of anything else, either.

Quickly I searched, and found all I needed. The old woodsman had store housed plenty of wood, which I clumsily stacked in the fireplace. He had a stockpile of tinder as well, so I used it all. Then I found his flint, as well as a tall jug of something that smelled like rotgut syrup. Hands nearly useless, I plunged a dagger into the jug, coming out covered in thick, eye watering, oily goo. Fingers numbing, eyes blurring, I dragged the flint along the blade, pressing against the central ridge to no avail. On the third strike, however, the oil caught. For a second I just gazed at the rod of pure heat that burned in my hand, relishing the warmth that erupted from it. I gazed at it trembling in numb hands until something deep inside me screamed and I jerked awake to shove the whole conflagration deep into the tinder and left it there. The fire came to life at once, and I dozed before it, letting the radiated heat leech the cold from my body.

Hours later, I awoke freezing. First I added as much wood as I dared onto the fire without choking it. Next I had to painfully remove my clothing and find places for it to dry. The cabin had warmed greatly, but the wet leather was stealing my heat. My feet and fingertips still tingled in agony and I nearly wept as I pulled the belt for the Phantom Angel from my back. The sword, against all odds, had stayed put. In the tightness of the underwater tunnel, it must have been the length of wooden sheath that had kept me from making the turn. My thrashing had destroyed the beautiful, white leather wrapped item. The flexible sword had bent and survived, while the sheath had not. It had been the last gift to me from the woman I loved, and shattering it had kept me alive.

There was something of my whole life in that one sentiment.

Finally, my gear was laid out to dry. There was pitiful little of it, in any case. My pack and supplies had been on the horse, and now the horse was with Raina and the rest of them. I found quite a few knives that had survived the swim, as well as a block of bullfist that had made it.

I found a drawer that contained moth-eaten, dusty blankets. I pulled them out and laid one down just outside the reach of the fire and then propped one up like a lean-to on my swords. This was meant to catch the heat of the fire while the rest I pulled on top of me. Almost immediately I dozed again, world fading in and out of focus.

When my eyes opened I could see the skeleton of the woodsman in the corner watching me, the fire, and the front door that I had braced against entry.

I felt someone lift my foot, push me out of my saddle.

What did you expect?

Sanity, like most human parts, is a fragile thing. I was unsure if I was asleep or not. I was certain the voice was in my head and not from outside. Sill I could not shake the idea the words were in a voice I had never heard, the voice of the dead woodsman. I looked up at the skeleton. It had not moved, it did not move.

Again, what did you expect?

I blinked, and the room was dark except for the hot coals in the fireplace. I reached for another log.

Is that necessary?

I paused. Then my hovering hand reached for the my jerkin lying on the stones before the fire. It was dry, or at least dry enough.

No. I thought. *It is time*.

I stood, the hours of warmth radiating from my skin into the chill air. The clothes pulled on dry but the thicker leather armor plates were damp and heavy inside. Still, I buckled the scratched pieces into place. Then I took inventory. I had one package of food, a small skin of water, a soaked fire starting kit, a small clay jar of weapon black, assorted knives, spikes, a few needles and rods, a shortsword, and the Phantom Angel.

And that is all?

I looked around. *No, not at all*.

I gathered cloth from everywhere, browns, stained whites, and greens. I tore off strips in many lengths and striped them across my body, leaving dangling tails to further break up my outline. I stuffed the bullfist: nuts, berries, bone marrow, and shredded jerky, into my mouth. I swallowed it without tasting and then drained the flask of water and tossed it aside.

So, son, what are you going to do now?

I tied the final strips across my face.

I am not a man of peace. I pulled the swords out of the dirt, coated the blades with thick black goo.

That, at least, is settled.

I strapped on the shortsword in its sheath, then hefted the Phantom Angel in my hands. *Was there ever any doubt*?

I took the bucket of dirt from the side of the fireplace and tossed it over the fire, smothering it and plunging the room into darkness.

Your desire is there, but there is penance yet to be done.

I kicked the brace from the door and it creaked open. The heat flooded from the room in an instant, and I looked back to the skeleton. *Will I ever be done*?

It is unwise to ask the past about the future.

And then I left, feet carrying me toward my destiny.

My feet ate up the ground, movement loosening the tight knots left behind by the abusive water ride. I found the road easily. There was no trace on the rocky ground of anyone's passage, but I knew their direction and had memorized the path. I was certain that neither Blondie nor Alexander Jaeger would stop using a scout now that I had found the traps, but they would not think to have a trailing group to pull him out of the fire if things got dicey, nor to catch even a singular blade following on swift feet to take revenge.

I found their first campsite. There were blood stains, and signs that there had been a struggle of some kind, but nothing more. No graves. Then I circled back and found the mashed down spots where someone had laid out a bedroll all night. Sixteen had left the inn, there were fifteen spots. I wondered who had been killed, then realized the missing man was myself.

I got back on the road and followed. Up into the mountains all but forgotten by man.

EIGHT

DEATH IN THE DARKNESS

IN ANCIENT days, dwarves had mined this area deep and long, feeding the riches back through the ports to their empire overseas. Legends written in Hundeausführer's notebooks spoke of dwarves obsessed with gold and jewels, leaving hidden rivers of copper, iron, and tin untouched and lying on the ground of their mines as dross. It was the force of these legends that drew the Untamed Barons to unite centuries ago and come raiding up into the mountains. It was the same reason the men of Hammarfall were marched into the mountains to stop them. Only after years of death and misery was the truth discovered. It was a land of good rock, but empty of riches, with stunted trees and sparse cropland. Both sides claimed victory, but really at a certain point they ran out of men, saw the land for the worthless patch of turf it was, and stayed home next season. It just took twenty years. Twenty long years of needless bloodshed.

After the first year, losses were so nightmarish that neither group bothered shipping their dead home. No, they buried them on the battlefield where they fell. As I crested the next rise, I saw what that meant for the Battle of Stierlichtung, a massacre that had left only two dozen men standing. It was a tale of woe, and families from both sides made the trip here to visit the field of the dead. With no way to know who was buried where, they began leaving lonely stones carved with the names of the loved.

Not to be outdone, the noble families commissioned stoneworkers to carve blocks from the surrounding mountains and make them into monuments of the dead. This began a need for every family that was worth any name to build a monument, and any family of wealth, and so on. This was how, where the land of Hammarfall met the sky, there was the Stierlichtung Necropolis.

I had been chasing them for two days, far too long. A determined man on foot can outstrip a horse at a walk easily. A fire, an anger, a short haired psychopath raged inside my chest kept me going from before dawn until far into the night. The man I was trying not to be was dangerously close to the surface, but it spurred me on to run for hours, to ignore my hunger and to not think what had happened to Raina. I had found no corpses, nor graves, but Alexander Jaeger was a common kind of evil, and it was easy to see that soon what he would do to her.

I stopped by a spring and drank my fill, topping off my flask, urinating away from the stream, and then drinking again. I pushed water into myself, for I did not believe I would stop again until murder was committed. Still dressed in rags tied over my damaged leathers, I avoided the ornate front gate of piled and mortared stones and scrambled over the low wall with barely a sound.

There was a power, a thrumming, in the air. My heart beat fine and clear, all the louder for how close I had brushed against Death's hem. It was a wonderful joy that refused to fade with time or sleep, it was a rhythm, and I could almost hear the symphony behind it. Then, just as that thought faded from my mind, I felt the first note. I had never heard it, never even seen the foreign language code that musicians learn to make music, but the instant it started, I knew it was *The Rage of the Dragons*. I felt like Annalirya was with me, and I became bold and hungry for revenge.

Ahead, a campfire lit a section of tombs like a flickering phantom. Bold as brass amongst the towering monuments to the dead, it crackled cheerfully as the wind picked up and howled. Forward, I crept amongst the stones as a wind amongst the shadows. There I took in the full measure of the situation, and saw the folly that had befallen the men who had betrayed me.

A full thirty men, dressed in somber colors but without crest or banner, held the Rakes captive. For their camp, they had picked an intersection of paths in the graveyard, clear of tombstones with plenty of space to tie up horses in a corral and chain the prisoners. Of the boys there were only twelve left chained together. I was excited to see Hanner, who was bound, and also Raina, who looked bereft of hope yet all but untouched. Alexander Jaeger wept openly, snot clotting his moustache and beard. Broken tooth slumped near his master, all fight beaten out of him.

There were piles of equipment out of reach of the captives, and the first I identified was the stack of shovels leaning upright against one another. Then it became clear what this was. The boys had been ambushed elsewhere, then lead to this place. It was known they were coming, and others might follow to find them. This, of all places, they could carefully cut and roll up the sod, dig the graves deep, bury the Rakes, Hanner and Raina, and then roll the sod back out to take root. Should they be found in five or ten years, what is one more skeleton or less amongst thousands?

This was the last stop in the quest for the symphony and for our ambushers. Strangely enough, they were as tired and road weary as we, ourselves. The captors were not fools however, and had set out a minimum guard pair of men high up on a mausoleum at the edge of the camp. They could watch the whole of the camp from their vantage, but still it was clear they feared the captured and not any kind of rescue. The men did not even turn outward, and with the fire right beneath them, their sight into the darkness would be crippled at best. In comparison, out in the womb of darkness, I could pick them all out.

Still, killing thirty men without a chokepoint to limit them or an ambush to thin them, was not possible. Not without confusion and chaos. I moved to a new vantage point. There were the horses, I saw the stack of iron jaws, and the packs of the captured. The music ramped to a crescendo within me and convinced me that with those, I could try.

Oh, don't get me wrong, I was- still going to die. One man does not take on thirty and live. But, at least for the sake of my apprentice and Hanner, I had to try. Perhaps a strike now to make them move, and then another, and another, whittling them down? I put it out of my mind. If I survived, I would continue to plan. For now I needed mystery and blood. The music was louder, blotting out thoughts of tomorrow. It sung of war and it wanted it now. I fought against it as I forced myself to move slowly, carefully.

The wind was picking up, but I ignored it. I worked out the problem as I went, first sliding amongst the rope-corralled horses, of which there were many. They continued to sleep as I slipped amongst them. I moved to the edge of the horse pen closest to the camp. There I found the massed pile of iron jaws and saddles. With painstaking slowness, I began to cull the pile of equipment. Nothing in my saddle and saddle bags had been disturbed, further proof these people were called by some higher purpose. To slit one's own throat is one thing, but to be above a little loot or scavenge? That takes dedication. I quietly saddled three horses at the far edge of the pack. Considering what was to come, I staked them down on short tethers. Little by little, the stack of equipment dwindled. I built my plan around havoc.

I moved, covered only by the nighttime nickering of the horses, the snoring of the men, Alexander's weeping, and the sounds of the herd relieving themselves in their sleep. For hours I moved slowly, carefully, placing iron death, cutting the lines to the corral. It struck me that a few of the Rakes were in the way of the horses, but that could not be helped. I reclaimed my white bow and arrows and moved off to a good spot to shoot from, well out of the light and behind a few chest-high tombstones. Hurriedly, I wrapped the bow in dark fabric from my rag kit. As much as it could be effective to look like a ghostly archer invisibly firing a white bow, I could not chance them firing blindly at the bow and striking me.

The music moved to the beat of my heart, and it hummed along my tendons. False dawn was coming, and with it my chances of success would approach nil. There was a noise from the camp. One of the captors awoke, and then staggered up. He tried three times to buckle on his sword, but then tossed it down in disgust, one of the watchmen jeered at him quietly but mercilessly. The soldier made a rude gesture and then came out past the ring of light. The sound of the phantom symphony hushed, a diminuendo that held its breath, waiting. He headed straight for where I was making my last preparations.

He may not see much color, but he could always see movement, so I froze and willed him to stop, to go back, to veer off, all thoughts that perversely brought him closer and closer to my spot until he was not a step away. I silently flicked a small knife from my sleeve into my hand as he unleashed a steaming stream of urine, willing, hoping, that I did not have to use it. The music told me I would, hoped I would.

And then he turned, took a step backward, and right onto my foot. No, I did not yell out like a moron, but he did look back and see me. He blinked, unsure of himself. It was in that space of hesitation that I leapt up, covered his mouth, and jammed the bladed spike into the base of his skull. He died without sound, and without fuss. He had, however, set a fuse. Soon the watchmen would notice he had not returned. Soon, someone would be woken to go find him, others to guard, to search. I needed to move and move now.

I became a shadow to retrieve the final two traps. Thankfully, they stored them the way I stored them – flat and ready to go with the bar tensioned but the safety pins in place. I barely got them into position when the dreaded words came.

"He's taking forever to piss," said One.

"Maybe he decided to take care of both ends while he had the chance?" suggested Two.

"Or maybe he fell asleep?" One's voice smiled about it. Then whispered as loudly as he dared, "Leoff?"

One was having none of it "Go check on him. If you wake the prince and get us extra watch tonight, I'm going to thump you."

Now the music flowed in ghostly rhythms that anticipated the drops of blood, the spray of death from a throat, and it beat upon me to move faster. I moved over ten tombstones, took out arrow after arrow and my jar of weapon black. Nicking my fingers something fierce, I spread the greasy charcoal all down the feathers, the shaft and head, turning one, two, three of Richter's beautiful white arrows black. I had to, for white could be tracked back to the source. Black would–

"I'm going to check on him." Two said.

I could hear One not only concur, but catch the tone of concern, "*Ja*, you do that."

I heard the bolt slip into the heavy crossbow, a bolt meant for me. The music was loud, very loud in my head. Time was up, this was it, because if I had picked carefully enough, when Number Two climbed down to check, he would come down the tilted sculpture for ease of footing. If he took that path…

Apparently he didn't.

I peeked up and saw he had slid down the camp side facing of the mausoleum. I took aim at the bowman. His eyes squinted toward me and I ducked down, cursing myself for a fool. I had knocked a white arrow, and the watchman had seen me. It was time to move, before–

If the clap of the iron jaws did not wake you, the sound of a man suddenly without a leg from the knee downwards would do it.

Far off, there was a flash of lightning and a peal of thunder. The rains we had thought gone for good were swallowing the stars to the west with fearful speed. I barely managed to knock a black arrow as our attackers leapt to their feet and burst from tents. The first was an older man, pugilistic beard jutting from a noble chin.

He asked the world, "Report!"

But what he said to me was, *I am in charge*.

The music moved like blood made of venomous serpents through my veins. A black arrow sunk in to his lung, missing his heart by two fingers. He collapsed as I ducked down and shifted tombstones. Number One on top of the tomb had started to point toward the sound of Number Two's screams, and so missed the arrow, missed his leader's collapse, and only looked back down to magically see him fallen into a pool of blood.

Another older man, bald and wizened, came out in only breeches, but slapped his old fashioned sword to the buckle at the center of his shield, "Rally! Rally! To arm–"

At this point what panicked men needed was the calm voice to tell them the obvious. What I needed was panic. My next black arrow slammed into his shoulder, spinning him to the ground.

The wind was starting to howl, and the campfire spread blinding sparks in all directions. Two men started to run to check on the urinator and the guard, and they hollered back tales of death.

"Calm! Arm yourselves! Lord Wetwegseemann has taught us well! Prepare yourselves." But the third black arrow shut him up, center of the chest, for good.

Then I ducked down and ran as fast as I could to my next position. Men were loading crossbows and firing them in all directions. The music whispered to me, and told me where to go. Bolts smashed into the headstones and chipped chunks off with earsplitting reports. I low crawled amongst the stone cover, the wind turning icy cold as it reached down into the space between the tombstones and pulled out the chill of the grave. The fire began to die down as men began looking for targets rather than firing blindly in every direction. I made it to the opposite edge from the horses, and knocked my last, white, arrow. I bent the bow with all my might and let the shaft fly into the chest of an enemy. His scream volcanoed blood as I dove back amongst the tombstones. A cloud of bolts slapped into the carved rock all around me. I needed a distraction.

I hastily untied a rag from the bow and pulled at the other end, unraveling the camouflage from the white wood. More bolts came as I heard windlasses click and clatter in mad laughter as the strings were drawn to reset heavy crossbows. I reached Richter's bow up and hooked it upon the hand of a distraught stone figure. It rocked there, an obvious target for the ire of these soldiers while the symphony spirited me away.

They launched two volleys, then drew swords and charged the bow. They moved in a wave, but within heartbeats men were screaming. Three dark knives whistled out of the night and buried themselves in sweating, tender flesh. I smiled viciously as they turned toward me in a flock. Then, again, the traps they had left to kill me culled their numbers. Iron jaws snapped on legs and severed them from their owners, adding to the cacophony of howling wind and sparks.

Again, I tried to disappear into the landscape, but a bolt whizzed by very close. Men rushed forward to help the injured, to find more of their own traps had been set out against them. I managed to get to the far end of the makeshift paddock. Men were circling around to search for me on one side when I slapped the rumps of the rear horses. Awake from the cacophony of battle and nervous from the smell of blood, it took only that to panic them into a run.

The horses exploded from the pen like grapeshot, the meager ropes used to contain them cut. The music was crashing like the laughter of a mad god in my head. They flooded into the camp, filling the open intersection, passing close to the prisoners as they slammed bodily into my enemies. What traps were not found by men were found by horses, their nightmarish wails adding to the storm. A knife flickered from nowhere and barely missed the watcher on the mausoleum, who in turn fired back blindly and hit one of the Rakes. Another knife came at him and he went to the far side of the tomb. He swung down the tilted statue, placing both feet momentarily in the last trap before he, too screamed into the night.

Men pushed at walls of flesh, the horses milling about in confusion and trying to find any clear path to escape. Out of the darkness I came for the Rakes, but to free them, I needed a hammer, a chisel, and about an hour. What I had was three seconds and the Phantom Angel. Risking everything on one, mighty stroke, I appeared above Raina and Hanner, slicing downward without pause. The chain end was wrapped around a tall monument and secured by a thick rivet to itself. The ancient elvish blade, forged of alloys beyond men's ken, bit the iron chain, throwing sparks out in a brilliant flower. Then the severed end fell to the ground. I yanked Raina to her feet, the stub end of the chain slithering through the rings on her manacles.

I pointed. "Packs and saddled horse, go!" Next was Hanner, "Packs, horses, go!"

And after that the Rakes pulled themselves free of the chain in sequence, but too late. One of the ambushers saw what was happening, and yelled out a warning. Again the music rose on a wave. He leapt forward, stabbing a Rake still bound, only to be cut down himself as I spun and lunged. The music ended, the tune taken up by unearthly phantom chants, screams, cries.

As he fell, weeping guts from an open wound, the horses parted in unison. Twelve men had met their end since the chaos ensued, but many more were left to fight and kill. Five of them saw me and rushed forward. I lunged absurdly far and brought the Angel around in a flat arc at waist height. It held them back for a few breaths, just a few breaths more. The music was becoming hectic, discordant. More horses were jockeyed out of the way, and more men were coming to join the line before me. Worse, one man had enough sense to grab and begin loading a crossbow. When it was done, I was dead. The voices of the symphony were crying, screaming in my head.

A soldier lost patience, and bounced within range with his gilded, engraved sword. Without ceremony, I slapped it from his hand and lopped off the arm at the elbow, giving up a full stride as I leapt backward to engage the next man rushing.

I blocked high and stabbed low, putting the blade crosswise into his boot and toppling him over, but the next was there, and I dove under his guard, slamming into the side of his head with the hilt of the Angel and then stepping off, swinging the blade in a tight arc that severed his head from his shoulders. I was already panting raggedly, already spent from days of running and a night of heavy exertion. The animal bits of me were fatigued beyond measure, my brain turning numb as it drowned in adrenaline.

Three more men died on the verdant grass, but now seven faced me, with drawn blades. Hair, grass, clothes, and the tails of rags whipped in every direction at once. I saw the man in the back slam a bolt in to the firing notch of the crossbow. Then, I knew it was over. He raised the heavy contraption to his shoulder as the sky let loose with a blinding flash and a deafening, stomach churning rumble. He aimed.

The music went silent.

And then the sky let loose with every bit of fury of the last week, concentrated into this spot. I threw myself to the side, but I never knew if he had shot at all. Suddenly the rain was so thick it was like fog, and every breath sucked in a few drops even through the rag mask I wore. Men shouted in rage, then in fear, and then sheer terror. I raised my sword, but I could not even see the tip of it in the beating drops. Every place they hit hurt from the wrath of the wind pushing the water to the velocity of a clothyard shaft.

The shouts became shrieks, the soldiers reduced to mere children by some, unnamable horror. I stumbled forward, swords and hands reaching in lieu of drowned eyes, and then I saw the shadow of two men locked in a deadly embrace. I blundered forward, through the obscuring walls of rain, until I was almost within touching distance of the two. Then there was a triple stroke of lightning that lit up the world in gut wrenching shades of white. One man gurgled blood from a terrible throat wound. His attacker nuzzled the wound like an animal, pausing and turning to me like the very vision of violent death.

It was a skeleton, completely devoid of flesh, and held together by the barest wisps of tendon. The teeth were broken to sharp points, and even now chewed hunks of throat flesh that dropped through the open jaw. The entire mouth was stained red, with pieces of gristle caught between the ancient teeth. Meat simply flopped out of the bottom of the jaw, staining the lower bones with splashes of blood. Then the flesh smoked and crackled, sizzling in an instant into ashes that dissolved under the fists of the storm. The rain tried in vain to sluice the creature clean, but the age chewed bones found pockets and pits to store the blood within, making it speckled with arterial spray. Within the pits of supernatural blackness that made the eyes, fields of bright blinking red stars. *No! Not stars. Eyes*. Hundreds of red, hungry eyes staring from some otherworldly place, driving the creature before me as an engine of unrequited desire. Heart thumping like a rabbit's, I stumbled backward and fell. The creature turned from me back to its feast. I took the opportunity to retreat. Well, being honest, I damned well *stole* the opportunity to flee.

Beneath the sound of pounding rain, I could hear the sounds of battle, or more truthfully, the screams of the massacre. It was with no thought to courage or fair play that I leapt to my feet and staggered to the location of the stolen packs. I swept four or five into my arms by the straps and started off into the graveyard.

A pale man, one of our attackers, glided like a ghost out of the darkness and pulled up short as he caught sight of me, dressed in gray tones and fluttering rags like an apparition. Then he found himself and pointed a sword at my heart.

"You will surely burn in the hells for what you seek–" Whatever other clichéd wisdom he wanted to impart was cut off as he was tackled by three red stained skeletons. They began ripping him to mouth sized pieces and stuffing him into their faces. The parts of him burned into ash, and he screamed as if he could feel it all, feel it forever. It was as if the mouths of these creatures were the gates of hell itself. I dodged out of arms reach and bolted for the saddles. Screams were all around, and the rain was becoming icy and frozen as it fell.

I fumbled forward and found the final horse I had staked out had broken free or been released when Raina and Hanner had taken their own. Another flash of lightning, concurrent with its thunder, blotted out all sound in the world except a thin tinny ring. Yet it illuminated a battlefield of utter, demonic delight. Men were dead or dying, the chains of the Rakes were empty, and now the horses were being feasted upon.

The final saddled horse was not five strides away from me, skittishly trotting in a circle where it was hemmed in by tall tombstones on three sides. It was clumsy with fear, eyes rolling in the sockets as if being savaged already. I managed to bound to it and get a hold of the bridle, but as it nickered and trotted away so I could not mount. The packs pulled me off balance, and I could not keep up as the damn animal moved its ass in a circle to keep me from the saddle.

It was then that I noticed that the screams under the pounding of rain had stopped. Other than the slushy splash of half frozen rain pouring onto the ground as if from buckets, no sound was made other than from the horse, and I.

Then the rain began to lighten, and I saw a dozen, two dozen, five dozen shadowy forms through the hazy curtains of water. It was right then I thought to myself: *to hell with the damned packs.* And in the newfound appreciation for haste over being eaten, I vaulted off of a tombstone onto the back of the mare. Without pause, I dug my heels in and goosed the beast to a full gallop.

The rain was still blinding, numbing, and the terror of being consumed pressed in on all sides. So when the mare jumped a tombstone, I hadn't seen it. She certainly hadn't seen the larger monument just past it. We crashed into the pillar at full speed, and I was dumped head over heels onto the turf. My head, protected only by a thin layer of cloth, cracked against a tombstone, and I felt wakefulness slip though my battered, tired, hungry fingers.

And it would be a lie to say I ever expected to wake.

NINE

THE UNEXPECTED

I WOKE.

I was wet, shivering, sore with a throbbing headache. But I was awake, albeit somewhat more slowly than I would like. Not only that, it was dawn, and I hadn't even gotten a good night's rest out of it. Though all of this really seemed like petty complaints: pain, cold, mushy reflexes, perhaps should be below notice to most when one didn't expect to even be alive, some would say. To hell with them, I say. I hurt, and it was the result of an unfair and uncaring universe no matter the opinions of lesser people.

I hated to admit it, but I was listening for the music, straining to hear the ghostly symphony awakened in my soul, and it was not there. The absence left me feeling lost, hungry, and alone.

Then I remembered the walking dead, rain hitting their backs white and pouring out their front in a flood of red. Burning flesh and screaming men echoed in my memory. My eyes snapped open and I scrambled to my feet. The world blurred and I had to quickly sit back down. I put my head between my knees and concentrated on breathing. Breathing and listening.

Far off, I heard the song of birds cavorting in the slowly lighting sky. Closer than that, the slight moan and whistle of the wind was never ending amongst the monuments. Nothing else stirred the silence over the graves of thousands. Finally, the world settled, and I slowly heaved myself to my feet, my hands automatically gripping the Phantom Angel firmly.

The camp had been leveled. Tents were in shambles. The corpses were worse. Strewn like broken toys, stripped of flesh, torn to pieces by time-sharpened bones and jagged teeth. The ground was disturbed, as if by the passage of thousands of burrowing creatures no bigger than a skull. I shivered, for there were no other signs of the dead that had attacked last night, nor any clue from whence they had come. Naught but the disturbed soil as if their bones had burrowed toward one common location above ground and assembled to slay without mercy.

Not that I could complain, for they had missed me, and had utterly wiped out those that stalked my company. In fact, as I combed the camp, I found the only corpses that had not been shredded to the bone were the men who had died early in my attack. Even those mortally wounded had been further masticated by the uncaring dead. I did not see Raina or Hanner, but I did find five of Von Snotleaken's men. None had been eaten, and mayhap had died before the attack of the dead.

I found a wrapped package of cured meat, hard tack, and dried fruit that the destruction, the rain, and the bugs, had all missed. I wolfed it down without pause, and washed it into my belly with a skin of watered wine. Off in the distance, a familiar white mare wandered. I recovered the poor, battered beast and brought her back.

I took less than a candlemark to saddle the horse, fill and pack saddlebags with supplies, then tie off several backpacks onto the whole. I was becoming despondent when I turned back to the camp and found the satchel of Hundeausführer's books that Raina had raided from his stores. I brought it and tied it off as well, then stole the opportunity to grab as many pouches of coin out of the wreckage of the dead as I could find. I even had the good sense to grab a sheaf of arrows that looked about the right length, half a dozen swords in scabbards, Raina's bright steel sword that had cost us so dearly, and Richter's white bow which still swung in the wind. My horse so overburdened, I mounted it (why should I be the only one to suffer?) and struck off toward the main path that wandered through the necropolis.

It was the whole day into evening again before I came upon them, but they were easily spotted. Raina was mounted, watching and awaiting the merest twitch in her instinct to send her galloping away. Hanner also stood guard near a crude fire, sharpened spear in his hand. He sat far too close to the fire, and stared inward towards it instead of away. I could read in her body that my apprentice wanted to be far from there. I could equally read in the stances of the Rakes that they were sullen, and not likely to go anywhere. Alexander Von Snotleaken was pale, and twitchy, hair in disarray and swatting at bugs buzzing about him alone.

I rode slowly, and the sound of the horses' hooves alerted them long before they saw me. I did not slow, but I came about half a crossbow shot away when I raised my voice to address them, "Hail the camp!"

Raina broke into a gallop, riding toward me and pulling up short abreast. She leaned over and smothered me in a hug, eyes glistening in the darkness as she smiled.

"I was certain, many times in the last week, that you were dead."

I shrugged and grinned. "If these idiots could kill me, I would be dead already."

"What happened to the nobles?" Her eyebrows shot up. "We listened to them for hours talk, wonder, and debate around their camp. They were not common men; they all spoke like high born."

I nodded, staring up into the starry sky and wondered what that meant. I handed over her sword in its scabbard, and she looked like a girl greeted by her favorite hound. "How? How did you get it from them?"

I shrugged. "There was no one left to object."

She stared at me, took in my appearance. I was still dressed in slightly damp rags from the neck down in varying shades of gray. Blood from my head coated one whole side of me, but I looked otherwise unharmed. She shook her head. "That's impossible."

I thought about the hungry dead and shivered. "You have no idea how impossible."

I nudged the mare into motion, and she came around to ride with me. Hanner smiled, but looked like a boy caught backsliding. The rest were not shocked. -They knew who had saved them, but they looked upon me with a mixture of exhaustion and pure hate. Seeing the bundle of swords behind my saddle, one of them bounced to his feet and rushed at me. I shifted the horse slightly, planted a boot in his eager chest and pushed him back. The Rake bounced off of the ground as I pulled the Phantom Angel from the crude thong that held it onto the saddle's pommel. The silvery blade glittered hungrily where it peaked through black grease, and held them back as easily as a shield wall.

"Who pushed me into the lake?" The words were like a thunderclap in the middle of the camp. The Rakes all stole glances at Blondie Broken Tooth and Snotleaken, who's face became masks of fury. "No? Well then I'll keep my steel if it's all the same to you."

Schwartzklippen stalked forward to me, his face attempting red but only managing it at the cheeks. The rest of his face was a jaundiced yellow green, with bright red bags under his eyes. "Don't be a fool, Crow. You will never survive out here without us." I brought him up short by putting the tip of the Phantom Angel in his path and giving him the choice to impale himself or stop. He stopped, but the current of air that continued past him held a nasty note of rotten meat.

My head began to pound as I felt my blood rise to match his insolence. "From where would my danger arise? For those that ambushed us are dead in the necropolis. Volker's men have never given chase. So the only danger to me that I can see is the man who tried to dump me into a sinkhole of swirling water and leave me for dead at the bottom of a lake."

Schwarzklippen sneered. "Now a wise leader would consider forgiveness to ensure the strength of the group."

"Forgiveness is fine, unless it becomes the reason that you have two bleeding holes instead of one. And the second you or your boys have a sword, I expect you to stick it as deeply in my back as you can manage." I cut the straps holding two heavy packs to my saddle and let them fall. "And while following a fool is supposed to be terminal, I brought you food, wine for watering, and daggers." Alexander Jaeger lunged for the pack, but the edge of the elvish blade interrupted him. "But my price is I don't want to see you again. Start back toward town. Get to Hammarfall."

He nodded an assent I didn't believe even for an instant. I moved the horse away from the packs. The Rakes fell upon them, pushing and shoving, a few to get at the food, more to get at the wine. They gulped the stuff without using it to purify water, which was proof to me that they hadn't changed even a bit. Only two ignored these gifts: Alexander Jaeger and Blondie. They dug to the bottom and had daggers in hand. By that point however, I was many manlengths away, stopping before the only Rake I could trust. Hanner looked away, face burning.

With his ears, there was no way to be subtle. I had to half shout. "Hanner, are you coming?"

Which brought dozens of eyes up from the discarded packs to the heavyset lad before me. He shuffled, shrugged, kept his eyes on the ground. He said, too loudly, "I need to stay."

And it wasn't a betrayal of me, no matter how it felt. I cut another pack free and gave it to him, then pulled a sheathed sword out of the bundle behind me. I handed it to him solemnly. "Be careful."

He smiled sheepishly and ducked his head in a half nod half shuffle. It was written on his face that he was glad that I was not angry, for we had fought and bled together. The only problem was I was a wandering nomad. These Rakes were his people. His future, if there was a future, lay with them.

I motioned to Raina, and we rode off into the night. We moved slowly, sparing the horses, until they started to stumble. We found a pool left over from the previous night's storm and let them drink.

Raina looked up and down the road, as struck as I was by the sheer abandonment of the area. It had once been paved. Now grass and weeds grew ankle high through the stones of the road, time buckling the pavers like broken teeth. Finally she ended the silence, "We need to stop here."

I nodded to my apprentice. "Can we afford it?"

"The horses can't afford us not to."

"Then how will we be safe?"

She thought on it for a moment, then she examined the moon in the utterly cloudless sky. "We won't get much more than a half a night between us if we mean to be off before the lordlings can come after us."

"You think they will come after us?" I interrupted.

"They'd be fools to do it."

"Are they still following the dictates of Von Snotleaken?"

"Yes, and so they'll be coming." She huffed. "Give me a hundred breaths."

Ninety-nine breaths later she was moving with purpose. She left the horses in the middle of the road, tied to the tree as the obvious bait. She spread circular patches of leaves and debris, purposefully putting the driest twigs between them. Then we climbed two trees. I had my bow and arrows. She had heavy gloves prepared and a rope tied to allow her a fast descent. We both drank our fill of watered wine and woke several hours later, well before dawn, with full bladders. Breaking camp took only minutes, and I watched her wisely obliterating the circular patches, meant to make them think we had hidden iron jaws. She left the twigs that would have snapped and given away the presence of those avoiding the 'traps.'

"All for nothing."

"Was it?" I watched her closely.

She nodded at me, hopefully understanding as she answered. "No."

I smiled and nodded at her. She glowed as if I had heaped gold and glory unto her name. This suited me fine, for any gold I could save was a boon to me. As we mounted I considered that moment carefully. I had spent almost all of my life caring only for results, and gaining precious little praise. In a life where you would sell any man, woman, or child for coin, there is less than no value in thinking or caring what is said of you. Yet now, first with the Lady Aelia's guardsmen a year ago, and now with Raina, I found that they respected me, that my words could move them to work better, harder.

It stirred something inside me, a hunger. It made them want to be better, to rise in my estimation. It was preposterous, but it made me want to be better, too. Maybe that was why I had not killed Blondie, or Snotleaken. Maybe I was learning mercy. Or maybe I was going soft.

In either case, we left earlier than I had ever seen the Rakes start moving on their own, and kept up a hard pace all day. They only had one horse, Hanner's, and Snotleaken was likely to be the one riding it. There was little chance they would ever catch us. Yet we pushed the horses every day and set up clever distractions and useless traps every night without fail.

After one week, we came to a long bridge. It leapt three times from peak to peak to span long drops into deep clefts. I took the opportunity to walk three paces in and skin the bark off a tree at hip height. Then I walked ten paces and marked another tree within sight. At the third tree I clambered upward and tied off a pack, heavy with food, wine, and the spare swords. While I did that, Raina walked fifty more paces into the woods, marking five more trees before coming back. Cache cashed, we made our way back to the bridge.

The next night, we found the ghost town.

Saddled high into the mountains, it was bereft of inhabitants. Every window had been blown in by one of a thousand storms, every door hinge had rusted through and discarded the barriers into the streets. Inside, tables, chairs, beds, chests all sat in various states of decay. There were pots, pans, plates, all rusting, chipped, broken, or overgrown. Whenever this town had been abandoned, it had been done without anything being taken by the townspeople.

Raina stopped by one house and looked in all directions, finally pointing. "It's early yet, but defensible. We stay in that attic, build a fire down here in this fireplace. If they come looking for us, we will be buildings away."

But my hair was standing on end, and my teeth buzzed in my skull. I shook my head, but it did not help. I looked in every direction and caught sight of a raven just at the edge of town, sitting on a tree and looking inward. Like climbing a skull, I reached into the wide empty sockets where windows once sat and went from hole to hole, then to the eves and above to the slate roof. The peaks all sagged, and some of the modest towers listed dangerously to one side. Still, turning in all directions, I picked one out after another. They all sat patiently, all watching me, all outside of town. I watched a murder of three take flight from the south side of the village. Rather than flap onto the wind coming toward me, they all turned and fought into the current of air, avoiding the town at all costs as they took to the evening sky.

I hit the ground hard. "We need to go."

Raina's brow furrowed, but she knew enough not to argue. We led the tired horses to the edge of town, over another bridge and out onto a wooded hillside. A small trickle that ran out of the woods and across the path brought about the discovery of a small spring in a well screened glade. The water was fresh and cold. We drank our fill, let the horses do the same, unloaded our beasts and ate. Even without a fire, the night was pleasant, and we both slept until well after dawn.

We refilled our stores of water and led the horses out of the glade and back to the road. Once there, we rode for three more days until finally we saw the castle of Annalirya Von Zeitheim, Enchantress of Strings, The Burning Composer, the Mother of the Symphony. Zeitheim itself towered over us, a crumbling hunchback of a mountain topped by the hilt of a castle shoved into its spine.

We, again, came to a series of bridges that skipped across closely grown chasms. Having no other cover, we slept there. And though we both lost half a night of sleep to keeping watch, in the morning we were both buzzing with energy. We had finally made it there, and though it was only halfway through the journey, the relief was palpable.

It took a full day of crossing innumerable bridges, climbing higher and higher, back and forth in front of the castle. Again and again we crossed from the southwest to the northwest face of the peak, only to double back, and back again. We spent the whole time within bowshot of the walls, but the straight line path was too steep for man or beast. At the midpoint of the switchbacks, there were wooden bridges. Though old and rickety, they held our weight. I pointed to the castle wall, where a massive crank sat rusted into uselessness. It looked as if nobles or freight could be loaded on a wheeled cart at the bottom and cranked up the steep ascent without wasting a day getting there. Everyone else would have to endure when invited, or else a rain of arrows that would blot out the sun, and that with stopping every turn in the road, because I surely would be the first to advise her ladyship to destroy all the bridges so they would have to be rebuilt. Assaulting this meager keep would be a nightmare. I was wondering how any army would even make it to the walls, let alone inside, as the sun set and we reached the gates.

The family line had died out a century before, and the whole mountain range not long thereafter. Knowing that, I'm not sure what I expected, but it wasn't the ruin before me. We crossed the permanent bridge across the last gap and paused to imagine what this fort had looked like in its youth. The outer wall was little more than a crumbling decoration, a garden for vines and lichen. Inside, the front lawn was grown out of control, hip high with mountain grasses and wild wheat. It so offended our horses that as soon as we slipped their reins they went to clearing the growth. There were enough pools from the recent rains we didn't have much worry about watering them, either. They might as well run free in the courtyard, for the stable was nothing but a collapsed ruin. The keep itself was of hardened stone, but the mortar was largely missing, the windows were gap-toothed patchworks of missing panes, and whole sections of the roof lay sprawled in the yard like fainting ladies. We checked inside carefully, but it was no better.

The night was crystal clear, and the door hinges were so eaten by the viridian teeth of verdigris that they fell apart as we pushed. The doors fell in with a thunderous boom, announcing us to naught but ghosts and regrets. The room was paved in marble, the walls so far apart they were lost in darkness, and the echoes went on forever and got lost and separated in the distance. Even a glance showed nothing with two feet had been in this room for long enough that a thick coating of dust covered everything and was deep enough I sunk a finger nail-deep into it.

Just like the town, everything was left behind. But here the items had held up much better over time. Outside we found some large nails, almost the size of spikes. Nearly corroded to uselessness, we scavenged them and drove them into the wooden frame of the main gate. Then we looped some of the rope we had back and forth three times to create a makeshift barrier against escape of the horses.

Next we removed the saddles and packs, taking everything inside. There were four fireplaces in the entry hall, and we chose one that was clear and near the door. There we took some ancient wood from the pile and tossed it in and got it going. We found a bench that fit the crossbar slot to the front doors, so we set them both up and used the impromptu bar to hold them in place. A table and a few chairs barricaded the door nicely. The only windows were high up on the wall, and would be difficult to get through without waking me. None of this would stop me from getting to a target, but luckily I was already inside and not considering suicide.

Both of us stripped down and brought old iron drying racks out of a cupboard and hung our clothes, both worn and packed, blankets, rolls, and packs. Though where we sat on a moth eaten rug was more or less clear of dust, and the fire roared before us, once naked and surrounded by darkness we both felt eyes from every side.

We practiced our silent signs. I pointed toward the scummed over and darkened paintings. Such was the degradation that all the pigments were nearly black or brown with age. Only the pale ovals and long circles of the faces could be picked out, and only after staring. The eyes, however, white spots with dark voids into infinity, stood out and seemed to follow wherever the watcher walked about the room. She pointed out the winged figures of victory that adorned every available space. I imagined these were muses meant to bring the Mother of Symphonies her inspiration. Whether the lighting, age, or purpose, they all looked carved in various shades of misery. I nodded, and shrugged.

I signed, *pass me a knife*.

She did something ineffectively distracting with her hands and slipped a knife from her pack over to me. *Not bad*, I motioned, though that was something of a lie.

How many paces to the door?

Five?

How many turns of a flying knife?

Two and a half.

We played a few dozen more rounds, testing both her hand's vocabulary and her knowledge before we pulled our bedding and clothes from the racks. The damp had been chased off and we laid out bedrolls and pulled on clothes that were toasty and warm. The rest of our gear we left drying. I pulled the Phantom Angel nearby, and slept a full night for the first time in weeks. The eyes of the dead were our only sentinels.

TEN

THE BONES OF GENIUS

SAY WHAT you want, but even a well made bedroll can't turn a marble floor into a feather bed. I got up and stretched stiffly. Raina soon did the same. We only had preserved rations, but at least we were able to toast them on a plate in the fire. The differences in taste were not always pleasant, but they were a change at least.

We slipped on our leather for protection, soft boots for silence, and a multitude of traps, tricks, poisons, and blades.

"Shall we?" Raina asked as she gave her bright steel sword a few swings to relish the balance.

"And we will do it silently."

Raina said nothing, but her shoulders dropped. In my training that would have called for a bit of blood. Worse than being lazy with training was the transgression of letting others guess at your mind. I decided not to mention it. She was not training to be an assassin. Not really.

I hefted the Phantom Angel in one hand and the oil lamp from our packs in the other. I will say that we were not silent at all. Oh we made far less noise than most people, but being silent in a place that has been unseen to for a century does not take skill, it takes magic. It was still good practice, and anyone more than a room away would not hear us moving. Yet, after a long, tense, exhausting day we had found nothing.

Fine, we had not found nothing; we found room after room of abandoned goods– rotting silks and linens, decrepit furniture, and time blackened paintings. There were beautiful frescoes and bas relief sculptures of various musical scenes spread everywhere, but none seemed to be of import. The castle was shaped like a bowed square, with the thickest walls toward the front gate and the steep drop to the switchback paths below, the thinner walls protecting the overgrown gardens in the center and facing the rising cliff of the mountain at its back. We were careful and thorough, but from the depths of the family crypts to the rickety walls of the upper towers, we found no trace of the last resting place of Annalirya, Last Lady of Zeitheim.

I felt a feather light brush on my arm and I turned. Raina touched her own eyes with forked fingers and pointed. I followed her direction out a broken pane and saw that the central gardens had even collapsed into some kind of oval sinkhole. The event had been old, for vines hung down into darkness from the gardens on all sides, but it did cut the heart out of the once beautiful respite.

Finally, we wound up back at the main entryway, our sinuses clogged with dust and nothing to show for our efforts. The whole of the next day passed the same. The first day was frustrating, the second was maddening. I sat in the front hall, staring at one of the darkened paintings, fire crackling in the night.

Raina had made a wine porridge out of one of the oat, fruit and nut rations. It tasted horrible, but at least the feel in the mouth was different. I set the bowl aside, half eaten, and just marveled at the master carpenter who carved a chair out of heavy, hard wood, and did it to make it feel like cushioned silk. I moved the Phantom Angel so it was tilted against one arm in easy reach, and once again considered the painting above us.

The more I stared, the more details slid from the background. The fire flickered and snapped, the sound repeated and distorted by the massive space on all sides. It became a beat, a soft percussion, the beginning of a melody. The face in the painting gained shape and depth, and as I watched, the sad eyes stared into my deepest places and pulled at the hollow caverns my melted sin had left behind. I could hear it now, more forceful and insistent, pushing the beautiful lady from the frame into clouds of wispy strokes that hovered about her like smoke.

I stood, heart pounding, though my feet were frozen to the floor. I tried to scream for Raina, but my throat was closed, and she lay asleep near the fire, blissfully unaware of the phantasm coming to hover before me. The music sung of such lost longing, of such desperate need, that my heart melted and throbbed in time. It was a harmonic understanding of the resonance frequency of my wounds, and it comprehended me in ways no mortal woman could. When the pale hands appeared from the cloud of smoky paint, I accepted them gladly, and when the eyes gazed upon me I wished them to flay me open to expose me to the Gods above and yet accept my darkness, my desires, and my tainted soul.

We moved as one, the music pushing us in dances I have never known. We glided along the dark marble, night rendered day by the power of our combined understanding. The desire in our steps became a need, no longer sweetness, but breath itself, and then to a frenzy. The music did not keep pace, rather it was the heartbeat of the universe on all sides. Glorious note combinations gave us wings to fly and my partner twirled and slid in a complicated duet as my muscles tried to throw themselves from their sockets with every turn. It was more than frenzy, more than a berserk lust to consume life whole from any throat that we could find, it was everything and all things beating in time with visceral addictions and the clattering snap of dancing on the cold marble floor. And that note, that full final note that peeled out like a bell out of the belly of the strings and held us together for breath after breath as our faces came closer and closer and the black strands of hair parted and our lips came together in the dark infinity that lay between our separate selves.

There was a ringing smash and I jolted awake.

Sunlight was invading obscenely into the entry room, or was it a feast hall? The painted lady was gone. It was daytime: I was in my chair and I was still asleep enough for rogue thoughts to collide in my skull. Raina was obviously long awake, and had been preparing food and sharpening her sword. Yet, this wasn't a kitchen, or an armory. I snatched up the Phantom Angel and darted to the center of the room. Now that I was looking, the staircases that raised on either side formed a large alcove, or an amphitheater of sorts. I ran to that section, trailing a curious apprentice. Once there, I drew my knife and, holding the Angel by the winged crosspiece, struck the elvish steel.

The ringing peal was bright and crisp, beautiful and perfect. Yet, it wasn't the sound, but the resonance of the entire room that gave me pause. The sound iterated out from here, filling the room from end to end. The note died and I stood there in silence for many moments.

Raina watched me for as long as her patience allowed. "What is it, Master?"

I spread my arms to encompass the room. "This is a concert hall. She built her entry room to be a concert hall, a ball room, a feast hall where she could share her art."

Again, a long pause. "Music was her life."

"Yes." I nodded to the room, now picking out everything that made it a musical centerpiece to the castle.

And then she caught up to me, "So, where did she do her compositions?"

"Where, indeed?" Like Lampedocht, she would need another space, and it would have to be as harmonically balanced as this one. A place we had not discovered.

We bolted breakfast and armed ourselves hastily. Again we cased the music themed artwork. We tapped, pounded, twisted, and pushed on every conceivable combination of pieces and parts of every musical flourish in the building.

For the record, there are three types of secret doors. There are the obvious ones. They leave scrapes on the floor, they do not line up perfectly with the camouflage, the buttons are poorly made or worn and easy to spot.

Then there are the unobvious ones. Those, you will not find without manhandling them, and even then the expert craftsmanship will fool you most of the time. Knocking for hollow spaces is as good as it gets, especially with a twenty waterweight sledge and maybe and axe to get through the door if the switches can't be found.

The good news is the third type, unobvious doors are normally turned into obvious ones given enough use and enough time. Yet, we came to the seventh floor empty handed, again, and it became clear that we had failed once more.

Raina looked out of the windows and down upon the horses in the front yard below. "Maybe the legend of the Opus is just a legend."

Then I had it. "Wait here."

I bolted from the room as if on fire. I returned a good while later, rope and grappling hook in hand.

"You think she used a rope and grapnel to get to her conservatory?"

I answered her wry smile with a puckered face as I pulled on heavy leather gloves. "Windows."

But that time I lost her. "What, Master?"

"The most begrudged person in any kingdom is the candlemaker. Anyone who can avoids paying for tallow or wax, simply because it is expensive, and once used it is gone forever. Better to wake early and bed early."

"Yet, this was a wealthy and creative woman, and would work whenever the mood took her."

I grabbed a moldy chair and put it through a broken pane of glass, shattering the remains and sending them showering into the garden below. "But even so, she would use all the light she could get when it was available to her."

"Did you find the room on the outside?"

I attached the grapnel to the rope, and walked to the front wall where a empty windowpane gave me a place to snag the hooks of the grapnel. "No, they all look like they are present and accounted for."

"The inside then?"

I paused, then continued trailing out the rope to the wall facing the garden. "No. All of those rooms seem to have accounted for the windows there as well."

Raina huffed as I used a dagger to shatter and scatter the last remnants of glass from the shattered windowsill. "Then why do you think it's on the inside? Why in this section?"

I sheathed the dagger, took out a section of braided leather and attached it to the Phantom Angel. "One, Nobles hate to walk, makes them feel like peasants. Everything precious is kept close to them, and the places they live." Then I slung it over my back. "In a miser's castle you will find a vault. In a castle of a mother, you will find the rooms of her children." I would just slip it through a belt with no scabbard if it were a mortal sword, but the blade would have an equal chance of eviscerating me if I bent wrong, or cutting the belt like warm butter. "And there is the obvious."

I stepped onto the sill as her voice rose in timbre. "Obvious?"

I pointed to the front windows, which were small, narrow, and reinforced to keep a man from just diving in from a siege ladder. Then she turned to the wide, inviting window I stood in. I shrugged and jumped.

I wasn't trying to elicit a cry from her. Really I wasn't, though it was warmly satisfying to hear she cared. No, I had to get past the lip of the sill with my hands, and there was just no easier way to do it.

I swung for a moment before bracing my feet against the wall. This entire space, the width of two men, was shielded from either side, above and below by the ridges in stonework. I went over a bulge in the facing, and found… more wall. I let the rope slide through my hands and thighs. I slipped downward again and… bare stone. And another and… well not what I was looking for. Windows, but with stairs barely visible beyond the filthy glass. Then again, I didn't remember those stairs.

It has always been my opinion that I would rather be right for the wrong reasons than wrong for the right ones. I started to reach around behind me to the pouch on my belt. I had spent good gold on this fancy new hook knife, and I thought this would be a good time to use it.

"Master?" I didn't have time at the moment, I was busy reaching around for the climbing hook attached to the back of my belt. It was a harder reach hovering in midair gripping a rope, than in a market stall in Hammarfall. "Master!" More panic, more volume, but that time I felt it, the line jumped in my hands. I kicked out desperately, smashing the glass and opening a hole. There was a fiery burn along my palm as my hand brushed the blade of the Angel, but there was no time to pause. I ripped the climbing knife out as the rope jerked again. "MASTER?!" I slammed the hook into the hole as the hook let go from above. I dropped, then the hooked knife caught something and I was yanked at the end of the chain to a complete stop, belt biting badly into my body and starting a whole new collection of bruises. Also slightly unplanned for– the chain ran to the clip on my belt, but was attached at the rear. So I hovered there, in midair, below my target window, oscillating back and forth facing awkwardly outward. Then again, it beat a three story drop.

"Master?" Raina called out again, "Master?"

I straightened up by bracing boots behind me and arcing my back painfully. I managed to find a part of the chain where I could wrap my left hand around it, and slowly, agonizingly, pull myself up. "Master?"

"Dear Gods, Apprentice, give a man a moment to suffer in peace!" I roared.

There was a slight pause. "So next time will you please figure into the plan three more breaths to check to make sure the sill isn't rotted and ready to pull out of the wall?"

There were times it did not pay to be born without a long sadistic streak one could visit upon taxmen and apprentices. This was one of them.

Balanced on the sill, I took out my thick-bladed dagger and knocked in the glass, pulling myself in and taking a few moments to sit on the stairs. I found a bandage and wrapped my palm, which was bleeding as if it had discovered a new trick and wanted to show off for a proud papa. I got it wrapped, but it bled through almost immediately. The cut was frightfully deep, and I would have to attend to it the second my legs stopped shaking.

Once I had recovered, I followed the stairs upward. As usual, the door that was impossible to find from the outside was easily operated from the inside. The body of a carved muse slid outward. I was on the balcony, overlooking the main hall in a location we definitely had not checked for this kind of thing. Within minutes, I was joined by Raina, who had brought the rope and grapnel from above.

I motioned for her to carry the heavy thing, then I reached down to recover the hooked climbing knife where it dangled on the chain. I smiled at her. "Useless, huh?"

She pointed to one of the chain links, which had almost pulled open under the shock of my fall. "Almost."

I shrugged. "I don't count the times I almost die."

"Really?"

"Can't count that high." I placed the hook knife gingerly, and painfully, in the pouch with one hand, leaving little drops of blood everywhere with the other. I shook my head. "I need to get this closed."

But the doing was harder than expected. The astringents I had must have gotten wet, for they were caked, and did not hold blood. The silver needle and silk thread held up fine, but the numbing agent I had was obviously a fake. So, there I was, sewing it off-handed and clumsy until Raina came to my salvation. If you can call it that.

Of all the women in all the world, I apprenticed the one who had not sewn a stitch since she was twelve. No matter how exact my instructions, the stitching wound up messy, crooked, but at least functional. I recleaned and rebandaged it, and then pressed the bandage to the frosty marble floor of the composer's keep. For the first time I cursed the lack of snow, for ice would keep the hand from swelling more surely than a dusty floor. It helped some, but the whole hand throbbed a bit, and burned with a disquieting cold.

I sat in what was quickly becoming 'my' chair and weighed the option of waiting for one more day. Sourly, I dug into the pouch of books and came out with what I thought was Hundeausführer's journal. It was not, but the next one was. I sat the first down and delved into Hundeausführer's lavish words laid at the feet of the queen of music. I found another page of musical notes, and I felt them decoding behind my eyes into sound.

I looked over my shoulder again at the balcony and clenched my teeth. Even the idea of delay made me twitchy, restless, and I kept looking upward to the balcony at the top of the flying stairs. I could not see the yawning door, but I felt it there, mocking me. Raina prepared and served some food, but I did not taste it. I stared at the fire, but I did not see it. My apprentice asked me a question but I did not hear it. I was lost in the ghostly sounds of string instruments crying in the sunlight, lost and forlorn.

Finally, I shot to my feet. I made a light pack to take with me, then I moved my right vambracer down until it immobilized the wounded portion of the hand and tightened the laces across the top of the arm and around the thumb. It was fairly useless as armor, but it just might help that cut to heal well even with me knocking it about. It was my primary sword hand, I needed it to heal well.

"Master?" I turned to find Raina ready to go, holding a lit lantern and wearing a lopsided smile. "I didn't think you were just going to leave it alone."

I took her shoulder with my left hand and squeezed. The insane pressure of the music slipped away, leaving me energized and determined. I pushed away the throbbing of my palm, and took up the Phantom Angel in my off hand. We began climbing the massive, flying staircase that hugged the orchestra pit on one side of the dance hall, and came to the opened door into the hidden staircase. The sun was still up, high in the sky, and I was thankful, but once we made one revolution on the stairs, we passed by my bloody entrance through the window, and then into utter blackness but for Raina's lamp.

The stairs were regular and easily traversed, and then another glow greeted us as we passed the first floor and a small rose window at head height illuminated the way downward. There was another secret door here that lead to the ground floor, behind a bookcase. We propped that open and continued.

Again, once we made two turns on dusty and forgotten landings, we were covered in darkness only relieved by the single, pitiable flame. We travelled downward over and over, the dark relieved only by slivers of light that sliced into the false night.

"So much for the candle theory," Raina murmured. Before I could stop myself I cast her a poisonous look.

By mutual and unspoken consent, we moved as silently as possible, which on flat, hard stone was pretty quietly. Only the glow of the lamp gave away our position, but it felt less like a precaution against discovery and more like an act of contrition for disturbing a holy place. The idea was ridiculous, but as we exited the base of the stairs into the grand, vaulted chamber, we could do nothing else.

Raina raised the lantern, adjusted up the wick to full burn, and opened the shutters wide. We had found her conservatory. In Hammarfall, Lampedocht had a room where he composed, a room he had called 'harmonically resonant' that housed dozens of instruments, writing tables and reference works. This conservatory was to his, what the Phantom Angel was to a broken bottle.

It was a natural cavern, worked only insofar as to be usable for the purpose. Stone teeth hovered overhead, dripping from the ceiling like the fangs of a thousand giant serpents. Thick curtains covered the west wall and moisture-warped instruments of every conceivable type were placed in cases and stands throughout the chamber. At one end, sitting just inside the curtains, was a massive desk. The paper would crumble to the touch. Countless candles had dripped down from the holders, creating long liquid streams caught forever in time. The inkwells were hardened into black iron pucks at the bottom of the crystal bottles. Even now, so many years later, every piece of paper, every instrument, every quill waited for her like a loyal soldier. This was her place, and as precise as her music had been, her space had been as well.

But, no clues, no tomb, no Opus Discordia. I started to mutter angrily while behind me, Raina reached up a hand to the dark curtain that spanned from wall to wall. She hovered just short of touching the thing.

"Warm," she said curiously. Then she grabbed a handful and lifted it. Our eyes, accustomed to the dark, were assaulted by the angry slash of light that appeared at the bottom. She staggered back into me and I caught myself on the desk with my bad hand. The curtain, however, had been holding on all this time simply as a matter of inertia. The second the delicate balance of forces was disturbed, it tore from the rings above in an explosion of noise and dust, filling the room with choking mold spores and dry-rotted cloth. It also exposed a wall of windows at least fifty paces wide leading to the central garden.

It was a colorful display of growing chaos that was impossible to enjoy, as the sunlight pouring in was blinding. But the moment passed, and we were able to recover enough to once again look out upon the–

No. Not the garden.

As we moved forward, we could see the huge, oval gash in the rock ceiling, the hole in the center of the garden of the castle. This, too, was overgrown, but the strangled admission of sunlight had it grow wild instead of explode in place. Without pause, and without asking for advice, Raina opened a door paned in glass and hinged on an old tin frame. The wetness beyond hit me like a fist, and I followed her into the… what? It was a cavern open to the sky. And all around, fallen seeds and stray cuttings had taken root over the centuries. Now it was a haphazard nursery. In the center was a waist deep pool, empty now. The walls were engraved with detailed carvings almost obliterated by time, the inner surface stained deep brownish black by rust.

I caught sight of a carving on the far wall, and like a hound unleashed I took the lead. In moments I was fording through waist high vegetation, still brittle from the winter. The slog proved impossible, and I leapt into the shallow pool, nearly falling and cracking my head open. Even moving in the relatively clear pool was difficult for the collection of debris there. Along the bottom the pool were a compilation of large, rounded stones and brittle white branches that grasped at the feet, collapsed into dust, or rolled from beneath secure footing. I stumbled, fell, stumbled again, but did not give pause to my weakness. I had fallen twice, catching myself on my right hand with shocks of pain, by the time I had reached the far wall.

Here was a splendid carving of a winged muse. I stared at it mesmerized, haunted by the pounding of my heart and the ache caused by the swath of time that separated us. I was utterly certain, beyond any doubt, that the face it bore was the face of Annalirya Von Zeitheim.

Music filled my soul as I reached out to her, but as I touched her cheek, I left dripping red trails from a hand where the wound had reopened. I yanked the bloody mess back, leaving her mouth brushed in crimson. I unlaced the vambracer and pulled it back up onto my forearm. The bandage was bloody and needed replacing immediately.

"Master?" Raina's frightened call drew my attention back to the wall. Annalirya Von Zeitheim was splitting down the center, the interior latches looking like teeth in a maw splitting down her center. "How?"

I shook my head as she held up the lantern. "I don't know. Maybe I'm on a pressure plate. Maybe I hit the switch by mistake."

However it had been activated, the yawning door lead to a chamber beyond. Inside, carved out of the native rock, was a dark mirror to the massive sarcophagus on the outer wall. This was not the beautiful muse of myth and legend, it was a skeletal reaper of souls. Organ pipes were carved out of the back of the thing and erupted skyward into the darkness. Notes were carved inside the swirling cape and hid amongst the bones of musical death like imps looking for scraps of flesh upon which to feed. In the hands of the skeleton, held out as if to present me with a gift, was a box made of glass panes, edges sealed in gold. Inside was a sizable wooden box carved with a mixture of scenes depicting music and death.

Raina played the lantern everywhere but where I needed it, instead asking the inane, "It looks like she is raising things from the dead? Or maybe summoning them? Are those demons?"

I glanced down at the carvings. "Horned helmets, probably barbarians. There are tales of her charming hordes with her music. Now put the light here!"

I am not naturally cautious; it was a trait I earned through gaining quite a few scars. Yet, I saw nothing obviously dangerous about the box. I took the glass sides gingerly, then dropped it to the ground. The shattering sound was musical and discordant, filling the cavern with a short scream. Then I knelt and opened the partially broken wood box, all sound around erased by the thumping of my heart. As I flung the glass and wood aside, I came upon a bundle of tight oilcloth meant to stave off time, water, and wildlife. Inside it all, I found sheet upon sheet of vellum marked with the strangely beautiful lines and notes that was the language of music.

I slung blood from my right hand and then motioned for Raina to wrap the bundle up. She slipped it into my bag, but I clutched it to my chest like a child as we traversed the white sticks and rocks that carpeted the ground of the stained pool. We snapped and cracked our way through it, up the stairs and back to our camp. There I leaned the Phantom Angel and slumped into the waiting oak chair. In an instant I popped back up. I went to the barricade of the front door and examined it closely, fearing some horror would snatch victory now that we had our prize. It did not matter. Nothing mattered. I had the Discordia and tomorrow we could start back toward Hammarfall. I immediately began disassembling the barricade.

"Master? Are we leaving tonight?"

The question shocked me. It would be foolish to leave tonight. Tomorrow we would have the light. "Don't be silly. Why?"

I drew the table away from the door, leaving only the bench in the crossbar hooks holding the whole thing together. Raina's tone bit into my pride. "Well, then, can't that wait for tomorrow?"

I paused for a second, the inescapable logic of her statement conflicting with some internal compass. I looked again at the moved furniture, saw the bloody handprints I had left, and the wound finally began to feel the sting. The world swam for a moment and I wondered if I had caught a fever. I stumbled back to the chair and fell into it. "Yes, of course."

Suddenly numb and supremely tired, I didn't eat. I didn't even feel Raina tend to my hand, but I know she had to tighten and tie off two ends that had broken and then resew the middle. She rewrapped it and said something to me, but I did not listen. Instead I closed my eyes, and slept.

I awoke upon the road, on the back of my stolen horse. The poor thing was wheezing, as if having been pushed to its limit. Froth was collected around its mouth and nose and I shook my head at strangely distant memories of galloping. Raina was nowhere to be seen. I was crossing one of the flying bridges that leapt to cross the numerous crevasses leading up to Zeitheim. Utterly disoriented, I tried to find my bearings.

It was sunset. I was coming to the ghost town we had hurried through. I shivered, then blinked hard, but the world continued to stubbornly suggest I was alone, coming to the dilapidated village, on the road, on a saddleless horse. I was three or four days from the castle. The horse was alive, so I had to have stopped, and I could not have galloped all the way here. The deep hollow put of my stomach said I had not brought food, nor water for myself or the animal. I struggled to regain control of my mind, to remember what had happened and why.

Panic flooded me. I felt the bag of books, including the Opus at my side, and waves of calm eased the tide panic back into its sea. There was a scuffle of boot on rock. I spun again in the saddle, reaching for the Phantom Angel...

It was not there.

That is, of course, when the rock hit my head.

Act Three

The Opus Discordia

ONE

CONFUSION

WELL, THE rock wasn't the first clue. The first clue was the bolt from the crossbow. It slammed into my chest, piercing the bag of books I clutched like a child, and rocked me in my seat. Dazed, I looked inside the bag and saw a thin volume cored from front to back and then stopped dead by the very first page of the Discordia.

My heart leapt into my throat as I tore open the wrappings. It was in vain, for the arrow had pierced everything with ease, but it could not even put the smallest scratch on the thong bound symphony. I saw that and was simultaneously chilled and relieved.

Understand that this was all happening while I was riding TOWARD THE ENEMY WHO WAS SHOOTING AT ME. To say I was a little off would be a kindness. For their part, those doing the shooting just stared at my continued survival, and then one of them tossed the rock that hit me in the head.

I fell from my horse. Don't laugh. A fall from the back of the horse does not seem to be far, but men have broken their necks doing it. Apparently, I did it wrong, because my neck stayed stubbornly in one piece.

"Bind him! Bind him!"

Now, I thought the rock was enough, and the instructions were to tie me up. Instead the bastards improvised. They beat me, and kicked me for good measure. Dazed, bleeding, I thought it was all a bit of overkill, but they were too busy hitting me to ask any questions. Soon, hands quested over me, and once they found all the obvious knives, they happened upon one hidden knife and then searched for them as well. They found most of them, but I had a few throwing razors and a heartpin left when they tied me to a huge set of crossed beams. Now if I could just reach the weapons, I could escape. Seems they thought of that.

The whole of my gear, including the books and the Opus, were dumped in the grass right next to me. They might as well have been on the other side of the sea. Two reasons. The first was it looked like there were fifty men spread out and encamped in the village. Secondly, it was hard to tie a man up correctly, but these bastards had obviously been practicing. They had soaked leather straps that they bound my wrists and ankles to the X shaped planks. They were tight now, but by morning they would cut off the blood to my hands and feet as the leather shrank. They had neglected to take off my boots, which might keep them functional for an extra day, but most torturers would remove them as soon as they got started. In a day or two, I would lose them to blood loss even if otherwise unmolested. *If* I lived that long.

As I was tied, I looked up into the dark caves every house in town had become. The chill I had first felt here came again and made me shiver. A few had fires lit in the hearths of abandoned homes, but the shadows were wrong. Angry, somehow. Suddenly I was not sure any of us would live that long.

The leader, a tall, clean-shaven man with beautifully bronzed skin, a gorgeous, massive mane of white hair, and the face of a street fighter, gave orders easily and effortlessly. Those that followed him did so as if their necks were slightly stiff from leading rather than following. Add to this, all the orders were given in a clipped, proper form of the language. These could only be nobility.

Oh my. The great and the good. I am saved, dammit.

They backed off as the commander stalked toward me. He didn't even pause as he reached way back, took a grip full of hair, and slammed his fist into the side of my head. I had just enough time and good grace to tilt my head into the blow. He connected with my skull instead of my jaw. Oh, it didn't hurt me any less, it just hurt him a hell of a lot more. He cursed bitterly and cradled his hand.

"You will pay for that, commoner."

Which tells me that in that nowhere place where watchmen go to learn to such gems as, *What do we have here*? Next door to that is an inbred little palace where the apprentice nobility master, *You will pay for that, commoner*. I smiled at him. Not the nice smile, the other one. "And here I was certain we would be fast friends, milord. It looks like you have me already trussed like a peasant lass for your pleasure."

He swung again, and this time all I could do is twist my head to lessen the impact some. There were still stars and the taste of blood. It lit fires inside of me, and if we had been on equal footing I would gladly do to this scion of some unforking family tree what he was clearly about to do to me. On the other hand I knew this– you call a man a rapist, and he is disgusted. You call a rapist a rapist and he reacts with violence.

He leaned in closely and hissed, "You son of a whore, what did you do to my son!"

Unable to stop myself, I spit in his face. I'm not saying it was a wise decision, but had he leaned in about half a finger further, I would have torn out his throat with my teeth. Let's just say I don't thrive in captivity. "I don't know who your son is you dung-eating moron."

He wiped off the spit, then backhanded me. It didn't connect the way he wanted, which told me he really didn't do this kind of thing often. Hitting a bound man, after all, was not an art, nor science. It just took a certain familiarity with violence. This was the kind of monster that used wealth and position as his knife and club. If I got the chance, I would gladly show him what a man who used actual knives and clubs could do.

He threw back his cloak and drew himself up to his full height, showing off the utterly inappropriate clothing from the golden brocade of his shirt, to the complex stitching on his boots. He was a big man, no doubt, and probably physically powerful in his prime. Now his mane of white hair was thinning abruptly, and his clothing made him look like a clown who had run off with the crown jewels. "I am Raymond Von Schwarzklippen. My son is Alexander Von Schwarzklippen. You will tell me what spell you have put upon him."

I sneered, "Your son was in charge, your royalness. So I have no idea where he is or what has happened to him. Of course he got himself captured twice, drunk quite a few times, and finally got sent back to Hammarfall with his tail between his legs, dragging his ass the whole way to wipe the stink of fear-squirted dung from his–" Then the subject of the conversation was there and I smirked. "Well, I see he didn't get that far. Looks just as I left him. Can I go now?"

Dirty, disheveled, and apparently drunk, Stinkleavin wobbled on his feet, but managed to glare at me over his no longer neat and trimmed beard. He was pale, yet flushed. I noticed he carried no weapon, and his clothes were stained from some kind of food and many kinds of drink. He leaned forward and slapped me. Then again, harder. Then again and again. Soon his fists closed. He tired quickly and staggered away from me. The smell that wafted from him, however, was indescribable, worse than rotting meat.

"Cure him!" The elder commanded, apparently to me.

My head was swimming from rage and pain. Now, looking at the sullen and spoiled face of Alexander Jaeger, only the leather and wood frame kept him alive. I managed a low growl. "Cure him? Of what do you speak?"

Raymond came just outside of biting distance and glowered at me. "Cure him, witch!"

I gathered every fiber of my being and forced a double lungful of air to rattle the sky, "CURE HIM OF WHAT?"

Possessed of a fit of utter abandon, Alexander yanked down his breeches and lifted his shirt, screaming, "YOU HAVE DONE THIS!"

The smell was indescribable. His entire genital area was blackened, green, swollen and oozing. Immediately I thought back the many weeks to when A.J. Von Rottenkranken had put his hands on me, and I had taken the bolt out of the belly of a dead man and jabbed into his groin with the tip. Apparently the iron head had nipped his flesh and infection had followed.

I was hurt. I was bound. I was injured. Yet, I could not stop my mouth, "Now I see the family resemblance."

Raymond Von SausageLimppen attacked. He may have been unfamiliar with hands-on violence, but he was a quick learner. He grabbed a hold of the bloody bandage on my palm and squeezed. I admit it, I screamed. Then he let go and put punch after punch into my exposed and skull-less gut. It went on for a minute, and I got that sick, slippery feeling inside my bowels that happened when I was ill, or there was blood escaping somewhere. My vision blurred and jumped with every impact, but for a heartbeat or two, I was certain that pale faces, distended and hungry with shadows, watched from every open dark portal in the village. Finally, panting, he backed off.

"Take this demon to the edge of camp so I cannot hear his vile mouth! Post guards! Tomorrow we will convince him to cure my son!" The elder Schwarzklippen roared, and when he turned to Alexander, his tone was only barely softened, "Cover yourself and go rest. We will clean up the rest of your mess tomorrow."

The man-child did cover himself, but he also dodged forward and grabbed the satchel of books from the ground. If the singular look inside did not tell him he had the Opus, the inarticulate rage that burst from my mouth would have.

He smiled through the sheen of pale sweat, and then made for the largest house with a fire burning. I continued to scream and lunge against my restraints, all thoughts driven from me in a mad, animal fury. Two guards dragged the standing X to which I was tied out to the edge of camp near the bridge. Then one struck me with the flat of his blade, knocking my senses far beyond my reach.

All in all, it was in no way hard to reason what had happened. We had been sending a steady stream of corpses back to Hammarfall. One had carried a note to call for a group to come for my head. And, poor bastards, they had answered with fifty men– nobles, squires, servants, and guardsmen to do the real work. They had prepared for me, but they were not prepared for what was coming.

My vision swam for hours, true unconsciousness denied me by some nasty twist of fate. Instead my eyes caught sight of corrupted figures slipping in and out of the shadows. Slipping is wrong, for they were unconcerned, upright, calm, and without hurry. Yet they appeared only where the eye could scarcely follow and then dissolved into some patch of shadow or around the corner. And their faces! Their features were corroded almost past recognition. Their mouths distended open like a snake's. The eyes and nostrils were gaping black pits. Every opening cracked the skin of the face so they all looked like screaming skulls, but far too human for all that.

Lies of the first book, the oldest book about Annalirya Von Zeitheim I had read, came to mind.

...and the Bitter Queen of the mountain palace screamed her rage at the destruction of her instruments by the boys of Opferhügel. She summoned her Riders through the songs of their kind, and sent them burning down the mountain with swords carved of the darkest night. But the boys had since confessed to their crime to the village priest. As the moon fell beneath the horizon, the priest met the Riders in the village square.

They surrounded him, dread destriers screaming into the night as they reared and carved runnels into the dirt with their hooves. For days the darkness lasted, the sun banished from the sky as the village priest continued to defy the Symphonic Siren and her minions. But he was but mortal, and his strength failed as the horrified people of Opferhügel watched.

Finally the priest lost all heart. In his despair he raised up his holy staff and cried, "Take mine life, but kill not one of these people of Opferhügel!"

The Riders accepted his bargain, and he broke his holy staff upon the ground. The Riders fell upon the priest with a horrible fury for vengeance delayed. They cut him to pieces, and their mounts stomped him into the mud. Yet they were held there by powerful order of their mistress. And so they turned upon the citizens of Opferhügel. They fell upon them with blades so black they could not be seen. They burned with fires so hot they froze the blood. They harvested the sinews of the folk as they had been bidden. And as they had bargained, none of the folk would ever die...

A little girl peeked from around the corner of a building. She smiled, but the smile continued to grow, her eyes sunk into burning pits, her mouth opened in a never ending scream as she slid from view.

There was only one guard now to watch over me, but he was watching the town instead of the road. He started.

I muttered through swollen lips, "Thomorgon's dusty balls, you see them, too?"

The guard winced at the God of Death's name. He stared at me with revulsion. "Send your imps away, wizard."

Despite everything, I chuckled darkly. "A wizard, am I? Should I have been caught so easily?"

The man swallowed hard. "Von Schwarzklippen told us of how you came back from the dead. How you slaughtered thirty men in the graveyard!"

"And so you think it wise to hold me now?"

"My cousin rode with Alexander. Did you sacrifice his soul to save your own skin?" The guard did not wait for an answer, but put down his shield and took a thick leather strap from his pouch. Then he stalked forward and wrapped it about my face, first filling my mouth and then tying my jaw shut and fastening it behind my head.

"No hexes, demon whelp!" The guard hissed at me.

Behind him, two dozen paces, I saw a little boy crawl like a spider across a roof. He stared at me with hungry, black pits and then leapt from one house to another. Midway, the moon came from behind the clouds, the shafts of light erasing him from existence. No! I was mistaken, for the boy appeared in the shade of the next house's second story, and slithered into the window.

All around the encampment, fires were lit, food was cooked and consumed, torches burned. Even yet, it would not be long. Then, staggering with the consumption of his courage, the broken toothed Blonde of Alexander's company left the safety of one lit home. He came on, staggering less as his plan puddled in the base of his skull. He dropped the bottle to the ground. At the base of the decanter, facing away from the lights, I thought I say an eye watch hungrily.

He came as close to me as a lover, leaning against me as his skin burned. He pressed against me for balance, hands groping along his belt until he found and retrieved his dagger.

"Alright you foul bastard," he slurred pressing the knife against my cheek, "where is your bitch? I never got my turn back at the conductor's house with a whore, so I figure you owe me a turn with yours."

My guard sneered, "Bodo, you are drunk, go to bed."

"Shut up, Stefan!" Blonde/Bodo railed, "Or I'll tell your mother the baby in your father's mistress' belly..." he lost the train of the thought in the deluge of alcohol,"...is?"

Though grammatically imperfect, the guard reacted as if shot. "Don't be a feltcher, Bodo. Anyway we caught him alone on the road. Nobody was with him."

Bodo turned back to me, the booze combined with the stumps of shattered teeth to lend his mouth a powerful reek. "You are never far from your bitch, Crow. Where is she? Huh?"

"He's gagged, you prat."

He pressed the edge of the dagger into my face. It hurt, it pinched, but the dumb bastard was as fastidious with his weapons as every other facet of his life; it couldn't cut butter. Then, far behind him, a nude woman wafted before a door. Though naked, she was as unappetizing a thing as I had seen in my life, all dark tendrils and puckered skin, sunken eyes and screaming lips. She was there, on display, and then she moved back into the darkness. Even with the dagger against my face, I started and stared.

As drunk as he was, Bodo could not help but notice. He followed my eyes to the empty house. "What? There?"

And without waiting for an answer he whooped and ran off for the building. Calling out his intentions toward rape in graphic detail.

"Shut it, you stupid bastard!" the guard called to no avail. He turned to me as Bodo disappeared into the house, speaking with some honesty. "If he doesn't find her there, and I doubt he will, I will be sorry for you then."

Then a blade, slim and deadly, snaked around his neck. The arm, draped in gray fabrics followed suit, its mate yanking back the head and clamping a hand over the mouth as the knife pierced the throat from right to left through the windpipe as she had been instructed. The body panicked, and the rag-draped ghost held on as he shuddered, slapped at her arms, voided itself, and died.

The ragman sprang forward and sliced the thick leather from my limbs with sure strokes. She even caught me as I fell from the perch. Over her shoulder she had rigged a makeshift sheath, and slung the Phantom Angel there. I laughed silently. My apprentice had found me.

Breath brushed against my ear, "You must move. We are not safe."

The clouds cleared again and pure moonlight shone down upon us. The whole, dilapidated town appeared edged in silver. Then, an undulating scream pierced the night. It's like had never been heard in the deepest crofts of the most perverse torturers in all the realms. It was a scream of such horror and pain, I had never heard its equal. I soon would.

I grabbed Raina's hand and sprang to action. Well, stumbled. My feet were half dead, and my hands all but useless after the straps, yet we bolted for our very lives. We made it behind the nearest building as men poured from the common rooms of each occupied home.

I pointed upwards and cupped my hands she shook her head and pulled me further into the doomed village. It seemed like our footsteps on soft earth rang like metal boots on marble. Men were shouting, echoes off the building making them sound like they were coming from everywhere. Finally, she stopped and jumped to grab the edge of a small addition onto the–

It was the village church.

–well, it was as good a place as anywhere. I felt a stab to my pride when Raina had to turn to grab half numb hands and haul me onto the small add on shed. From there, we scrambled onto the roof. At the peak, we could see Raymond ordering his men to search every building. Men fanned out in every direction and we ducked under the peak of the roof. I desperately pumped my hands into fists, trying to work life back into them. My wound was bleeding. Just then, the church bells rang.

Now, I am not an expert on remaining unseen. No! Wait! I *am* an expert, and I can tell you that if you do not want to be seen, having a damn church bell going off above you is not the way to do it. The clouds returned, covering over the moon, but it was not shadow enough to save us. I grabbed Raina's shoulder and rolled over to make for ground level, but cold nails of fear immobilized every limb. Raina turned, and gasped in an aborted scream.

Down at the edge of the roof, a hideously distorted face slowly, agonizingly rose out of the alleyway below and onto the roof. There was a scuffle in the alleyway and a voice cried, "What?"

The… thing, it turned to whatever luckless bastard spoke in the alley, and descended toward him. There was a scream, and a heartbeat after, the sounds of a dog eating a bird. Fans of blood flew into the air. By mutual and unspoken consent, Raina and I scrambled to the peak of the roof again. There, the sounds of shared horror could reach us undisturbed. I paused, watching as men entered dark buildings, searching for me. Distorted creatures would appear from the murky shadows and…

I turned away, retching, but Raina did not hesitate. She leapt to the base of the church's bell tower and scampered up the decorated side. I spit a gob of bile to the roof, then followed. Fear must have had my heart beating like a jackrabbit, for my hands were stinging with pins and needles, but functional. At least functional enough to get me to the bell tower. The return of use had my wounded palm in agony, but I could not listen to it.

Half to herself, half to the things in the dark, Raina muttered, "We are in the church. They can't come here. We're in the church."

I was hoping the dire spirits knew the rules as well as she did.

Regardless, we had an even better view of the carnage, for carnage it was. From one house a geyser of blood vomited onto the street. Into another, one man ran. His screams brought three more, who disappeared inside. More screams joined the first, and only after they stopped did four skinless brutes jog out onto the street and attack more of Raymond's men. Their blows were powerful beyond imagination, and they did not die until plied with fire and oil. And then they screamed.

The half-seen herd of horses that had borne the men to this place added their panicked noises into the night. They dissolved into a cloud of bones and vaporized blood from the corral.

Alexander then appeared in the street. Empty handed, only half dressed. He fled down the street, his cries mingling with the sounds of suffering all around. He stayed in the open street, snagged a fleeing horse from the group, mounted bareback, and fled toward Hammarfall leaving his father and all the rest. My eyes tracked back to the house from where he had appeared.

The words that escaped me steeled my purpose, "We have to go get the Opus."

But Raina sounded in no fit state. "Oh Gods. Oh Gods. Oh Gods. Oh Gods. Oh Gods. Master…"

"What?"

"There is no bell."

I looked upwards, into the darkness of the tower, to the empty, hollow, shadowed area which should have contained a big brass bell. The damned bell that had rung only moments ago. Instead it held only eyes. Eyes and mouths.

In that instant, Raina rolled out of the tower, grabbing the edge and almost leaping downward from ledge to ledge. I was too weak. I would never make it. But I could buy her precious heartbeats to make her escape. As her head disappeared from view, I dove and grasped the handle of the Phantom Angel. I yanked it free of the makeshift sheath, and unwittingly unleashed a blade of hot blue fire that seared the eyes and flared into every corner. The specters flashed into black ash that evaporated with the smell of burning flesh.

I squinted at the blade, only remembering it doing this once before, and that in the presence of a twisted demon get. But that had been a candle flame to this raging fire.

The cloud passed the face of the moon, and silvery light carpeted the town again. The screams and moans were dying, and I gave up all pretense of stealth to shout, "Raina!"

She reached the roof and turned. I threw the Angel like a spear, lodging it in the roof by the impossibly sharp blade. As she pried it loose, I swung down and made my way to the peak. She held the burning sword to the sky, casting light in all directions. I reached for the Angel, and she recoiled. I took a double handful of her shirt and pulled her masked face close.

"Give me. My sword." Trembling, she handed it over, but her eyes darted everywhere, and I knew wherever she looked she saw fresh horrors staring back. I let her go, then moved my hand to the back of her neck. I pulled her head to touch mine, our eyes locked. "Stay close. I am going to get you out of this."

Her brilliant green eyes, frightened and alone, focused upon mine. Her irises opened a fraction, and she nodded.

I let her go, and made for the corner of the building. I heard her right behind. I leapt from the roof of the church to the smaller add on. I swept the blue burning blade in an arc, and the shadows erupted into ash, ambushers incinerated by the light of the elvish blaze.

Another inhuman shriek tore the night, the gravestone for another lost soul, as we made the edge of town near the wooden X that had been my prison. It was instant, one step we were cold, fearful, and hunted. The next, the cool night touched our sweaty bodies and kissed burning foreheads. The Phantom guttered out.

I took Raina's hand. "Get your horse and supplies. Get back here, and if you don't see me do not, DO NOT leave this bridge until morning." I turned to head back into town.

"Crow? Where are you going?"

I took one step. The feeling of utter hopelessness, of unquenchable anger, of bone chilling cold returned. The Phantom Angel flared with blue fire from tip to crossguard. "I must get the Opus." I heard the steps of the two remaining skinless thugs. "Run!"

And then I readied my sword, taking a deep breath of foul air, exhaling all hopes and doubts. Dripping blood, sheathed in bleeding muscles, they rounded a house at a run.

Then they charged.

These were not creatures of talons and smoke, but flesh and blood, and required more than just light and flame to dissolve them. I obliged. I batted the sword of the first to the side, then took that arm with a vicious swipe. I dodged past the silent thing to plunge my sword hilt deep into the chest of the second. That was it. It should be over. If life were fair.

And it isn't.

I felt a hand grab onto the nape of my vest and shirt, tossing me like a spoiled child tosses a kitten that has scratched him. I flew end over end and landed on the ground, rolling to a stop of brand new aches and pains. I staggered to my feet, but they were already coming, skinless feet leaving bloody footprints in the dirt.

I managed to stand and slipped a hidden knife into my hand. I ducked the bare knuckled swing of the weaponless thing and then rolled to the side to avoid the sword strike of the next. He was moving slower, and continued to suffer as the Phantom Angel blazed in his chest cavity, blackening everything and turning his torso into a lamp. I flicked my knife, burying it perfectly in the face of the second bloody corpse. He did not stop, nor drop, or even pause the least little bit with four inches of steel in his face.

"All the hairy balls of every Lord in–"

I may have had something pithy to add to that complaint, but the one armed beast caught me under the left arm with a powerful blow. The arm went numb, my breath whooshed out, and only the awkwardness of the backhand that hit me next kept it from severing my spine. I rolled to a stop again, and they both were coming. One fast and armed only with his phenomenal strength. The other slower with a sword. No! He still had two swords. One of them, the one in his chest, was mine.

I struggled to my feet as the first ran at me. I never made it upright, but instead dove from a crouch to the side, then back behind him. I gripped the Phantom with one good hand and desperately heaved upwards. The blade cut through the thing and left its body, ringing off of its own down cut and deflecting the blow. I did not stop, I leapt backwards with a desperate, blind chop.

The Phantom bit deeply into the charging thing, blazing and burning a path and turning bleeding exposed muscle into useless coal. I rolled to the side, and with two more slashes, it was done. Their heads rolled on the turf, but it was not this that stopped them. Wherever the blue fire feasted, it continued to crawl, destroying the bodies completely and turning these beasts of destruction into ineffectual, flopping pieces.

Wounded hand screaming at me, I held the blazing sword high, dispelling the shadows and coughing against the cracked ribs that ached beneath my left arm. A fat drop splashed into my eye. My right hand was bleeding again. Cursing, I used the blade to slit the tattered wrappings and pressed the ugly, clotted, twice-sewn wound to the blade. It burned and hissed, and I held it only for a few beats of my heart before pulling the right hand away.

In some poxy bard's rendition, I'm sure it would be hale and healthy, whole and ready for more. What it was in real life was seared shut and still wailing in pain, but at least the skin did not look charred or burned in any way. As magic goes, that's as friendly as it gets in my experience.

Finally, finally, I was feeling human. I walked tiredly to the house Alexander had been cowering inside. A light still flickered there. As I came closer, I could make out the voice of the elder Von Schwarzklippen.

"Back! Back! Damn you!"

Sword high, I walked through the doorless mouth of the house. There, Raymond stood in the remains of a camp. Bedrolls were everywhere, packs and saddles strewn by hasty feet. There were five bodies, or parts of bodies strewn as if kicked by a mad god. They had not been simply murdered, but shredded by hate both ancient and everlasting. Blood was knuckle deep on the floor. Someone had kicked the emergency water bucket into the fire, extinguishing it by accident, I was guessing. Raymond Von Schwarzklippen had foregone his sword, and instead held a torch in each hand to chase back the shadows. When my blue light began to overtake his orange torches he spun to face me.

"You!" In that word was all the accusations of a lifetime rendered down into poison.

I looked about, and on a chair in the corner, moth eaten and time stained, sat my satchel with Hundeausführer's books and the Opus.

"You heathen bastard! What have you done? What have you done?" He was near tears, past rage, somewhere near the intersection of despair and insanity. I ignored him and retrieved the pack. I winced, lifting it with my left arm, but got it around my neck and shoulder all the same.

"Come back for your grimoires?" He ranted, teeth bared in a snarl. "Well today you have made a very powerful enemy. The Von Schwarzklippen family will hunt you down unto my son's, son's, son, demon!"

Against my better judgment, I paused in the door. "You know, in all this country I have met many bad men. The worst, however, has got to be the product of your loins."

The old man spat, holding the torches before him like a protective wall. "Go to hell, peasant."

Without missing a beat, I swung the Phantom in a tight, horizontal arc. The heads of both the torches splashed into the lake of congealing blood at his feet. They hissed like snakes–

"You first, father of monsters."

–and went out.

My light went with me. Shorter than a sword thrust later, his shriek started high, and then moved higher, and higher, and higher, climbing the scales of music into the realms only gods of pain and agony could hear.

I exited to see them, all of them, every single lost soul surrounding me with corrupted faces and caustic eyes. I raised the sword high, and they stayed out of its light. I moved, and they gave way.

I nodded grimly at the horrors, fatigued past fear. "Yeah, you stay there."

Then, a gentle glinting caught my eye. It lay in the middle of the street, right in front of the church. I walked the ten paces, the bubble of specters moving with me, a hungry circle of doom. I came to the spot, and saw the little telltale flake of silver winking at me. Uncovered by some hoof or boot, I knelt and dug around the thing with a dagger, loosening it from the soil.

In moments, it came loose into my hand. I had to knock dirt free, and slowly, slowly, I revealed a blazing sun, metal corona making a wicked point, behind a crudely cast crossed scythe and sword. It was a symbol of one of the old gods, worshipped by farmers in the wild. It was pitted, and green copper peeked from beneath the flaking silver finish. The thing was probably worthless, but out of habit I tossed it into the satchel with the books. My arm was aching, so I shoved the sword tip first into the soil, then took the time to check for the Opus.

Some hidden sense tingled at the nape of my neck, and I ducked. The creature using my shadow to sneak up and consume me was blasted by the elvish light. I struggled to my feet, cursing and clutching the Opus to my chest.

There arose a massive wailing from the assembled crowd. I spun to see them from every side, and as I turned more sounds of unholy lament were raised. Then, as if snatched by giant hands, they were yanked back into the shadows and sucked back into the nether worlds from where they came. Quite without warning, I was alone. The Phantom Angel guttered out.

I blinked, pulled the sword from the ground, and made my way back to the bridge.

There, Raina was waiting. "What happened?"

"They just," I searched for a more complete answer than, "went away."

"Are you sure?" she asked, voice shaking. I placed the Opus into the satchel and held up the Phantom Angel. Other than the almost unnatural sheen to the blade, it looked decidedly mortal at the moment.

"Come on." She handed me the makeshift scabbard. I had to unwind the leather thongs to get the blade in, and then rewind them to keep it snug. We exited the far side of the village as I slung it upon my back.

We left the dead, fresh and uneasy ancient both, well behind before we stopped again. When we did, we found the body of Hanner. It looked like he had been beaten to death, then strung up like a criminal. They had taken everything from him: his weapon, his clothes, and his dignity. He may have left me when I needed him, but if there had to be a punishment for that, he had paid it tenfold. Now I thought of the dumb bastard that had let him go so easily, left amongst a group of jackals who would turn upon him the moment his protector was out of sight. That bastard was myself.

I shared some measure of blame. I would purge my sin when I found Alexander Jaeger Von Schwarzklippen. I would do things to him that would make the Gods weep, and then bathe in the tears. I turned wordlessly to Raina. She was crying. I wanted to snap at her for being weak, but I would have had to wipe my own eyes to see her clearly. And I was not that kind of man anymore.

Burying Hanner took much of the morning, and so we only found our cache toward evening. We climbed the tree, and recovered the bundles. We packed up everything we had and moved as fast as we could. It was far faster returning than getting there. Our ambushers were dead, we were no longer saddled with the anchor of the Rakes, though we were once again reduced to one nameless horse. I let Raina ride without comment, working my hand every day to stretch the knitting muscle.

Still, the silence was building a pressure between us. Normally I prized Raina for her ability to simply watch and wait instead of nagging me with endless minutiae, but so much had happened, the quiet was like stone yokes weighing us down.

When she spoke, it was soft and out of nowhere. "I understand that I have not known you that long, Master, but I had hoped I was doing a satisfactory job."

I chuckled, waving her off tiredly. "You rescued me from the edge of an armed camp of men, approached without being seen, and struck down a soldier without hesitation." I noticed she shuddered. "You did better than anyone could have asked."

"Then why abandon me?" Simple words, but barbed. Betrayal barely beneath the surface.

I shook my head. We continued onward, almost a thousand paces before I could even hazard a guess. And even then, "I know not," was all I had. "I left without a pack, without food, without a saddle, and without my sword…"

But as I spoke, a desperate weight coalesced and hung from my guts, pressing them toward the dirt. My steps lost their forward push, and carried on only on momentum for a few tiny strides. She brought the horse to a stop.

"Why would you do that?"

I looked at her, and my face, the face I had practiced and trained for years to show nothing, to give away nothing, to admit to nothing... fear bubbled to the surface of that face. I trembled and clutched the bag with the Opus tightly to my chest.

A defiant fire kindled within me. It flickered, and burned, and then raged. I took a deep breath. "It doesn't matter. We have a pile of gold waiting us at the end of this road. Let's get there and get paid."

She nodded sadly. "I could do with paid."

"And then," I sighed and began walking again, "we find a sane city to spend it in."

"If Volker isn't dead."

"Oh, I don't think he's dead." I brought out my skin and took a drink of watered wine, wishing for some honey to sweeten it. "That would be far too easy."

Two

Poison

NO MAN has ever died because he has prepared for the worst case scenario. He may have died anyway, but that is another matter.

My apprentice was sleeping fitfully, speaking less. The cause was easily diagnosed– She had lived a life training for battle but existing as a watchman. City guards use their clubs far more than their swords, but out here she had killed at least four or five men, and maybe more. Harder to come to terms with was the one killed from behind, in cold blood, in the middle of the night. Then came a night of unspeakable horrors… When I was her age, I would have rebuffed any offer of help. So I pursed my lips and waited for her to ask.

There is a tradition from a far away country; The porcelain bowls used by nobility are expensive, made by master craftsmen, and colored a beautiful blue. When they are broken, they are not discarded, but instead are brought to another crafter who seals the wound with gold. The object may be broken hundreds of times as it is passed down the generations, with scant veins of gold appearing in a web-work across the thing. It is considered just so with people, only people are repaired with steel. Fracture them enough, and eventually they will never be shattered by anything, ever. Pain is a forge that strengthens us, and renders us more powerful as long as we refuse to stay broken. I did not know how to comfort her, for it was my life she saved. But when she found her own way, the steel would begin to seal the wound and bind the cracked parts of her psyche together.

We had left Hammarfall with more than two dozen men and horses, a huge noticeable train of noise. We entered Hammarfall as a rider and a horsewoman. This time we avoided the main gate and circled to the seaward side where, for only an outrageous fee, a boatman let us aboard and took us to the southern docks. Once there, we could take the southern gate from the docks directly to the Lord's Quarter. When we arrived there were dozens of boats taking on or dropping off passengers. Some brought food. Others brought luxuries. I had prepared Lampedocht's signet from my pack to get us past the guards, but in the past weeks this had apparently become so routine the guards at the waterfront no longer even asked.

I shook my head. My apprentice, quiet all morning, shook her head as well and spoke my mind, "How do they expect to keep Volker's men out?"

"There is no way," I responded. Less than a quarter candlemark later, were moving toward Lampedocht's mansion.

We arrived dirty, tired, smelling of sweat and horses, but before we could even be announced, the conductor was there. I have seen men engaged in long campaigns coming home to newly minted wives who had pined and yearned for their safe return. That was how he looked at me: frightened, hopeful, and hungry.

There was no exchange of pleasantries, no questions of health, he nearly trembled as he asked, "You have it?"

I found my hands were made of lead as I reached into the satchel at my side. They shook as I pulled out the four finger thick bundle of bound pages. Lampedocht reached for the sheaf, saving me from having to fight to give it to him. I felt a terrible hollowness inside me as he turned away and rushed to a side table. He brushed bric-a-brac away, clearing a surface and sending an ancient vase crashing to the floor. He spared it neither a moment nor thought as he unwound the strings and brought forth the first page.

Penned in a delicate hand, scribed in dark brown ink, the conductor began to weep with joy as the words were revealed: *The Magnum Opus Discordia*

Then he considered the massive stack of papers the symphony entailed, and shook his head. "Master Crow, you shall have your coin. Please, make yourselves at home. Have the servants draw you baths. Please excuse me, I have to study this. I will see you…" He began flipping through loose pages, his eyes going wide as his voice trailed away, "...at dinner. Will…see you… at dinner…"

A serving girl, as confused as we at the conductor so focused on the pages standing up in the middle of the hallway, smiled glassily and motioned for us to follow. I expected to be shoved into the attic where the Rakes had been put. Thusly I was surprised and pleased to be put into what amounted to a suite in the upper stories of the mansion. Raina would sleep in the anteroom, my room on one wall, the next door was to the bathroom and garderobe, the walk-in master closet on the last wall. My room had only the one door, and then colossal windows, as tall as two men and covering the other three walls. I was too numb to see anything except vulnerabilities. I closed the massive curtains, the only light come streaming in through the high arched window tops above the curtain rods. I reached for wire to bind them, and remembered that the only thing I had of value was with Lampedocht.

We divested ourselves of our gear. The girls produced robes for us while they took every scrap of clothing we owned and our boots for cleaning. I had taken a long while to turn mine over, for I had to remove a dozen razors, blades, needles, and a few hidden coins, so they could be washed in safety.

A coal fired furnace in the basement had been heating water since we arrived, and the girl worked the winch that turned a screw mechanism in a pipe that brought the water all the way to spill into the tub. I had never seen such a thing. Raina was delighted and clapped to see it work.

I checked on the bags of coin and the secreted bag of gems from Alexander, and found them unmolested. I took out one shining silver disc and held it up. "King or sigil for the bath first?"

She snatched the coin from my fingers, and we both stared at the empty hand for long moments after. I was overcome with a weird, raw terror. There was no way she should have been able to take that coin. *I should have seen it coming. I should have read her intent long before she moved. Was I losing my touch? Was I that tired? What was wrong with me*?

Raina tossed the coin onto the table, "No, you first."

The servants retreated, and Raina dropped her robe to the floor with only a hint of modesty. Maybe she was trying to prove a point. Maybe she was glad to be alive and thought to share the feeling. But she stripped my robe off in a very businesslike manner and led me to the bath. It would have held four people easily. Even with her helping me in and then taking up position behind me, there was room to stretch.

Instead I just sat there. I could feel her cinch up behind me. A second later she slathered cool, gooey strings of soap across my shoulders. It should have been pleasant, it should have been relaxing. Instead all I could do is stare at my traitorous hands.

"That wound is healing nicely."

I opened my hand. The weeks on the road left an angry pink welt, well on its way to becoming a scar. All I could do is stare at it, and feel the huge void inside of me where something used to be.

Raina washed me, and then herself once she had ejected me. She pulled the plug at the bottom of the tub and the black water sluiced down the pipe and out of the wall. After, we both stood in our robes. I could feel the rising tide of anger in her, and I could feel the gaping hole widening inside myself.

When our clothes arrived, we were summoned to dinner. We ate alone. Lampedocht never left his conservatory, where he had retired with the manuscript, and Winifred was nowhere in evidence. We finished our meal. I walked to my bed as a man with no soul. I shuffled through the door to the pitch blackness of my suite and collapsed, face first on the bed.

From the doorway, I could feel more than see Raina's glowering form. "What is wrong with you?"

I didn't answer. I couldn't answer. Every step toward the Opus had been more sure than the last. The way back had been numb, as if burning with the power of the pages I carried. Now that the Opus was gone, and I knew it belonged with Lampedocht above all other men, I was hollow, empty, a shell. A scream came from my deepest soul and exited my body as a silent sigh.

I closed my eyes and prayed I would never open them.

The world was in color, bolder and richer than I had ever seen. The fir trees on all sides towered above, but not as high as the leaden monuments of marble and limestone. These towering monstrosities were marked with screaming faces carved by every violent storm, these the only remains of the names and dates they had borne in memoriam.

I turned to see the Phantom, hooded and inscrutable. It spread its arms and pointed behind me through the towering tombstones. I looked back and heard the faint strains of a symphony on the wind. At the edge of sight, the ground roiled, the growth twisted, and some horrible transformation was happening. I turned, and the Phantom was gone. Fled. That was the word that felt true–fled.

I was running without knowing why. I was moving with such intensity that my entire body hurt. That is not true, I was in utter agony. My lungs burned and my legs screamed, and all the while the music became louder and louder. I looked over my shoulder, and saw the corroded faces peering from the dark places. I turned back and there were thousands of them there, rictus grins from every shadow. There was a burning sting on the back of my neck.

I screamed and fell into the lake.

Water pressed in on all sides. It crushed me, smashed me into rocks. The tunnel caught me, held me, and I could not breathe. I could not wiggle free.

Raina slapped me with all the mercy of a falling rock. I snapped awake, rolled up in blankets tight enough to choke, and I vomited blood upon the floor.

"Master!" She shook me again, moving me so I could empty my lungs of the crimson torrent that threatened to drown me. She pulled away her hand from behind my neck, and it was covered in dark blood. "Master! You are cut on your neck! There's something brown in the wound."

I heaved from my lungs, diaphragm pushing with all my might. The wound was nothing, it was the poison therein that was killing me. Even my last healing draught would do nothing to stave off my death. Eyes pulsing with red glanced at the windows I had not personally secured, and one was cracked open, the wind stirring the curtain. I sucked in a ragged breath, "Church!"

"What? Master, what?"

"Church!" I vomited again, then drew in another breath through a throat too small to breathe, "Thomorgon!"

The music was back. Soulful, sorry, it was a goodbye. The music was getting louder.

I tried to breathe and failed.

I passed out.

***

I awoke.

The priests were at a loss, and Raina held them at bay with naked blade and a face that said she would use it if called to do so. My mind simply caught the current of the words, but not the words themselves. My heartbeat was too loud. My breath squeaked as it passed my burning throat, and I startled them all by raising out of the pool of blood and crawling along the marble stone floor on my hands and knees.

People were speaking. I could not make sense of it. I sucked in air as if lifting a horse on my shoulders. There simply was no time... no time.

I got to one of the braziers burning charcoal just beside the altar. I pushed myself onto the altar, head thumping, pulse pounding, knowing if I failed now, I would never wake up again.

I reached out and scooped up the bowl of widow's root. There was a shout from behind me, I heard footsteps to intercept me. Raina yelled something.

I fell into the marble half pillar that held the bronze bowl of burning blackness. I dumped the shaved widow's root in. There was a flare as they caught, then they cooked in the heat, releasing thick, oily tendrils of purple smoke. I sucked in a feeble stream, then a meager trickle, then a half lung full. I turned from the pot and vomited blood and ropes of long, stringy mucus from my lungs.

My next breath was almost normal, and I fell from the bowl, sweat streaming down my face as I coughed violently, heaving from my lungs dark red ropes that splattered to the floor. There was an eternity where that went on, then my throat began to close. With desperate will, I lunged back to the smoking pile on the coals, sucking in as much as I dared before sitting back upon the altar. I didn't notice nor mind as much as everyone else did.

I breathed in a third lung-full. Finally one of the priests ventured, "My son, that root is meant for tiny doses. It is poison to consume it so."

I nodded, already feeling the root's secondary effects as they took the spikes of panic and clear cut them into a denuded calm. "Thank you, father. I know. Please, this batch is nearly burned. I can pay, but I need as much as you can manage from your stores. And a pipe, while I am begging. Please, I must have it now or else expire." One priest was simply confused, but the junior of the two bolted toward the store room to fetch me my request. I shifted bloodshot eyes to my apprentice. "Go, pack quietly. Gather everything we own and bring it here."

"Here?!" The elder priest exclaimed as Raina bolted from the church.

I turned back to the smoke, which was becoming thinner and thinner, like the sands of life draining through an hourglass. I could feel the side effects of the root crash into me like a herd of wild horses. Given in small doses to the grieving, it pulled my emotions from me, and silenced the far off strains of symphony. It also dissolved the mucus in my chest and nostrils, and opened my lungs to work properly. "I have grave need of your hospitality, holy man."

He shook his head, bald head gleaming, extra chins wiggling, everything not covered by black robes shimmered with cold sweat. "Perhaps the Hospice of Mercy is a fit place for someone such as you and your… your…"

"Apprentice." I finished, face buried in the dwindling lace of smoke. Then I took my face away and coughed up a fist sized chunk of yellowish phlegm laced with blood.

He startled. Apprentices belong to those with skills to teach, skills that are worth money. "What is your profession, may I ask?"

I tossed a caustic glance at the raven in flight carved above the altar. I hooked a thumb at it. "When he tells me, I will tell you."

The younger priest returned then, a clay tavern pipe in his hand from Gods-knew-where, and a pouch of the shaved root. As he worked, he offered, "Your shirt is caked with blood. Please let me cleanse it for you."

"Gerald!" his superior snapped. "You are not his manservant."

Gerald used a pair of tongs to break up a tiny piece of coal and drop it into the bowl of the pipe, then sprinkle in a few flakes, speaking as he did so, "But do the scriptures not say that we are servants to all men, even elves and dwarves should the need arise?"

The elder exploded, "That does not make us launderers!"

Still dressed lightly from dinner, I wiped my mouth and balled up the shirt to keep my blood from Gerald's hands. I shivered in my pants alone as I passed the bundle to the junior priest and accepted the pipe. I sucked on the stem, and felt all my emotions get even further away as my lungs opened to the nourishing air. It was like being severely drunk, without the euphoria booze has the decency to provide. It was an inside numbness brought on by the drug, but it would keep me alive for a few hours. Again, I tried to settle against the altar, but Gerald gently maneuvered me down the dais and to a pew. He slowly turned me to sit.

"Look at him, Gerald! He's a warrior, no doubt. Look at those scars. He..." The elder swallowed and stumbled where he stood, all feeling having left his legs. "Oh Merciful Father of Eternal Peace."

Gerald started at his master's reaction as I sat down. He left me sitting and rushed behind me to aid his master to another seat. "Father, what..?"

The elder pointed a shaking finger, which Gerald followed to the ugly, blackened, raven shaped scar splattered across my back where the assassin tattoo once was. I drew a long, pull on the pipe and turned to look at the two priests. "A chill is taking me. Could I beg a covering from you two?"

What they wound up doing for a few heartbeats was just stare.

Raina was back within a candlemark, and that was far faster than I had expected. She negotiated with the priests to place the horse in the yard in the back of the church, unpacked our gear, and was shown to one of the spare priest cells where she dumped the load. Through it all, I just sat and sucked on the pipe less and less, huddling into the blanket far more. The widow's root, like a mercenary, was defending me, but at a dear cost to my body. I was at the delicate point where the cure was more dangerous than the malady.

I was offered rest and food, but it was drink I craved more than anything. All of us retired to the small kitchen. It was odd to transfer from the somber blacks, blues, purples, and browns of Thomorgon to the utterly mundane living quarters in the far rear of the church. The coal in the pipe had gone out, but I waved off another. Instead, I breathed deeply of the steam from a cup of tea. The whole time, Raina watched me across folded arms, her jaw set in obstinacy against relief. At least she waited until I had finished the first mug of tea and my mouth felt far less like the inside of a mattress.

"What was that about?"

I took another drink, and set down the heavy earthenware cup. "Poison. They cut my neck. blade was probably coated."

The elder priest sat in the corner, as far from me as one can get and still be in the room, but Gerald leaned forward, fascinated with this break from the daily grind. "Poison? Who could do such a thing?"

"The Assassin's Guild."

Everyone was more shocked than the elder priest, who calmly asked, "Who would pay to have you assassinated?"

I could not help but look slightly embarrassed. "There is something of a list."

Raina finally grabbed her mug and took an angry swig. "And that's what's been wrong with you since Zeitheim? Poisoning?"

I shook my head, tried to stand and failed in a coughing fit. I leaned the candle over and sucked on the pipe. The concentrated smoke entered me and eased the fit. I stood and stumbled off toward my monk's cell. I left because I could not answer her. I did not know.

Once there, I dug through the books left in the satchel. I stopped, stunned. The holy symbol from the priest in the village was still there, tossed in absently and carried back to Hammarfall. It had survived centuries in the soil, discarded and forgotten. Now it was a lump barely recognizable, silver plating flaked black and corroded. I knew in my heart it had sat in contact with the Opus Discordia. I discarded it.

I passed on Hundeausführer's journal, on the more recent sycophantic ramblings. I went to the old writings, the ones written during or just after the life of Annalirya Von Zeitheim. The rest of them left me alone as I poured through the stories, dwelling on the abominations caused by the beautiful, dark haired seductress.

For seven days I smoked, and read, and dozed in the halls of the dead. I ate little, I spoke less. One day a ruckus lead me to find Raina practicing her sword work in the back yard. I could not gather the will to join her. Instead I returned to my cell. And again I dove into the books as if for the first time. It went long into the night, and as the candle burned down, I think I had finally assembled it all in my head.

It started with the death of her unloving husband, and then the mysterious disappearance of her young daughters, dead from the plague. That was when she wrote her first symphony. Her large family residing in Zeitheim dwindled as her works soared. When her family was finally all gone, a long, dry spell took her. Critics and kings alike lamented ever hearing her compose another note. Then came the war.

It was to become her golden age.

Whole armies marched inside of her walls, swallowed by the gates and then never to be seen again. There were tales of her bathing in blood of virgins before embarking on a symphony. Of entire towns obliterated at her whim by nameless knights, now that I read with clear eyes, these warriors seemed far less mortal than at first blush.

The words echoes inside of me. I had read them before. I know I had read them, but somehow I had discarded them within my own mind. A cloud was lifting and the searing light of truth caused me to squint, to blink and drop the book to the floor. There was smoke everywhere. I rubbed my stinging eyes.

Cold fingers slid into my hands and gently pulled them aside.

She was there, so beautiful she glowed. I remembered her from every book, from every darkened painting of her home, and from her cold tomb. We had danced for hours in the darkness, and I felt our courtship as a heavy weight pressing us toward the powerful depths of union. She was a tiny woman, barely as tall as a teenager, rapier slim with long blue-black hair spilling from her head in shining waves. Her green eyes bore into me and laid hooks like eggs inside of my very being. Her sharp features, her small stature, were nearly elfin. They whispered lies to me of purity and loveliness... and the music, the music was everywhere.

Then she was against me, cool and distant against my burning need. Her mouth was against mine, tasting of cold strawberries and blood. I swelled in her presence as her golden robes dissolved into vapor. Her frigid hands embraced me, but touched the scarred flesh on my back. It erupted as with fire and I shrunk from her, but she followed me, cupping my face in her hands and murmuring comforting falsehoods. Again she kissed me, and I felt her essence invade me.

One hand found her tiny, firm breast and the other mashed her to my powerful chest. She leeched the heat from me and pushed me down upon the bed. Something hard was there, and I pushed it aside to give us room for our passion. My hand contacted metal.

The Phantom Angel burst into violent blue flame, detonating like thunder as the makeshift scabbard flew apart. The specter of Annalirya screamed, digging clawed hands into my shoulders to hold onto me. The sword continued to flame, leaving bed and cloth untouched, but causing a hurricane gale that ripped the ghost of Annalirya from me. She was forced away, through the wall, and my head instantly cleared.

Bare chested, unshod, I snatched the elvish sword from the bed and burst from the cell.

There she was, pushed down the hall, but flying toward me in a cloud of lost souls. Her sharp features, once so elfin and benign, twisted into something awful and demonic. I bolted for the chapel, but the ghost caught me at the door. With casual distain she pushed me into the worship hall, sending me sprawling onto the naked marble, pews hurled before me as if by a massive explosion. Trained reflexes pointed the blade away and turned an uncontrolled fall into a roll. I came to my feet.

She was already there, screeching as she sunk needle-like fangs into my shoulder. The cold burned and I screamed like the dying. I started to shiver uncontrollably, barely retaining the coordination to sweep my sword in a tight, flaming arc along the front of my body. Her victorious shriek became a dissonant cry as the strings of her symphony were pulled apart. Yet, she did not die; she instead hurled towards me again.

I saw the priests and Raina burst into the chamber as I sailed over the altar, then down behind it, and into the passage there. The Phantom Angel flew from my hands and we both skittered down the steep ramp.

This was a place seen by few living men. After laying on the altar, the dead were brought there for preparation to be interred. Fitting, then, that I would be there.

I came to my feet dizzy, groggy, but the Angel burned like a blue sun and I bolted for it. Claws of cold raked my chest, and left blue scars threaded with veins of black across my chest. I recoiled, shaking as I feinted left, right, and diving back and knocking tables of reagents to the floor. I came to my feet with few wits and less energy at my call. Annalirya opened her mouth and pounced upon me.

I raised my left arm and she latched upon it like a hound. She was ice itself, but weighed nothing. Yet, I recoiled from her attack, tripped on the edge of a pool, and plunged in totally without control.

The slippery, oily surface embraced me completely, and I sunk into its depths almost gratefully. The warm fluid flushed the cold from my body. Then I felt the barbed hooks buried deep in my soul rip free, tearing pieces of me as they fled. The pain was blinding, but finally I could see. I suddenly sensed the chains that had been upon me for weeks, months. They had infiltrated so subtly, carried on the strings of her music, that I had not noticed. They spoke to me, lied to me, sang to me, used me. Their removal numbed me with pain, and yet I could finally feel. The reaction with the spirit was nowhere near so peaceful. She exploded from the pool, sending the contents spraying in all directions. Ropy strands of oil dripped from her and she recoiled like a maiden dumped in a midden. Then she saw me climbing from the pool, and she roared in discordant frenzy.

"CROW!" Raina was there, holding the burning brand of the Phantom Angel. She hurled it toward me. Heartbeats extended into infinity.

Annalirya's black tresses became a halo of obsidian razors. Her mouth distended and her needle teeth became daggers. She lunged for me, and I rolled to the side. I came up with one hand lashing out.

The spinning, burning form of the Phantom Angel slapped into my palm as if placed there. I continued the motion, never daring to pause as I brought the sword in another deadly circle. It connected with the angry ghost. My free arm grabbed at her, crushing her spectral form to me. But by then, the oil that infused her was burning. It coated me; I was burning. Yet all I could do was stare into her beautiful green eyes and hold her tiny body to mine.

I could hear her music. I could hear it speak to me like we were two halves of the same person. Her mortal visage returned, she stared at me through the flames. Love, unconsummated, thundered within me for a kindred soul that had fallen and never found favor again. I don't know when it had started, but it was real, and it was a chain that would bind her hell bound soul to mine, and mine to hers, for all time. A tear slipped from her cruel eyes and burst into steam on her cheek.

"I am sorry," she said.

"It is far too late for that," I replied.

Armored with a blanket against the flames, Raina crashed into me and the blow carried me into a pool of sweet, scented water. I came up for air, my own sins extinguished, but the composer left to burn alone. Her screams seemed to go on forever, even long after she disappeared and left naught but a burning pool of oil behind.

The instant she dissolved under the water, the Phantom Angel extinguished. The only light now remained in the hands of the two priests. Accustomed as they were to the dead, they stood in shock.

I did not need them for comfort. I needed no sign from the Phantom Angel. I knew the spirit was gone. The music had gone with her.

I reached down for the Angel and climbed out of the pool. I put out a hand and helped Raina out of the depression. Gerald came forward, candles in the holder fluttering as he moved. "Is peace your business?"

I felt the blood drain from my face, and my irises become pinpricks. Then I glanced back at the burning pool of blessed oil. "No, I guess it is not."

I started to brush past him, but Raina called, "Master! He asked if it is all over."

I looked at the burning pyre again, and felt something ache in my heart. A want for kinship, of knowing. The need for another soul as dirty as mine to understand and forgive me. "The answer is the same."

We retired to the kitchen, frazzled and strained, but unready for rest. I slumped into a chair, running a hand through the sizzled and oiled locks of hair left to me. Within moments, Gerald had a cup of steaming tea in front of each of us. The elder priest took them all and dumped them out. He replaced them with the same warmed cups filled with golden brown spirits, a dollop of honey, and a squeeze of a lime brought on a ship from far away. It was harsh, and burning, peaty and soothing all at the same time.

The older man chased Raina out of the seat opposite me and sat down. More bold than he had been all week, he stared at me in the eyes like a challenge to battle. "I am Father Castor. I have served the Lord of Death for over a generation, and I have never seen the like of that shade before."

I took another sip, wincing at the strength of the bourbon. "Well, Father Castor. What do you need from me?"

He shook his head. "If I'm not mistaken you were under the influence of that spirit. Do you know who it was?"

Raina piped up without hesitation, "It was Annalirya Von Zeitheim." She turned to me. "Wasn't it?"

I nodded.

A look passed between Gerald and Castor. The elder refilled my cup and eased back in his chair, sipping his own mug peacefully. "You need to start at the beginning."

Parts of me railed, doors to my innermost self slamming shut against intrusion. Then a hard, sword-calloused hand fell across mine. I met Raina's green eyes haltingly. "Why did you abandon me at Zeitheim?" she asked.

And I started to remember.

It did not begin at Zeitheim, but weeks before. It was the music. It had always been the music. It had lit the need, the fire inside of me. It had driven me onward when caution would have me walk away. There had been a hollow place inside of me and the spirit had settled in and worn me like a warm winter cloak. That was the reason I had braved death. That was why I had put up with the insufferable Alexander Jaeger.

I shot up from the table, but Castor was at my elbow. "Breathe, my son. You must go back, you must remember what fell deeds you were forced to commit."

I shook my head and looked back to the room of three that sat like a triumvirate over my sins. I waved them off. "It wasn't like that. It didn't force me, it only provided…"

Castor nodded. "A downhill path, an easy way to mold your steps to its own desire."

My brows clouded, fists clenched. "Who are you, Father Castor?"

He retreated before my fury, giving it space to evaporate as he sat and sipped at his mug. "I am a simple priest now. But in my youth, I was an exorcist. I never did see a real possession until now. Though I caution you, speak now. Best unravel it fresh to find any wrongs you can put right before it is too late."

I was about to snap at him when an image slammed into my mind, shouldering in like a broken dam letting loose a tide of ice water. I looked to Raina, hands shaking. "Outside of her tomb, the pool was not stained with rust. Those were not bleached sticks that filled the bottom."

These were not questions, for I had seen bones many times before.

We sat and talked the rest of the night, Raina being the truthful eyes to my memories. The stories that I had read about The Burning Composer had varied wildly in tone. The books written in her lifetime described her as a monster, but the further from her lifetime they went, the more fawning they became. The authors had heard her music, and had fallen under a spell that had outlived her in death… as had I. The red brown stains of ancient blood in the rough marble pool outside her conservatory, the bones stacked up inside, these were proof of her monstrosities. Those very things I had missed or dismissed because of my own infatuation with the lady.

Even so, I had more to tell of myself, to myself and all. I described the undead in the graveyard, and how they all but ignored us, and attacked our enemies. How they had left me alone even while senseless. I described the dance with Annalirya in my dreams. How the specters of the massacred villages had recoiled from the Opus even more than they had from the light of the Phantom Angel.

"And your blood opened the tomb. Almost like you knew, like she told you. At every step, you were safeguarded, Master. She needed you," said Raina.

"But after I had the Opus, after I slept that night, I awoke on the road without you…" I finished, the words feeling slightly hollow in my mouth. "...three days later." I shook my head, uncertain. I coughed, lungs still less than perfect.

Castor frowned. "After it had what it wanted, it did not need Raina, if ever it did. It took you and brought you on your way back here."

Gerald's hands shook, ever so slightly, "So it was the playing of the music that caused a… a… receptive state?"

Castor frowned mightily, having grown from a cowering man in the face of blades and poison to a giant in the face of supernatural horror. "It would appear so. All the telltale signs of possession are there, Master Crow. Though from your story it was when you were ill, and then nearly drowned, that you were most vulnerable to her, and she became stronger within you."

Raina shook her head, trying to fit these strange new rules in her head, "If one of her songs, played by some random group–"

Castor objected, "Hardly random. Chosen by a master conductor and played by expert instrumentalists."

She shrugged. "As you say, Father. Yet, I ask if he can instigate a possession by a damned soul with strands of her normal music, what might happen with her greatest work?"

Castor flipped through the provided histories of Annalirya. "So you managed to find the tomb and recover her Great Work of Discord. Where is it now?"

I shook my head clearing dust from inside my skull. "The what?"

Castor frowned. "The Magnum Opus Discordia, it means–"

"The Great Work of War," Raina and I finished.

"No." Gerald shook his head, still pretending to drink from his cup. "Many centuries ago, perhaps. During the time of the composer, however, Magnum Opus Discordia would have been translated as The Great Work of Discord, Chaos, or Havoc."

And the difference between those two words, a dark and perhaps demonic composer, a city in tatters ready to explode into violence, was everything. I murmured, "We had been told it was a work that would tell the horrors of war. Move the city toward some resolution of this conflict."

Castor pursed his lips. "Unlikely." He stood, slapping the table to gather us from shock. "Now, right now, where is the Magnum Opus Discordia?"

Raina and I shared a look. "We delivered it to Swan Lampedocht."

THREE

POSSESSION AND PURPOSE

I HAD a thousand worries on my plate, but one had to take ultimate precedence: Lampedocht. I was exhausted, cranky, and my body felt ravaged by the last vestiges of the poison that sought to chemically collapse my lungs into a bloody froth. That put me in the perfect state of mind to go brace Swan Lampedocht and very likely get into a fight.

We suited up, but we did not dress for a formal meeting; we went dressed for battle. Thick leathers, hidden knives, and freshly honed blades. I did not want to kill Lampedocht, but I was taking no chances at this point. We left as soon as dawn broke, plunging into the streets of the noble quarter as soon as it seemed practical.

Raina knocked on the door, but I reached forward and twisted the knob. Polite niceties all aside, we were here on a mission. Two servant girls bumped into us in the foyer. They looked at once scandalized, startled, embarrassed, and worried as we intruded. Truth be told, I don't know how I would react if I had an armed man who had thrown up blood all over the guest room barge into the home while fully armed. I saved them the stammering. "Lampedocht."

They glanced at one another, passing messages in the secret and silent language of staff everywhere. "Allow me to take your things and Sylvia will go to the conservatory and–"

"I know the way, thanks." I turned and bolted up the stairs, Raina following grimly behind. One servant pursued with a series of protests. I knocked on the conservatory doors, but only waited a heartbeat before finding the lock engaged and putting my shoulder to the door. Ornate, beautiful, elegant, none of these were synonyms for strong. The door popped open and flew wide, exposing the room beyond.

I ignored the panicked prattling of the staff as I walked swiftly to the center desk of the music room. I found the conductor quite absent, but the Opus was on his desk. No! I leaned down and found the symphony now was printed in drab, black ink upon fresh pages, not brick red ink on ancient vellum.

"Find what you came for, Master Crow?"

I turned back toward the door, to the voice both familiar and alien. It was Lampedocht, but not. His clothes were not just in disarray, but stained and misbuttoned. His gray hair and beard were not just splayed, but tangled and greasy. He had none of his strangely self deprecating and conciliatory demeanor. Now he was acting like a lord. The man had gone from absentminded genius to slovenly, mad ruler. Chills played along my spine.

I snatched the Opus copy, thick as the king's taxes, and held the massed bundle in one straining hand. "Lampedocht, the symphony is cursed. How many copies have you made?"

He stared at me with blazing eyes. "There are two hundred and seventy parts, each with their own distinct piece to play." He swept from the room stalking downstairs like a predator. "No harmonies, no duplicate parts. I don't expect you to understand."

I paused for a second, stunned. "There are two hundred and seventy copies?"

Lampedocht stopped to give me a look of utter contempt before leading the way back down and through his house. "I TOLD you that you could not understand. There are two hundred and seventy pieces of music played by two hundred and seventy instruments. Only when brought together will they create the symphony as a whole."

I felt my guts freeze inside me at those words. "Lampedocht have you done it?" I bolted forward and forcibly turned him around, gripping his arms in my steely hands. "Have you played the music all at once?"

Showing more power than I would have ever imagined, he shrugged me off, pushed me back, and continued toward the ground level. "Impossible! The tuning for specific sections, the timing, the combined melody must be perfect before they can be joined into a whole. And that won't have time to happen until we play it."

"Lampedocht, you cannot play that music." As we came down toward the smoking room, I caught a cloud of powerful perfume and the distinct whiff of something rotten. I put it from my mind. "It is a spell, or a curse, or something that means no good for the mortal men and women of Hammarfall."

"We are performing at the king's command at the Grand Temple of the Muse. It is settled. Now as for you, wizard–"

Raina and I exclaimed as one, "Wizard?"

"Oh I have heard all the things you have done to try to keep the Opus from my possession."

"Swan, I was the person who delivered it to you!"

Lampedocht actually paused at this contradiction, then shook his head as if to clear it from the buzzing of flies. "And yet here you are, trying to take it back! No matter," The conductor opened the sliding doors to the smoking room, "I have true allies that shall protect the great work of the Mother of Symphonies."

The doors parted, and there, clouded in perfumes with an underlying reek of rot, was Alexander Jaeger Von Schwartzklippen. He was pale, sweaty, drawn, with a rictus grin of obsession, and the wide irises of a man drowning in opiates. His finery was finally immaculate again, but he was hunched, almost bent double around his crotch which bulged as if containing a ridiculous tuber of massive size. He was walking only with the aid of two canes.

"Hello, bastard."

I suppose you are asking yourself why I was not saying hello back with the aid of daggers of varying sizes, weights, and sharpness? Well, that's because I had not mentioned the royal guard. Yes, not city, not personal henchmen, but THE royal guard. The second the door was opened the two rushed out and grabbed me by the arms, pulling them outward, twisting slightly and putting restraining hands on my shoulder to keep me in place. These were not thugs or functionaries, these were the best kind of soldier a man could buy. "Oh, I see you have noticed the men lent me by my good friend, the King. You murdering my father gave me his seat and power. You killed half a generation of nobility that were in his service and it has made you a vile enemy in the eyes of the crown."

I looked slowly at guard one, who was all kinds of thinking about how to take away the Phantom Angel without losing his grip. I looked at guard two, who was glaring at Raina in a silent order to GET BACK. Then I turned to Alexander Jaeger, who was clomping slowly toward me. "You think it's going to be easy as that?"

"Your legends do not scare me, Crow. You may have survived everything up until now," The mask of sanity slipping, Alexander stopped just outside of biting range, the stink of him so powerful it nearly killed me. He collected his canes into the hand that was missing a finger, then a small twist to one and pulled out a razor sharp blade, long and cruel. "but I promise, you only delayed your doom. I will see you cut and stabbed, and flayed, and burned, and shot, and finally, finally, drowned as I intended all along." He laid the blade against my cheek, pressing ever so slightly. "What do you say to that?"

I gave the only warning I could, sucking in a double lungful of air and expelling a tiny fraction in a dozen small words, "I don't know. I can hold my breath a long, long time."

Alexander was nonplussed. He looked to guard one and guard two for some clarification, then stared back at me, sure he was being mocked, but not sure how. During this whole mummery, his blade came away from my face. That's when I hauled off and kicked him in the groin with my hard, traveling boots. To be fair, it was not so much a kick; it was months of built up frustration, hate, and disgust. It focused every muscle in my body into a severe arc of violence that connected with the sound of tearing meat and a bursting wineskin. It was every bit of emotion focused at the end of a steel shod boot. It was, in every sense, an act of the gods.

As I applied force in a shockingly fast manner, the massive bulge in Alexander Jaeger's pants erupted and vile fluids exploded along the inside of his pants. I had held my breath, so I cannot describe the secondary effects to you, but I can say that both guards began to retch uncontrollably. I levered the first into Von Sausagemissing, and kicked the knees out of the other. I bolted from the room, past the vomiting Lampedocht and gathered the green faced Raina, who had not quite understood in time.

We fled the house and raced to the street. We stopped long enough to get our bearings, then rushed for the gate to the lower city.

"Was I like that? Like Lampedocht?"

"Sometimes," Raina grimly replied.

And then it became crystal clear. "Dammit, he's possessed."

We came up to the gate, the guards giving us suspicious but unknowing looks. Raina tried to control her face as she hissed, "Is there anything we can do?"

I took out Swan's signet and the doors began to open. Assassins and revolutionaries, rebels, and royals all collided in my head, making a right fine mess of the whole thing. "I need time. I need to think."

"We don't have much time, Master."

Behind us, there was a shout. "He's a dark wizard wanted by the king, get him!"

Now, it is important in times of stress to give clear, concise orders. Screaming, "Get him!", is good. Screaming, "He's wanted by the king, get him!", even better. Calling out, "He's a dark wizard (and thus may melt the flesh from your bones just by looking at you) wanted by the king (who isn't here to do anything to your flesh just this second), capture him!", gets a little addendum, (or, you know, let someone else try first!).

That was why I got to shoulder the first guard aside and my apprentice and I dove through the gap to old town. Now, in the poxy bard's version, that would be it. In reality though, it is that guards: city, personal, or royal, are pretty much the same. And every one of them figure that if someone is wanted, they may be wanted alive. But *dead* is still better than escaped.

Our only blessing is that guards practice with crossbows about as often as they bathe. When they do practice, it is against a big scary round target that sits there and waits for them to shoot. This is not to say they can't hit anything. In fact, I had painful memories of betting they could not hit me. That is the advantage of twenty men firing in a volley and just one striking from a distance. So, I took a risk. I skidded to the stop, turned and held out my hands, and roared arcane sounding gibberish. Every one of them ducked behind the wall.

There was nothing but utter silence on the street. A young man who looked for all the world as if he had been waiting on a bench for me to appear, darted off into the streets with the speed of unencumbered youth. I cursed and we ran.

Just a few heartbeats after that, however, once none of the guards were frogs, they came back over the wall to aim at us only to find we were long gone. In a perfect world, that would be that. However, somewhere weeping on the floor and leaking snot out of each nostril like a raging river, was a madman. He was giving the orders at the moment, and he had a royal warrant for my arrest and execution. The guards on the wall got the word to reinforce and give chase. They sent up a white rocket followed by two blue and red fireworks. I couldn't decode them word for word, but I bet the general idea was, *We hate Crow so much! Get over here so we can kill that charming, handsome bastard.*

Which is largely untrue. I am, instead, an orphan not a bastard.

Royal guardsmen appeared behind us, moving at a run. About twenty of them ringing and jangling in half-plate armor. This may have completely precluded them hitting us with crossbows, but greatly increased the likelihood of them stabbing us with swords. Rather than slow down, we sped up. We were able to outdistance them a fair bit and lose them around the gentle arc of the belly of the city, but let me remind you that Gods have completely different ideas of 'lucky', 'helpful', and especially, 'funny'.

That was why we were busy looking backward when the mob of half armed and mostly unarmored rabble appeared ahead of us. Raina and I, gasping for air, slid to a stop less than ten paces from them. I coughed up a phlegmy rope of blood, and at first saw the boy that had seen us outside the gate and run off. So, then this was our welcome back into the kingdom of the revolting commoners. At their head was the armored lieutenant halfwit and then the purple avenger himself, Oleg Volker the Volker (something he came up with, so don't blame me). He stood like a prophet, arms outstretched, at the head of his stunted column of thugs and bullies. He projected clearly and forcefully to the whole of the quickly emptying street.

"CROW!" he either demanded, declared, or interrogated, depending on your point of view, "Crow, I am the future of Hammarfall. I will have your final answer, or I will have your blood! Will you join the good men of this city, or will you fall before them?"

I wheezed. I gasped. I held up one finger while doubled over as to beg for just a moment's pause. Gone to her haunches, my apprentice was no better off, but she met my eyes. I glanced behind us meaningfully. She rolled her eyes, but smiled like a cat batting at a tasty mouse.

I stood straight. I coughed more bloody phlegm. I gasped a few more times. Coughed again. Then tried to project solemnly, "I shall serve you, and then your men serve me?"

Volker nodded grimly.

"I accept!"

There was a moment of stunned silence. I smiled and waved to the men as if accepting an award. I drew my sword and went to one knee presenting it to him, yet not quite giving him the time to grab the blade before I stood and sheathed it. Still, Oleg Volker smiled triumphantly, the lieutenant frowned, and one or the other was the signal for the Volker's men to cheer, drowning out the sounds of approaching metal. I nodded humbly to his men.

Volker had added a new twist to his 'everyone is a common man' hierarchy. He handed me a badge of office. Simple, rough, with a massive V in the center of the crude scrollwork. I put it on and the cheers rose more intensely than ever. That was when the guardsmen showed up at a weary jog, and the sound of celebration died on the street.

"MEN!" I shouted in my best military voice, "SERVE THE VOLKER! KILL THE ROYALS!"

And I'll give them this– Volker's men were not smart, but they were loyal. To be clear, about one quarter were pissing themselves, one quarter were still confused and getting caught in the rush, one quarter were grimly prepared to do what they thought the Volker wanted, and the last quarter, after months of being fed on a diet of every evil the royalty may or may not have ever inflicted upon the common folk, were in a killing rage at the sight of the guardsmen. You can guess who lead the charge, but in the end, they were all pulled forward by a shared hate and the press of bodies.

I grabbed Raina's hand and we dove into the nearest alley, avoiding the crush of battle. Behind, a guard pulled out a bundle of fireworks and unwrapped a slow burning match from around his glove, but a thrown spear took him in the chest. We sprinted to the end of the alley and turned right. I caught sight of another problem looming overhead. Raina started to slow, but I pushed her back into a run. She glanced at me, puzzled and I yelled to her, too loudly, "Konrad's!"

She wanted to ask if I had gone mad, and that was a fair question, for Konrad's was halfway across the city. Yet, I pressed her to a run. But it soon became apparent her lungs were flagging. A cart rattled by us, forcing us to stop at the intersection of another street and I caught sight of another Church to the God of Death. This one was far more simple, and serviced the common folk of the city. I pushed Raina toward the tall, black walls and purple stained glass. She looked back to me, eyes like a wounded hound.

"Go!" I shouted. "I will catch up!"

And then I was gone, hoping that she followed my advice as a shadowy, wispy doppleganger I was not meant to see sprang back into action. I ran forever, through alleys and down streets. I was the fox, and the damned hound had to feel the thrill of the hunt for my escape to work. I found a set of close in walls and, lungs burning, legs unsteady, I scrabbled up the corner intersection. I rolled over the lip of one of the walls and fell the five hands to the roof, an ill advised *tink* of a missed throwing blade telling me my pursuer had tried to end this already. I rolled almost drunkenly to my feet and I ignored the scrapes to my hands, ignored the screaming of my thighs, and the ragged stitch in one lung. My pursuer threw a bundle of fireworks just to one side of my face and the whip-cracking explosions nearly turned me from my course. Instead, I bulled through the explosions. Ahead, just short of Konrad's inn, two black bundles dropped and erupted into walls of smoke, obscuring my target. I ignored it all as I vaulted from one roof to another, made a clumsy attempt to sneak around the tilted roof, and as my predator came through the smoke and into view, I opened a small shutter and threw open the window. She tried to get out a throwing knife dripping with ooze, but heedless of any danger, I dove in. My pursuer, feeling her chase was at an end, drew two nasty short blades and dove through the waiting window into darkness. Eyes dazzled by the bright outside and utter dark inside, she unwisely dove through the opening.

She meant something acrobatic, I am sure. She never got there, for there was no trail, only death. One armored forearm slammed into the back of her neck, turning her graceful dive into a common sprawl. The other fist, clenched around the Phantom Angel, pinned her to the floor like a bug. It went through her spine between the shoulder blades. Even so, she took a few minutes to die, but she did it quietly so I backed off and let her get to it, allowing my ragged panting to subside. Nobody else came through the window, and once I was certain life had fled her, I shut it without a puff of sound.

The inn sat like a tomb around me, and I kicked the wreckage of the impromptu scabbard to the side (I had destroyed it drawing the weapon) and crept downstairs. Konrad's inn was a shambles. Every cask, bottle, rasher, or bag of food and booze had been taken. Chairs had been thrown, and tables overturned. I felt guilty tension turn at my shoulders, tightening the ligaments to a thrumming rage. Without even checking, I knew I would find across the front of the building a painted crown with a red X across it.

I went back upstairs.

I wanted to be gone, but this woman was a valuable resource. She was dressed in the familiar suit of rags, and bore the mark, but that was no surprise. I had no use for the two short blades, but I was able to replenish my long lost supply of poisons and hidden knives, for those not used on idiots and rogue noblemen had been lost in rivers and fires and all manner of dire adventures.

Several sheaths were sealed in wax, showing the knives inside were coated in death. She had a pouch of fake coins to use as a distraction as I had used my gold back in Forgeringer. What was far more useful, and an even larger surprise, was the pouch of shattered obsidian and dwarven alkaline metal shavings that she had. I took that for certain, and liberated several handfulls of smoke bombs and finger-sized explosives. I had never taken to the use of the small distraction devices, figuring they mostly drew more attention than I wanted, and a knife to the face was distracting enough.

Leaving the rest, I returned downstairs and shouldered open the back door, which had been nailed shut. I kicked it closed and wearily trudged into the yard where Raina and I had sparred and from there out into the city.

I had been less than half a candlemark with the body, so I was still suffering from great exertion followed by none at all. My legs wanted to cramp, my back was aching, and I was beginning to wonder if a nap in the middle of the road might be better than taking even one more step.

Yet, I pressed on, back to the commoner's Church of the Dead that abutted the cliff wall upon which stood the royal quarter.

I walked in, and when my eyes adjusted to the darkness, I saw the body slumped in the bloody pool. Then I recognized the face.

Gerald, the younger priest of Thomorgon lay in a pool of his own blood. We had left him in the cathedral in the upper section of town. What he was doing here, murdered, was beyond me. Yet, here he was, cleft from shoulder to sternum in a strike I was certain that Raina had not done. Aside from the power needed, she was much more likely to stab a man, not to mention the dull brown ooze that flanked the wound.

Here there were nothing but questions, so I slit the laces to my boots, slipped the heavy things under a pew, and lit out for the deep reaches of the chapel. I paused by the altar, quiet but menacing voices drawing me down into the sunken preparation room under this church. I moved like the wind, quiet and swift, but it took precious moments to catch my bearings.

Like the cathedral, behind the altar was a ramp that lead into the ground. Here there were pools and various equipment for interring the dead. Here, however, at the back of the chamber, instead of a passage going down, there was one going up. I took to it without any thoughts but swiftness and silence. The light faded on all sides and I was forced to slow. I felt my way to a smooth corner that continued to arc up and around, finally coming to some amount of light, and a scene out of a nightmare.

This was a catacomb that serviced the entire city. Long ago they had run out of places for caskets. Now they had room for only urns of ashes or the fleshless bones of the deceased. All along the walls, bones had been used to create massive displays of disturbing beauty and elegance. The next ring toward the center were a line of cairns constructed totally of bone, as tall as three men. Perfectly square, as wide and deep as two men with arms outstretched, thousands of skulls studded the outside, each with a name and year etched in a bronze slip that was nailed to the skull. The next line was the same, and the next. Giant mountains of bone that marched rank upon rank toward the lit center.

"Take off your clothes." The voice was like a bear had gargled with broken glass.

"But why? You said yourself that your quarrel is with my master, and not with me." Raina, defiant.

"Silence, wench. Your master betrayed the One True God of this world. You see this? This is Godstongue. First I am going to undress you, then I will take and seed you. Then I will murder you with

Godstongue so you will serve me forever in the hereafter. And when your master finds your broken, violated body, he will come to me, and I will kill him too."

And with those words, I broke into a run. Two torches burned. One was on the floor, the other had been tossed into a brazier of charcoal, lighting the fearful scene.

Raina was nude in the center of the chamber, backed against an altar. Most of her clothes were in a heap on the floor, her sword and dagger meticulously set on the altar next to her. She covered her crotch with her shirt, but there was something defiant in the way she held the cloth. She was not thinking about her nudity, but about killing, and I took heart.

The man opposite her would make the innkeeper Konrad look tiny. His muscles were built into mountains on his form, straining the seams and defying even the need for armor to contain them. In his hand, a long shard of golden night dripped pitch onto the floor like a slavering beast. Meant for two handed use, he held it easily in one massive paw. He flicked the sword out, shearing the bottom off of the garment she held for modesty.

"Drop the shirt. Make this easy for me, and I'll make this quick for you."

I was still sprinting when the flickering light illuminated the floor. I skidded to a halt, aware of my folly. Around the altar, aligned east and west as the real thing, a miniature of Hammarfall, the city, had been made of bones. Every building, every street, every church and even the palace had been rendered in polished, fit, but otherwise unaltered bone. For a man without boots, it was a field of razors waiting to happen. And a man with no sure footing would die before the sheer might of the assassin. So I did all I could do.

"Looking for me?"

Like an animal he shifted his attention, completely and without reserve, toward me. His nostrils fared, eyes widened to take in every detail before I died. He smiled with manic energy around one, baleful word, "YOU!"

And then the knife sank into the massive wad of muscles at the base of his neck. The assailant roared blood and staggered, Raina throwing a second knife concealed by her modesty shirt. It bit deeply into the belly of the bestial man. Without pause she spun and drew her sword free from the sheath on the altar as the gargantuan foe made a fearsome overhead slash with his pitch-darkened blade. Raina bent low, legs spread like a water skimming bug, and the strike rang against the altar behind her. The giant recoiled and she flipped her sheath off into the face of the brute. He batted it away with an indignant, crimson roar that cut short. Ended, now and forever, by the bright steel sword shoved into his heart.

Completely nude, but clothed in determination, Raina jerked once, sawing the blade viciously in and out. To this day I am not sure if I was meant to hear her say, "Quick enough for you? Oh, but it seems I broke your heart."

With that she kicked the huge man in the crotch, sliding his numbed body off of her blade, down upon the sharpened ribs that made the vaulted walls of the palace of the king. These sharpened bits took him through the neck, and his body flopped uselessly, destroying entire model city blocks in his expiration.

I took my time walking around to the open end of the horseshoe of Hammarfall (the model). Raina had time to gather her clothes about her and cover herself, though she did it in a manner of business, not desperation.

"Do not touch anything spattered with the bile of the blade. Wipe anything metal clean, discard the rest." Raina picked up her jacket of plates, which had absorbed the worst of the momentum splash when the blade met altar.

I shrugged. "Leave it. It's more danger than protection now." She did as I bid without speaking or protesting. She dressed in clothes and padded tunic. I walked up the dais in the center of the model, and looked down upon her handiwork spread out like a giant in a city of the dead. I nodded at the corpse. "You have learned well."

She smiled at me grimly and retrieved her guttering torch from the altar. "To tell the truth, I thought all the nude games were just so you could look at me naked."

I smiled impishly. "There can be two reasons for things."

She managed that same grin, but it was strained. "Is it bad to be afraid?"

I quelled the urge to hold her, to hug her. She was not a woman right now, she was my apprentice, and if her business was a blade she had better get used to this. "No. This is the perfect time to be afraid, once it is over."

And then she was in my arms, holding me tightly as if for dear life. She wasn't holding a master, or a father. She was not weak, or dainty. She was afraid, and she needed contact with a comrade. I forcibly relaxed, and held her close to me. Maybe there weren't hard and fast rules for this after all.

I would like to have left right then, but there was a matter of the sword left behind. Fashioned of iridescent gold metal, the scorpions that made the hilt appeared to be an oil wash of colors. The blade no longer wept black ooze, but it was dried on the metal and I was sure even touching the stuff was deadly. There seemed little doubt this was an artifact of my old master, the Lord of Murder. We manhandled the unnamed assailant off of the model city enough to get his scabbard from his waist and wipe the blade on his pants before sending it home. I had no idea what we would do with it, but we couldn't leave a thing like this just laying around.

Raina explained that she had met Gerald down here when she had come in, and then the giant had burst in moments later. She had time to learn that the Cathedral was connected to the church through the main burial chambers. Still bootless, we continued upward. We went through three similar caverns, these with offshoots that lead to similar caverns, until the spiraling ramps brought us to the cathedral in the royal quarter. Within moments we had located Castor, and told him the awful news. Peotyr, the young novice that normally dealt with the lower church scurried off to begin preparation for Gerald's body. I stashed Godstongue with our gear and returned to the chapel. There, both Raina and Castor were praying.

Now, I don't want to sound insensitive, but if any of the Gods were going to do something for Gerald, it would have been better it happened long before now. Besides that, halleluiahs of praise have got to be better than wining petitions for help. Both those facts taken together, and you have the inescapable fact that none of the Gods care even a little for us, living or dead. Still, I waited, and waited, patience wearing thin.

The clanking of armor broke the moment. A shadow appeared at the door that quickly disappeared. Patience gone, I levered Raina to her feet. "We have to go."

Far, far too late.

It seemed less than a breath later the man in clanking armor was again at the tall double doors to the cathedral, riding a white stallion into the chapel at the beginning of the grand isle that ran the length all the way to the altar.

"YOU! Puppet of evil! Consorter of demons!"

I hung my head, shoulders slumped, but my voice carried as loud and clear as his did, "You have the wrong man."

"I do not!" And though the mounted knight had no lance, he had a long spear he was setting up with his heater shield to come my way.

I shook my head and cursed bitterly, "Every fool and fop wants to kill me tonight, it seems. Get Castor out of here." Hardly a necessary order, as Castor could face down things from all seven hells, but fainted at the idea of blood, especially his own. He and Raina made their way to the door past the altar that lead to the living space for the priests. I took out the Phantom Angel gingerly from my belt and held it lightly.

"I see it is true. You have stolen an elvish blade. It will serve me well, *fornicator*."

Something about the way he said *fornicator* let you know he didn't mean women. It has never once worked in the past, but I am always ready to be surprised, so I tried mercy. "I am going to give you one chance. Stand down."

In response, he slapped down his visor and charged his horse right into the church. Not to be outdone, I charged back.

Alright. I was tired, I was cranky, I was well past hungry. I had lost a friend, been chased, and nearly lost my apprentice. In exchange I was able to kill an assassin, assist slightly in killing another, but mostly the highlight of my day was kicking a lordling in the crotch so hard his genitals exploded in a shower of sewer water. While that last was both satisfying and spectacular, I was spent and ready for a nap. I was not in the mood for any kind of fight, but here he was. And since he didn't act like he was from the assassins, Volker and his rabble, or Sausagemissin and the city guard, he could only be from one other place. So understand when I batted aside the tip of the spear, jumped into the pews to avoid being trampled, and then threw back the hooked climbing knife off of my belt. It was not an act of desperation. The hooked knife had no chance of piercing his armor, but it did catch on the flange of his knee cap. This was pure genius, for it pulled him off of the horse and wrenched his leg into uselessness.

Now the knife was attached to the back of my belt and it may have yanked me to a dead stop at the exact moment it did the same to him. And such a reaction while in the pews MAY have pulled me ass over teakettle into the pew in a most painful and undignified way. It also may have snapped that bent link in the chain that attached the knife to me, but sir asshole had a broken leg and I was just bruised, so I still won. And thus it was still genius.

That's my story and I'm sticking to it.

FOUR

THE DESECRATION WALTZ

THE KNIGHT was unconscious, and unlikely to awake for hours. His leg was the least of his problems. His head had been insufficiently padded inside that steel helmet of his and when he had come off the horse, it had rattled around inside. It is not appreciated by many that the steel keeps you from the edge of a weapon, but not the force. I have no idea what inspired him to remove the padded hauberk. When he awoke I could ask, if I cared. I didn't.

We had all spent through the night. Raina had the knight tied to a bed and Castor was tending him. It left me free, since I had only two days to the concert and a temple to topple if I was going to stop it. Not that I was an expert at temple toppling, or even had the vaguest idea of what to do once I got there, but time was running out, and cowering in the catacombs was not going to stop the coming disaster.

It was no secret that the Temple of the Muse was the site of the concert. Well, if it were a secret, it was horribly kept. The Muse was a goddess of a more civilized time, or at least an older one.

Imagine Hammarfall as a horseshoe of rock facing Hammarbay, ramping from ground level on the north leg to the heights of the palace on the south leg. The Temple of the Muse sat in the belly of the curve a hundred feet above the city below. It occupied a delicate finger of rock festooned with columns and vaulted ceilings, of open air and curved walls. The orchestra sat on the very end of the finger of rock, backed by a massive wall of curved marble. The sound projected back toward the noble quarter. It is said that the sound of a symphony would fill the homes of the rich like butterflies born of sound, but did not die there. The Muse was a Goddess for all men, and more of the sound splashed against the curved back of the wall behind the audience. It echoed outward, and cast itself out like light across all the dark places, from northern leg to southern leg, painting every house and soaking into every ship on the water.

This was the temple I had to destroy.

As you may be able to guess, dressing in black and sliding around in a building armored in white marble would not be very effective. You know, I am sure, that stealth is not about not being seen, but about being dismissed. It only took minutes to find a girl selling worn clothing for coppers out of a cart. As a bonus, the fleas were free. I tied back my ragged hair, scuffed my boots, and changed into the rough spun clothes. With so little clothing, I only managed to secret two long knives on myself, practically naked. On the other hand, I was sure that no sword was going to decapitate the temple from the city above.

There were at least fifty men working on the Temple when I arrived. Some were replacing weather stained curtains of the deepest red, stringing them like sails between the lower columns. A massive pile of stained and warped wood lay dejected outside of the main entrance. The king was sparing no expense to mollify his people, or at least have a good time. You know which I was betting was the motivation. A few workmen were even taking in carpets to quiet the steps of patrons, and a large knot of them were mindlessly taking hastily prepared cushions from a large wagon and going inside. Two buildings had been built blasphemously close to the temple, and the one on the right was decorated enough to be a fast climb. Not useful today, but good to note just in case. I waited for a half heartbeat break in the flow, and then grabbed a stack of plush cherry-red cushions and followed the last man inside.

The interior, normally a sparse field of columns and stone benches, had been transformed into a maze of man-tall curtains. I slid from the line when stairs appeared and climbed them to the balcony ringing the whole of the floor. I dumped the cushions into an aisle and walked confidently the whole circumference of the balcony. I could see the work continuing everywhere, and I felt what was wrong.

Once you stood back and watched all the disparate work, it stopped being random. It fell into a pattern, and there was a music to it. I could not believe I was just seeing pictures in clouds, but instead I could see the subtle influence of, if not the Mother of Symphonies, then the darker powers that hid in her shadow.

The ancient design was alive with workmen, far more than I would ever have guessed. The center audience chamber was open to the air, but long poles had been brought up and reinstalled in the worm-eaten brackets. From these poles cloth had been strung, open to let heat rise and escape. They could also iris shut when pulled from the pulley system if weather turned foul. Vertical drapes were hung to funnel the sound and dampen the tiny reflection from the stone into something more lifelike for the rest of the city.

Even as I watched, workmen dropped the last planks onto the carved hollow of the stage, hiding the space beneath and finishing the performing area. Almost without pause, more wood was gathered, dropped, and began to assemble into lofty, raked benches for the orchestra. That cheap thrill, like catching a married woman eyeing you slowly, ran through me. If I could collapse the stage, there would be no way for the performance to continue. I needed to see that stage.

No man challenged me as I walked past them. Their eyes were glazed as if from far too much labor, and they neither spoke, nor joked, nor whistled. The atmosphere was heavy with dire potential, much like the midnight graveyard, the haunted village, or Zeitheim itself. The Burning Composer, or whomever she had sold herself to, was weaving itself into the essence of this all but abandoned temple.

I found the stage, and marveled at the complex system of pulleys and ropes that formed a spider's web of confusion above. The flurry of activity only ten paces from me as men hurriedly built the benches, masked my movements from casual eye. I crossed the stage and on the far side found a mostly rotted wooden door that had not been replaced, and aged stairs beyond. I took them without pause, careful to lower the door quietly.

It was then that I remembered I had nothing that resembled a source of light. Carefully, I shoved at the door, delighted when the bronze anchoring bolts, shriveled and green beyond use, came out of the stone and allowed me to move the door to the side and let daylight stream into the place. Even so, when I returned I was faced with blinding brilliance and unending shadow. I had to plunge into the depths of the stage further and sit quietly with my eyes closed to adjust to any detail.

This was not as easy to do silently as one might believe. This was no empty, echoing chamber, but instead mashed full of the bric-a-brac from thousands of performances down through time. By the doors, forgotten braziers sat empty and disused. Costumes were stacked in musty heaps, and props were dumped in barrels. Old curtains and carpets, decaying ropes and puppets, instruments and tools and pieces of things too broken to identify. There were pieces of ships, rocks made of painted wood, a bell from a church, angels of all sorts, every Lord and Lady as well as every deadly fae or beast that roamed the wilds built to draw laughter or screams. And everywhere, everywhere, there was mold.

Hidden from the sky, drawing from the damp, feeding on every forgotten scrap of cloth, even the movement from replacing the floor of the stage, and thus the ceiling of this place, had kicked up enough spores to become a dense fog. I took a spare cloth from a rag pouch and wrapped it around my nose and mouth. I could still smell the sickly, bitter, dry clouds, but at least I no longer felt like choking and dying on them. My eyes watered and stung fiercely the deeper I went. Of course I discovered that all this suffering was for nothing.

The hollow beneath the stage had been carved from the natural rock that overhung the city below. The designers had placed great thought to the artistry of what they had done, but also the practicality. They had the stairs, as well as thick pillars spaced with long slabs of stone, all carved in place, that ran counter to the lay of the planks to support them from below. It would take dozens of barrels of cannon powder, or a few ogres with mattocks, to destroy the supports. Care and handling of ogres aside, it was not even as practical as blowing up the entire orchestra, even if I were willing to sacrifice possessed but otherwise innocent people, which I was not. Fine. I may sacrifice a man or two, but an entire orchestra?

I shook my head in the darkness, teeth chattering.

Only, it wasn't my teeth chattering.

In an instant, my heart went from standing to sprinting without my feet moving at all. I turned slowly, but there was no one at the doorway. The sound was closer, much closer than that in any case. My head snapped to the nearest figure, a mannequin listing like a ship frozen on the sea. The smiling face beamed its idiocy at the ceiling, but the dead, black eyes stared directly at me. Again the wooden chattering began. I freed a knife from my sleeve, but it felt useless and puny in my fist. Mortal, even.

On the wall, the carving of an immense kraken, tentacles rotted and broken, swayed slightly as hungry eyes bored into me. I edged around the pole, where a giant sized wooden wolf head grinned at me with yellowed teeth. The eyes followed me wherever I went. Again, the chattering, but now it was a chorus. I spun again, and dove backward, away from dozens of dead doll eyes. Hung on the wall were puppets the size of a child, dressed in wild clown colors muted by time and despair. It was the glass eyes that moved with me, that had me breaking out in a cold sweat. The eyes, and the mouths that fluttered open and closed with enough force to snap off the end of a finger.

I could feel her here, and all of her love for me had become the deepest hate as could be found. The dolls shook there, as if lunging against the hanging cords that held them in place, against all the laws of nature. I would say I have a fine sense of timing, but that is a bald faced lie. I do, however, have a sense of when the goblets were being set aside and the poisoned dirks were being drawn. That, right there, was that moment.

I bolted for the exit like a ferret– ducking, leaping, and slithering around obstacles only half seen. Then a shadow blocked the light.

"He says check, we check." I skidded to a halt as a second shadow skipped down the steps and joined the first. The voice was familiar, the shadows fanciful, with frills and thin, fashionable swords. There was a half pause, where I was all too aware that the terrible life had fled from the prop room and it was only me, in a mask, carrying a dagger, facing a bastard I knew slightly less than he knew me. The proof was when he drew his sword and hissed, "Crow!"

Without thought, I gripped a painted backdrop, black with mold, and flipped it into the faces of the shadows. The room exploded like a overripe corpse, spores instead of flies choking out the light. The fanciful men hacked and coughed. One suddenly fell quiet, and then the other. I stood over them, blood dripping from the end of the thick bladed dagger. *For Hanner*, I thought grimly. I saw them clearly now, and knew them to be two of the last Rakes in the employ of Alexander Jaeger Von Sewerknickers. I took another rough cloth from my pouch and dipped it in the blood of one corpse, then wrapped it around a hand as if injured. The dagger I wiped off on my mask and moved it up to cover an eye, providing a mask that was not a mask that hid most of my face.

I walked with purpose, hand cradled, blade secreted just at my fingertips. The workers still moved in time of some song only they could hear. I walked past them, unnoticed. Outside, city guards were being dispersed at the order of the bent, dual cane-wielding form of Sewerknickers himself. He was moving watchmen around in a haphazard manner, their numbers levied with a few of his old Rakes and a dozen new fools.

He caught sight of me leaving and pointed one cane. "You! Where are you bound?"

I stopped and turned, squeezing the soaked rag in one hand and causing blood to run in rivers into my shirt.

He saw and recoiled, dismissing me with a wave. "Bah!"

I hurried off, pausing only at a glass window. I stripped the bloody rags off and dropped them into the sewer. The window, however, showed a far more effective disguise. Black mold spores had turned my skin an elderly gray, peppered my black hair with advanced age, and collected in the folds of my skin to add line deepened wrinkles. I would have smiled, or laughed in triumph, but I had lost my likely chance to plant any kind of trap that would stop the performance. Now it would have to be done live, in person, and I had only the vaguest notion of how beforehand.

But I did know that I had run out of friends, and I would now have to start recruiting enemies. I had to question the broken legged knight.

After a bath.

FIVE

ENEMIES UNALIGNED

THEY SAY all bars are alike, but they have never been in this one. The Book of Knowledge was part bookstore, part library, part tavern, and part meeting hall. In the north, men gathered in secret societies where they wore dark robes and moaned gibberish into opiate-laced incense. They did this because they were rich, and they needed reasons for them to be rich and everyone else was not. This, however felt even older, like one of those societies where they were finally rich enough to stop asking.

The similarities were still there. The Book of Knowledge had guards on the door and one of those cultured stewards whose business it is to guess your weight, age, and approximate access to bullion before letting you in. I had no time for that. So again, I took to the roof, in through a window that a thin slit of metal easily made unsecure, and then from this storage room to the third floor. Walking like a man of means, with direct upright strides, allowed me to blend into the sparse, shadowed populous. There were a few other cloaked men, after all, even though the room was burning with two fireplaces. Each was more cultured than the last, perusing glass fronted cases of books, without men with clubs watching over them I might add. Of course none of them had an elvish longsword, but people are usually far less attentive than they get credit for.

From across the room, I saw my target for the evening. The table, like everything else in the place, was covered in carved lions, old as dirt, and probably quite valuable. This description also covered most of the patrons. The man I was looking for was no exception. His clothes were fine linens, golden rings, chains, and buttons winked in the lamp light. His face was papery and wrinkled, his hair shorn until it was like a white mist upon his age-spotted scalp. He was feeding himself from a small, roasted bird, the scent of buttered potatoes and barely cooked greens leavened with crisped bacon, making my mouth water. He sipped from a silver cup by a silver decanter filled with a white wine with just the barest hint of gold to it.

He overlooked the entire establishment, seated as he was at a table by the railing that bordered the central balcony. From there he could look all the way down to the floor, see all the comings and goings, and was perhaps the reason he started when I came from the direction of the storeroom.

I graciously introduced myself by dropping the stupid knight's helm onto the middle of the table. It crashed to the wood and drew the attention of everyone in the place, but he did not flinch further. He simply looked up from his meal, across my war gear and to my stern face.

I had my dunk in the lake to thank for losing most of my leather and chain, as well as my sheath. After the failed trip to the temple, I went back to the temple of the dead to the knight, Sir Violently Dismounted by Crow, and questioned him. Vigorously. He told me this man would be at this place, at this time. I had then made a quick shopping trip through the chaos of the lower city. New sheath, new armor, and many assorted surprises. It had not been easy, but Lampedocht's bags of coin opened many doors that would have rather stayed locked and may have bought me just a hint of a chance.

I was dressed for war, but it did not seem to register. The old man opposite examined the helmet for a second, then continued his meal. Even without an obvious signal, I noticed the bully boys from the front door start at a mild pace toward the stairs.

"Do I know you?" he asked in a tone that made me want to ensure he could only blow his nose by passing gas.

Without being bidden, I took a seat. A flicker of annoyance finally crossed the old man's face. "Yes. And I have felt your presence every step of the last few months, Lord Reynard Zeißtein." Again, a flicker of something. "Yes, I know, the Redemptive Order has all those rules of honor, loyalty and silence, but oaths only mean so much," I tapped the helm, "after one's leg is dislocated at all three joints."

"You murdered Raymond Von Schwartzklippen." It was not a question.

"Actually, that was the people of Opferhügel," I protested.

"The people of Opferhügel have been dead for over two hundred years," He spat, showing his hand for the first time that night.

"That made it all the worse for him and his men," I replied darkly. Boots were getting closer, one floor down now.

"You killed fifty good, highborn men."

"You sent them to kill me. Should I have simply given up in deference to the blueness of their blood?"

"You don't strike me as a man who bends his knee easily to anyone," he snarled.

"And don't you forget it," I replied, voice pitched hard and low.

Lord Zeißtein calmly chewed the bit of squab, swallowed, wiped his mouth, drank from his cup, swallowed again, and then replied, "You should know you will get nothing out of me thorough torture."

Stupid people always say that, and are always wrong. I heard heavy boots coming up the stairs. The time for flirtations was over. "Don't be coy, Zeißtein. You are the one who sent a small army of men to kill me without explanation. I would like to bring to your attention that despite having been subjected to your tender mercies, Von Schwartzklippen is still breathing, so your death sentence was obviously based on noble standing. Yet despite this, here I sit and you yourself are still breathing. But I swear that if either of those two boys behind me lay a finger on my person, I will put out each of their left eyes." The boot falls stopped behind me. Carefully, arrogantly, purposefully, I picked up the silver cup at my empty setting, filled it and then drained it. It was a delicious, winter sour wine. "Or you could try talking to me for once."

A dozen heartbeats covered the time where anything could happen, and nothing did. Then Zeißtein made a small motion, and the heavy boots receded. I refilled the small silver goblet and drained it again, before filling it and toasting him. "Good choice."

Zeißtein was unamused, "Those men could have torn you limb from limb even unarmed."

I shook my head and sipped the next cup. "No. They really couldn't. Now tell me why The Redemptive Order is looking to murder me in manners most foul?"

Again, to his credit Zeißtein continued eating as if nothing were going on but a visit from a particularly disfavored cousin. He ate, drank, and cleaned himself rather mechanically. "You are a fornicator with demons, a pawn of evil. You have carried doom to my city."

I waited a few breaths, nonplussed myself. "That's all?"

Finally he colored and threw down the fine linen napkin. "Is that all? Boy, you retrieved the final symphony of..."

I interrupted, "Annalirya Von Zeitheim: Enchantress of Strings, The Burning Composer, and so on, and so on."

His color moved toward red. "She was more than just a composer, she was..."

"Demonologist, perhaps necromancer. In any case, she was evil beyond measure..." I took out a knife and began cleaning my nails, more to look unperturbed as he interrupted.

And then purple. "And now..."

"We brought the symphony to Lampedocht where it will be played..."

"Tomorrow night. But it is not a symphony..."

"And while nobody knows what it really is, or what it does, it is likely to destroy the city," I finished, finally finishing a damned thought. "You couldn't tell me this in the beginning?"

He scowled. "The Redemptive Order has existed in secret for..."

"Hundreds of years?" I rolled my eyes. Maybe the school for watchmen and nobles was a university of clichés. "Look, I don't care about your secrecy, or your traditions, or your illustrious order. What I do care about is stopping Lampedocht before he assembles the symphony and plays it."

He looked at me through narrow eyes. "And why should I believe you?"

I drained the wine again. "You sent ten men for me, and they died. You sent thirty, and they died. Raymond Von Schwarzklippen brought fifty and they died. Why else would I be talking to one old man in this place if I were not honestly looking to help?"

Eyes never leaving me, he picked up his cup and sipped from it. He dutifully wiped at bloodless lips and smiled coldly. "You may be here to call off the assassin we hired."

"Which one did you hire? There were two." He blanched at the word 'were'. "Never mind. The assassins guild already wants me for their own reasons. Nothing you can do will call them off. So, tell me, what have we done by bringing the Opus Discordia to Hammarfall? How do we destroy the manuscript?"

The old man shook his head, for the first time truly looking old and perhaps a bit feeble. "The pages are enchanted. Indestructible. We already tried a fire at the concert hall. The pages were all that survived of the desk. An archer tried to assassinate the composer, but he was carrying the pages home in his coat and they stopped the arrow without a scratch. They are penned in blood and written on human leather." The lord's words, gaining in panic and momentum, finally calmed again with visible effort. "You have doomed us. She will enter every noble there, every man at arms within reach. Her generals and knights shall be brought back from the void of nothingness to serve the king, and that power will corrupt him into a monster. Our order has existed since her time, and we know the breadth of her calamity. Now it has returned, and we do not have enough blades at hand to stop them."

"The Redemptive Order is that shallowly manned?"

The Lord hissed, "We recruited one from each generation of the noble families, knowing that it would give us a fighting force of over fifty expertly trained men. You killed them!"

I beat my fist against the table. "I would that you gave me a choice. And it was much more Annalirya than I that dealt them death. Her ghosts and fiends safeguarded us every moment I was in her thrall."

The man leaned back, meshing fingers over his belly. "And so it comes out, then."

"Don't smile at me, you pale ghost. Your men are still dead. Your cause is still lost. And I have proven I am more dangerous than any of them still by virtue of one trait."

"And what is that Master Crow?"

"I survived." I drank the last cup of golden white, then slapped the cup face down like they do in the seaside pubs. "So, you have no men?"

"A pittance. Ten, and only five of those are any use in combat."

I thought for a second. "Get one of them with two fresh horses outside the city tomorrow night. I will have a list for you to give them to fill. Get the others into the Temple where the concert is being held. Get them dressed as servants..."

"They will not be able to carry weapons."

I huffed, "I don't want weapons. Have them smuggle as many bags of charcoal as they can manage. There are braziers under the stage. Fill them and leave the excess. When the concert begins, get them to bring out braziers of charcoal into the outside aisles and light the damn things."

"You think making the nobility sweat will end this all?"

"I think that her power is music and if we wish to win we shall have to change the tune. Make sure they set them up as everyone is being seated. Light them just before the concert starts. They might want cotton for their ears, but I don't know if that will work."

"We are not here to fill your pouches with gold, northman."

I stood and leaned close to Zeißtein, my eyes digging into him like talons. "Are your men going to do it? All I hear from you is doomed, and failed, and can't. So give me what I need, and give me the materials I need to do it. I will get the Opus back, and then I will return it to that bitch and put it back in her grave."

He chewed the words bitterly; he did not like the taste of bluntness or truth. "Fine. But how will you get past The Volker? He has been hunting you for weeks now. And the concert, even now there are royal and city guards along every wall and on the roof of the temple. You will never get close."

I shook my head. "I will handle Volker. I will handle the guards. I may even be able to handle a bit more." Plans were spinning behind my eyes, plans within plans.

Finally Zeißtein could wait no longer. "What?"

My chain of thought snapped and I scowled at him. "I will handle this. Just never make the mistake of thinking you are the good and righteous, Zeißtein."

He pursed his lips and prepared to drink again. "Oh no?"

"No," I spat, standing, "because sacrificing a few people in order to save a lot of people is only an act of heroism if you have the right to sacrifice the small group at all. Otherwise it's just murder in the name of self preservation and don't you fool yourself into thinking differently. I'll send a messenger to drop that letter off at your estate tonight. Don't forget the braziers and charcoal. Nothing works without those."

"What are you going to do?"

"Right now?" I cracked my neck and adjusted the Phantom Angel on my hip. "I'm going to steal an army."

I left, this time by the front door, and I felt oh, so posh doing it.

I returned to the Churches of the Dead. I assembled all of our equipment, Raina and I spoke at length, and plans were laid. She delivered my message to Zeißtein. A quick foray into Volker's lower city confirmed the bloody skirmish between the royal guard and Volker's men had ended. Another trip to the royal quarter confirmed that the massive Cathedral to the Muse was preparing for the concert. One more trip to a filthy, straw-haired man with bug eyes and burnt fingers, and I was ready to make war against music itself with a full satchel and a lighter purse. It took no talent, only ears to learn that most of the surviving upper crust would be there. After months besieged in one section of the city, this distraction would command the presence of everyone not manning a wall.

Afterwards we ate a sparing dinner. I slept, but in the morning, I was certain my apprentice had not. There was nothing for it; there was no time left. I was either going to doom this city, or save it.

Seemed unfair that, in either case, it was going to try to kill me.

SIX

THE LORD OF VIOLET

OLEG VOLKER'S meeting hall was a hive of activity. Well, perhaps not a hive, perhaps a pigsty. Yes, that was it– the grunting, the rooting around in troughs, the basic lack of shit cleaned off from one's person. Volker and his people were living in a pigsty. I entered and the men parted before me as if I were a lord from on high come down to pass judgment. My hard boots clomped on the stone floor, my new armor creaked slightly and my weapons jingled softly, but it was the purpose of my stride that made them give way.

As I have said, the place had the reek of hundreds of unwashed bodies and unwiped nethers, but that was not all that had changed since I had last been there. The tables that had once made islands in between the moderate crowd swallowed by the gargantuan building had been rebuilt. Now they were a pitiful two boards wide and vastly multiplied, both to service and leave room for the throng that now choked the room to every wall.

Speaking of the walls, they had once borne a line of simple paintings of lords and kings being overthrown by the common man and the sufferings of the latter under the former. Now every surface was covered with them. In fact, the artist, regaled in expensive purple as he sloshed paint upon the wall, was even now working on a painting. It depicted many commoners faced with a hulking, black figure. I started when I realized that it was me.

The room behind me had already fallen from the general rumble of men drinking idly to the hush of men expecting death to visit in some horrifically unknown way. I came nearly to the bottom of the ladder when Volker's Right Hand (I never did get this moron's name) moved to intercept me. He came to attention in my way, the way he figured a knight in plate and chain should, and rang one metal boot against the floor.

Volker looked from his incomplete work, frowning fiercely.

"The traitor returns!" Those words alone slit the throat on every voice in the room and brought every eye upon us. I stood patiently at the end of the upraised hand and extended arm of the fool in his shining armor. Volker scoffed and began to take the steps downward to my level, but slowly, in time with his words, which were thrown as if on a stage to reach every corner of the room, "I had never thought to have you back here, traitor. I was certain we would have to root you out of the hands of the nobles with a hoof pick."

I pitched my voice normally, but it still carried in the echoing silence, making everyone want to lean in to catch every word. "That is a fitting welcome, Milord."

The lieutenant burst forth with, "Traitor! Condemned by his own tongue!"

Oleg Volker smiled greasily, picking at the dried paint that dappled his hands and flicking it at me. "Oh, you know that we eschew the titles of the past. We have forged a new way without all that barbarity."

Behind me I heard a knife slowly being drawn. I needed this to change direction, fast. "Barbarities such as ingratitude, *your grace*," I said with an audible sneer, promoting him to king.

The muscles in his jaws danced as he chewed out the word, "Certainly."

"Then why do you treat me so shabbily, as a king with a pet commoner?" Those words rang like a slap in the emptiness. Too bad Volker had to fill up the silence with his own voice, pouncing upon me.

"How else, faithless wretch? You brought noble guards into our part of the city and then set them upon us without much word of warning. We lost twenty eight men!" He threw his arms wide and took one step up upon the bench beside him to be able to play to the crowd. "Twenty eight men doomed by this scoundrel! And where was he? Gone! He fled as the battle commenced to save himself from the slaughter we had to endure."

A groaning cheer of displeasure went up around him, agreeing with the obvious sentence.

"My apologies, Volker, but while you and your men were taking on the royalists, did you even once ask yourself why I had come to you in such a hurry?" Believers and thugs looked about, nonplussed. There was something of a crack in Volker's confidence. I shook my head sadly. "I was, indeed, in the noble quarter. And there I found out a plot against your life." And this, Ladies and Gentlemen, is why I try to be honest with myself. I am one of the world's best liars. "And while you and your men valiantly engaged the royal guard, I ran to intercept a far more dire threat. Assassins!"

The room gasped, but the plate and chain hero scoffed, "And what proof..." I held up a small vial above my head and then set it on the table with an audible *tink*. "You could have bought that at any chemist..." Another vial. "You..." And another and another and another. The lieutenant roared in indignation, "You expect me to believe that these are all poison?"

My calm reply rattled him to the bone. "Drink one."

Again, the silence closed in like a funeral shroud. The men looked from me, to Volker, to the poisons. It is important to cater a good lie to the people you need most to hear it. As long as this had lasted, it was entirely possible, even slightly surprising, that an assassin had not paid Oleg Volker a well deserved visit. On the other hand, the king was terrified of assassins, and would likely both avoid them expecting to meet his end at any bargaining session with them. Any noble that was found to use them on such a high profile figure as Volker would by necessity admit they knew how to contact the Assassin's Guild and thus not live too much longer than the target under such a paranoid ruler.

"Wait," one of the peons interjected, "you *killed* an assassin?"

He was roundly ignored. Volker continued, "That makes use of the first day, but what of the rest of your absence?"

Slowly, deliberately, I pulled off the sheathed greatsword from my back. I held it up to their leader and Oleg took it with a face full of marvel. "I tracked down the other assassin as well, to keep you safe, Volker."

Hilt shaped like a fist full of scorpions and eyes with two tails as a crosspiece, Volker slid the blade forth by three handspans. Immediately, the slick blade began to weep vile pitch. He started to hand it off to his lieutenant when I spoke.

"Do not touch that. You hold Godstongue, Volker. It is the only truly magical blade I know of." I lied, but he still snatched it back to himself. "Forged in an age long past, it is one of the most deadly instruments to ever cut a swath across the battlefield." I sighed, "It seemed dishonest to hold it back from you, who could wield it in the name of the people in a way I never could."

Which just goes to show that sometimes you *can* polish a turd. I suppose that is unkind. Most men only ever hear about magical swords. And, as a leader, now that he had one, he was one step closer to transforming himself into a legend. Dressed in his royal purple, Volker held up the sword above his head and the whole crowd cheered in deafening waves. I glanced behind and up, on the far wall, where a king in violet held a sword over a cheering throng of knights who stood on the bent backs of the peasants. I looked over the throng, and saw the noble women forced to work the fires and kegs, bringing food to their masters. One in particular, a small, angry woman, stared at me with promises of painful death. It was Konrad's wife. Well, to hell with her. I didn't have a mandate to salve her hurts…

I nodded to her slightly. She looked surprised.

…yet.

I completely ignored the armored man in front of me, concentrating all my will upon the figurehead just beyond him. I watched Volker balance there, teeter on his better judgment, such as it was. Then he looked down to the sword, and knew that if I were tainted, so would be my gifts, and he so wanted this one to be taint free. I saw him land on my side, but what pushed him there I would never hazard a guess.

"Welcome back, Master Crow. You are truly a cunning servant. It is good to have you among us."

The people cheered, save the slave staff and the armored buffoon. For his part, his arms popped up in a questioning gesture, which was the most public doubt he had ever shown his messiah, and then slapped gauntleted hands against armored thighs in frustration like a child. I never heard the dagger behind me disappear back into the sheath, but apparently it did, and that meant it was time to press again.

As soon as the crowd quieted, I pitched my voice in the stage shout as Volker had, purposefully bringing the whole host to our council. "I do not bring wholly happy tidings, Oleg Volker. Tonight there is to be a concert at the Temple of the Muse and..."

The lieutenant gazed loudly down upon this offering, "We know this already, Crow."

I nodded and began to move back through the crowd. "Excellent, then the men are ready. I will begin divvying them up into squads."

Volker, braced to watch two of his middle men make each other bleed a little, suddenly found himself mired in a policy decision. "Wait! Explain!"

I looked back to him. "Summer is half done, Volker. We have control of the food, but we will need to secure weapons, mounts and armor to face the armies that are coming for us from the other cities. We outnumber the guards, and now they have only the city partition gates to protect them, not the palace itself." I spoke to the lieutenant as if he were a child. "We move quickly, and we can have all the noble's gold, the guards weapons, and the palace to have extra walls come wartime. But we must have every single man you can spare, it must be tonight, and we must act swiftly."

Again the room was stunned to quiet. They all looked to Volker.

And that's the thing about lies. If you can spin one, make it so obvious as to be common sense, to tie in all worries and qualms and preconceived notions, then what you have is a trap. And it is as deadly as the dwarven jaws that had been left for us on the road to Zeitheim.

Again, Volker saw the sea of men expecting him to act like a hero, the sword that marked him as a hero, and he shouted wordlessly and raised the weapon in the air.

And in the excitement no one even asked where Raina was.

SEVEN

THE OPUS DISCORDIA

AS I HAVE said, there were two gates to the raised noble quarter of town. They were not particularly close, which was good, but I would have liked three, four, or perhaps a hundred better. You see the defenders only had so many men, and with the king in evidence, most would be within earshot of that man. The rest of the forces would have to be split between the two gates. I would have rather faced one to ten percent of those forces than half, but I'll take what I can get. Granted, we could avoid the guards entirely by taking one of a dozen secret ways, but I needed to thin some of the ranks of Volker's men. We outnumbered the guards heavily and I had to play this just right.

The concert began, and you could hear it all through the city. It was the signal for the first group to attack the main gate to the city. Again, I had split my forces under the guise of tactics. That was why one hundred men made a show at the first gate, throwing rocks and cheap spears, firing the odd arrow from cover. As soon as the first gate blew a horn to draw men from the dock gate, we struck. Well, I say we. I mean my lackeys.

Again, there were rocks, and spears and a good many more arrows, but this time there were four hundred men, almost every last body Volker had. I winced at the presence of so many boys and elders, but it couldn't be helped. Tonight was going to be bloody, no doubt.

The horn sounded at the dock gate as the fifth ladder went up on the city side and men were making it over the edge before being cut down. We lost at least twenty, but the gates were opened, and then the twenty were balanced by the guardsmen who then died as we swarmed their position. Like with a flood of insects, the guard house, gate, and corpses were scavenged clean of anything of use in minutes. We marched on the dock gate, hitting five guards who had been dispatched back to answer the call, and then we rolled over the seventy men on that wall from the wrong side. We lost thirty, but all the gates were ours.

Volker made some kind of inspiring speech I did not listen to. Instead we formed the men quickly and the moment he hit more than a half breath, I ordered them to move out.

I have to admit, the equipment was a mishmash, the lines were ragged and sloppy, the faces distant and almost in shock, but there was a growing kernel of something violent in them. Then, of course, I heard the music again. I could feel the song permeate my mind, and this time I could shake it off. It was mindless and martial, spiked and fanged. I could guess what it was doing to Volker's men, but I had no way to be sure. Still they were obeying orders and that was all that mattered for now. I did notice, however, that they were, for the first time in their lives, marching in time, I am sure it was to a beat in their heads.

I turned and liberated a shield from a nameless man. I waited and let the crowd slip around me until I was mostly at the rear of the formation next to the Glorious Hero of the People. I pointed to Volker and shouted, drawing him out of a dreamlike fugue in D minor. "This is it, Volker! No matter what you must keep them moving! You must keep them moving!"

He nodded enthusiastically, saying something revolutionary that was lost in the tumult. Though at this point I wonder if he could stop them. The men had even stopped eyeing the houses on every side hungrily and were now following the music back to its source.

I broke from ranks and skirted the main group to range ahead, for if there were anything I was useful at, it would be as a scout. And what is a scout, but a fancy word for bait?

The music became clearer and even more powerful. It took some concentration to keep the notes from invading my head. The audience must be in some kind of total stupefaction at the moment, to be sure. That was good, I needed the distractions. It was also extremely bad, I did not personally need the distractions. I patted the heavy, bulged slingbag I carried and hoped the surprises inside would do the job I needed done.

Again, the music came. It was the product of hundreds of hands and mouths, disparate, discordant sounds that blended under the guidance of a master into a powerful song of furious oppression. It sunk fingers into the brain and whispered every instance where one was owed, every time one was wronged, and it pulled a red film over the eyes to block out proper perspective and self control. Fights would already be breaking out in every alley and bar house. Married couples in trouble would be screaming and household goods would soon be flying. Young men would not only start fights due to bravado, they would actively seek them out for any imagined slight and no apology could be given, let alone accepted. I had less time than I had imagined. Much longer, and the city would surely burn.

I shook my head clear and found myself in the square outside the Temple of the Muse. Torches flared like watching eyes over the eerily still bodies of two hundred city guards and a dozen Rakes. I glanced left and right, disoriented for just a second as a crossbow bolt slammed into the outer edge of the shield, punching through as if it were not even there. The lordlings, at their prime, unaccustomed to the discipline of battle, pulled away from the main force, whooping and screaming the names of their royal houses. Easily another fifty guardsmen, themselves almost boys, broke ranks and sprinted for me with naked steel.

This, for the record, was my plan working a little better than I had wanted. I spun and bolted like a fox before the hounds. The guards cheered my demise, roared to the heavens their approval, adding a barbaric chant to the baseline of the symphony. Their voices become tired, and they sank back into the muddled, angry torpor of the song blaring behind their heads, and waited for the men to bring back my corpse. And waited. And waited.

But then Volker's army appeared, freshly armed with the mail and weapons of the Rakes and the guards. Fresh rents and bloody steel aside, they looked like a pack of mad mongrel dogs set to kill and mount every bitch in the kennels, and probably in that order. And over it all the song, the Magnum Opus Discordia pushed upon them, increasing the pressure of hate with every note, scattering thoughts. All leadership broke down as Volker's men charged in a wave. In heartbeats, men were fist to fist, and dagger to dagger, rolling in gutters that ran red with blood. Training and thought had been discarded by brains baked to insanity by the heat of fury.

I scaled a nearby building's decorative façade. From there it was only a long jump over an alley (the bottom a fatal fall, granted) that separated me from the Temple. From above, however, the grand melee took on a more sinister pattern, for as men fought and died, they became less and less rational. Men were not fighting enemies, but anyone within reach. Guardsmen tumbled on the ground, knifing each other in the eyes. Volker's men bit at jugulars, tore at eyes, and thrust steel indiscriminately. And the blood, the blood did not run in the gutters down to the sewers as it should. Cold terror gripped me as I saw it flow uphill, and into the main entrance to the desecrated temple. All the while the winged figures of the muses had faces transformed to despair and defeat by the flickering torchlight.

"What have I done?" I stared, but the voice was my own. For however cleverly I had planned this, I too had played into the machinations of the master plotters in hell. The sky was darkening as the final lights of dusk faded and the crimson curtains that irised at the top of the temple light gaped like a scream. Music leapt from it like a corpse from a grave. It blasted into the air, and highlighted one, two, then a dozen, then a hundred black shapes, all circling the scene of death about to occur. It was a cyclone of black feathers, of harsh caws, as if I had any doubt of what came next.

I gathered myself and tied a rag mask to my face. Then I sprinted to the edge of the building and leapt to the ring of stones around the temple.

The music below was oppressive and like two hands, crushing my skull. Here it was a rockslide burying all thought in the discordant explosions of its crescendos. I staggered under its impact, but held my mind together though force of will.

The iris was the logical choice of descent. I rushed to it and looked down. Torches had been lit, and to my utter delight, more braziers than I could have hoped for had been set up from stores and lit. The light and heat blasted through the opening, curtain pulled as wide as possible, but I could still see the travesty below.

The stage was filled by the orchestra, who played madly with unseeing eyes and fingers bleeding from the strain. Lampedocht was there, conducting like a man with a foot caught in a wasp nest. My worst fears were not to be realized. The guards inside were slack jawed and glassy eyed. Likewise the ushers and nobles of the audience were entranced, enchanted, unresponsive. These last had appeared in all the finery a cool summer night had offered them access to, but none had budged beneath the beating heat of the braziers.

I positioned myself over the hole leading down to the balcony and, donning heavy leather gloves, I slid down the system of ropes. There was a sickening lurch, and then a sinking sensation that poked around in my bowels for any loose stool to evacuate. I held on, fighting panic until it stopped and I slid the rest of the way to the balcony seats. I drew my shortsword, but none moved. Above the stone hole, twenty paces wide, had been choked off by my weight on the ropes, curtains closing the hole to five paces. I landed on my feet, sweat already sprouting on my face.

I glanced left, glanced right. No man nor woman moved toward me, though I could feel the ghosts of Discordia slamming into my mental walls. More telling I could feel soft, feminine fingers foraging in my chest for the heart there.

Good luck, you bitch.

I sheathed the sword and sprang to action I passed a bronze bowl of burning charcoal but I was too busy running and I couldn't reliably dig in my slingbag for my secret weapons. As one, everyone in the section I was passing and the section I was coming to turned to stare at me. Tiny veins in their eyes were snapping, spreading crimson throughout the whites even as the irises remained vacant and dead. They opened their mouths as a single being and toneless, undulating sounds joined into the symphony.

That was, of course when something icy cold slapped me in the face like the love kick of a mule. I went sprawling back into the brazier, dumping live coals onto the carpet with abandon. I rolled away, saved from losing even a single hair by the coating of ice that the unseen blow had left in place of sweat across the whole of my head. I shook myself and rolled backwards to my feet. The carpet began to smolder and as the traces of smoke wafted into the scorched air, it trailed around the form of my assailant, a ghostly knight.

Fine, I say knight, but a knight taller than any man, with screaming faces that undulated under the surface of his liquid armor. The unearthly steel was made of spikes and razors and points all around, with gaping tooth-rimmed maws where his palms should be. For a second I remembered the tales of Annalirya and her fearsome knights stripping the flesh and souls from her enemies, and I knew I gazed upon one of these fearsome thralls from beyond.

It lunged again, and I leapt a pace back, getting the Phantom Angel clear of its new sheath. Smelling the foul taint of corruption, it came forth haloed in blue fire. The light and heat of the blade hit the knight like a hurricane force, but far from disintegrating like the ghosts on top of the mountain, it simply leaned into the gale and continued to advance. This was not the bad news. Or rather, it was the bad news, but the answering scream from behind me was worse.

A single glance saw a second knight, as horrific as the first, floating toward me, arms outstretched. I struck at them, and it seemed to disrupt them like a stone thrown into a pool. It certainly caused them pain, but it did not stop them from creeping toward my throat and the end to my life.

Then it was me. Just me. Me, my sword, and a bundle grabbed from my slingbag. I had dozens of the canvas wrapped things, as large around as a man's spread hand and surprisingly light. I cast all hope that if these would disrupt the large song, they could disrupt the smaller ones, and tossed it on the spilled coals. Immediately, I dove over some seated singing patrons, boot clipping some poor woman in the head, and I rolled down the stairs to the raised lip and rail at the edge of the balcony.

Mortal opponents would be forced to come at me down the row one at a time, but these specters could fly. They simply walked through the bodies of their summoners, turning faces blue and in some cases killing them outright with their unearthly, hellish cold. I felt the heat ripped from the air as they got closer and closer. I shook icicles of sweat from my hair and held the elvish sword before me like a wall. Sadly, it would never be enough.

Then, on the floor, there was a flash. The canvas lit and burnt like a tiny torch for just a moment. Then, with the sound of a cracking whip, the bundle flew apart.

The sound was distracting, but gave the creatures no pause. Then there was another, and another, and then a string of three, two more, three more, one more. Harsh smoke began gushing from small paper and clay bundles on the floor as the fireworks continued to detonate in a random string. Inside, this close, they were unbelievably loud, and they drowned out the meter and rhythm of the Discordia. People began to blink, to wake from the dream. The song of summoning died in their throats and the knights faded back into the hells they deserved.

Others took up the song, but the harsh smoke choked them, and they could not be forced to match the exacting frequencies that could call creatures from the beyond. Men and women were standing in confusion, a clear path before them to panic, so I sheathed my sword and fled to the stairs. I took them three at a time, dumping little packages of Hammarfall's beloved fireworks, bought from a strange purveyor on the docks, into the braziers as I went. My little eggs hatched loudly, spitting fire, smoke, and thunder into the air and adding chaos to the discord, stripping it of harmony and power.

Nobles were waking, coming out of their stupor, but the reach of the fireworks was nowhere near as far as I had hoped. Each was a finite bundle of sound, and they would run out. The smoke, however, was far more irritating, and far more lasting, filling the curtained walls like a haze that sought to wake the sleeping audience. Yet the forces I faced were far more insidious and, though long perished, could still move against me. Move they did.

Far off, there was the triple crackle of thunder. A summer storm beyond the bay, coming fast. Yet it was not lightning strike, nor terrible rain that wrought Annalirya's will, but a shrieking gale that buffeted the temple with no gentle mercy. At one moment I was running down the side aisle, tossing bundles into braziers, cloaked in the thick, purple smoke born of these fireworks and smoke bombs. The next , a hundred crimson banners ripped from the floor like wing muscles peeled from the white marble bone. They flapped in pain as the wind blasted through in a silent roar, and the music, oh the music was louder every single heartbeat.

The wicked wind slapped me in the face, but rather than recoil, I charged to meet it. Bundle after bundle found burning coals, and I reached the broken doors to the understage. There the music was a physical force, the wind as angry as hornets. Still clad in the thickest of leather gloves, I grasped the nearest burning urn and carried it bodily to the stairs, where I dumped it in. If all else failed, I hoped the dry memories of a thousand past plays and operas would provide enough food to end this before the city was doomed. As to myself, well, I am a suicidal idiot. For, as I looked up onto the stage, I knew I could not leave the hundreds of artists and their leader simply to burn. This evil was not their doing. It was mine.

I made to leap upon the stage when something firm caught my empty slingbag. I lurched to a halt and was carried backward onto the aisle floor by the force. One set of hands, far too eager, sought to restrain me, but I responded a bit breathlessly with a salient point at the end of a dagger. My argument struck home and the gaily dressed Rake reeled away from the mortal wound I imparted. Worse yet, he had brought more men who needed to debate with steel and I had to roll to standing to escape a counterpoint embodied by a long thin saber. Without pause, I was up on stage and out of the cramped sunken aisle at the side.

There the music was everything. It displaced the air and seared the sweat from the body. It was the fuel for the muscles and the impulses as well. It was everything and everyone and I could barely reach forward to grab a fraying rebec from the hands of a player and smash it to the ground. We both stared at it for a heartbeat, and then he began to sing his hideous part as if the sounds were being ripped from his insides by clawed hands.

I heard the call of a raven and dove to the side, barely in time as the Rake behind me missed and cut down the newly minted singer before me. For a split second, the whole concert blared his death scream, and then the music went on and on. There were six surviving Rakes, and the no-longer-hobbling form of Alexander Jaeger Von Schwarzklippen.

They circled me in steel as I drew my Phantom Angel, edging me out into the light. Even the briefest of glances past the lime lights showed that one in ten, perhaps one in five, of the furthest from the music had escaped. Here and there flapping curtains had caught the braziers and burned in an undulating panic. It did not matter. The rest, even the King, sat in silent admiration, feeding the Opus with their very lives even as it tunneled into them like worms into a fruit and controlled them.

Alexander Jaeger laughed, but it wasn't just *his* laugh. The hollow, worthless man was something else now. He was carrying a massed bundle on his back, and he pulled it off to reveal Godstongue had found its slimy way into his hands, "Well, Crow. I finally get to see you get what is coming to you."

I had something prepared, I really did. Something along the lines of, *No, don't do it*, or *You fool, you are all being controlled*. But in the end, these were the men who had killed Hanner. Hanner had, in his way, loved them. He had trusted them enough to throw his lot in with them when times were at their hardest. He had earned for them: food, blankets, and a sword for defense. Rather than share, they had murdered him and taken it all. I leapt backward and swung blindly, killing the first Rake with a blow to the face before they even realized I was not going to speak at all.

The second came in and I felt my concentration diffuse. I saw everything, heard everything. A man charged from behind and I sidestepped his thrust. I blocked another sword and grabbed the first Rake's hair. I bent him backwards and then brought the blade down to decapitate the stupid boy. The next got a head in his face, which he caught, and then I brought the Angel down like an executioner's axe and severed his partner's thigh. Head-bearer dropped the grisly present in time to catch a sword in the eye. A thin, fast saber, made for thrusting, was swung at my armored back. It slapped into the kidneys like a kick, but failed to penetrate the sewn metal plates there. I pommeled my attempted executioner viciously in the face, and spun around him. Two swords, made for my heart, pierced him instead. I kicked the body back toward the two thrusting lordling, then pierced one in the groin, the other in the heart, then the first one in the throat as he screamed in agony.

Six young men. It is quick to tell, but it happened far more quickly still. By some miracle, I had survived. The air was redolent with the smell of bowel, pierced and evacuated, and blood. And then it was just me and Von Schwarzklippen.

He held up the favored blade of Isahd, God of Murder, the way a child holds a sword. He may have had some semblance of skill with a light, fast blade, but this was a great two-hander, and he barely had strength to lift it. I stalked him like a wolf, circling him as he sought in vain to find a place of control on the long, carved handle. Whatever magic of the music had returned him to health, it could not grant him skill, could not bring him luck, was incapable of matching the world ending rage that consumed me.

"You and me, then, peasant," he spat.

"I know you to be a thrall of the symphony, fool."

"And why is that?" And, trying to catch me speaking instead of fighting, he came forward with a series of clumsy thrusts each more ridiculous than the last. I parried, stepped to the side, slapped the blade hard enough to ring, and then blocked one, two, three slow cuts that wouldn't have hit an alley cat.

"Because you did not piss your pants, beg for your life, or run away once your men were dead." And then, without ceremony, I whipped the end of the blade in a shallow arc and slapped Godstongue into his own face. He went rigid and dropped the sword.

The cut on his cheek was thin, so thin it only beaded blood and did not trickle. But the poisoned spit of the tongue of the God of Murder was nothing if not efficacious.

Von Sausagemissin seemed to find himself there, at the very end. His nine fingers went to his face and tried to tear it off as his plaintive wail became a full throated scream. He stumbled into the rough circle of dead Rakes and he fell into the center. His body began bucking and kicking as he shuddered in death. I turned my attention to the audience, who seemed no clearer for having watched my masterful display, nor care much as I collected the sheath of the magical two-hander, put it home, and sling it over my shoulder. He had stopped moving by the time I was done.

The world had not paused even for a breath. The wind still shrieked in all directions, the music formed fists that smashed all complex thoughts. It filled me and penetrated me like a hail of arrows. It was as if the death of the Rakes on stage had crossed some threshold. Heat from below warped the wooden slats of the stage and smoke rose from cracks between the boards in instantly shattered streams. And that, ladies and gentlemen, was my cue to go.

I could not save the orchestra, the conductor, the audience. All I could do was escape with my life, and the Opus. Back stinging, legs rubbery, I lurched to the conductor's podium. There Swan Lampedocht flittered his wand from beat to beat, section to section, eyes glazed, hair sweaty and tangled.

His single-mindedness had offended me in the presence of his needful niece, but then I wondered how long he had been in the thrall of the Mother of Symphonies. Try as I might, I could not hate him, and in a flash of humility I understood I had little right to pass judgment upon him.

"I'm sorry, Master Conductor," I said as I reached for the pages.

There was a terrific force that bowled me back and slapped me to the stage. Searing heat and elastic wooden slats sent panic messages to my brain and got me moving. I blinked away duplicates of the confused world and saw there the pages of the Discordia trapped in a cyclone of force. The pages spun faster and faster, red notes resolving into the image of a beautiful woman, rendered in bloody ink as they spun. She gazed at me with pity, the kind of mourning one can only truly give by seeing someone walking the same troubled path five steps behind. Music crashing, fire crackling, wind howling, pages fluttering, she held out a dainty hand to me, offering me all I wanted now: someone to understand and accept my evil, to give me some measure of finality, of stability, of peace.

I struggled to my feet, glancing to the lost souls on every side. I knew I would never leave without those pages. I shook my head and I drew the Phantom Angel.

She dropped her arm to her side. Her silent eyes asked the obvious question.

"Peace is not my business," I replied.

And then I struck.

I might as well have been swinging at gnats, for all the effect my sword had. The cyclone coughed into a cloud, and then spat itself onto the ground. I leapt forward, slashing at the floor, but the pages were moving too randomly, too quickly. I stabbed downward, shattering a board, and had to leap back. The larger whirlwind barreling like a bull into the Temple, the steam poured over the stage, part bled off into the under stage where my fire raged. Now, provided with an outlet, the wind rushed in gulps to the prop room and came out of the hole like a volcano. I wiped my eyes, clearing the heat and ash as my enemy appeared before me.

A growl forced itself out of my mouth, "I am tired of killing you, you damned bastard."

Alexander Jaeger Von Schwarzklippen, dead and gone, wasted and hollow even while alive, stood. He was armored from head to foot in the indestructible pages of the Opus Discordia and surrounded by a fluttering cloud of the remaining symphony. The mummified corpse raised its arms and the pages collected into long, curved blades made of immortal vellum.

With the idea firmly entrenched inside me that doing something violent this instant was better than waiting to see what some unknown thing would do to me, I leapt forward. The Phantom Angel burning, I slapped aside the two blows meant to dice me into pieces and tucked it like a lance, whole body behind the thrust that caught the corpse in the very center of its chest.

The tip hit the pages and came to a full stop before it disturbed the first layer of ink. The elvish sword bent double, and then a page armored fist broke against my head like a wave on the beach. It tossed me to the side, Angel flying, limbs sprawling. I landed hard on the quickly cooking floor. I shook my head, but clarity refused to come.

The concert thing opened its fists and the blades flew into swirling sheets. Impossibly strong hands picked me up from the floor. One held me tight as the other struck me once, twice, three times in the belly. The force of the blows were so great that Godstongue, slung loosely on my back, bounced against my spine with every hit. The creature pulled me close, as if looking into my eyes to find when life finally fled.

Perhaps it was the pain, maybe the heat, could have been just delusion, but every bloody note on the paper held the tiniest face. Millions of tiny souls screaming as the concert came to its ultimate crescendo, and doomed the city with it. Then, I actually looked at the armored face.

There was a line, from brow to cheek, razor thin, where it was turning black as necrotic flesh, veins in the ancient leather paper taking the venom from that spot to the rest of the page, consuming notes as it went.

Then I was lifted and slammed to the floor. My left shoulder exploded into fiery pain. I rolled away as the musical corpse smashed the boards where I had been. They crumbled away, smoke and ash erupted in coarse clouds. I rolled to my feet, and I remembered how Von Schwarzklippen had died.

The creature lunged at me, and I spun, moving to the side as I awkwardly drew the great two-handed sword from its sheath and slung it in a weak, one-handed slash. The blade slapped edge on against the creature, and it paused as if shocked. A dozen musicians made screams with their instruments. They tumbled from their seats, but the conductor and the symphony went on.

I overbalanced and fell, but even in recovering my feet I could see that the magically murderous blade had failed to cut through even one sheet of eldritch paper. I cocked back the blade, but had to angle it from my face and body, increasing the strain on the screaming joints in my dislocated arm. The sludge seeping down the blade brooked no argument to this. Yet the closer the eye and the scorpions on the crosspiece came to my ear, the more I could hear dark whispers, threats of vengeance, and offers of reconciliation.

The creature reached into the cloud around it and pulled out its swords of paper, but I quickly leapt forward and snapped the blade downward. It blocked with both swords, but the poison bile slid from the blade and splashed from Godstongue onto the thing's shoulders and across the blades.

More musicians screamed and fell. A few more audience members found their minds and fled. The music itself stuttered and faltered as blackness covered the pages and filled them like the flesh of a living thing. These past pages, parts of the symphony but read and gone, still ripped through the room with their ghosts, weakening the spells but too little, too late.

Above the stage was a face, a thing, a being so horrible it would swallow all things and digest them for all eternity. It was a creature as black as any of the Dark Gods, and it was so close to being here, so close it roared in impatience to see so much to consume just out of reach.

Then the smoking foot of the symphony beast slammed into my already injured shoulder. I sprawled backwards a dozen paces and lay there in a fog of pain, my right hand locked around Godstongue of its own volition.

"It doesn't have to end this way. Come back to me, Simon."

The bodiless voice cut through to my deepest parts and I yanked myself to my knees. The creature was pulling pages from the cloud around it, patching the dead and dying pages on its body with new ones from the cloud, spreading the infection and killing more notes that would never be played again. Finally, I understood.

It turned to me, knowing that with my death, all resistance ended. Godstongue was not even held as a weapon. Instead it was across my lap, my heavily gloved hand stroking it like a dying hound. My breath came only in ragged gasps, hair stringy with sweat that stunk of fear, and my skin both flushed from the barbaric heat and pale from pain. The blade, I held a hair from my throat. The beast dove for me, but I was not there.

Everything I was, I threw into one, desperate lunge. I dropped Godstongue. I threw away any chance to escape. I discarded my own life as I reached out two heavy gloves dripping with the spit of the God of Murder. I felt two impacts as the creature sought to beat me, but my hands slid down its body, smearing hundreds of layered pages from shoulders to ankle. It crashed on top of me, then palsied as I rolled away.

There was an explosion of screams, instruments crashed, and the music died.

I staggered to my feet, pulling one glove off with the other and then cutting the first free so I did not touch the deadly, black ooze. I watched the pages flutter like broken wings from the corpse of my enemy. They circled weakly there, casting a shadow of Annalirya's face. Beaten and hurt, I limped to Godstongue, shaking off more bile from the blade before sliding it home in its sheath taken from my back. The Phantom Angel was next, but by then the boards were blackening and flame peaking through the cracks. I looked back to the pages of the Opus. Her face was still there, eyes showing nothing but the deepest sadness, the most vile betrayal.

"We cannot forgive one another for what we have done," I said to her. "That is not our place."

And then the pages began to brown and wither from the intense heat. Those on the stands of the musicians burst into flame directly, adding their light to the cleansing of this forgotten tribute to beauty. The enchantment was broken for all time, the Opus lost to the flow of fate.

Some musicians and many of the audience, including the king, would never move again, but the rest had fled as the smoke sought to steal their breath. I found Lampedocht and slung him over my good shoulder, stifling a scream as the other was jostled by the movement.

The streets outside were a scene of bloody chaos. All men, attackers and defenders had discarded swords and knives, and descended to fists and teeth. They had fed the Opus with their violence, but thankfully it was far harder to beat a man to death than most believed. The audience had entered the moaning carpet of revolutionaries and guardsmen, collapsing from heat and whatever insidious feeding the symphony had taken.

Winifred, Lampedocht's niece found me in the crowd. I staggered across the street, the sound of burning cloth far too loud by the temple. I slid the conductor to the ground gently, but as he touched the brick wall, Winifred recoiled. Immediately, I drew off the swords and let them clatter to the ground. I used a dagger to slit my vest of plates. They fell to the ground, revealing the splash of blood where I had indeed been cut by the rake, and only a finger away the black patch where the poison was seeping in to the garment to kill me. This is where the poison had come in contact with the composer's cheek and killed him as I carried him clear.

Winifred reached for the spot, and I grabbed her hand, shaking my head. She wept for him. I wish I could have, but there was too much pain, too many things left to do. No, that is a lie. I did not weep, for this was the last thrall of Annalirya, the last copy of the Opus in his mind. I had tried to save him, but he could not live through this if the danger was to pass over Hammarfall.

"What shall I do?" she asked, weakly.

I meticulously checked the sheaths and sword belts for any trace of poison. Finding none, I slung them. "Tell them he died in the fire. Find his compositions. Make sure they see the light of day." I stood. "Do not let him be remembered like this."

She stood and I thought she meant to slap me, but instead she embraced my soot and blood stained face and kissed me deeply. She was warm, wet, wanton, and tasted of honey and strawberries. It was a woman's kiss from such a young girl. I kissed her back.

"I will tell them the truth of you."

I shook my head. "Save yourself the pain. My reputation is not worth it and can only put you in mortal peril. Live well, and you honor me enough."

I turned and left.

EIGHT

THE CREATION OF ALL MEN

OF ALL things I did not want to hear, "My sword!" was easily number three. Number two would have been anything out of the mouth of Oleg Volker. Together they made number one, easily.

The whole of Volker's temple to himself was devoid of slave, master, fellow, or thug. Well, all but the purple clad moron and his tin plated dog. Of course the dog was barking.

"Bastard, son of a bitch, whoreson, and traitor!" The armored lieutenant stalked toward me, sword drawn and pulled back to cleave through my shirt and skin with equal abandon. The Phantom Angel leapt from its sheath and flashed at the end of my hand. It sent his sword spinning away with the first strike and split his plate and chain as if made of cheesecloth with the second. Just like that he was drowning on his own fluids.

I had changed. I took no joy in his noisy and fitting demise. Well, maybe I was just tired. Regardless, I picked up a rag from a nearby table and wiped the bright blade, sliding it home.

Volker finally found his courage. Not enough to go get his lackey's sword, but enough to sneer at me. It had always been his best weapon anyway. "So, what now? Do you serve the king? Or are you looking to usurp my station amongst the people?"

I walked to a keg, grabbed a stein, and turned the tap on the heavy bier. It filled the cup quickly, heavy foam head annoying me. I poured it onto the floor and then drained the supremely bitter concoction in one pull. I looked to Volker, who still stood as if something uncomfortable was working its way up his bunghole.

"Every conversation we have ever had revolves around you. Did you know that?" I tossed the stein aside, "Every time you spoke to your people it was all about freedom. But freedom stops where you start, doesn't it, Oleg?"

His jaw clenched, his spare frame trembling with honest indignation as he spat, "I don't know what you mean." Again I looked at the purple tyrant on walls all around. Oleg had drawn them all, and even resplendent in bloody, violet robes he could not see what he had made of himself. I sighed, which set him off into one of his prewritten collections of words used to move the uninformed. "You have ever doubted me! You have ever stood against me, vile betrayer! Everything I have done, I have done to preserve the lives and dignity of the defenseless! The abused! The downtrodden!" The sound of a crowd coming from the rear of the massive meeting hall gave fresh fire and certainty to his eyes. "And now you shall see! You will be chained and forced to watch my ascension at the head of an army of common men before you die."

But the crowd that came from the rear of the building was not of thugs and miscreants, but rag wearing, weak, and beaten slaves, serving girls, and prisoners. Men and women of noble blood. Freshly armed, freshly freed, they poured into the room like a tide coming in. Volker made to dart for the doors, but they too darkened, and the ragged royal mob blocked him from all escape. He backed away from them all, face pale and covered in a sheen of sweat.

"These people look abused and downtrodden. Try them," I said, and made my way outside as the tide of people he had enslaved enveloped him. His screams lasted a long, long time. Can't say it was adequate, but it was payback of a kind. I am told the legend of his treachery lives to this day, and criminals are saved all year to be put down on the anniversary of his death. I was just able to squeeze out of the door when I met a familiar face.

I paused for one second to meet the eyes of Konrad Pferdmann, chef and innkeeper. The gentle giant was changed, hardened, blood spattered. A stained sword shook in his hand. He nodded solemnly, but a whistle made us both turn. There was Raina, with Konrad's wife beside her. He dropped the sword to the street as they raced to one another and hugged fiercely. I gave them a moment, then tapped him on one massive bicep. He looked down to me where I slipped him a small pouch of golden coins and shook his hand. Then I gave him back the sword he had dropped. He met my eyes again and nodded. Raina and I wordlessly met up and went to the gate. There, Father Castor and Pyoter, his novice, waited with the rest of our equipment and the horse.

I stayed apart as Raina and the priests exchanged goodbyes. Finally finished, I motioned my apprentice along. It was only Castor's voice that caught us up short. "Crow?" I turned to the holy man, stomach suddenly in knots. "Is peace your business?"

I felt myself shrink a little. I had no idea if that was really what he had asked or not, but at this point there was little choice but answer, "No, Father. It is not."

He nodded. "Someday it may be. The Father of Eternal Peace is unforgiving, but he is scrupulously fair."

I nodded back, and we left town quietly as dawn rose.

We stopped once out of sight of the gate. I had Raina pull viciously on my arm, resetting it into the socket. Call me vain, but I didn't want anyone to know the scream that followed was mine.

Thankfully, at least she found the whole thing extremely amusing. We traveled for a few more minutes in silence before she broke it. "How did it go?"

"The symphony was some kind of gate to hell. We stopped it. Schwartzklippen and Lampedocht are dead. How about you?"

"You managed to convince him to all but strip his prison and slave pens of guards. I released one and armed a few, and from that point we rolled over them all, just like you said."

"Good, next time… you get to face the demon," I groused.

"I did face the assassin," she reminded me peevishly.

"One of two!"

"Mine was bigger."

"You never even saw mine," I protested.

"The one I killed was the size of a horse. Was yours bigger?"

"No," I admitted sullenly, shoulder still throbbing. I handed her Godstongue and let her tie it off on the pommel.

"What do we do with this thing?"

"One thing at a time," I said, resigned.

We went in silence again, until the sun was higher in the sky, then she had to know. "Is it always like this?"

I cinched down my belts, and settled in for a long walk. "Not at all. Most of the time I am *running* from the city."

After an hour or so, next to an abandoned farmhouse, three men waited with four horses. We approached cautiously, but I saw that one was Zeißtein, while the young man and the old man were remnants of the Order.

"Where's the Opus?" Zeißtein demanded.

"Destroyed," I replied, explaining that the poison of the God of Murder works on all living things, symphonies included.

They handed over one of the horses, laden with supplies for a long journey. It was so black as to be blue, with a fierce spirit and far too intelligent eyes. I sighed. I hated horses who thought they were smarter than I. It only meant trouble.

Zeißtein coughed delicately. "I would be lying if I said I ever wanted to see you again, Master Crow."

I mounted, taking two tries as the damned horse sidestepped away. "That's a hell of a way to thank a man."

The old lord affixed me with a cold stare. "Did you do it for thanks?"

"Hardly matters, it being done."

And with that we walked our horses away. We had been paid as much as we were going to get for this disaster. Sorting out everything else: The Redemptive Order, who would be king, the doling out of the Schwartzklippen estate, and much else would be no business of mine. That was the best part about being disreputable.

We came to the sheltered crossroads where we had slept with the Rakes waiting for Alexander Jaeger. On the signpost, a raven sat quietly.

Raina waited three heartbeats as we sat astride our horses. "Which way?" The raven flew off at the sound of her voice, heading north. "That answers that."

"Wait," I said, "the raven is wrong."

***

A day later, I knocked on a door in a tiny village. A teen boy answered, his mother looking worried over his shoulder. They just looked at me, afraid and alone.

"The Gundersons?" I asked.

The woman refused to answer but the boy nodded. I handed him the Wolf's bow, from the street duel near the mule. He also accepted the skinning kit and the empty quiver. I gave over the bag of silver he had earned for trying to kill me, and then added ten heavy gold coins with, "I had to use his arrows," as the explanation for the gross overpayment.

I turned to leave as the mother began to cry quietly inside the hovel. The boy spoke up, voice filled of defiance, "How did he die?"

I mounted, damn horse trying to side step on me again. Once settled I nodded at him and answered honestly, "He died providing for you. Fox hunt went bad."

Then we returned to the crossroads and followed the raven north. Farther north than either of us would imagine. For one of us had lessons left to learn, and the other had debts beyond counting.

At least there were two less debts, now.

The End

Epilogue

White Arrows

HE WAS tired, bloody. He stumbled and fell, raising hands as a great shadow fell across him. The rag-clothed bastard pulled a throwing knife from his thigh with a twist. The bald man on the ground with the long moustaches groaned, red leaking from a dozen expertly administered wounds.

"The Crow. Where is he?"

His answer was silence.

"I can cause you unimaginable pain," the ragman promised.

Nothing.

Behind the mask, you could hear the smile. "Good. I like this part." He raised an arm theatrically, knife in his hand.

An arrow and bolt left at that moment. Two shots that converged upon the bundle of rags. I got the lungs, no screaming for him. Raina's bolt took him in the heart. *Show off.*

We appeared out of the forest just the way Richter himself had taught me, and once his eyes could focus he grinned, then giggled, then laughed. "In the village… three more. They look for you. Question everyone."

The valley was in the middle of summer, a riot of green so deep and rich Richter's red blood was obscene in the face of the clean life. I opened the concealed flap at the bottom of my pack, removing the flat silver flask and putting it to his lips. He drank the healing waters greedily, his wounds closing.

Richter blinked hard as the potion worked its miracle upon him. "What… what now?"

I put a hand on his shoulder. "It is morning. You will sleep until nightfall." Then I took off the quiver and laid it beside him along with the white bow he had given me. Once he awoke, he would be by far the most dangerous of us.

"What then?" he asked.

I looked to Raina, but she was ready to follow me, as she ever had been into whatever bloody teeth may come.

I smiled at my friend as he faded in and out of healing sleep, mentally flipping through the ways to kill city-born assassins in the rural village of Matron's Rest.

I smiled– hunter, scavenger, trickster, warrior, Fox. "We kill them all."

About The Author:

James Daniel Ross is a native of Cincinnati, Ohio who first discovered a love of writing during his education at The School for the Creative and Performing Arts. While he began in simple, web based vanity press projects, his affinity for the written word soon landed him a job writing for Misguided Games. After a slow-down in the gaming industry made jobs scarce, he began work on *The Radiation Angels: The Chimerium Gambit* as his first novel. Soon after came *The Key to Damocles, Snow and Steel, The Last Dragoon, Whispering of Dragons, The Echoes of Those Before*, as well as many novellas and short stories. His most recent work is the first book in the Chronicles of Rithalion, *Elvish Jewel*, and he is currently working on the second installment, *The Fireheart*.

OTHER GREAT BOOKS TO ENJOY:

Imagine living over one hundred years without a home, without a family, without responsibility. Imagine being alone in the wilderness with nothing but memories of the long ago past. Imagine dreaming of the day you might find something worth living for... worth dying for.

Elvish Jewel.

The legendary Pact of Bakharas has been broken and daemon and dragon-kind are free to make the world of Shandahar a battleground in an epic struggle that has lasted centuries.

Young sorceress Aeris Timberlyn is burdened with the task of persuading a new Talent to return to the academy to pursue training in the arcane arts. Accompanied by her brother and their companions, she travels through dangerous lands in search of him.

Being the descendent of the Grimm Brothers doesn't make life a fairy tale... it's a curse.

Once upon a time Janie Grimm thought she led a normal life, but her father just died, her stepmother Evangeline is evil, and a frog named Bert keeps talking to her. Janie learns her father's death was due to a fairy trying to restore the magic bound by Janie's ancestors, the Brothers Grimm. Janie has only the members of the F.A.B.L.E.S. organization, and the promises Evangeline made to Janie's father before his death... but will it be enough?

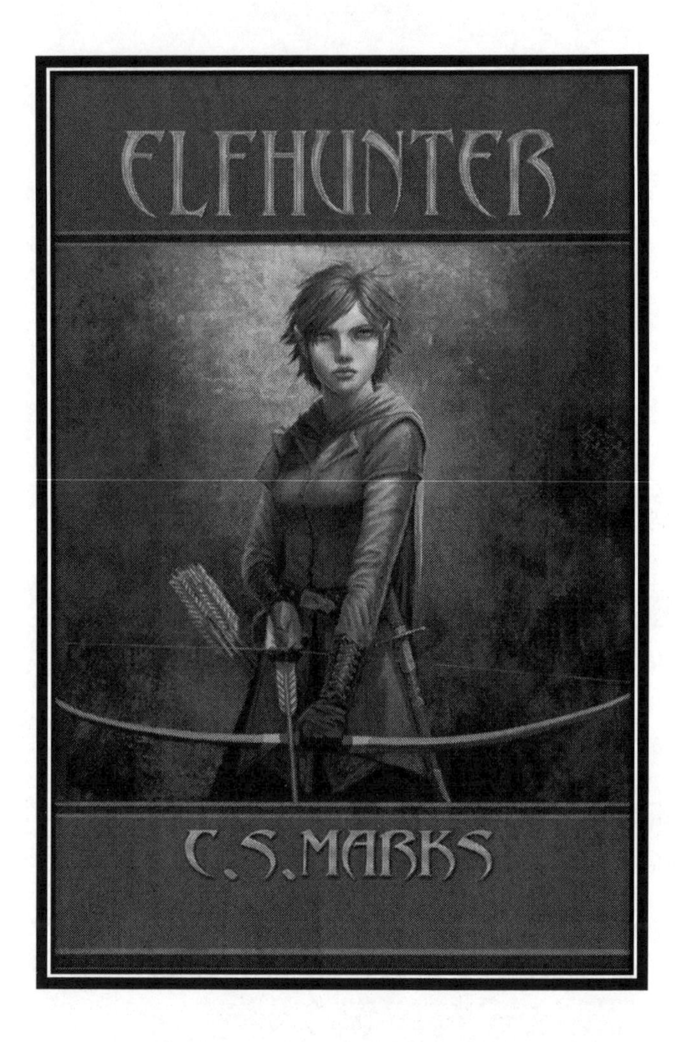

This is the tale of Gorgon Elfhunter, a monstrous, mysterious creature who has sworn to destroy all the Elves of Alterra– until none remain. It is the story of Wood-elven heroine Gaelen Taldin, who has sworn to rid her world of the Elfhunter even as she is hunted by him. The conflict between them creates a tangled web that blurs the line between Light and Darkness, love and obsession, free will and fate.

Time Traveled Tales is an exciting journey through stories of time travel, possible futures, and supernatural and alien beings from this world and many others. They are experienced through the eyes of bards like Timothy Zahn, Aaron Rosenberg, Tracy Chowdhury, Kelly Swails, Maxwell Alexander Drake, and twenty more. Each story is beautifully illustrated by renowned artist, Matt Slay.

Made in the USA
Lexington, KY
11 September 2019